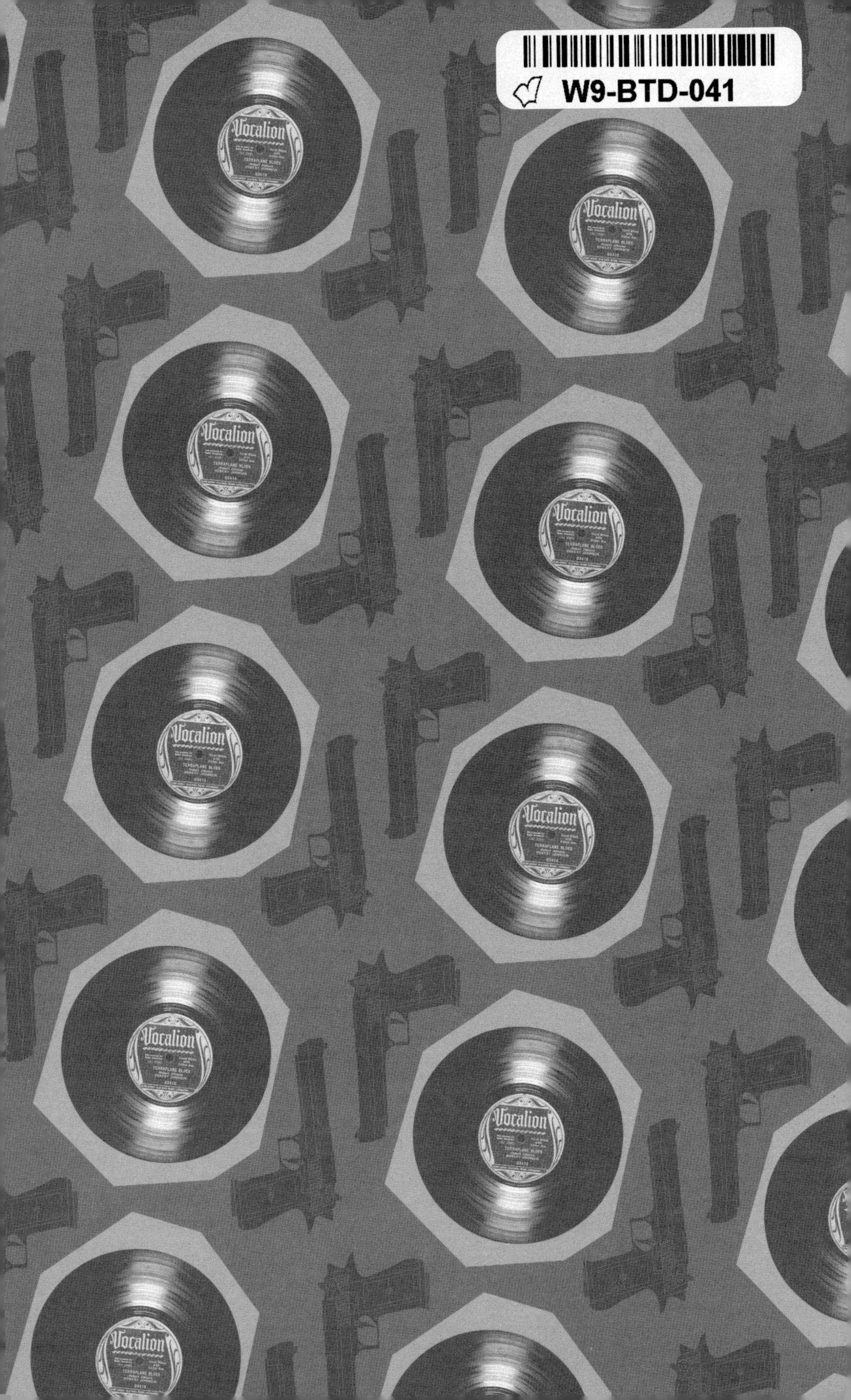
Vocalion
TERRAPLANE BLUES
ROBERT JOHNSON

IMAGE COMICS, INC.
Robert Kirkman: Chief Operating Officer
Erik Larsen: Chief Financial Officer
Todd McFarlane: President
Marc Silvestri: Chief Executive Officer
Jim Valentino: Vice President
Eric Stephenson: Publisher / Chief Creative Officer
Corey Hart: Director of Sales
Jeff Boison: Director of Publishing Planning & Book Trade Sales
Chris Ross: Director of Digital Sales
Jeff Stang: Director of Specialty Sales
Kat Salazar: Director of PR & Marketing
Drew Gill: Art Director
Heather Doornink: Production Director
Nicole Lapalme: Controller
IMAGECOMICS.COM

12-GAUGE COMICS, LLC
Keven Gardner
Doug Wagner
Brian Stelfreeze

www.12gaugecomics.com

/12gaugecomics
@12gaugecomics
/12gaugecomics
/12gaugecomics.tumblr.com

Book Design by Jonathan Chan

ISBN: 978-1-5343-0648-6

CROSSROAD BLUES: A NICK TRAVERS GRAPHIC NOVEL.
APRIL 2018. FIRST PRINTING.

PRINTED IN THE U.S.A.
For information regarding the CPSIA on this printed material call: 203-595-3636 and provide reference #RICH-783367.

For international rights, contact: foreignlicensing@imagecomics.com

IMAGE COMICS presents

a 12-GAUGE production

CROSSROAD BLUES
A NICK TRAVERS GRAPHIC NOVEL

Story **ACE ATKINS**

Art **MARCO FINNEGAN**

Cover **CHRIS BRUNNER**

Letters **TROY PETERI**

Editor **KEVEN GARDNER**

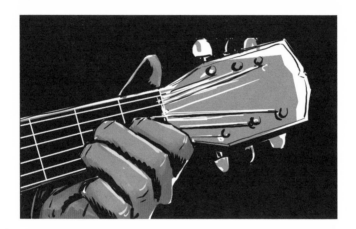

Jesus of Nazareth. King of Jerusalem. I know that my Redeemer liveth and that He will call me from the Grave.

Written by Robert L. Johnson,
shortly before his death in 1938.

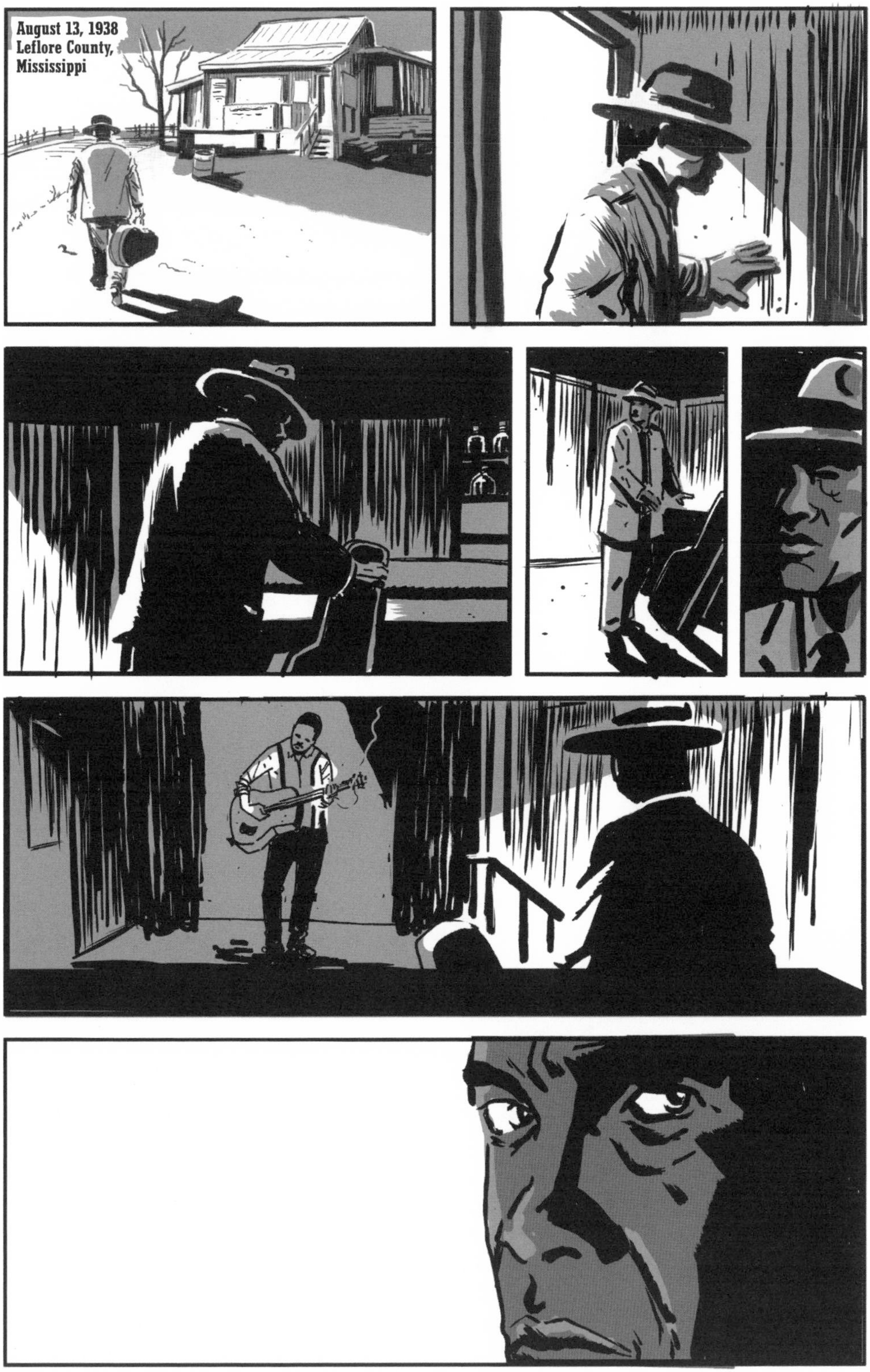
August 13, 1938
Leflore County,
Mississippi

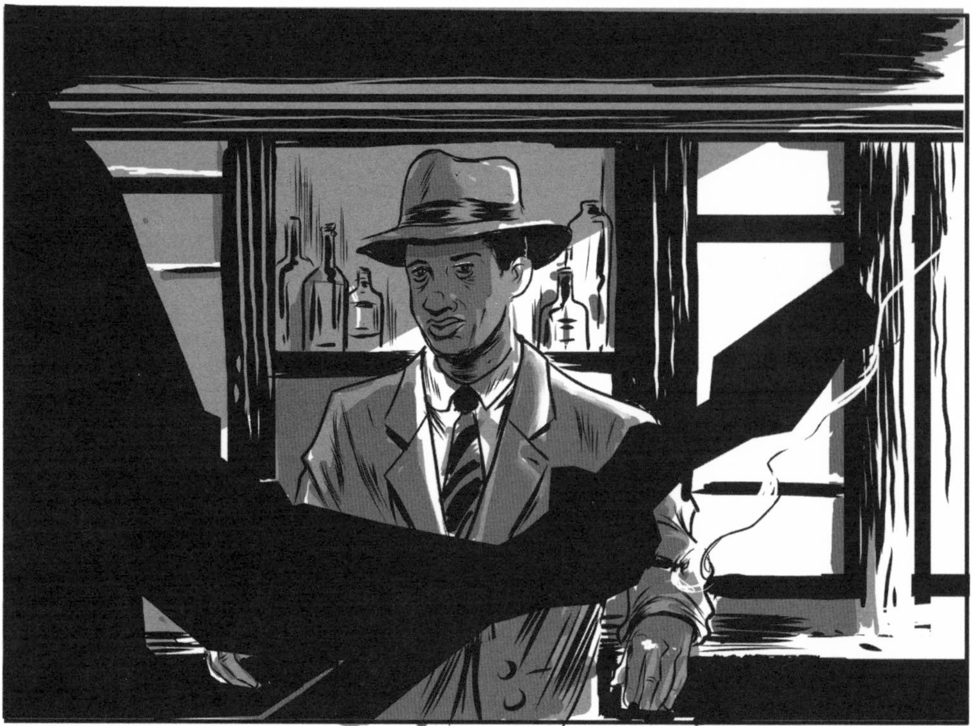

CHAPTER ONE

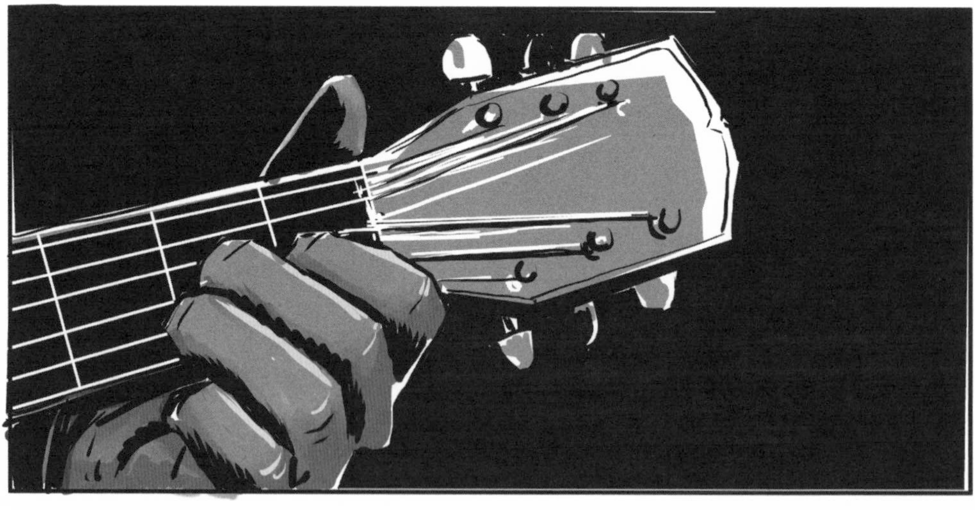

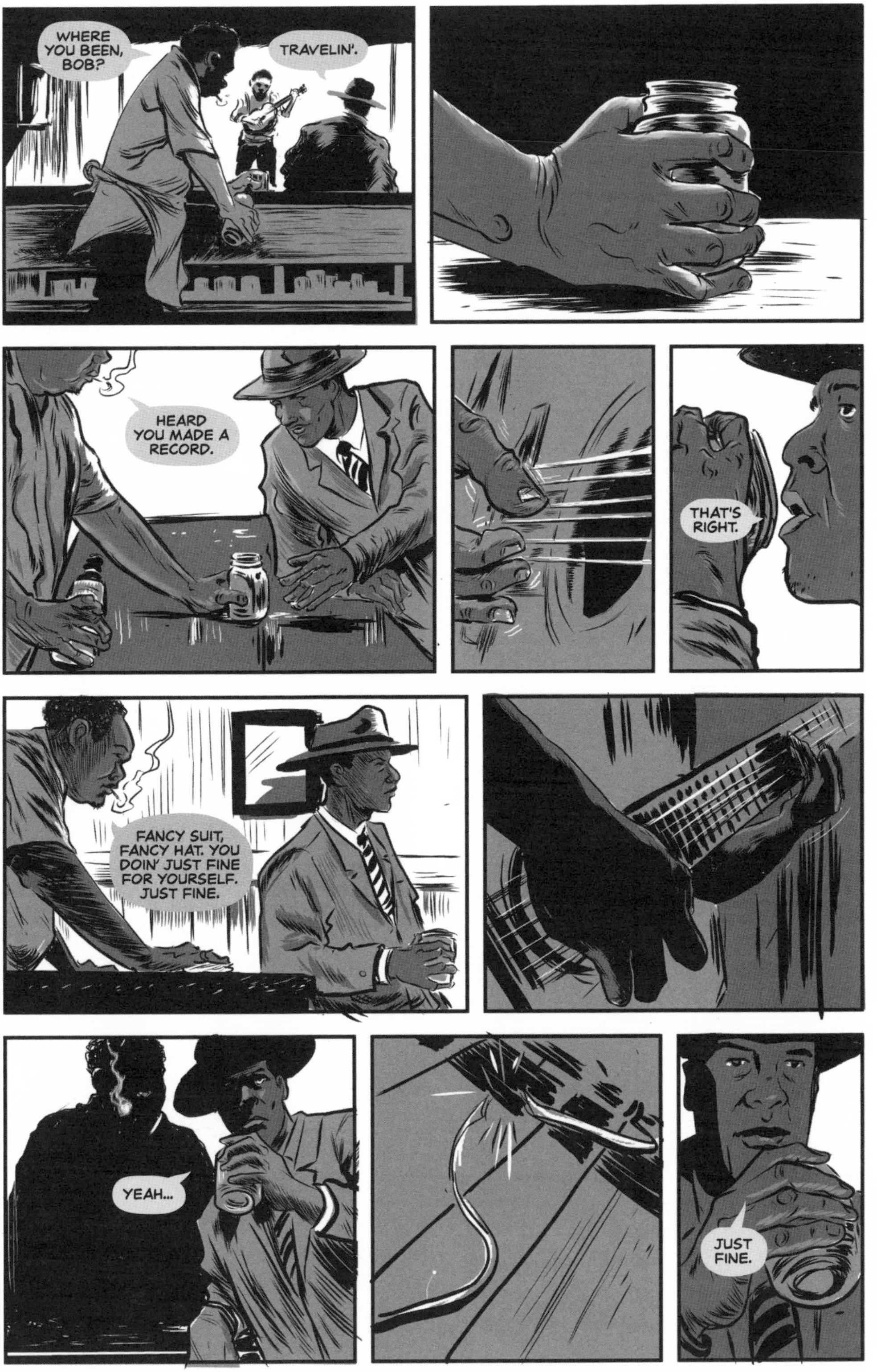
WHERE YOU BEEN, BOB?
TRAVELIN'.
HEARD YOU MADE A RECORD.
THAT'S RIGHT.
FANCY SUIT, FANCY HAT. YOU DOIN' JUST FINE FOR YOURSELF. JUST FINE.
YEAH...
JUST FINE.

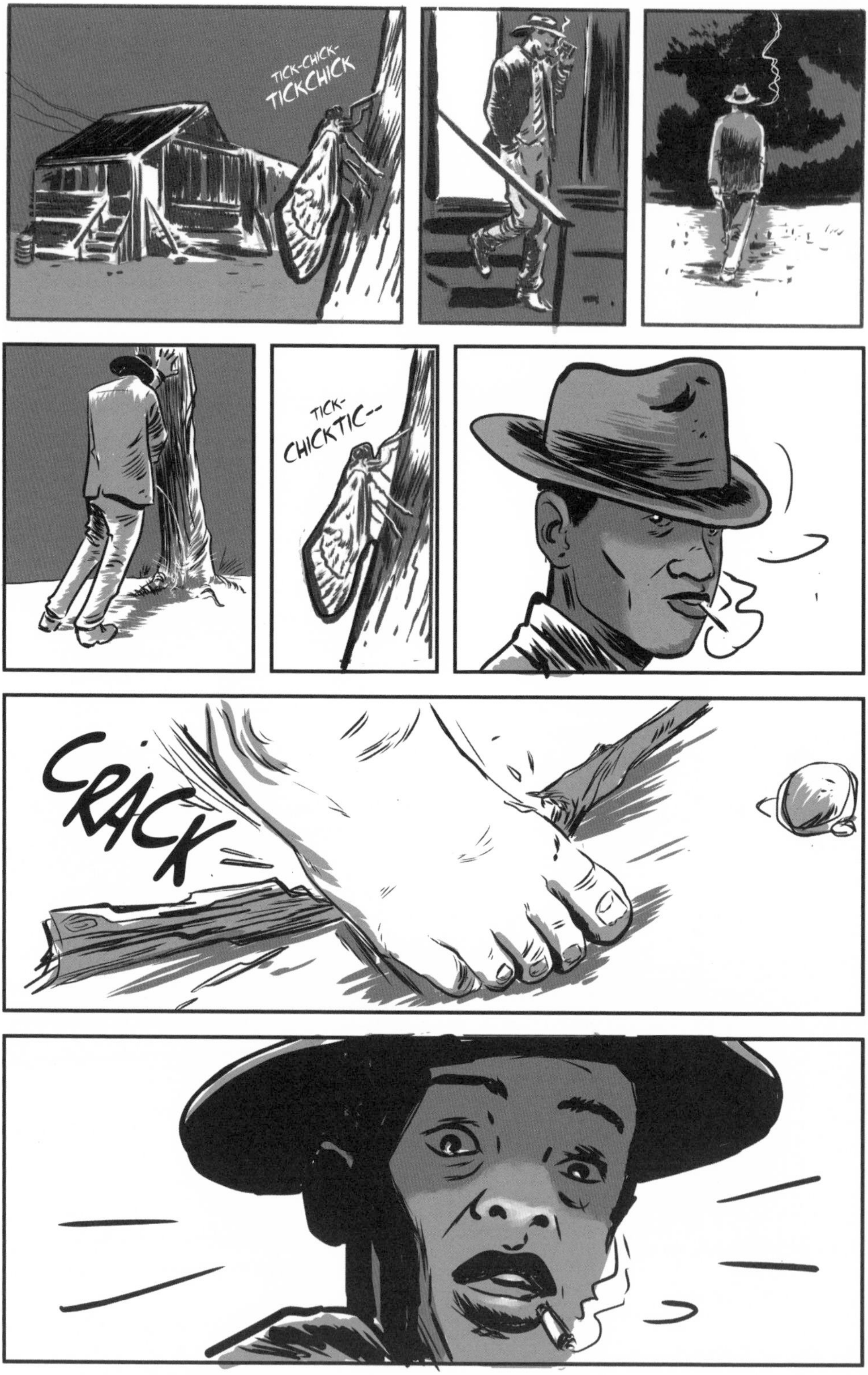
TICK-CHICK-
TICKCHICK
TICK-
CHICKTIC--
CRACK

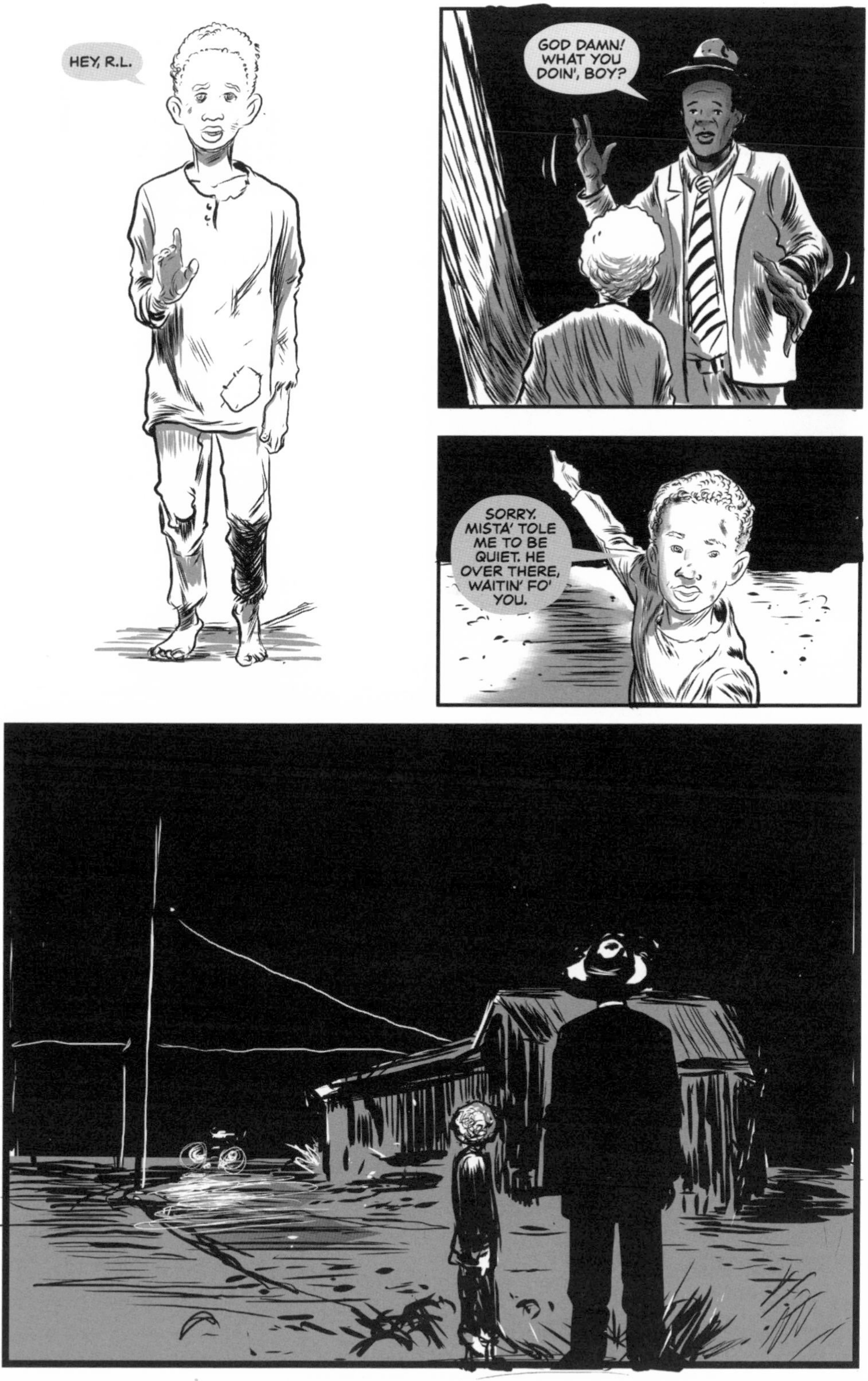
HEY, R.L.
GOD DAMN! WHAT YOU DOIN', BOY?
SORRY. MISTA' TOLE ME TO BE QUIET. HE OVER THERE, WAITIN' FO' YOU.

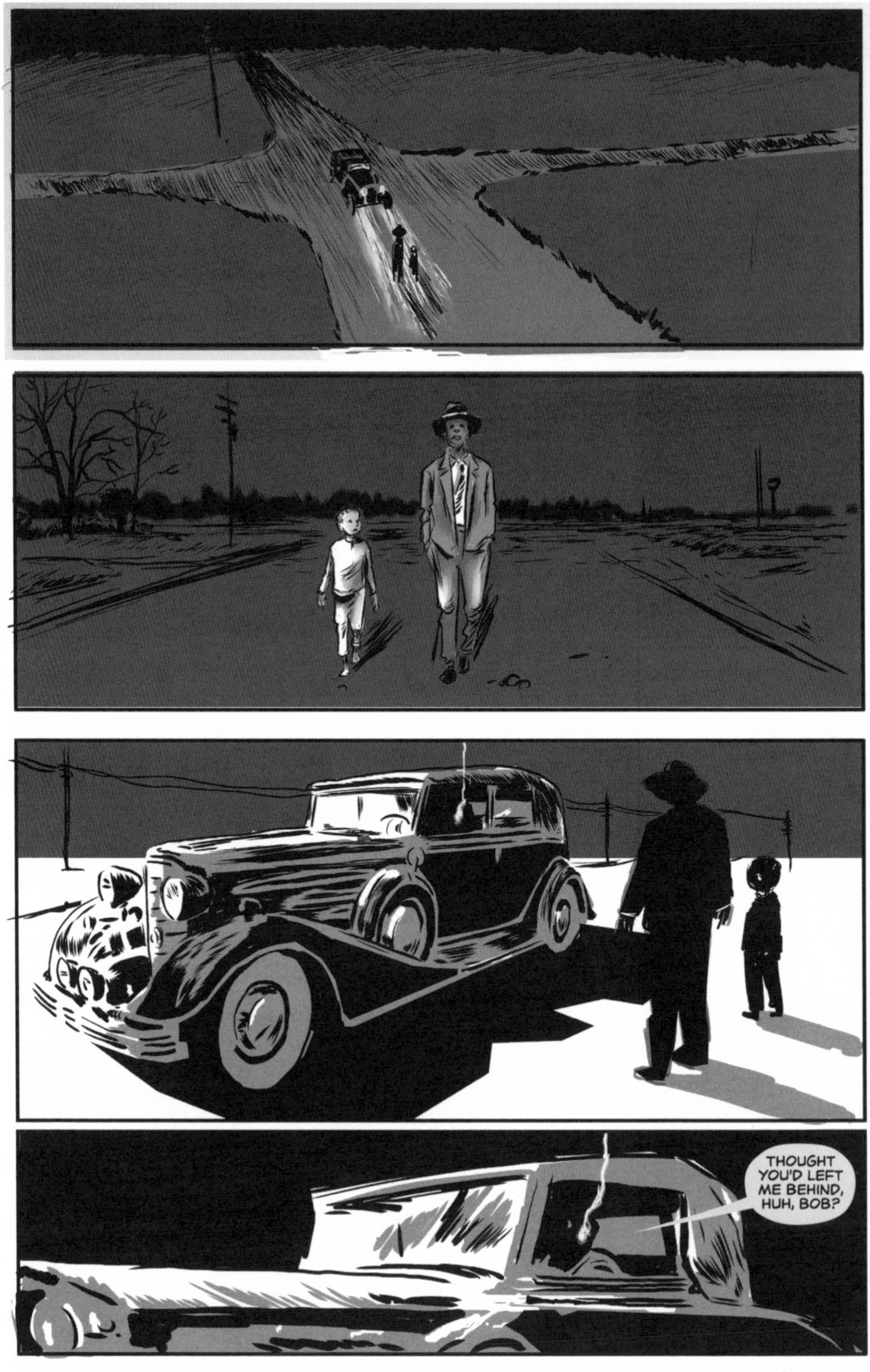
THOUGHT YOU'D LEFT ME BEHIND, HUH, BOB?

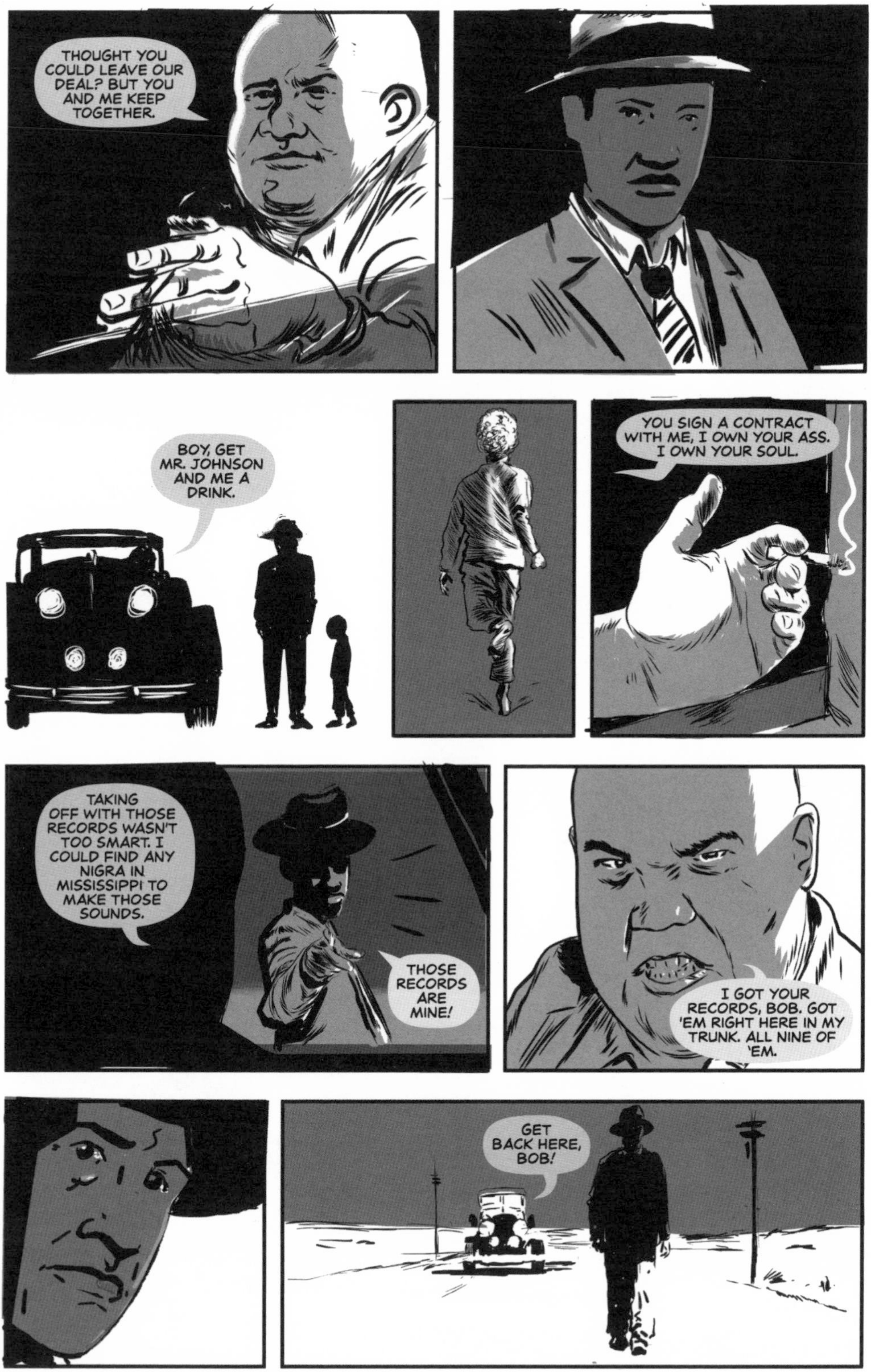
THOUGHT YOU COULD LEAVE OUR DEAL? BUT YOU AND ME KEEP TOGETHER.
BOY, GET MR. JOHNSON AND ME A DRINK.
YOU SIGN A CONTRACT WITH ME, I OWN YOUR ASS. I OWN YOUR SOUL.
TAKING OFF WITH THOSE RECORDS WASN'T TOO SMART. I COULD FIND ANY NIGRA IN MISSISSIPPI TO MAKE THOSE SOUNDS.
THOSE RECORDS ARE MINE!
I GOT YOUR RECORDS, BOB. GOT 'EM RIGHT HERE IN MY TRUNK. ALL NINE OF 'EM.
GET BACK HERE, BOB!

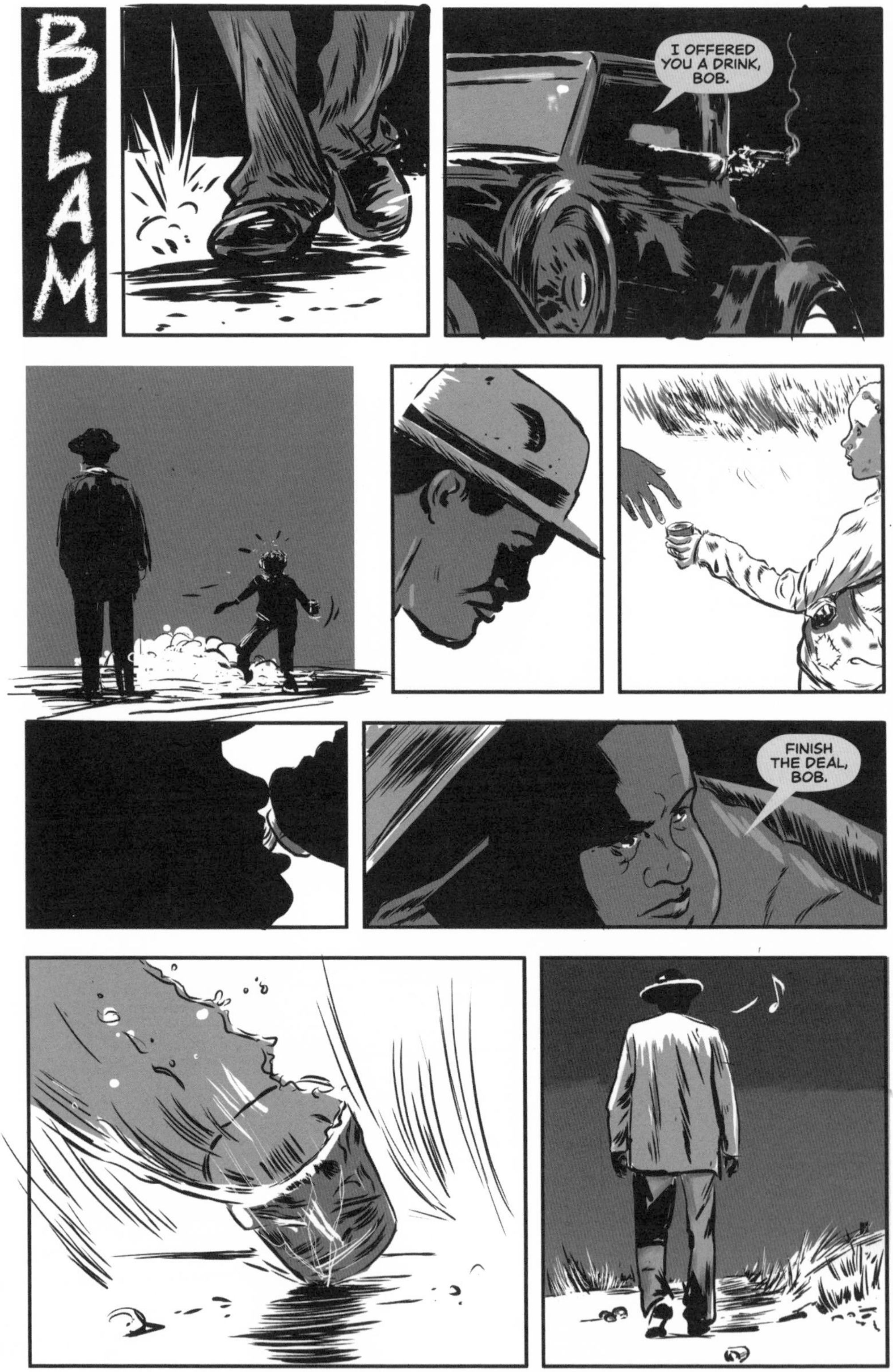
BLAM
I OFFERED YOU A DRINK, BOB.
FINISH THE DEAL, BOB.

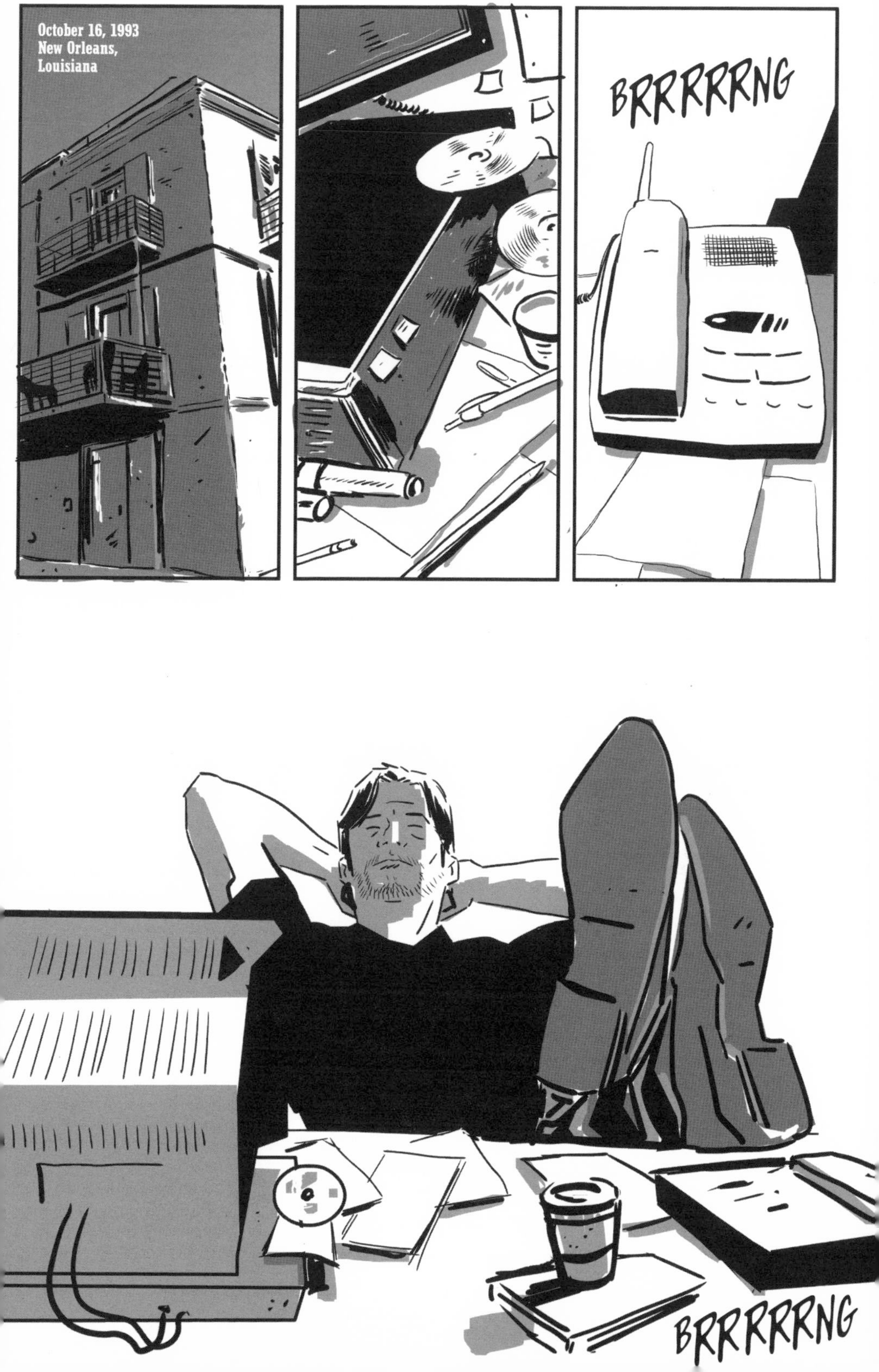
October 16, 1993
New Orleans,
Louisiana
BRRRRRNG
BRRRRRNG

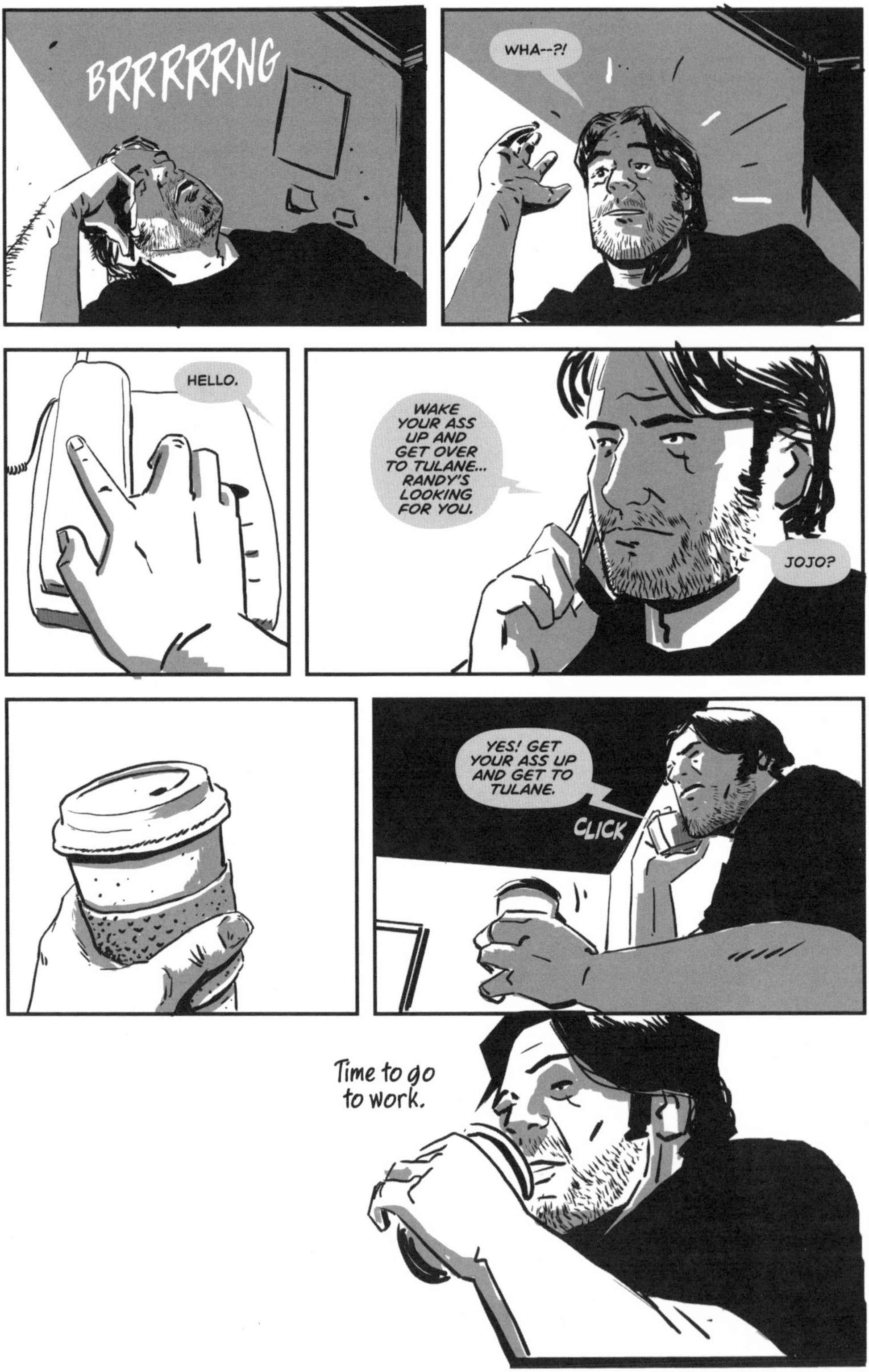
BRRRRRNG
WHA--?!
HELLO.
WAKE YOUR ASS UP AND GET OVER TO TULANE... RANDY'S LOOKING FOR YOU.
JOJO?
YES! GET YOUR ASS UP AND GET TO TULANE.
CLICK
Time to go to work.

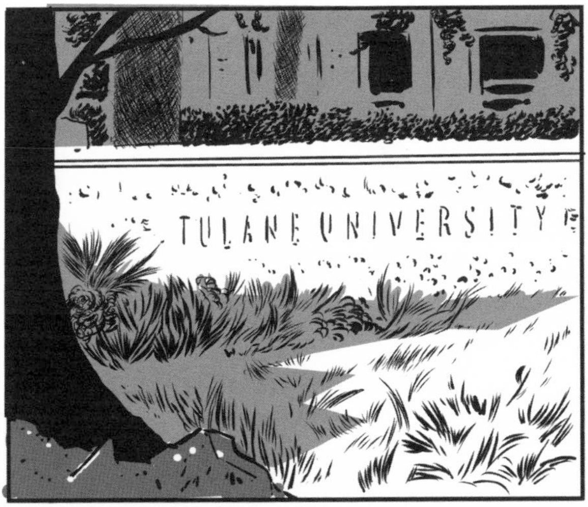
TULANE UNIVERSITY

Besides solving problems for friends and strangers to make ends meet, I also taught a class or two on blues history at Tulane. It wasn't a living, but I loved it.

Professor Randy Sexton, head of the Jazz Archives, had no anterooms or secretary, just a small, simple office with sagging bookshelves filled with magazines and biographies.

There was not a man alive who knew more about the development of New Orleans music than Randy Sexton -- author of more than a dozen books on early jazz and the roots of African music, from Congo Square to Satchmo.

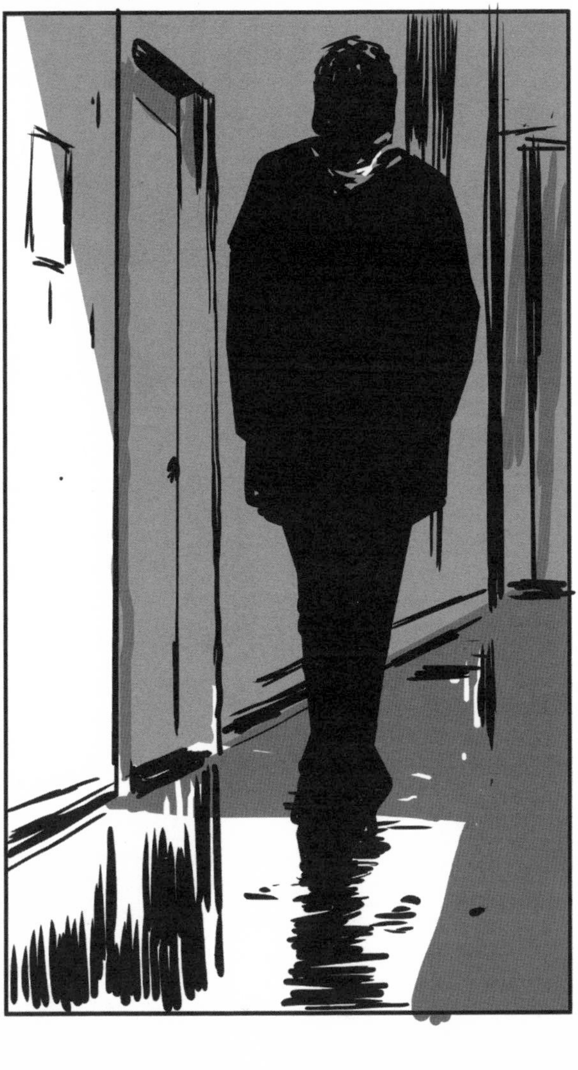

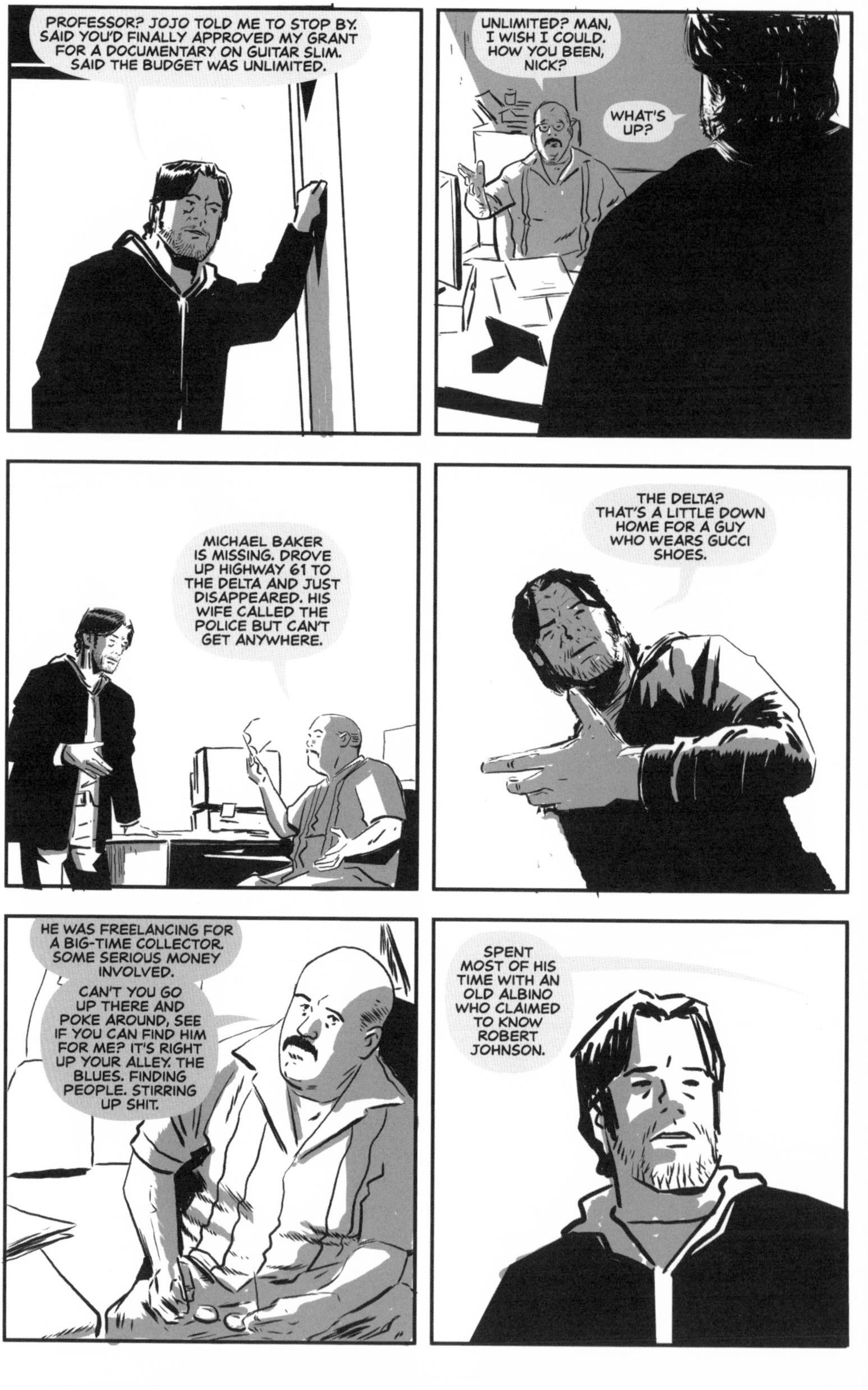
PROFESSOR? JOJO TOLD ME TO STOP BY. SAID YOU'D FINALLY APPROVED MY GRANT FOR A DOCUMENTARY ON GUITAR SLIM. SAID THE BUDGET WAS UNLIMITED.
UNLIMITED? MAN, I WISH I COULD. HOW YOU BEEN, NICK?
WHAT'S UP?
MICHAEL BAKER IS MISSING. DROVE UP HIGHWAY 61 TO THE DELTA AND JUST DISAPPEARED. HIS WIFE CALLED THE POLICE BUT CAN'T GET ANYWHERE.
THE DELTA? THAT'S A LITTLE DOWN HOME FOR A GUY WHO WEARS GUCCI SHOES.
HE WAS FREELANCING FOR A BIG-TIME COLLECTOR. SOME SERIOUS MONEY INVOLVED.
CAN'T YOU GO UP THERE AND POKE AROUND, SEE IF YOU CAN FIND HIM FOR ME? IT'S RIGHT UP YOUR ALLEY. THE BLUES. FINDING PEOPLE. STIRRING UP SHIT.
SPENT MOST OF HIS TIME WITH AN OLD ALBINO WHO CLAIMED TO KNOW ROBERT JOHNSON.

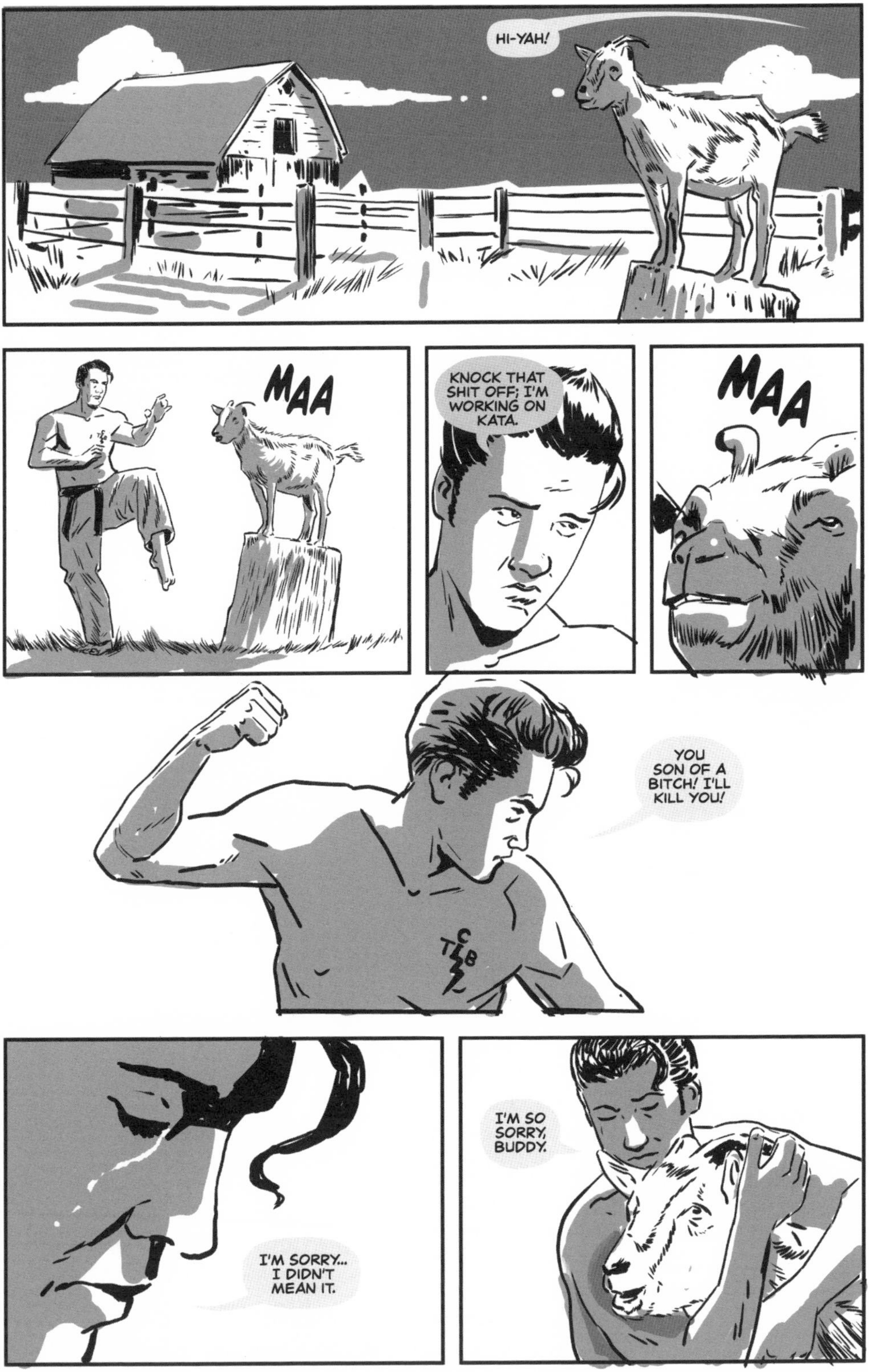
HI-YAH!
MAA
KNOCK THAT SHIT OFF; I'M WORKING ON KATA.
MAA
YOU SON OF A BITCH! I'LL KILL YOU!
I'M SORRY... I DIDN'T MEAN IT.
I'M SO SORRY, BUDDY.

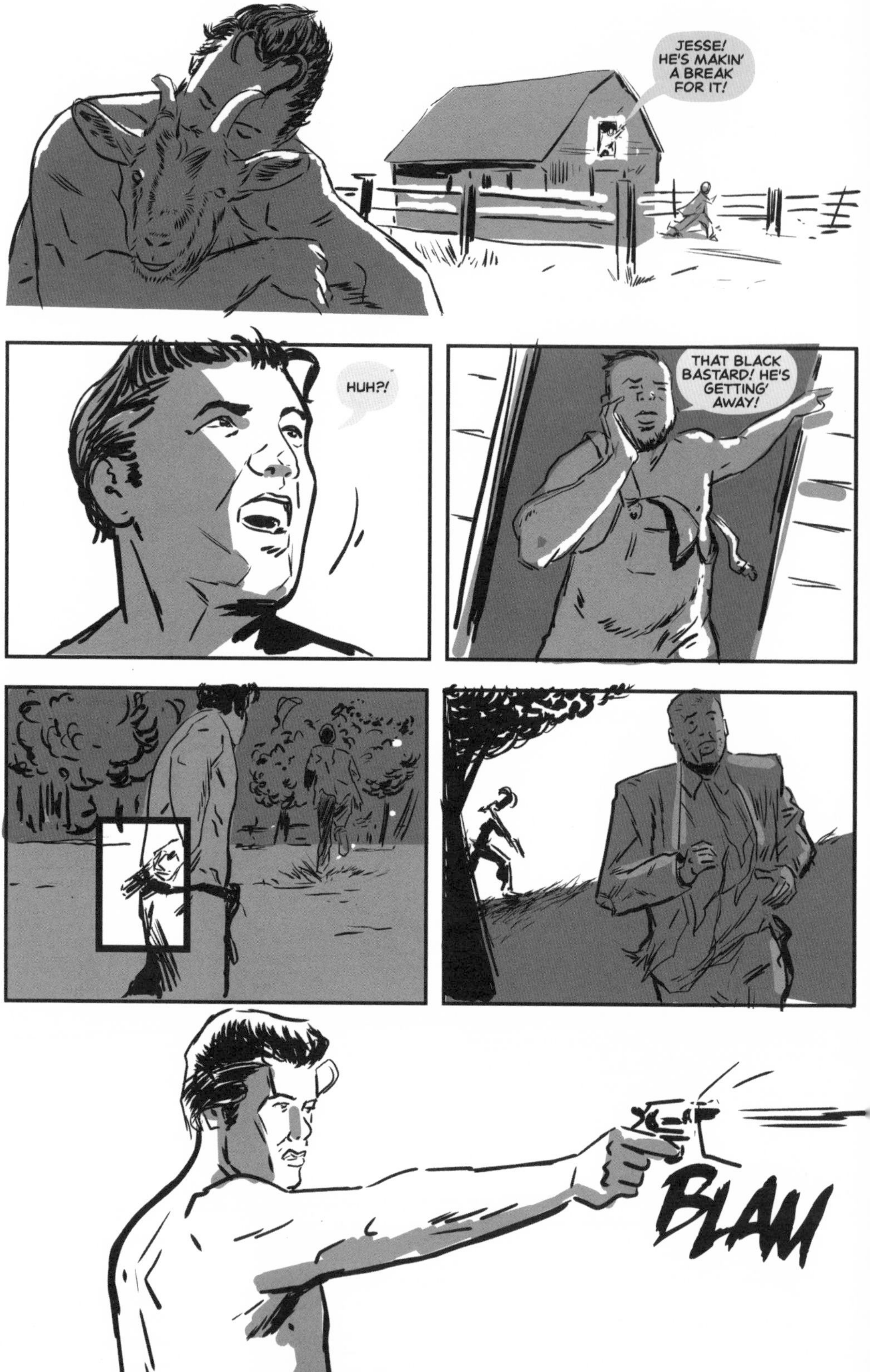

JESSE! HE'S MAKIN' A BREAK FOR IT!
HUH?!
THAT BLACK BASTARD! HE'S GETTING' AWAY!
BLAM

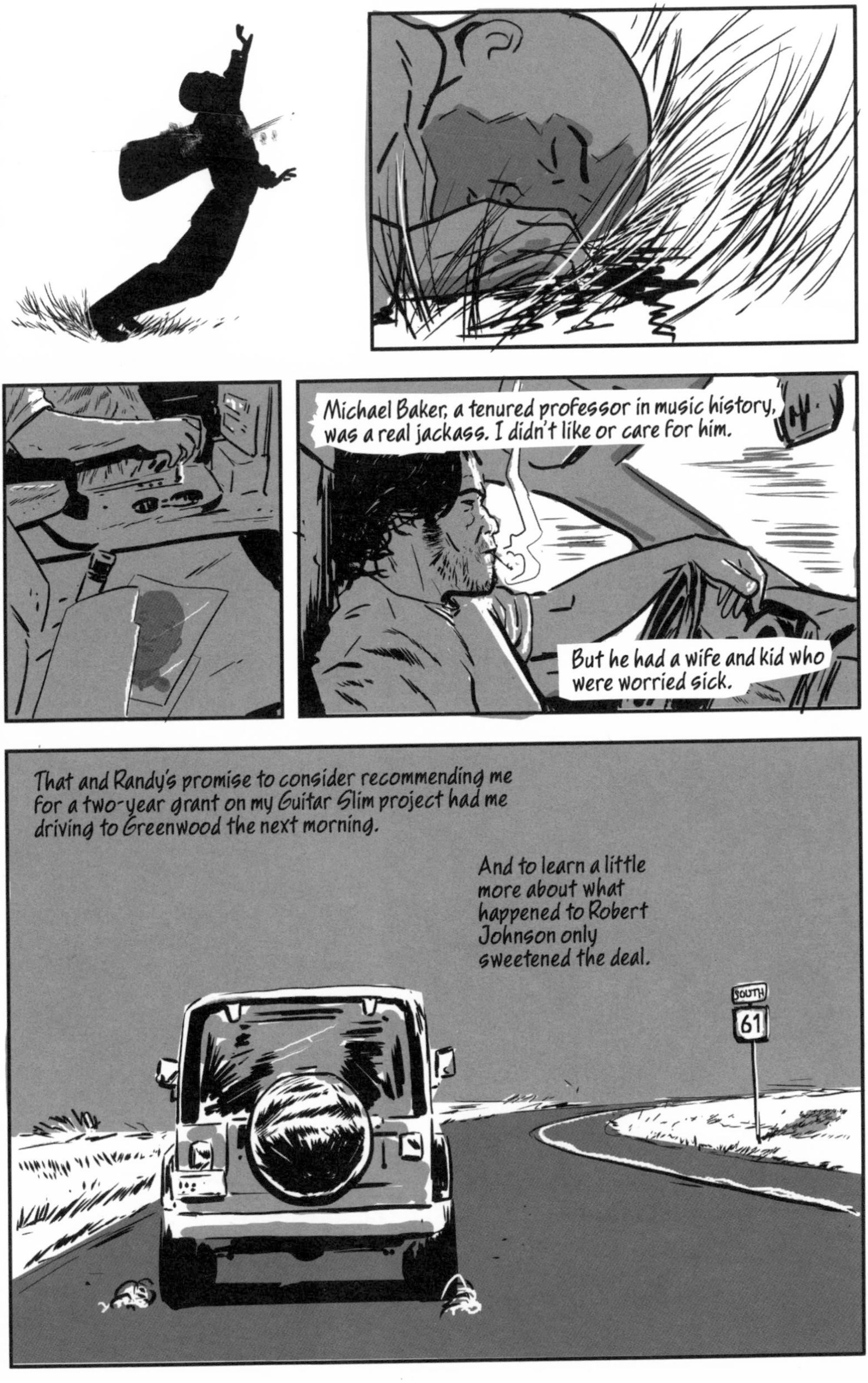

Michael Baker, a tenured professor in music history, was a real jackass. I didn't like or care for him.
But he had a wife and kid who were worried sick.
That and Randy's promise to consider recommending me for a two-year grant on my Guitar Slim project had me driving to Greenwood the next morning.
And to learn a little more about what happened to Robert Johnson only sweetened the deal.
SOUTH
61

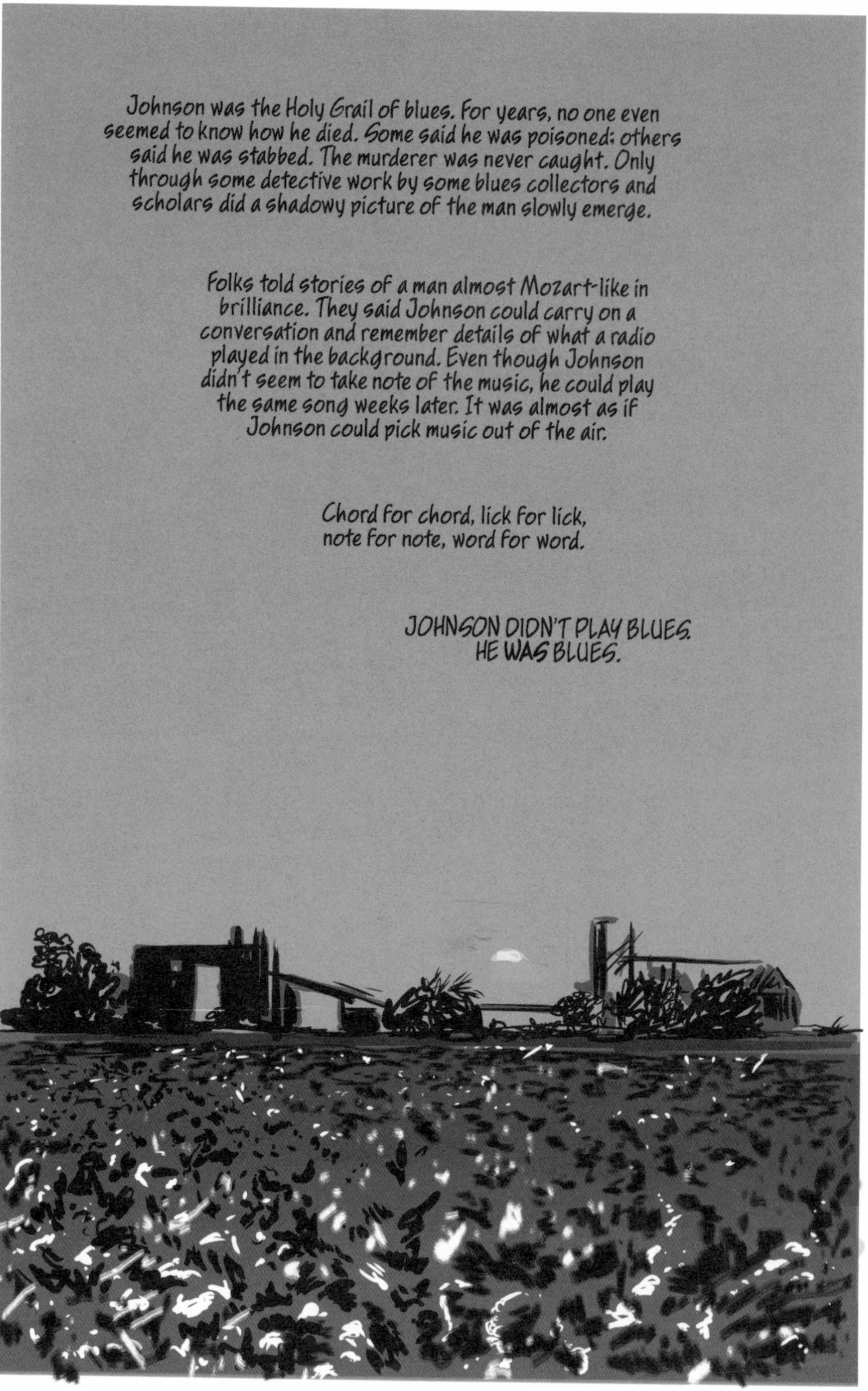
Johnson was the Holy Grail of blues. For years, no one even seemed to know how he died. Some said he was poisoned; others said he was stabbed. The murderer was never caught. Only through some detective work by some blues collectors and scholars did a shadowy picture of the man slowly emerge.
Folks told stories of a man almost Mozart-like in brilliance. They said Johnson could carry on a conversation and remember details of what a radio played in the background. Even though Johnson didn't seem to take note of the music, he could play the same song weeks later. It was almost as if Johnson could pick music out of the air.
Chord for chord, lick for lick, note for note, word for word.
JOHNSON DIDN'T PLAY BLUES. HE WAS BLUES.

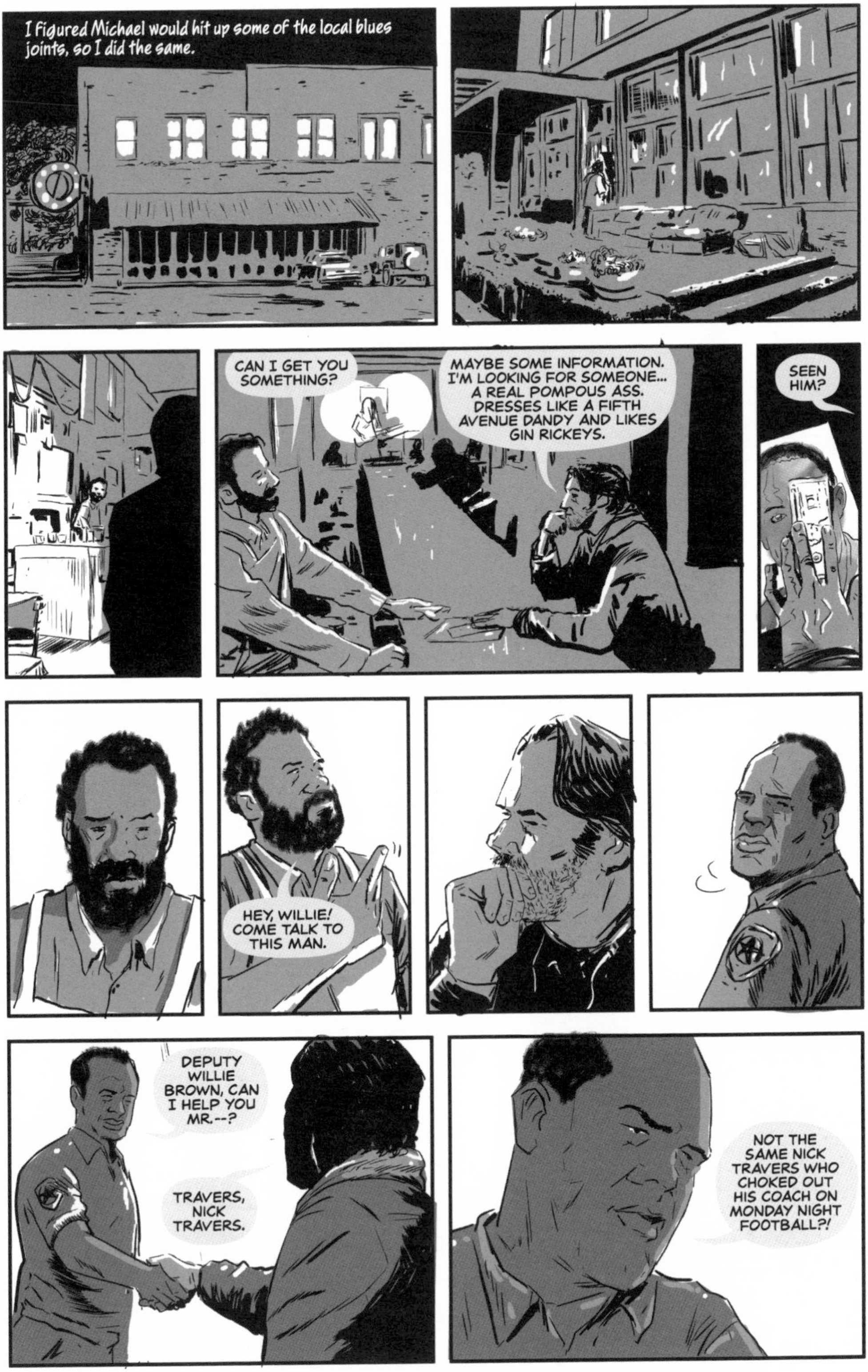
I figured Michael would hit up some of the local blues joints, so I did the same.
CAN I GET YOU SOMETHING?
MAYBE SOME INFORMATION. I'M LOOKING FOR SOMEONE... A REAL POMPOUS ASS. DRESSES LIKE A FIFTH AVENUE DANDY AND LIKES GIN RICKEYS.
SEEN HIM?
HEY, WILLIE! COME TALK TO THIS MAN.
DEPUTY WILLIE BROWN, CAN I HELP YOU MR.--?
TRAVERS, NICK TRAVERS.
NOT THE SAME NICK TRAVERS WHO CHOKED OUT HIS COACH ON MONDAY NIGHT FOOTBALL?!

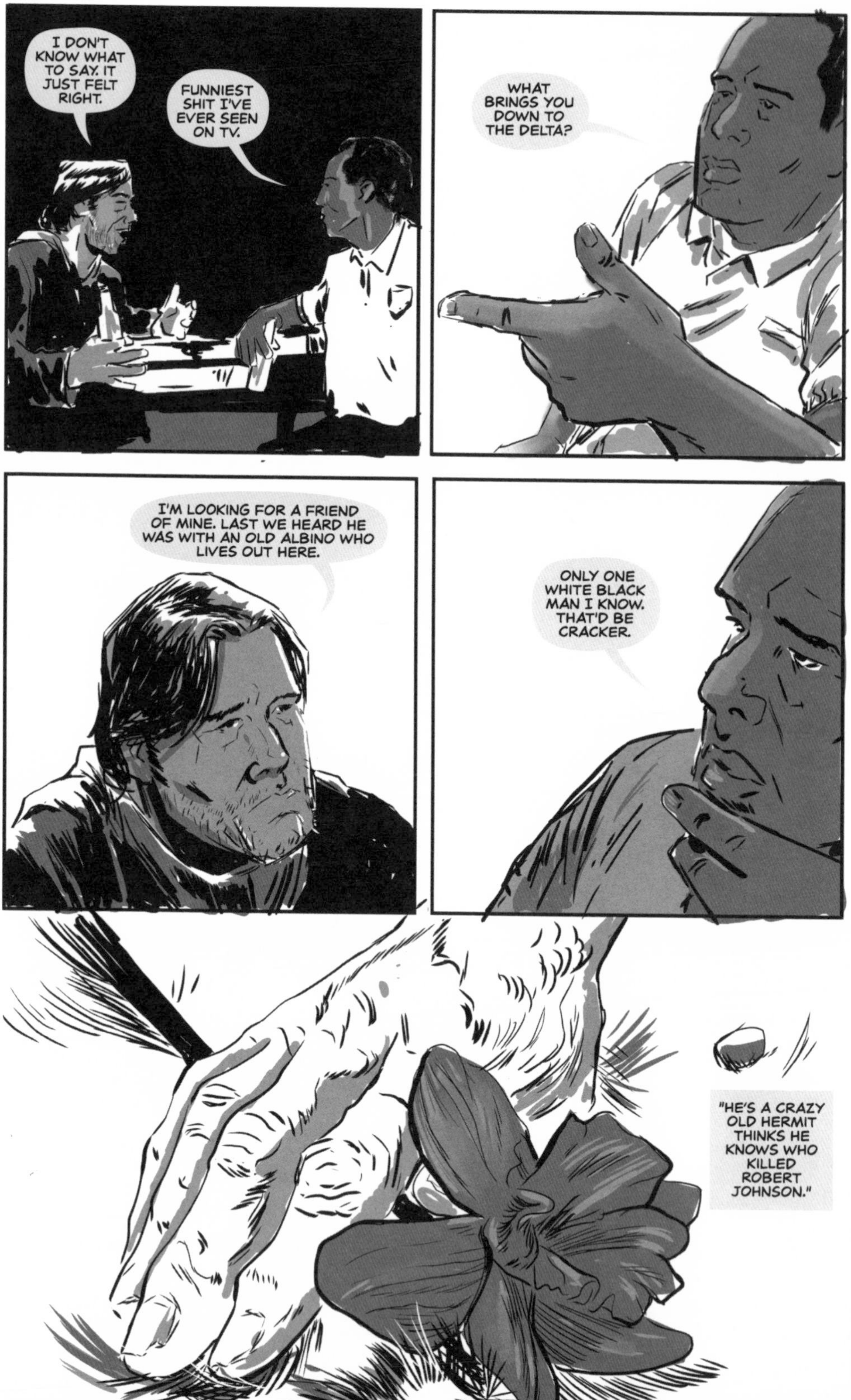
I DON'T KNOW WHAT TO SAY. IT JUST FELT RIGHT.
FUNNIEST SHIT I'VE EVER SEEN ON TV.
WHAT BRINGS YOU DOWN TO THE DELTA?
I'M LOOKING FOR A FRIEND OF MINE. LAST WE HEARD HE WAS WITH AN OLD ALBINO WHO LIVES OUT HERE.
ONLY ONE WHITE BLACK MAN I KNOW. THAT'D BE CRACKER.
"HE'S A CRAZY OLD HERMIT THINKS HE KNOWS WHO KILLED ROBERT JOHNSON."

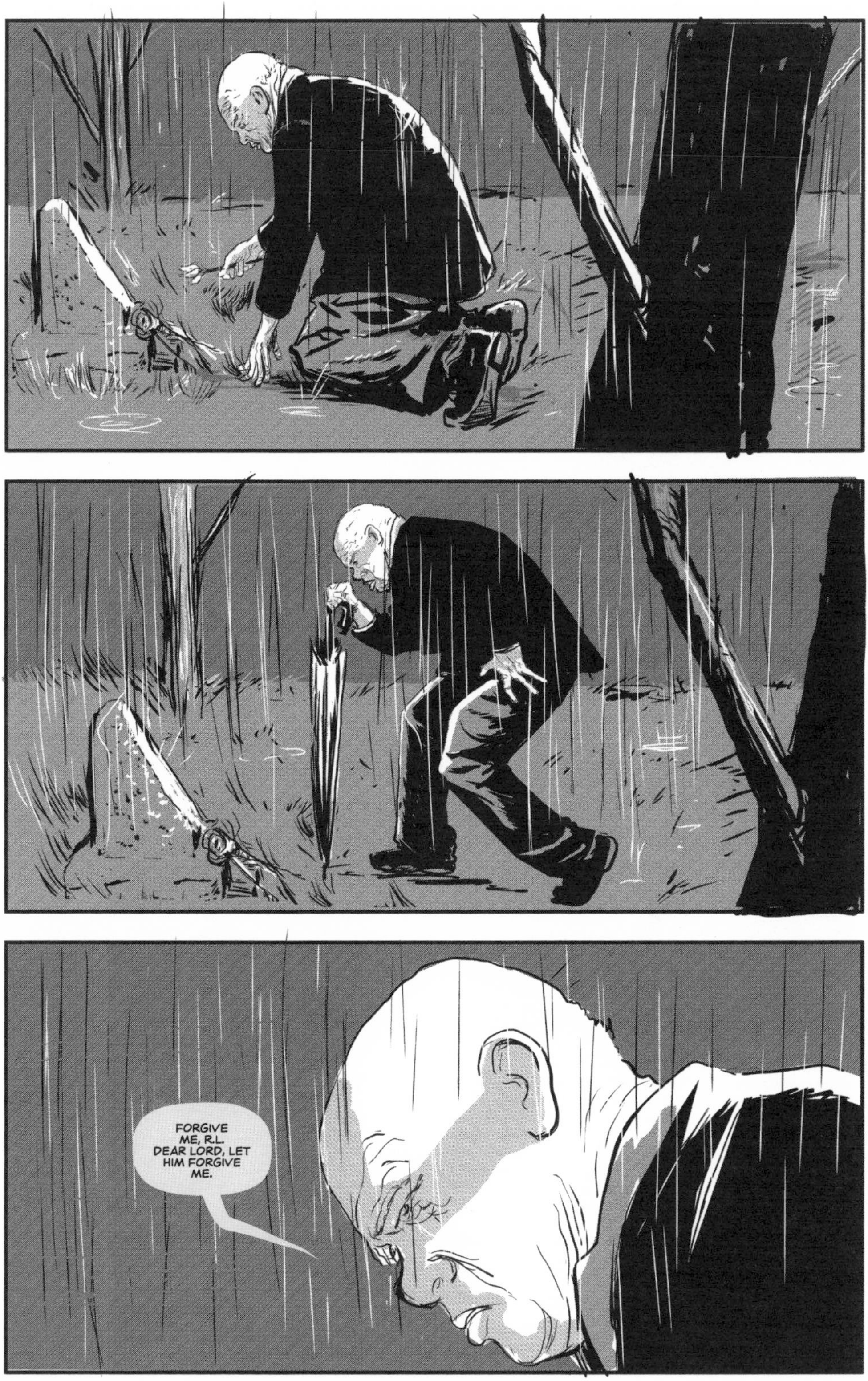
FORGIVE ME, R.L. DEAR LORD, LET HIM FORGIVE ME.

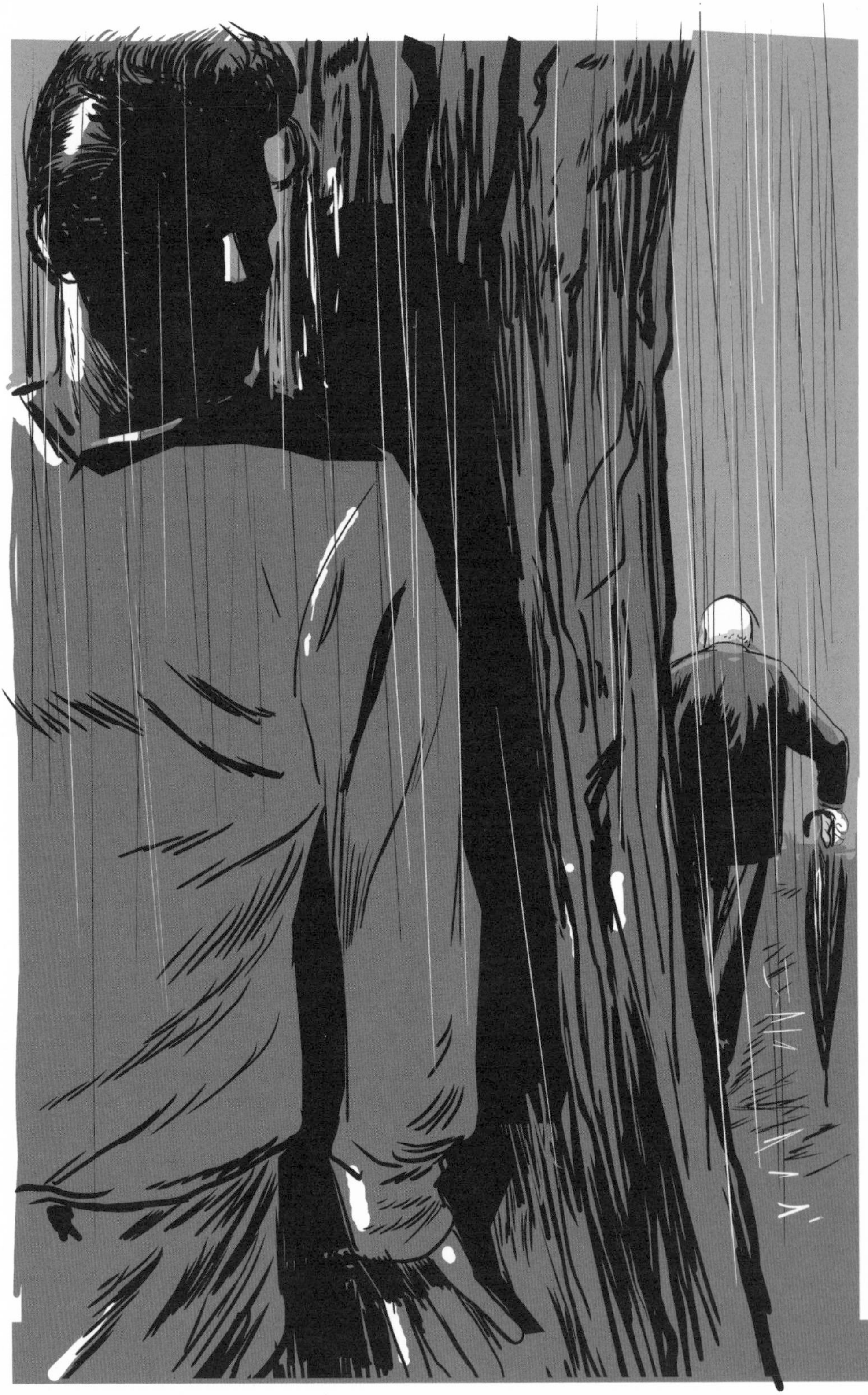

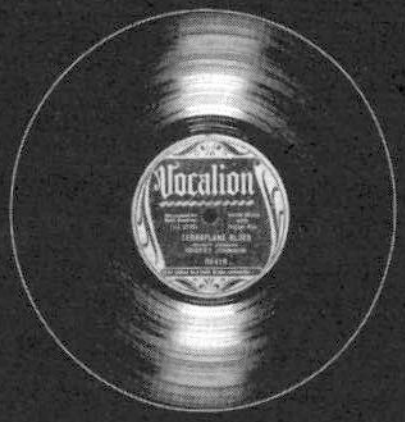
Vocalion

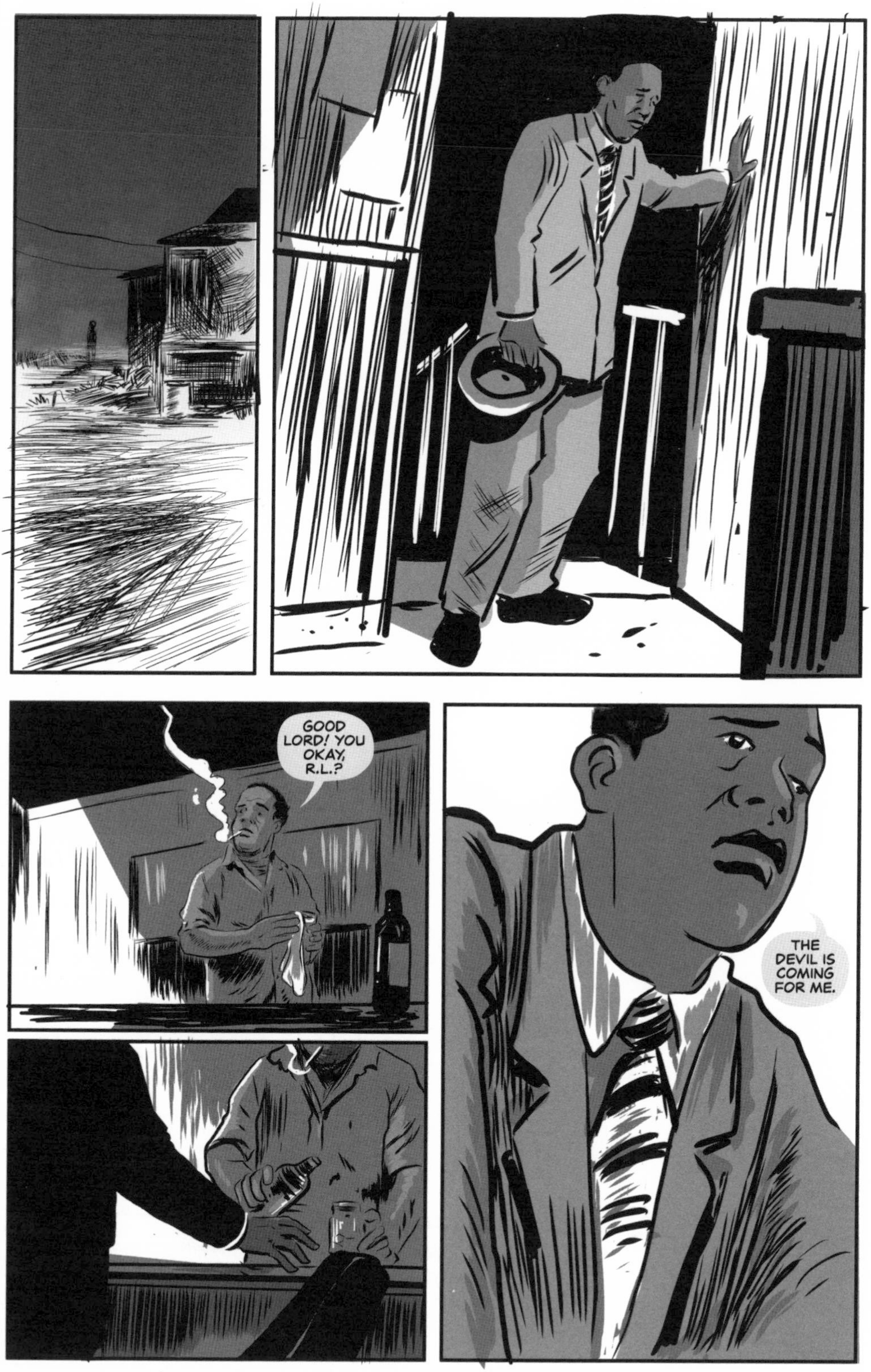
GOOD LORD! YOU OKAY, R.L.?
THE DEVIL IS COMING FOR ME.

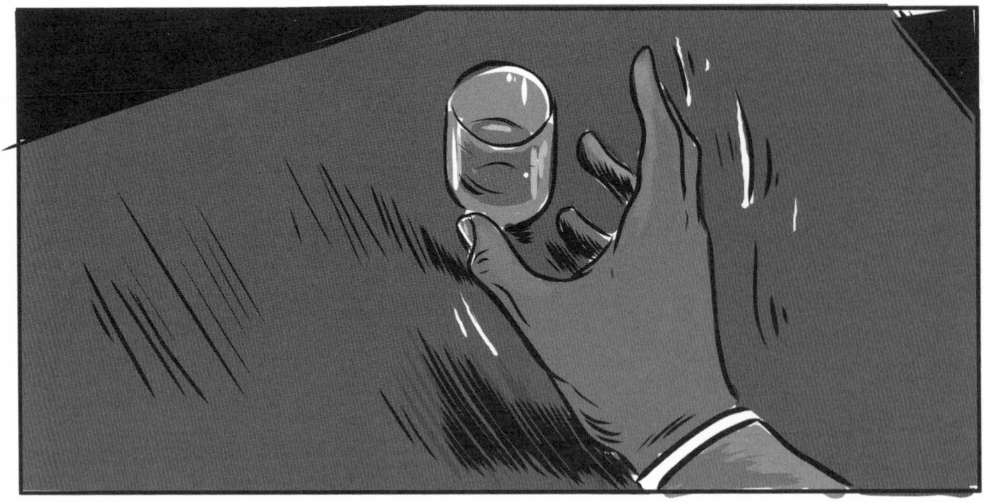

CHAPTER TWO

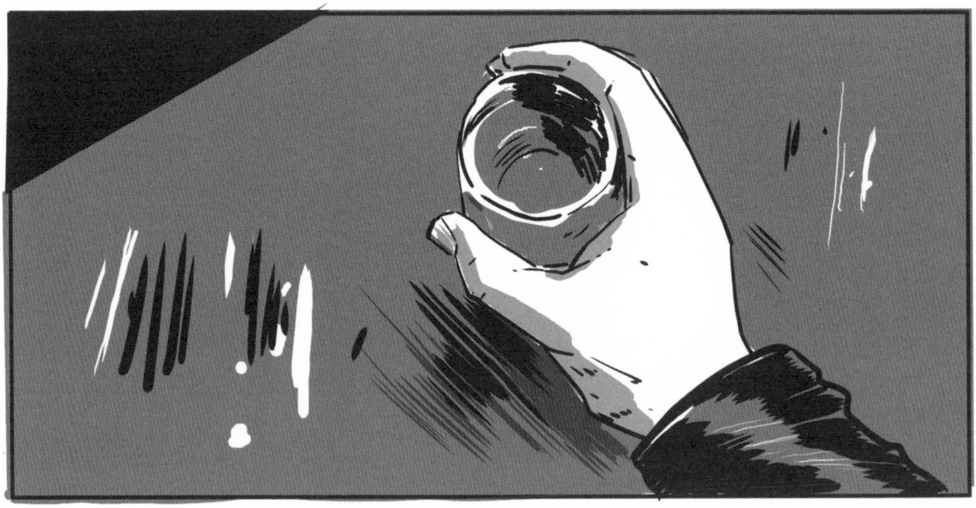

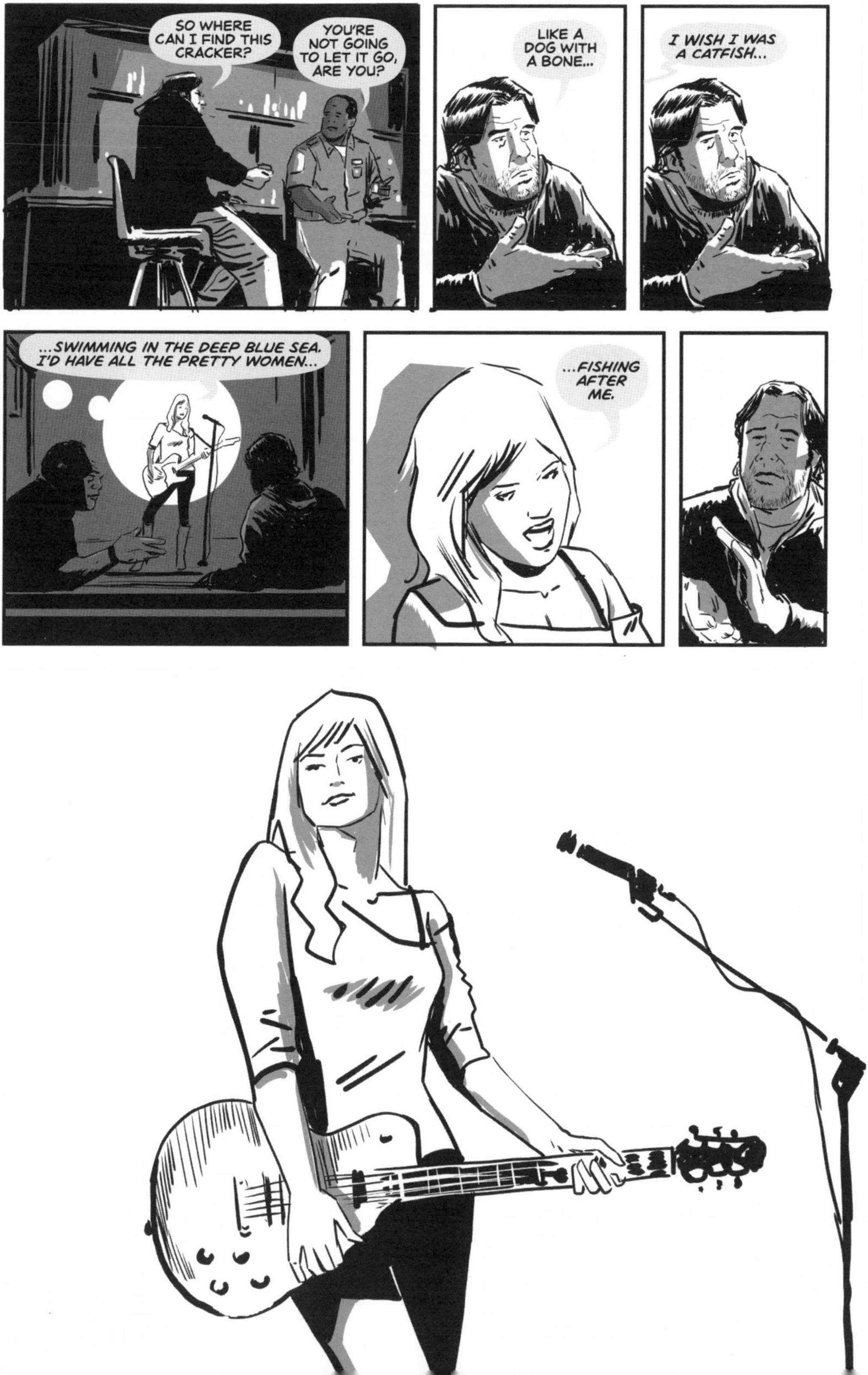
SO WHERE CAN I FIND THIS CRACKER?
YOU'RE NOT GOING TO LET IT GO, ARE YOU?
LIKE A DOG WITH A BONE...
I WISH I WAS A CATFISH...
...SWIMMING IN THE DEEP BLUE SEA. I'D HAVE ALL THE PRETTY WOMEN...
...FISHING AFTER ME.

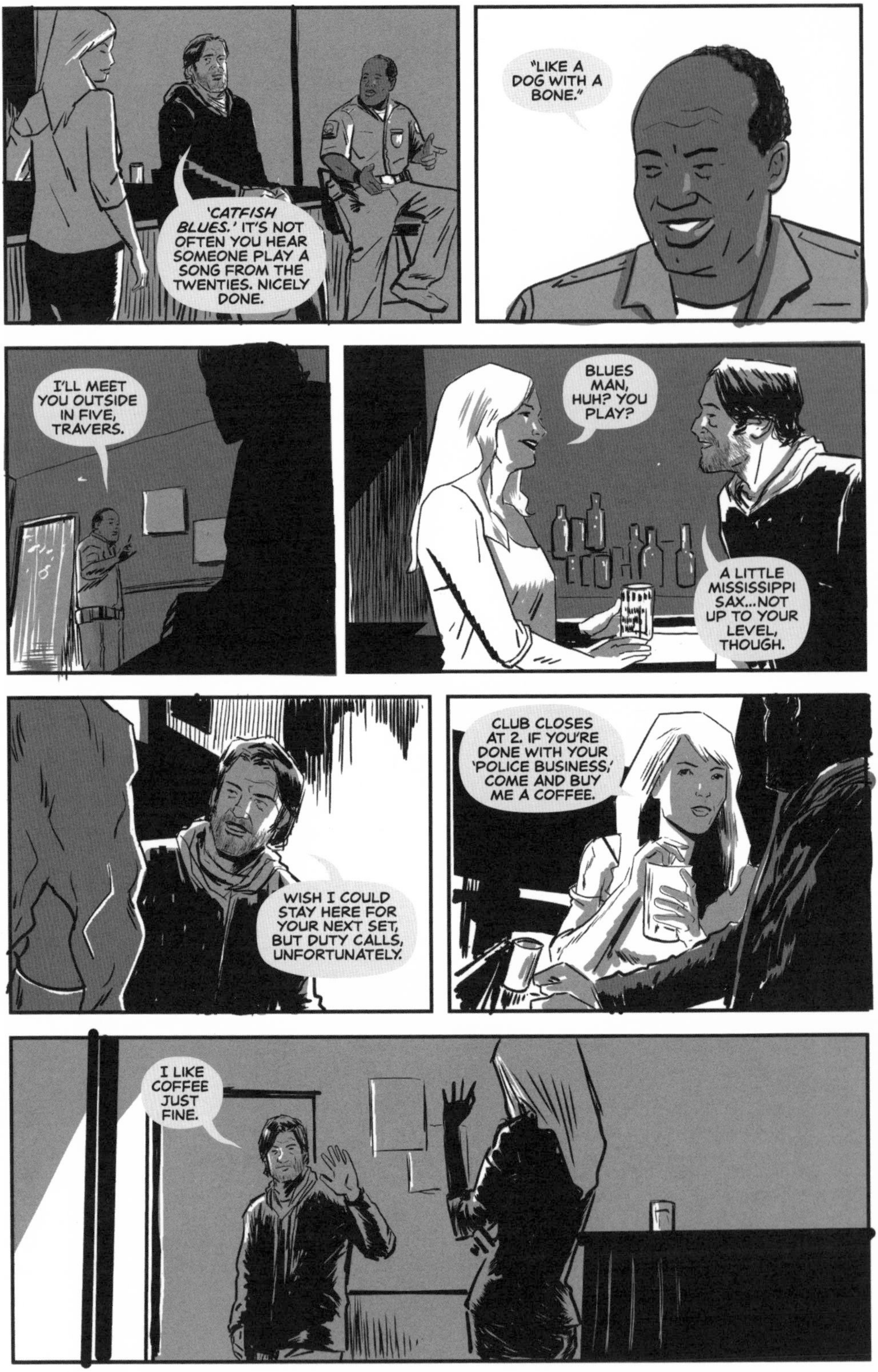
'CATFISH BLUES.' IT'S NOT OFTEN YOU HEAR SOMEONE PLAY A SONG FROM THE TWENTIES. NICELY DONE.
"LIKE A DOG WITH A BONE."
I'LL MEET YOU OUTSIDE IN FIVE, TRAVERS.
BLUES MAN, HUH? YOU PLAY?
A LITTLE MISSISSIPPI SAX...NOT UP TO YOUR LEVEL, THOUGH.
WISH I COULD STAY HERE FOR YOUR NEXT SET, BUT DUTY CALLS, UNFORTUNATELY.
CLUB CLOSES AT 2. IF YOU'RE DONE WITH YOUR 'POLICE BUSINESS,' COME AND BUY ME A COFFEE.
I LIKE COFFEE JUST FINE.

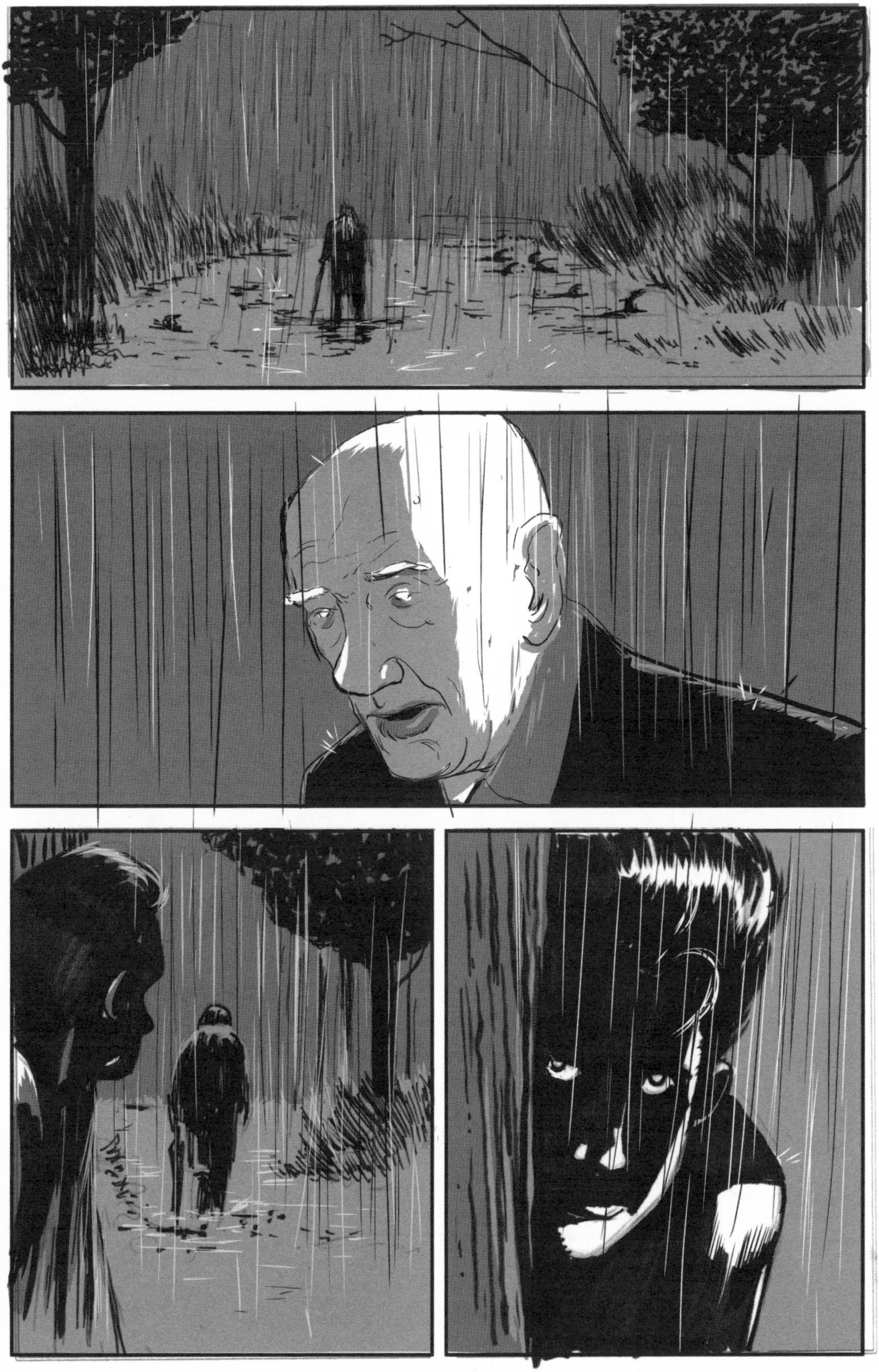

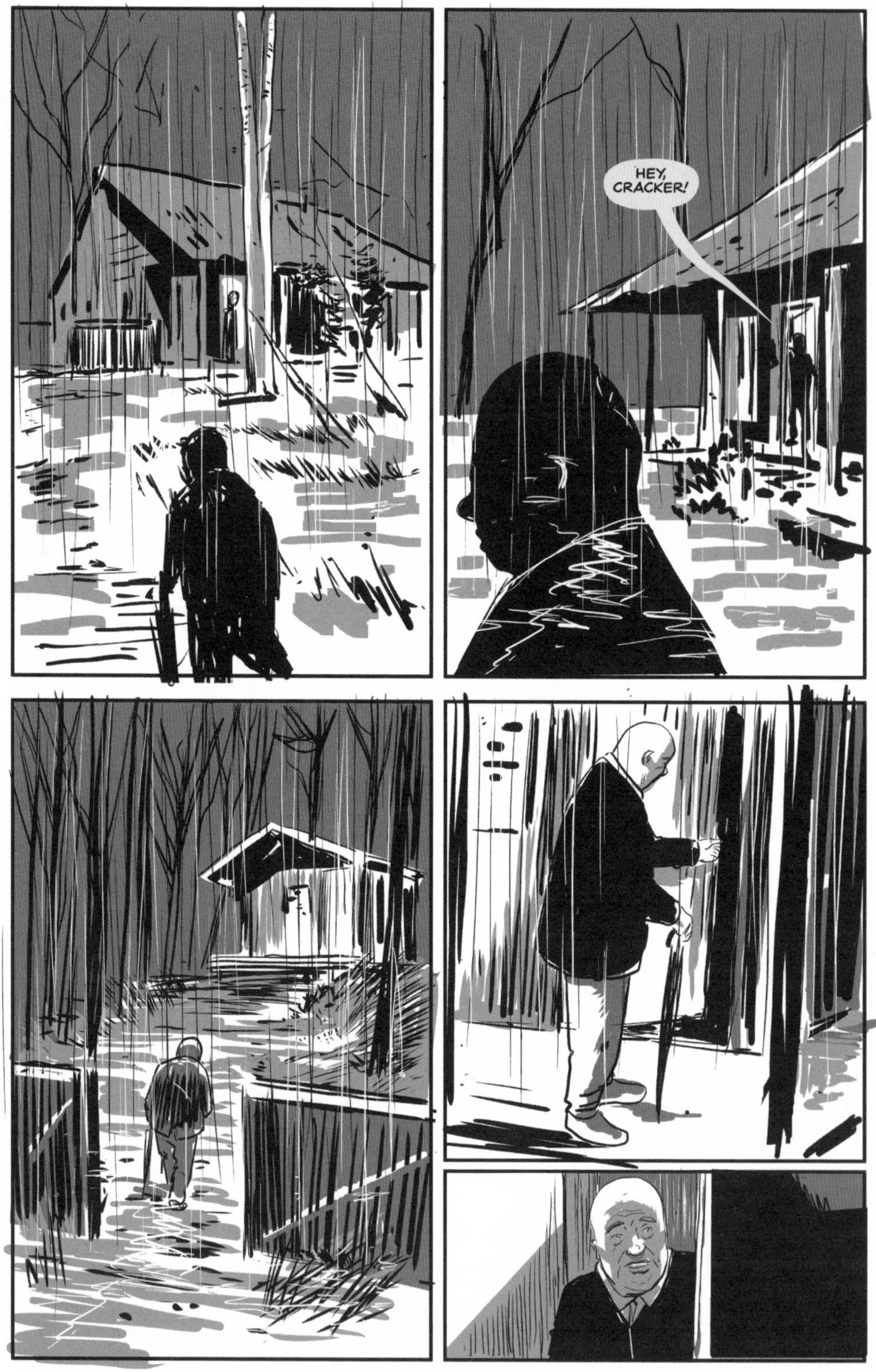
HEY, CRACKER!

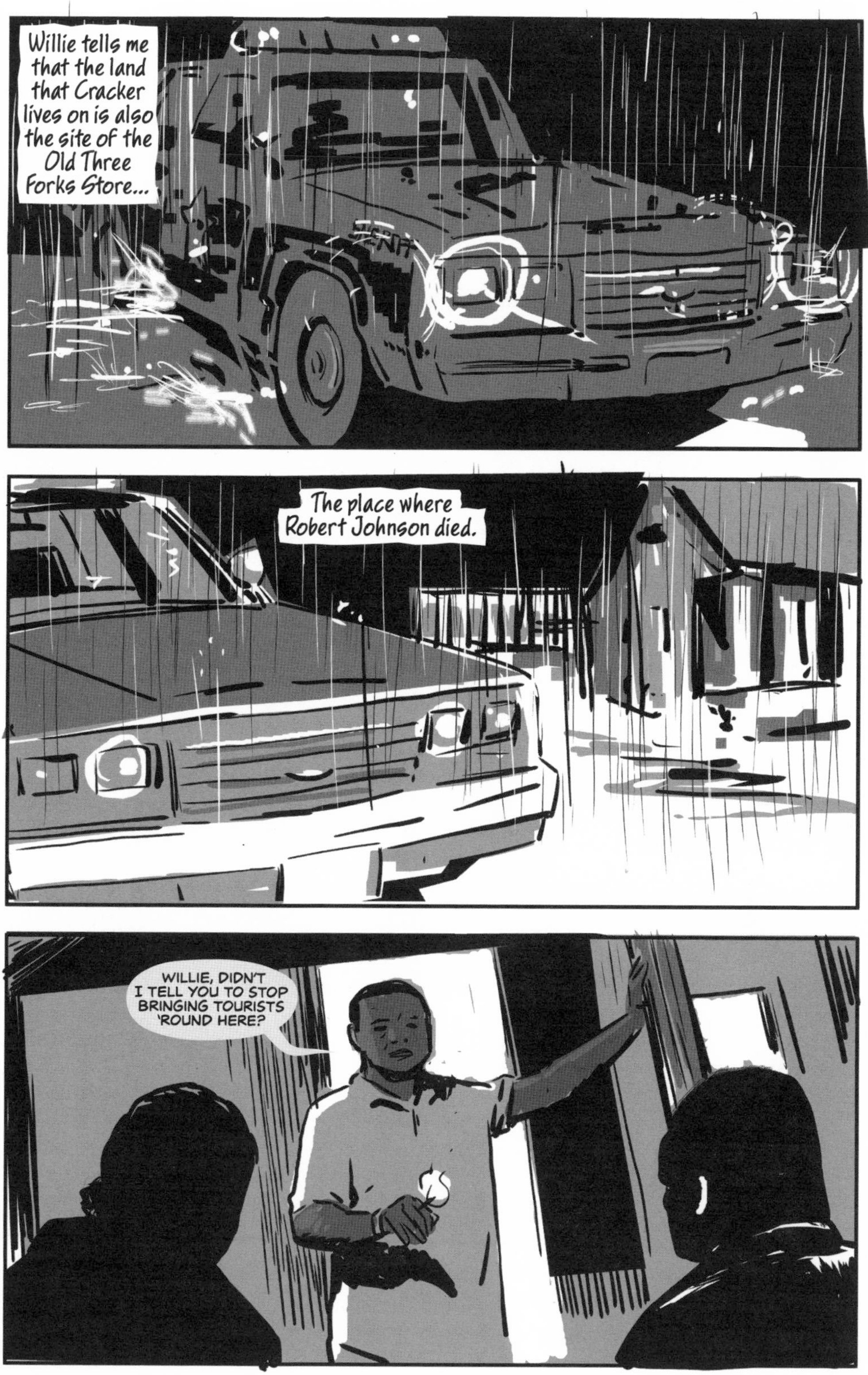
Willie tells me that the land that Cracker lives on is also the site of the Old Three Forks Store...
The place where Robert Johnson died.
WILLIE, DIDN'T I TELL YOU TO STOP BRINGING TOURISTS 'ROUND HERE?

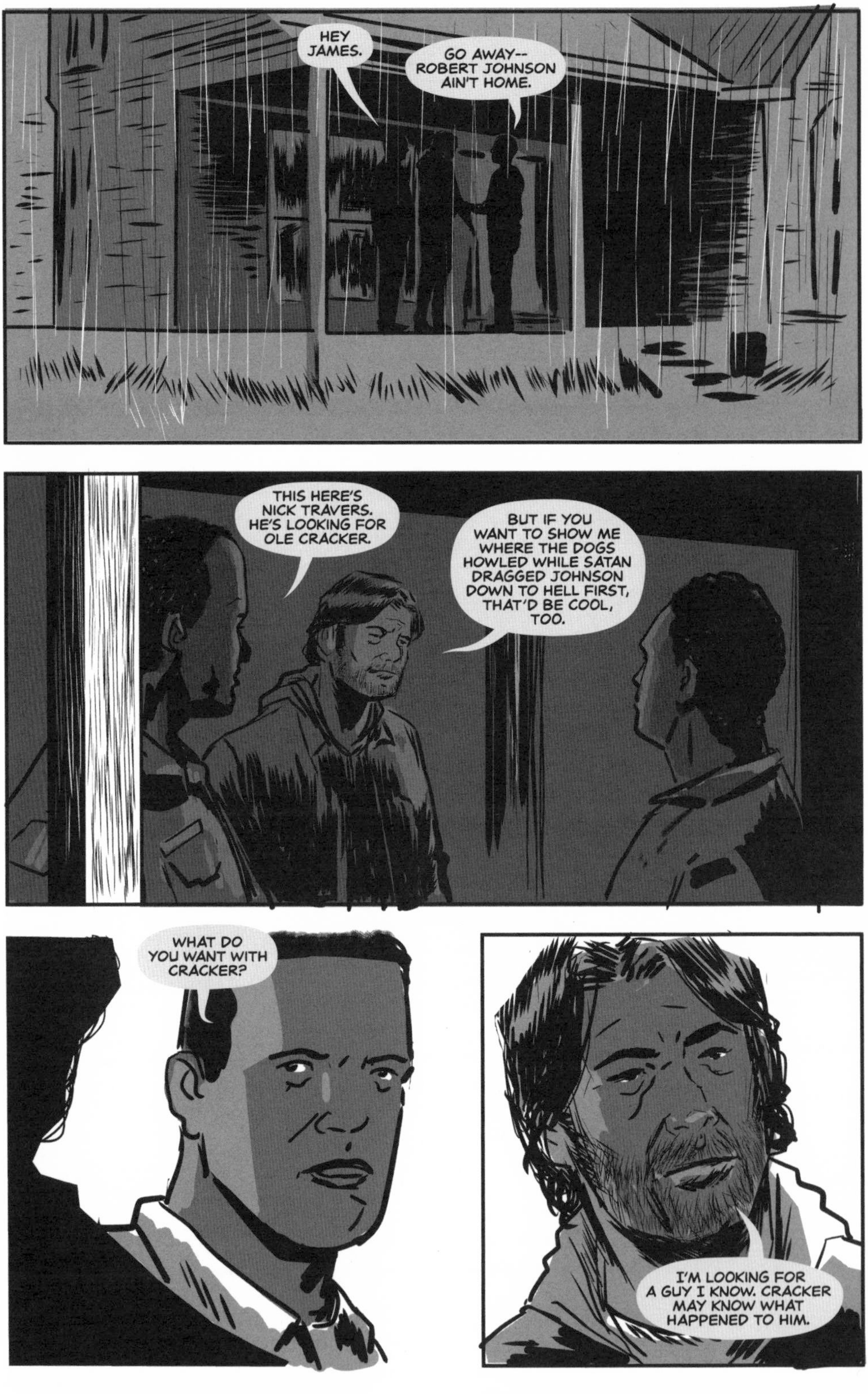
HEY JAMES.
GO AWAY-- ROBERT JOHNSON AIN'T HOME.
THIS HERE'S NICK TRAVERS. HE'S LOOKING FOR OLE CRACKER.
BUT IF YOU WANT TO SHOW ME WHERE THE DOGS HOWLED WHILE SATAN DRAGGED JOHNSON DOWN TO HELL FIRST, THAT'D BE COOL, TOO.
WHAT DO YOU WANT WITH CRACKER?
I'M LOOKING FOR A GUY I KNOW. CRACKER MAY KNOW WHAT HAPPENED TO HIM.

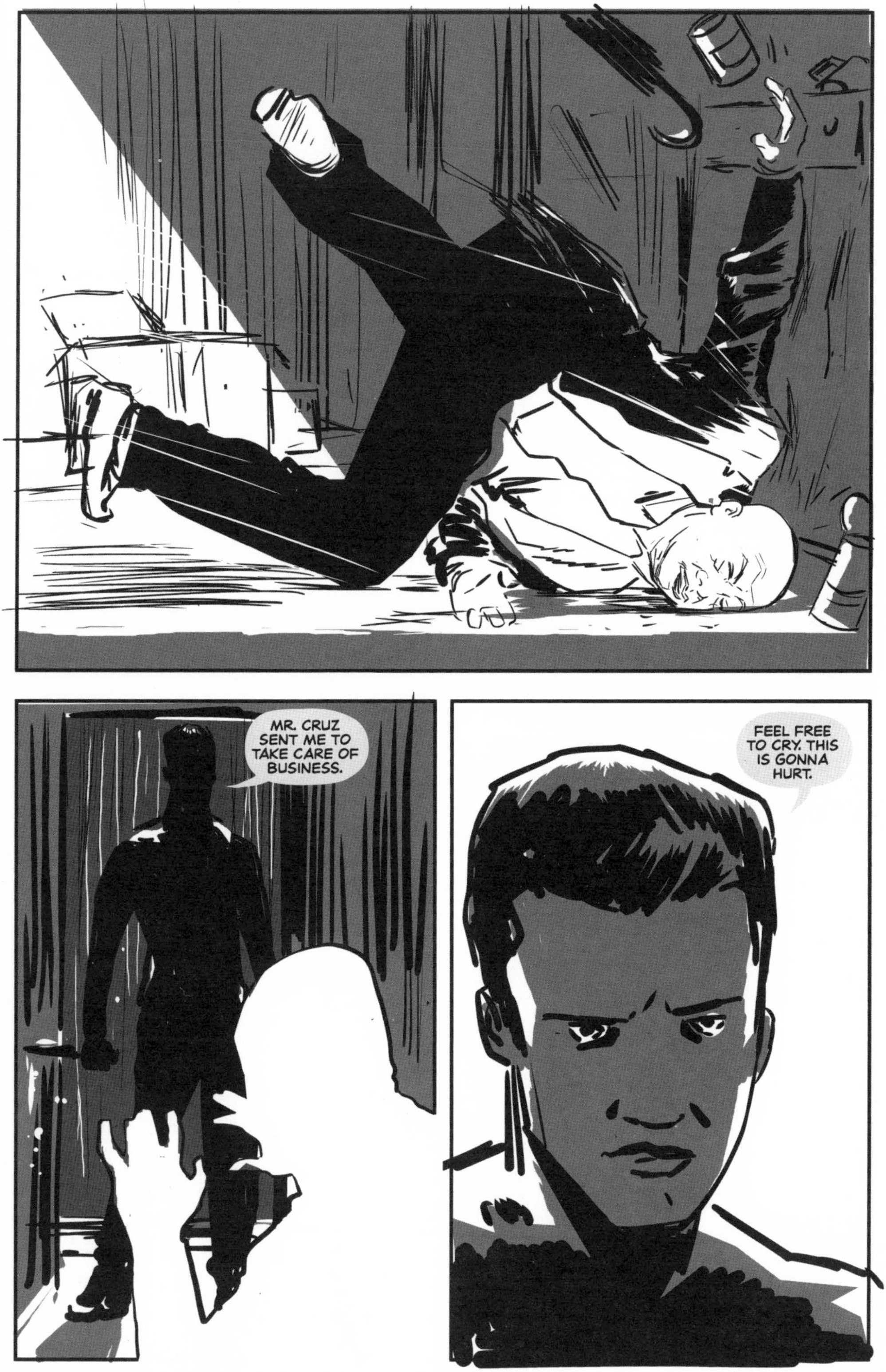
MR. CRUZ SENT ME TO TAKE CARE OF BUSINESS.
FEEL FREE TO CRY. THIS IS GONNA HURT.

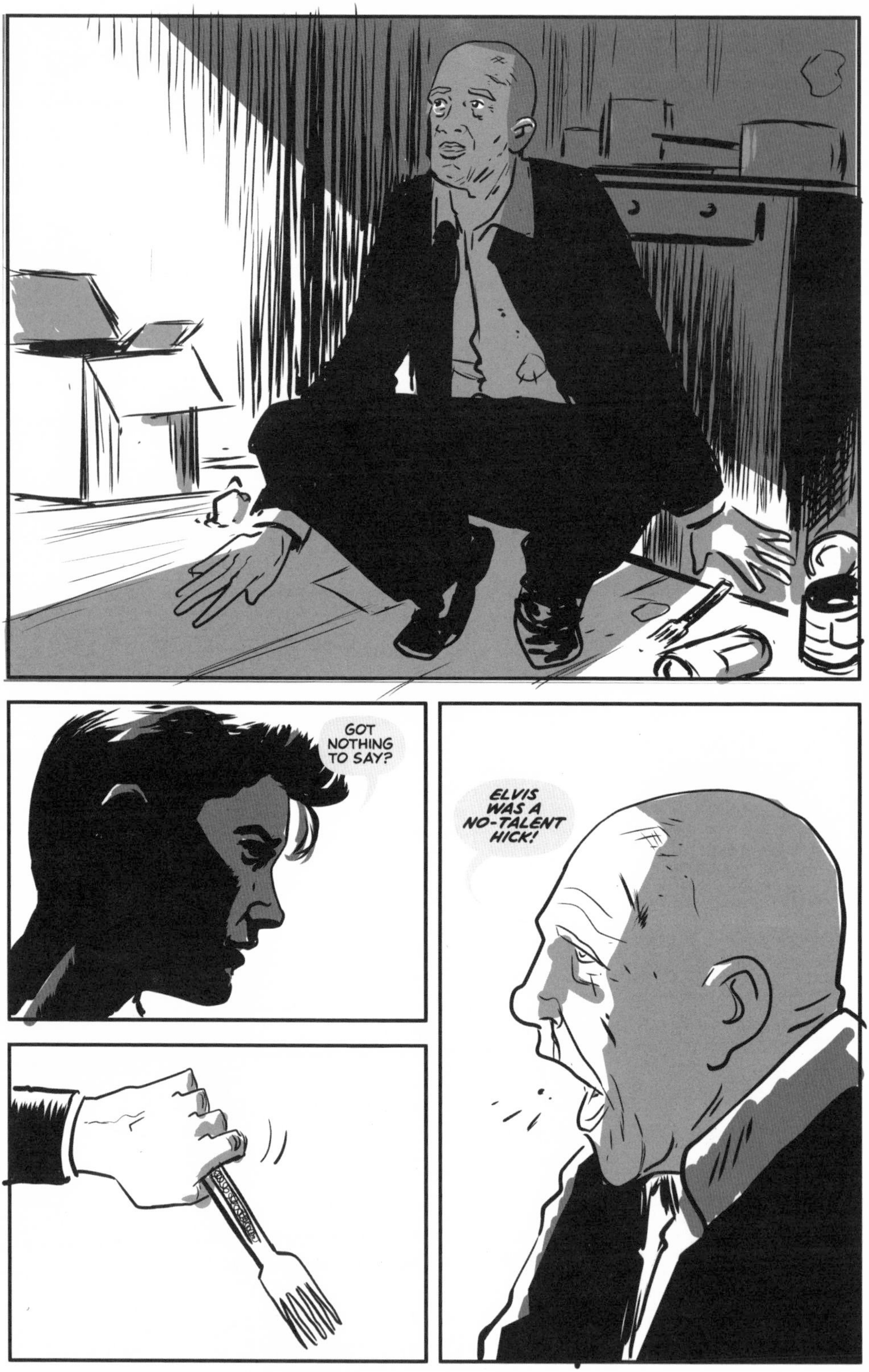
GOT NOTHING TO SAY?
ELVIS WAS A NO-TALENT HICK!

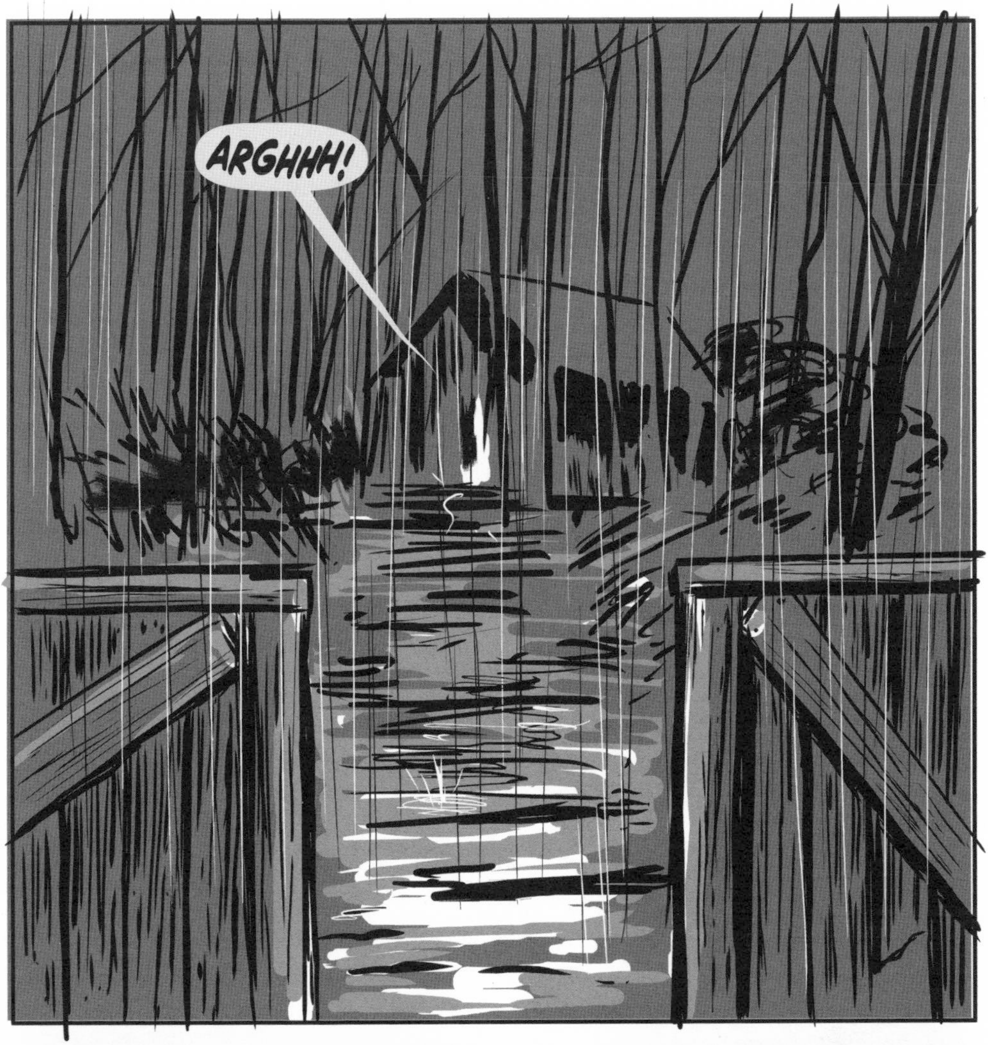
ARGHHH!

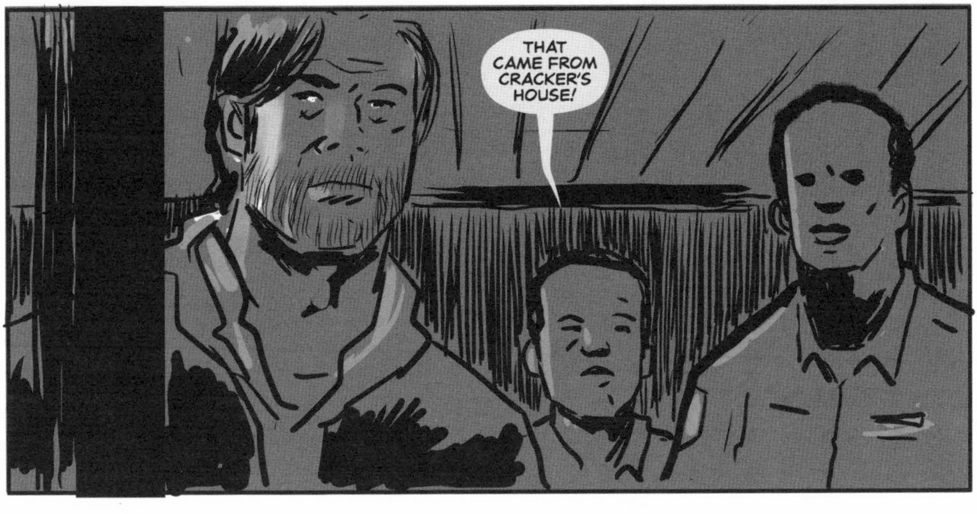
THAT CAME FROM CRACKER'S HOUSE!

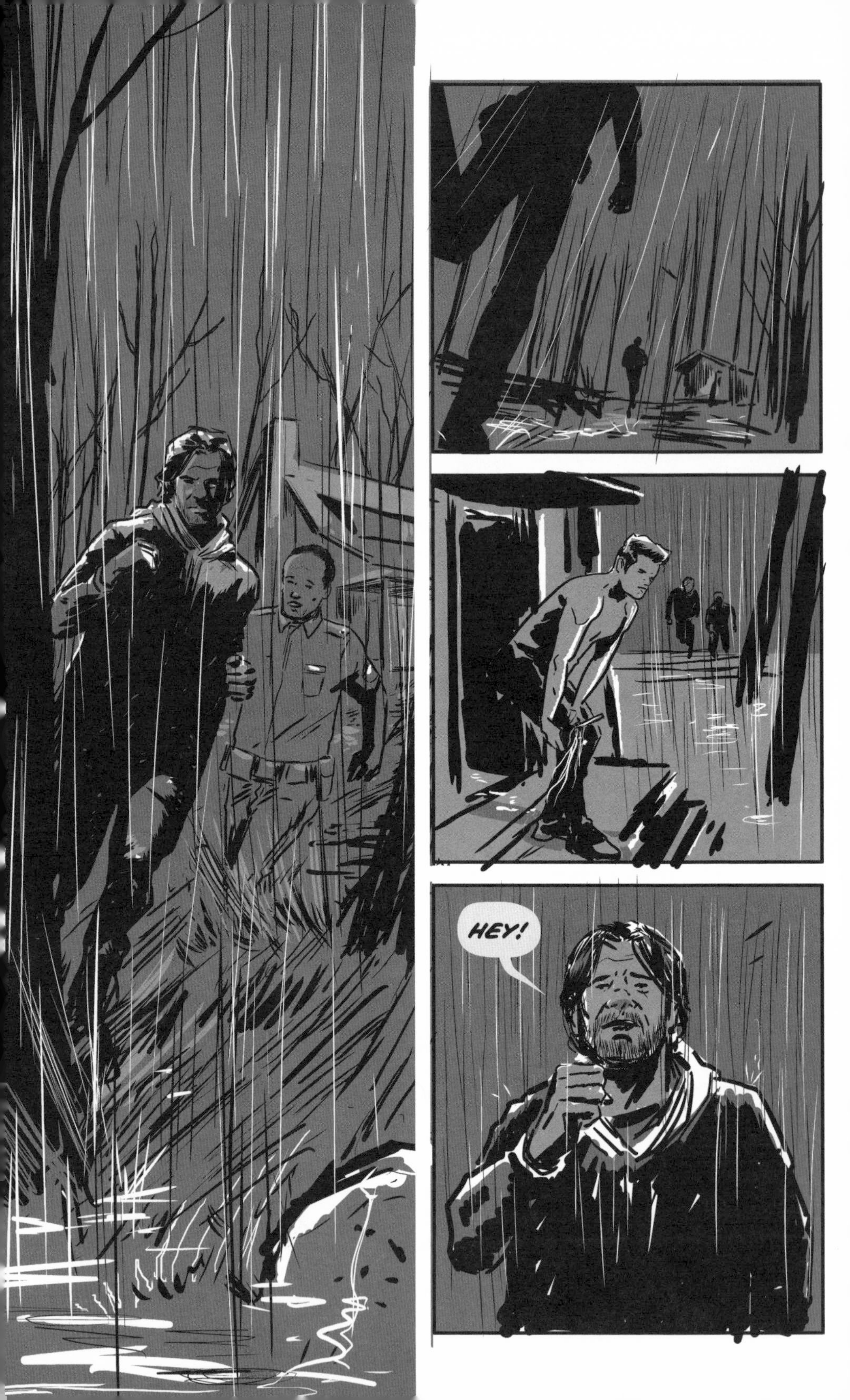
HEY!

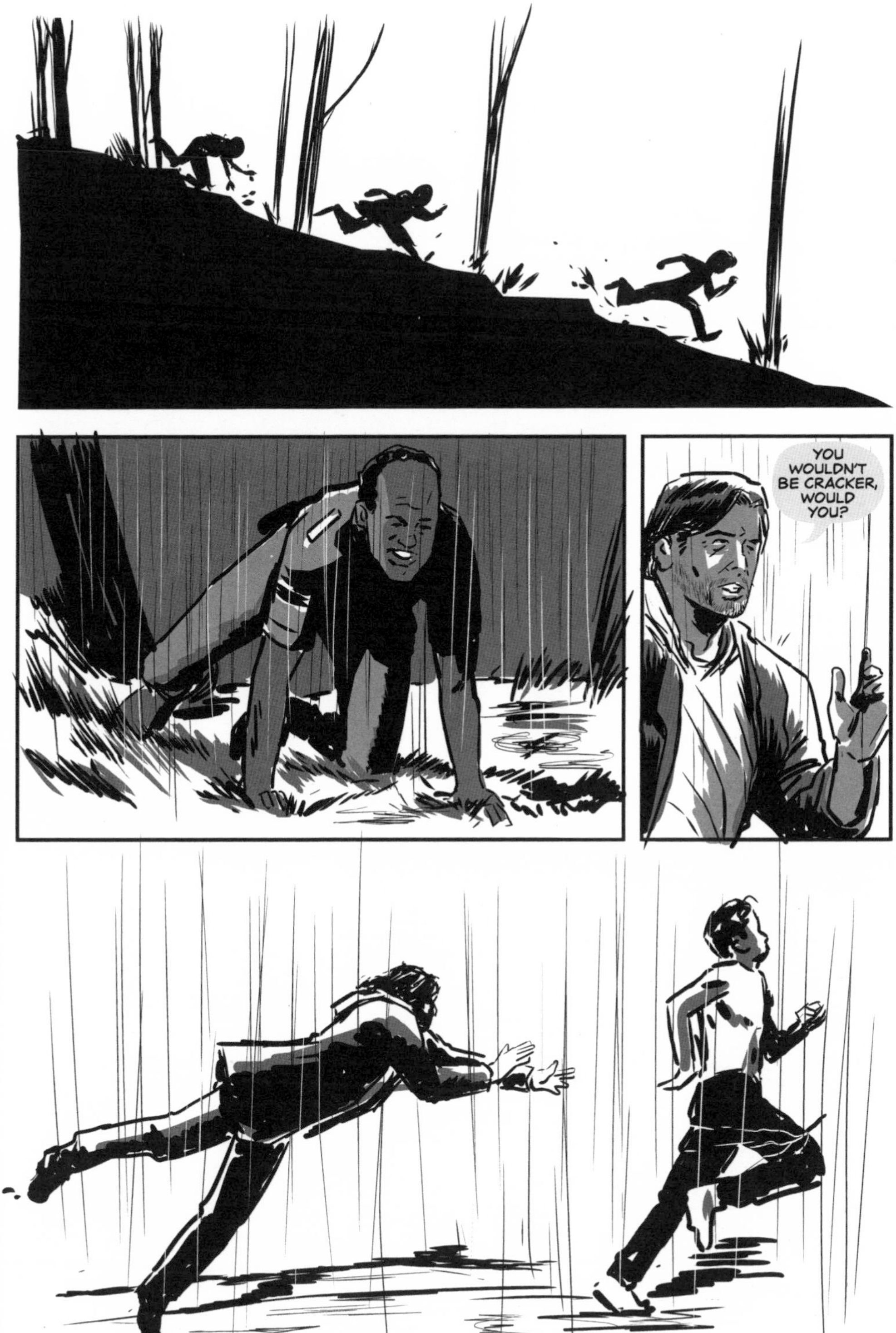
YOU WOULDN'T BE CRACKER, WOULD YOU?

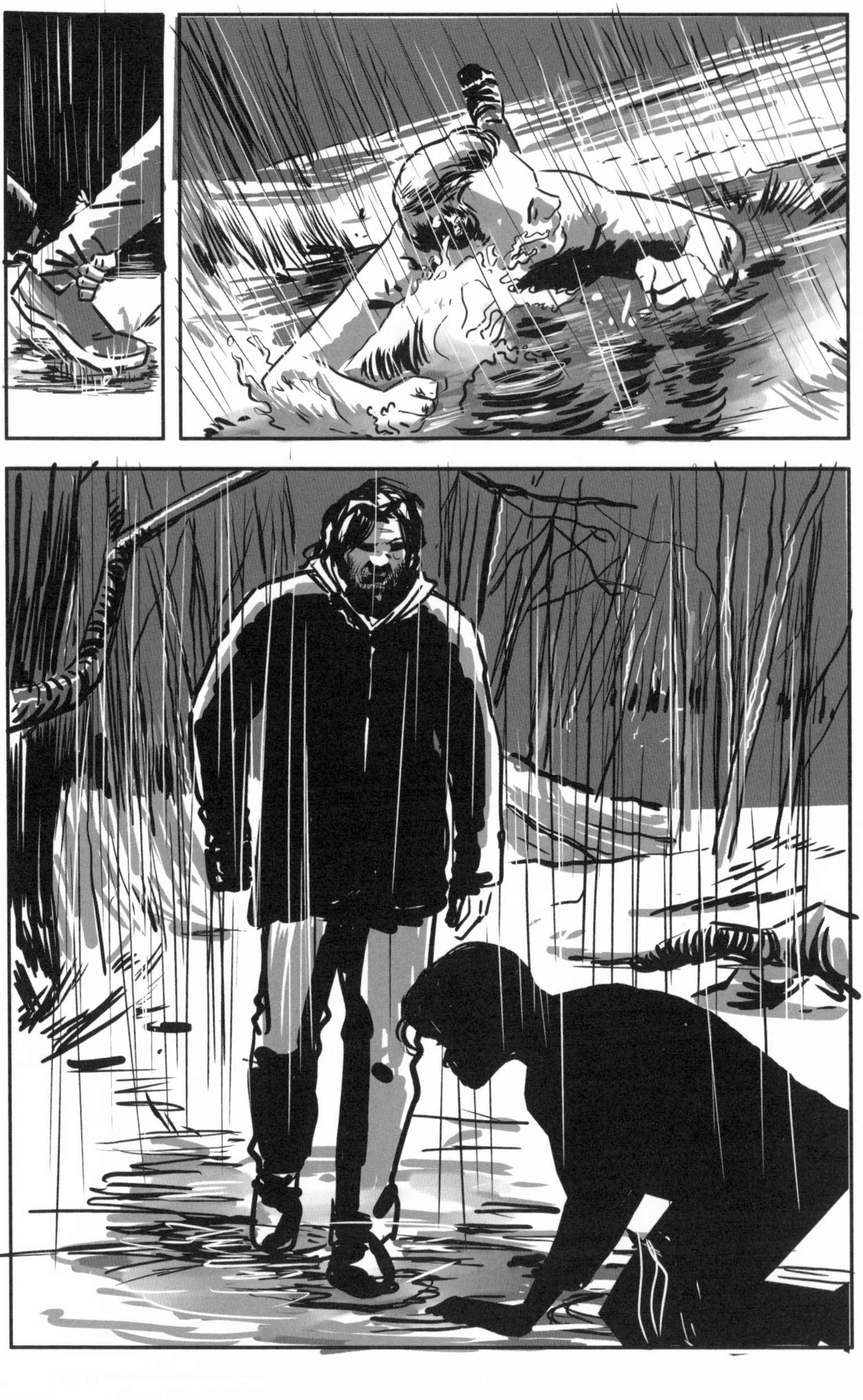

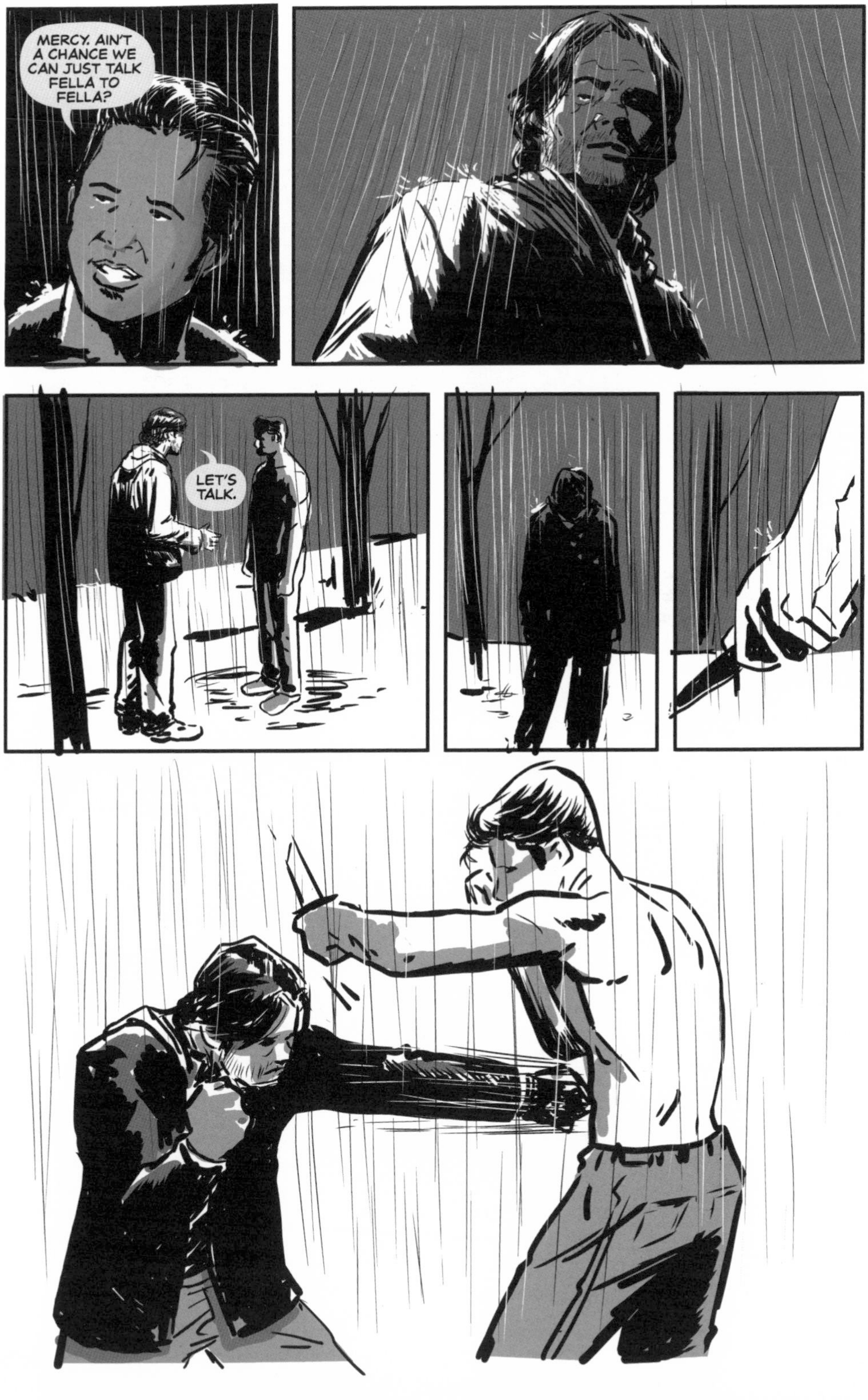
MERCY. AIN'T A CHANCE WE CAN JUST TALK FELLA TO FELLA?
LET'S TALK.

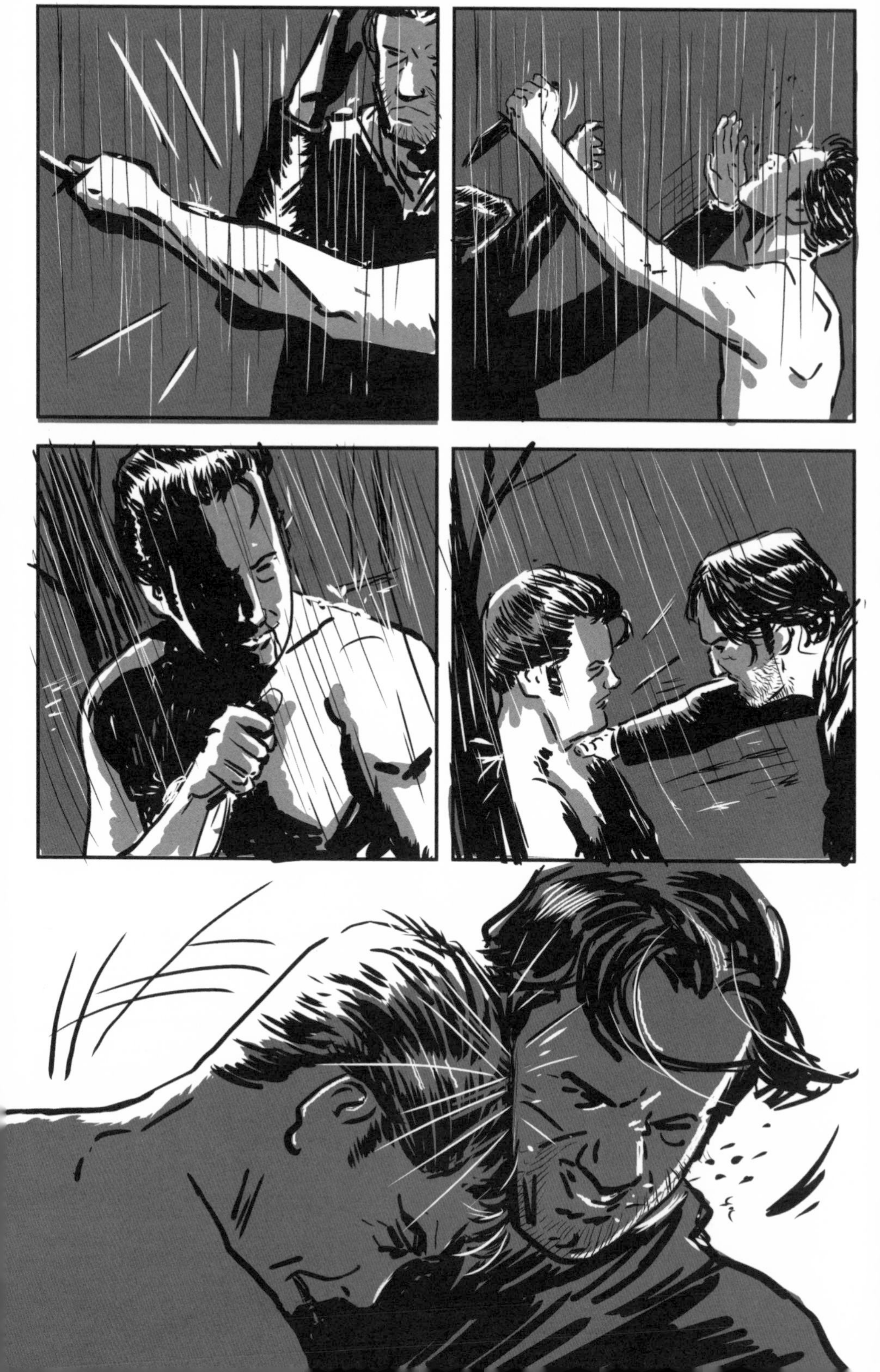

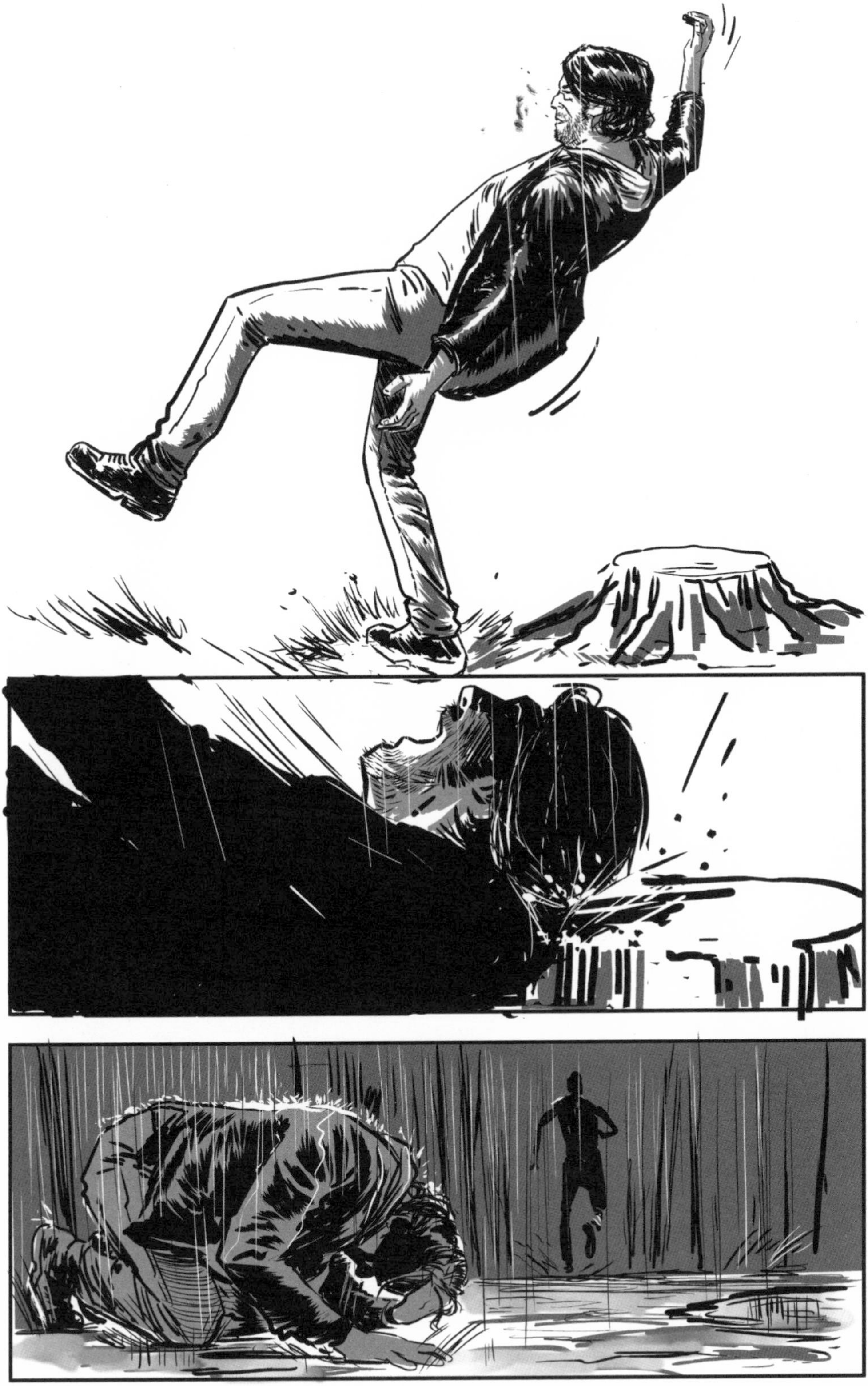

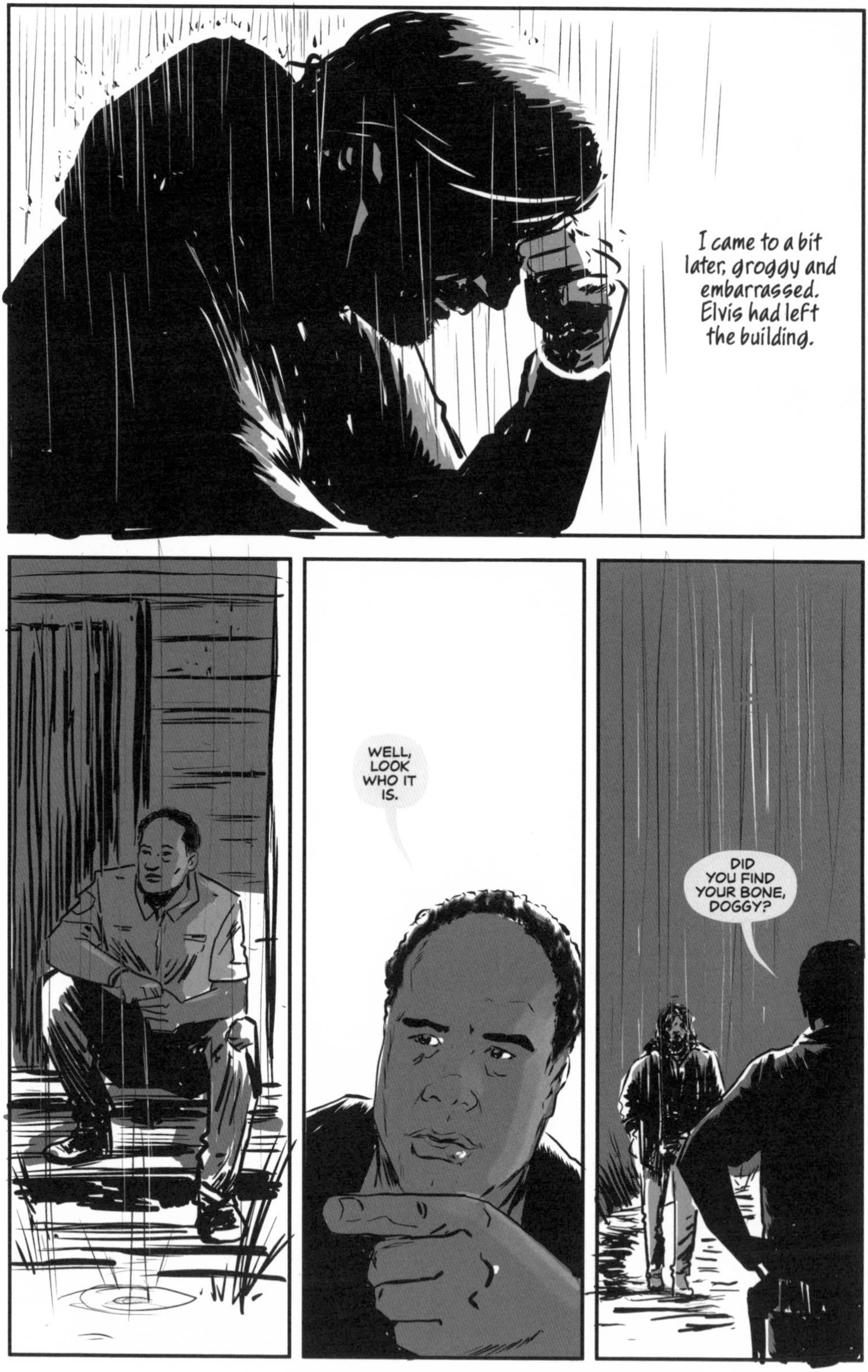
I came to a bit later, groggy and embarrassed. Elvis had left the building.
WELL, LOOK WHO IT IS.
DID YOU FIND YOUR BONE, DOGGY?

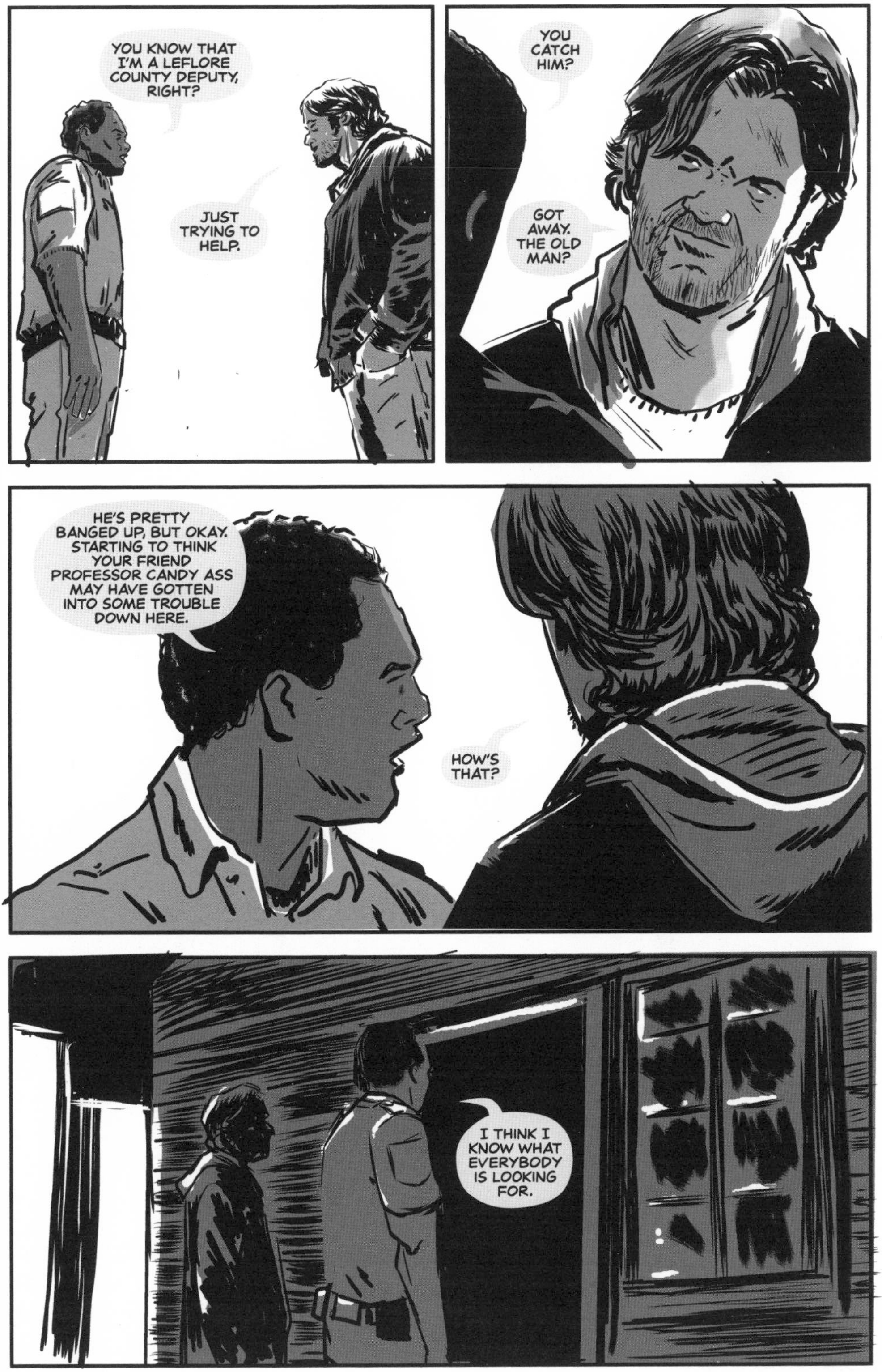
YOU KNOW THAT I'M A LEFLORE COUNTY DEPUTY, RIGHT?
JUST TRYING TO HELP.
YOU CATCH HIM?
GOT AWAY. THE OLD MAN?
HE'S PRETTY BANGED UP, BUT OKAY. STARTING TO THINK YOUR FRIEND PROFESSOR CANDY ASS MAY HAVE GOTTEN INTO SOME TROUBLE DOWN HERE.
HOW'S THAT?
I THINK I KNOW WHAT EVERYBODY IS LOOKING FOR.

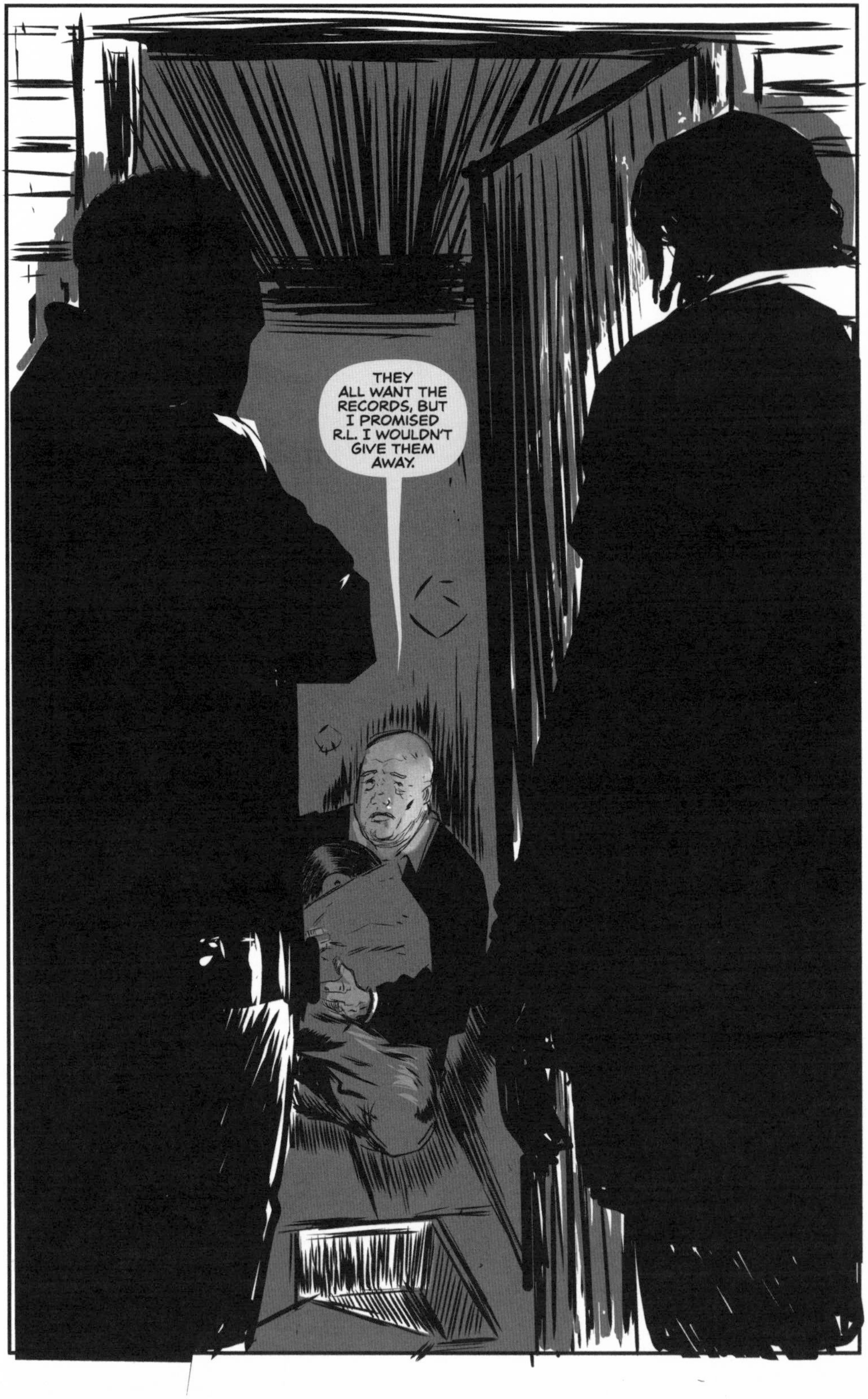
THEY ALL WANT THE RECORDS, BUT I PROMISED R.L. I WOULDN'T GIVE THEM AWAY.

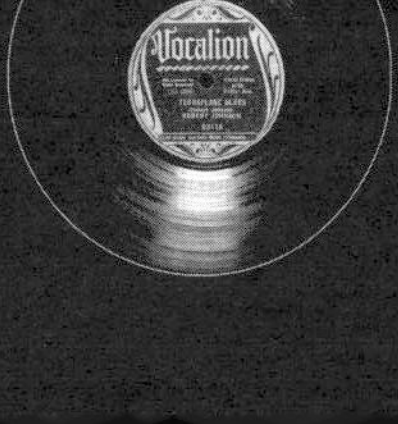
Vocalion

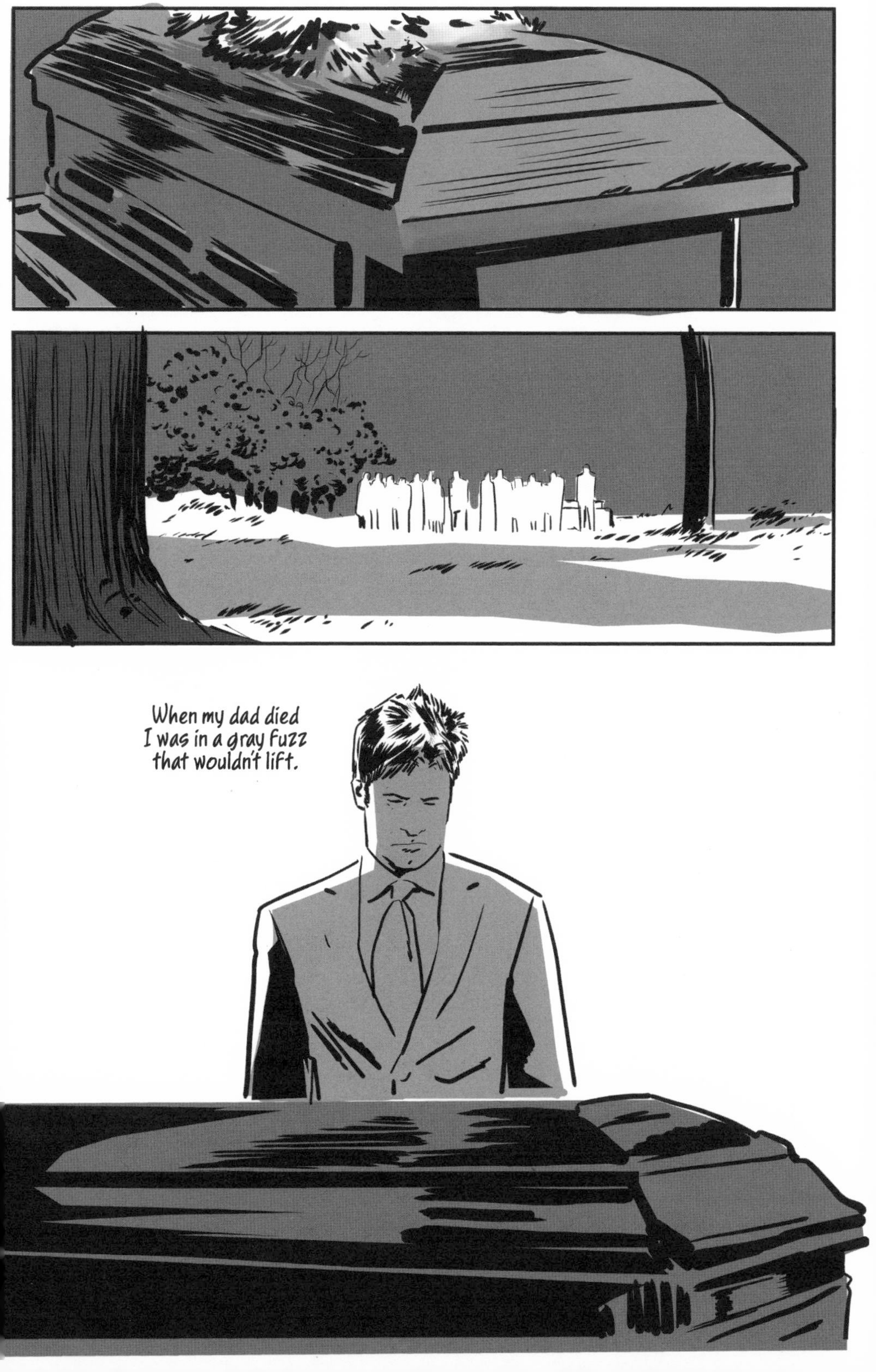
When my dad died I was in a gray fuzz that wouldn't lift.

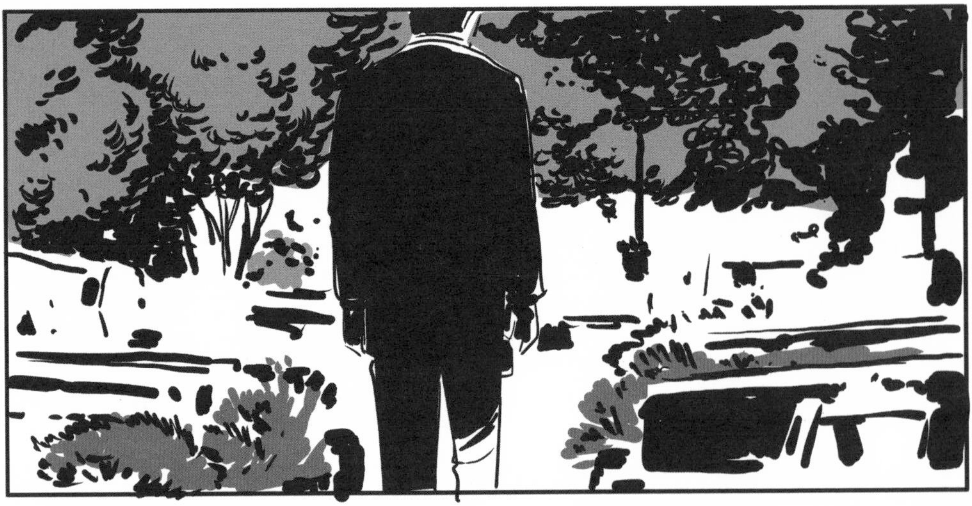

CHAPTER THREE

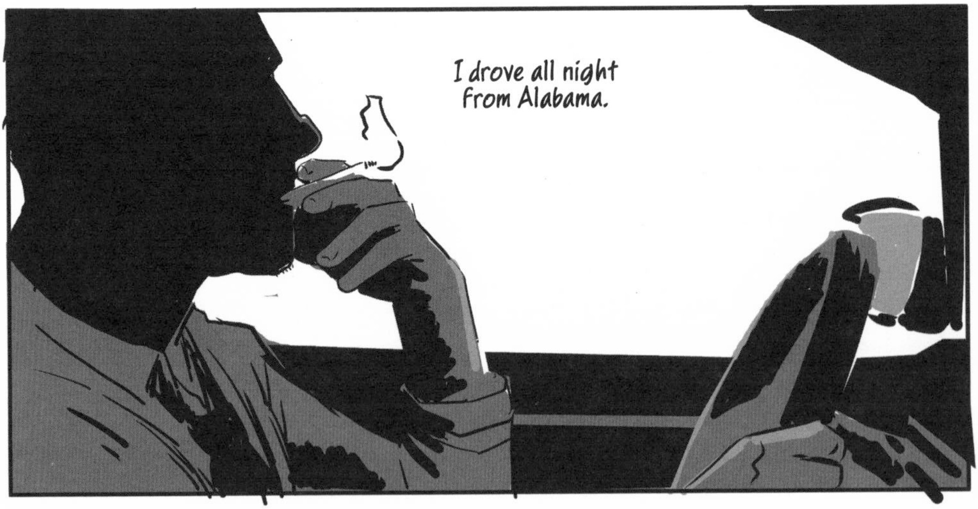
I drove all night from Alabama.

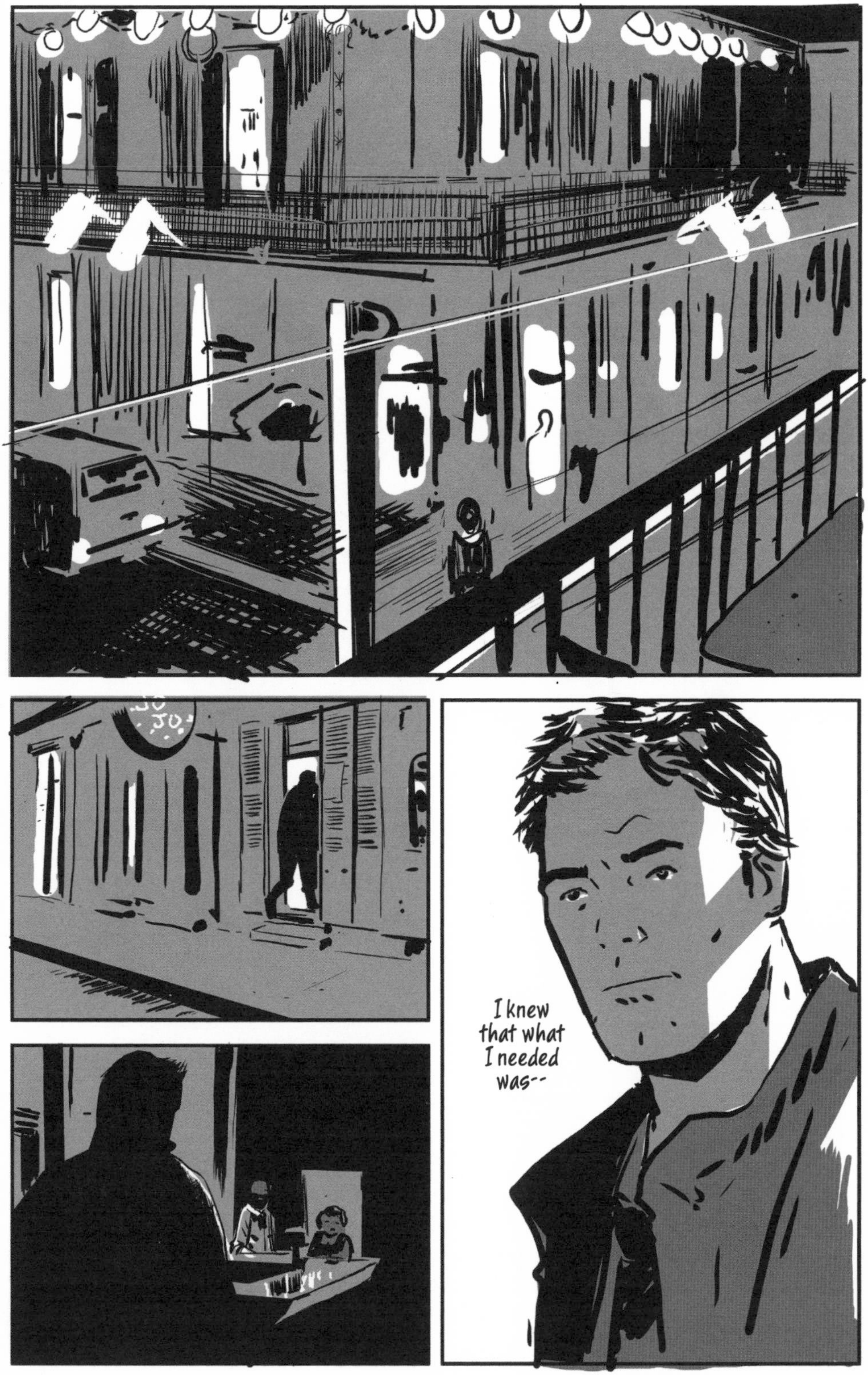
I knew
that what
I needed
was--

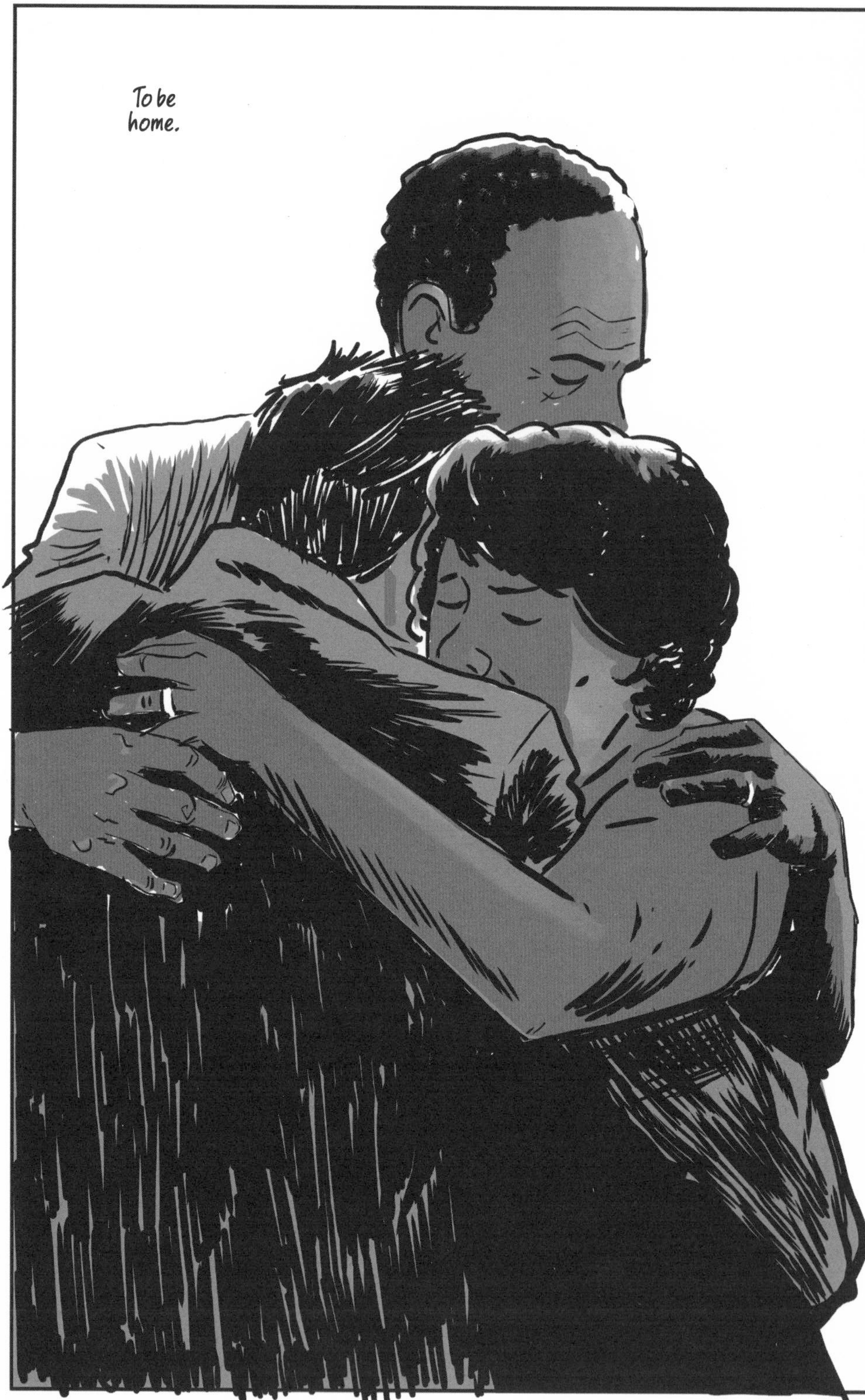
To be
home.

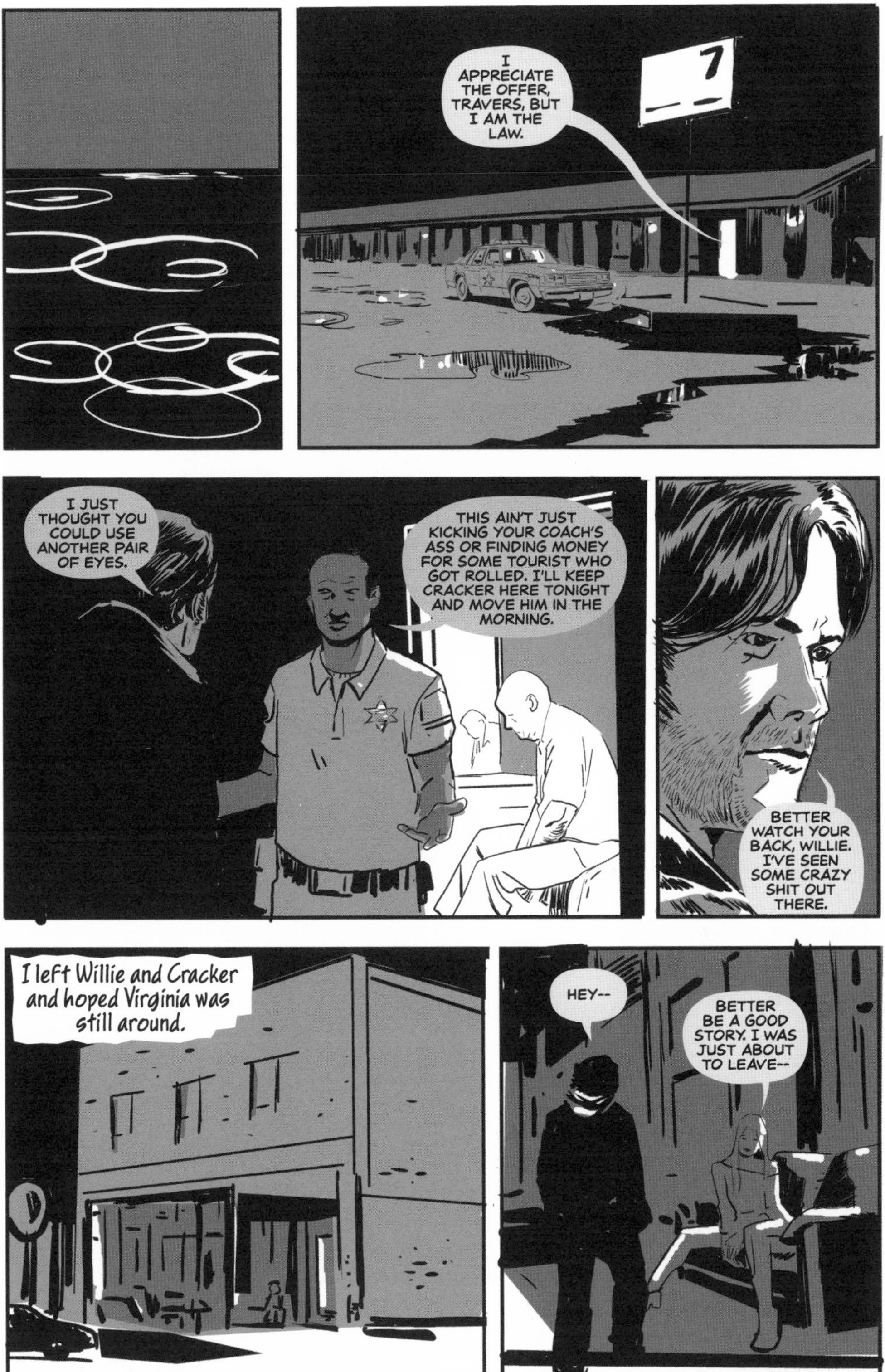
I APPRECIATE THE OFFER, TRAVERS, BUT I AM THE LAW.
7
I JUST THOUGHT YOU COULD USE ANOTHER PAIR OF EYES.
THIS AIN'T JUST KICKING YOUR COACH'S ASS OR FINDING MONEY FOR SOME TOURIST WHO GOT ROLLED. I'LL KEEP CRACKER HERE TONIGHT AND MOVE HIM IN THE MORNING.
BETTER WATCH YOUR BACK, WILLIE. I'VE SEEN SOME CRAZY SHIT OUT THERE.
I left Willie and Cracker and hoped Virginia was still around.
HEY--
BETTER BE A GOOD STORY. I WAS JUST ABOUT TO LEAVE--

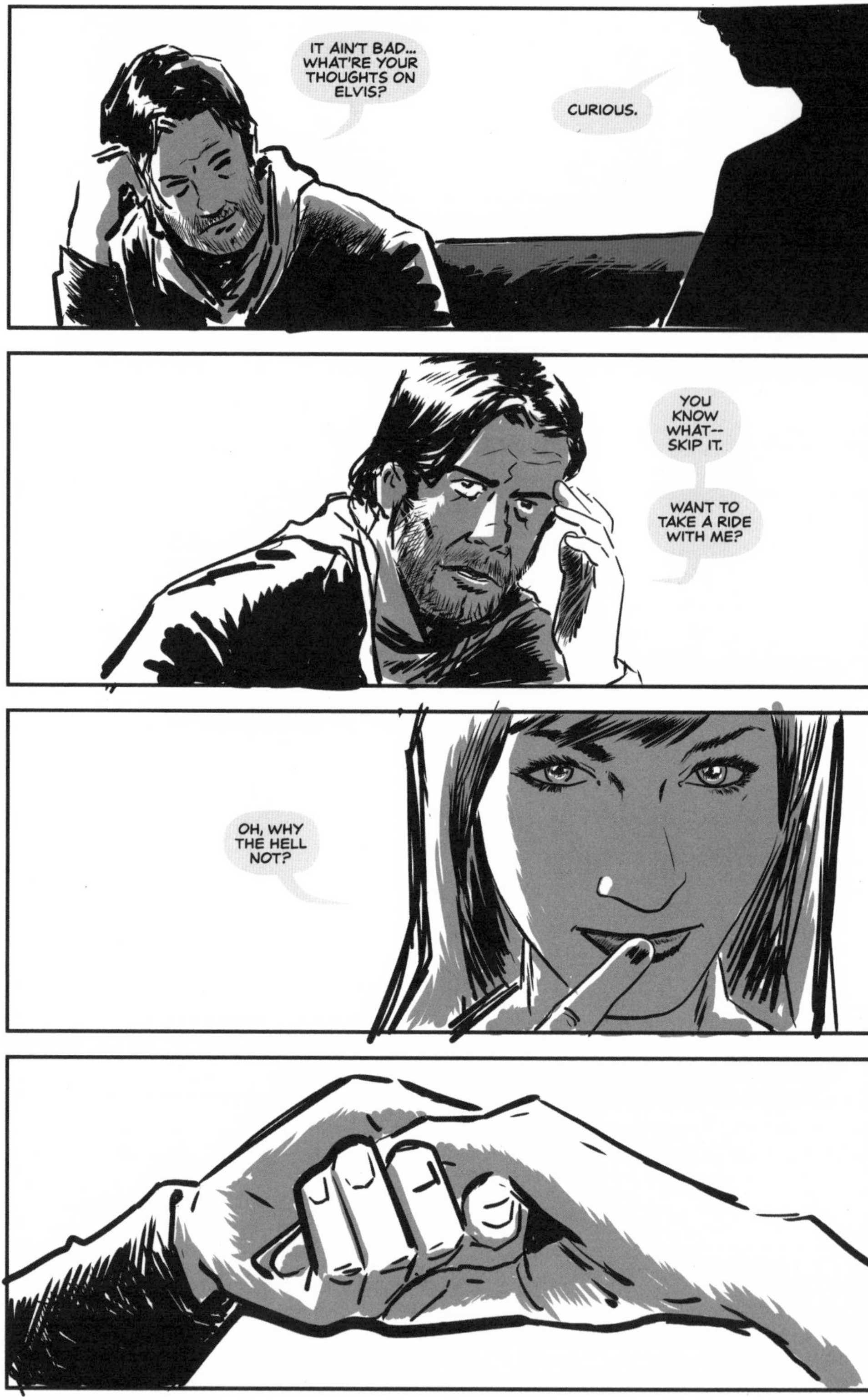
IT AIN'T BAD... WHAT'RE YOUR THOUGHTS ON ELVIS?
CURIOUS.
YOU KNOW WHAT-- SKIP IT.
WANT TO TAKE A RIDE WITH ME?
OH, WHY THE HELL NOT?

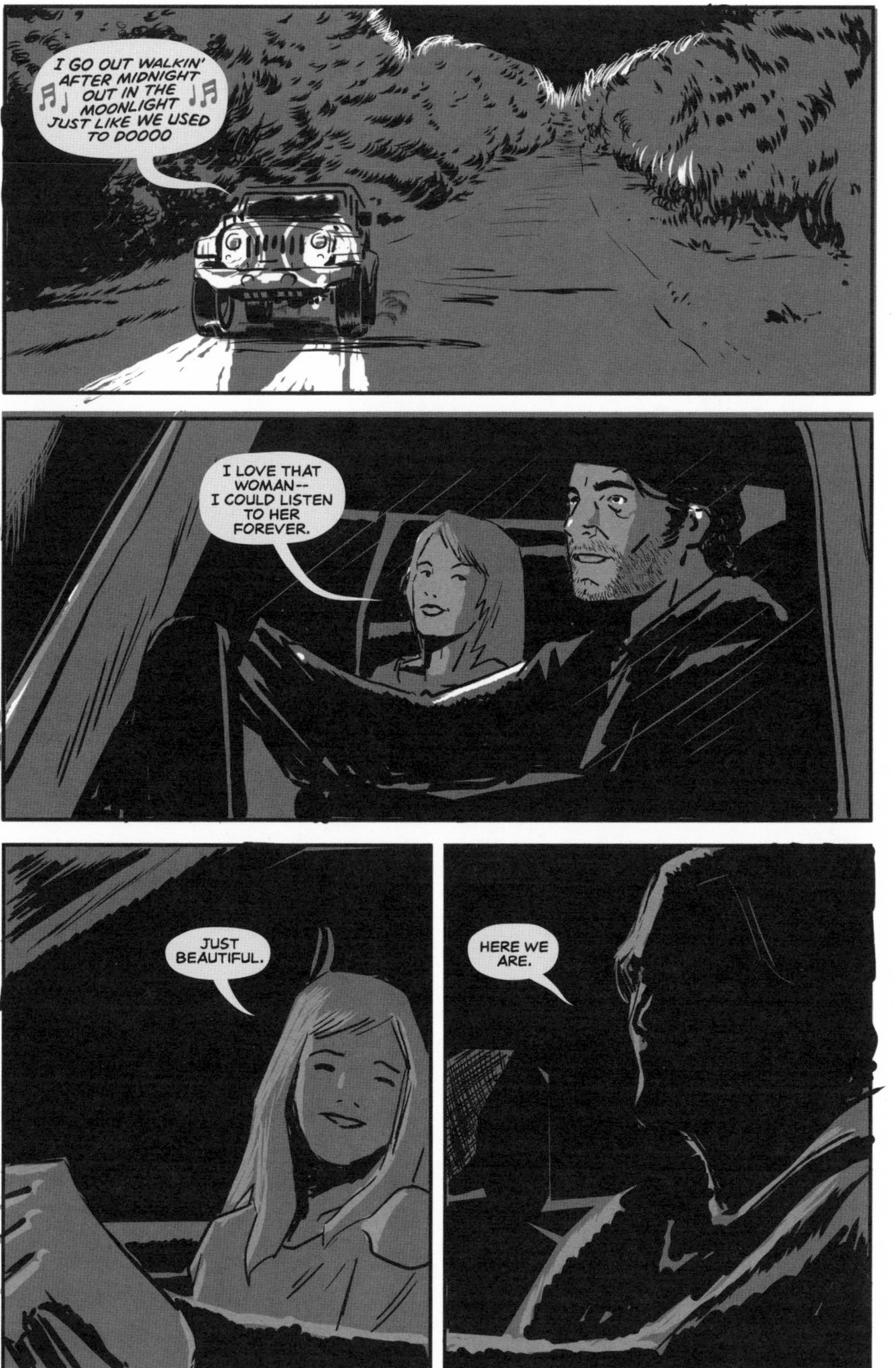
I GO OUT WALKIN' AFTER MIDNIGHT OUT IN THE MOONLIGHT JUST LIKE WE USED TO DOOOO
I LOVE THAT WOMAN-- I COULD LISTEN TO HER FOREVER.
JUST BEAUTIFUL.
HERE WE ARE.

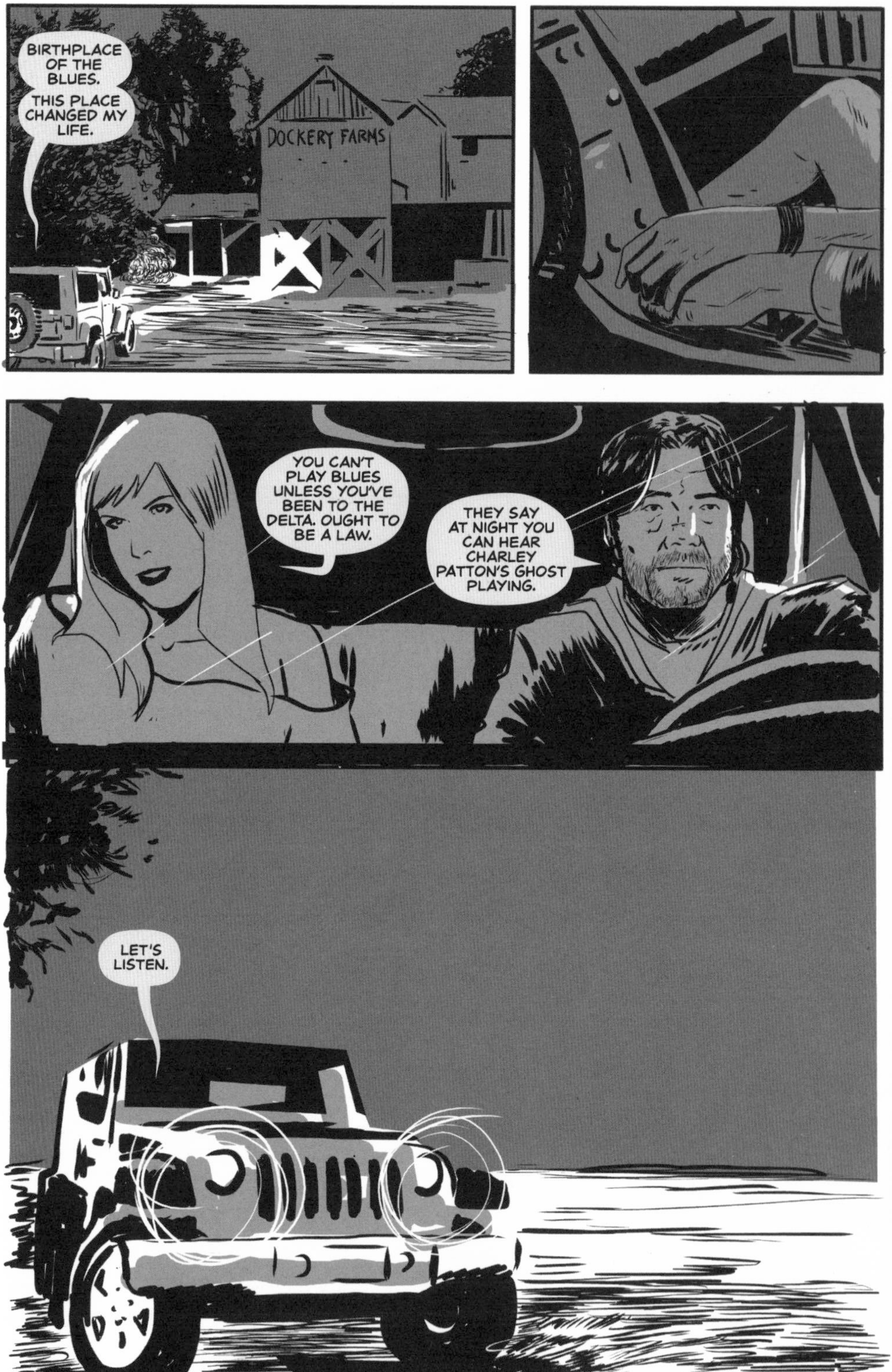
BIRTHPLACE OF THE BLUES.
THIS PLACE CHANGED MY LIFE.
DOCKERY FARMS
YOU CAN'T PLAY BLUES UNLESS YOU'VE BEEN TO THE DELTA. OUGHT TO BE A LAW.
THEY SAY AT NIGHT YOU CAN HEAR CHARLEY PATTON'S GHOST PLAYING.
LET'S LISTEN.

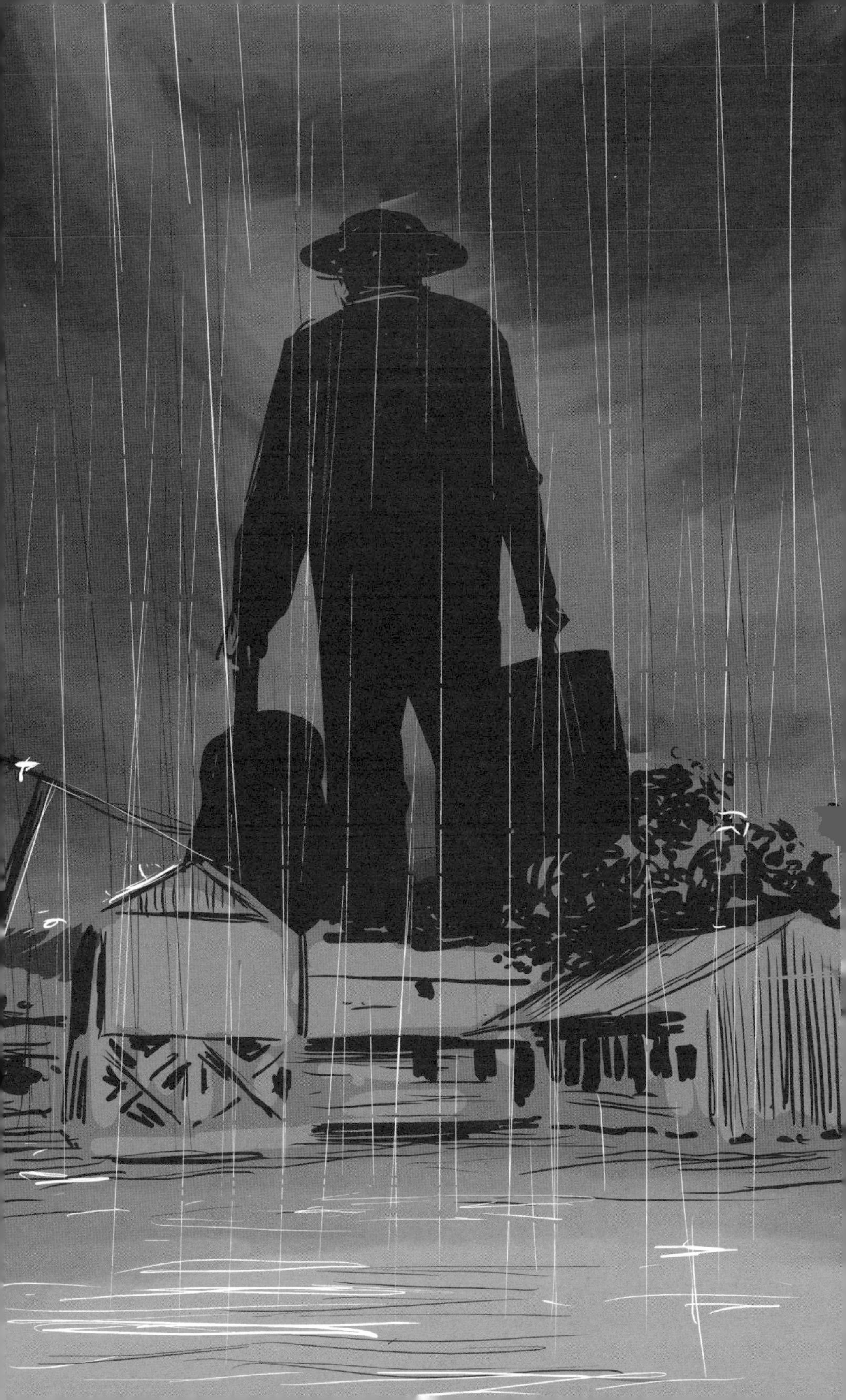

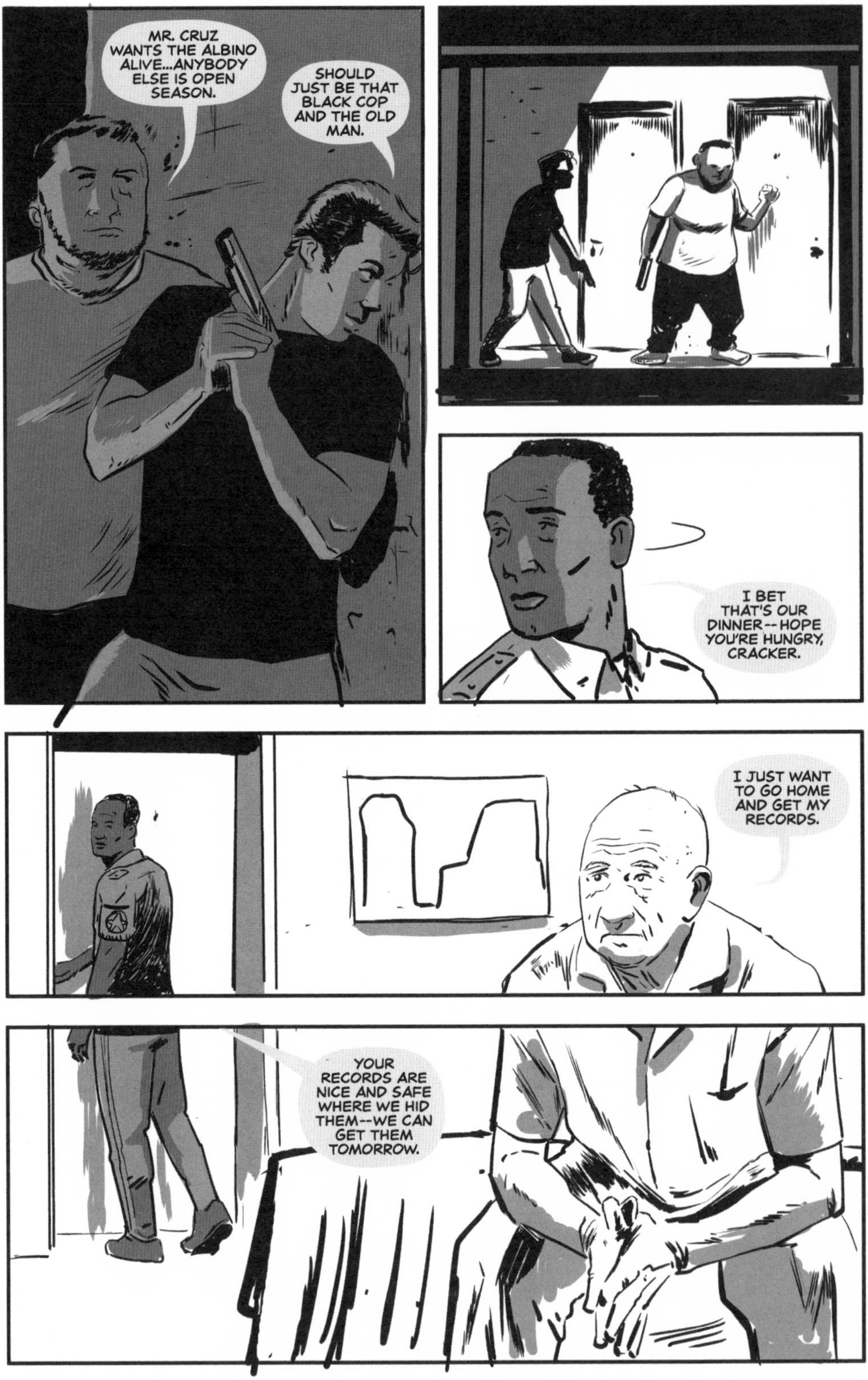
MR. CRUZ WANTS THE ALBINO ALIVE...ANYBODY ELSE IS OPEN SEASON.
SHOULD JUST BE THAT BLACK COP AND THE OLD MAN.
I BET THAT'S OUR DINNER--HOPE YOU'RE HUNGRY, CRACKER.
I JUST WANT TO GO HOME AND GET MY RECORDS.
YOUR RECORDS ARE NICE AND SAFE WHERE WE HID THEM--WE CAN GET THEM TOMORROW.

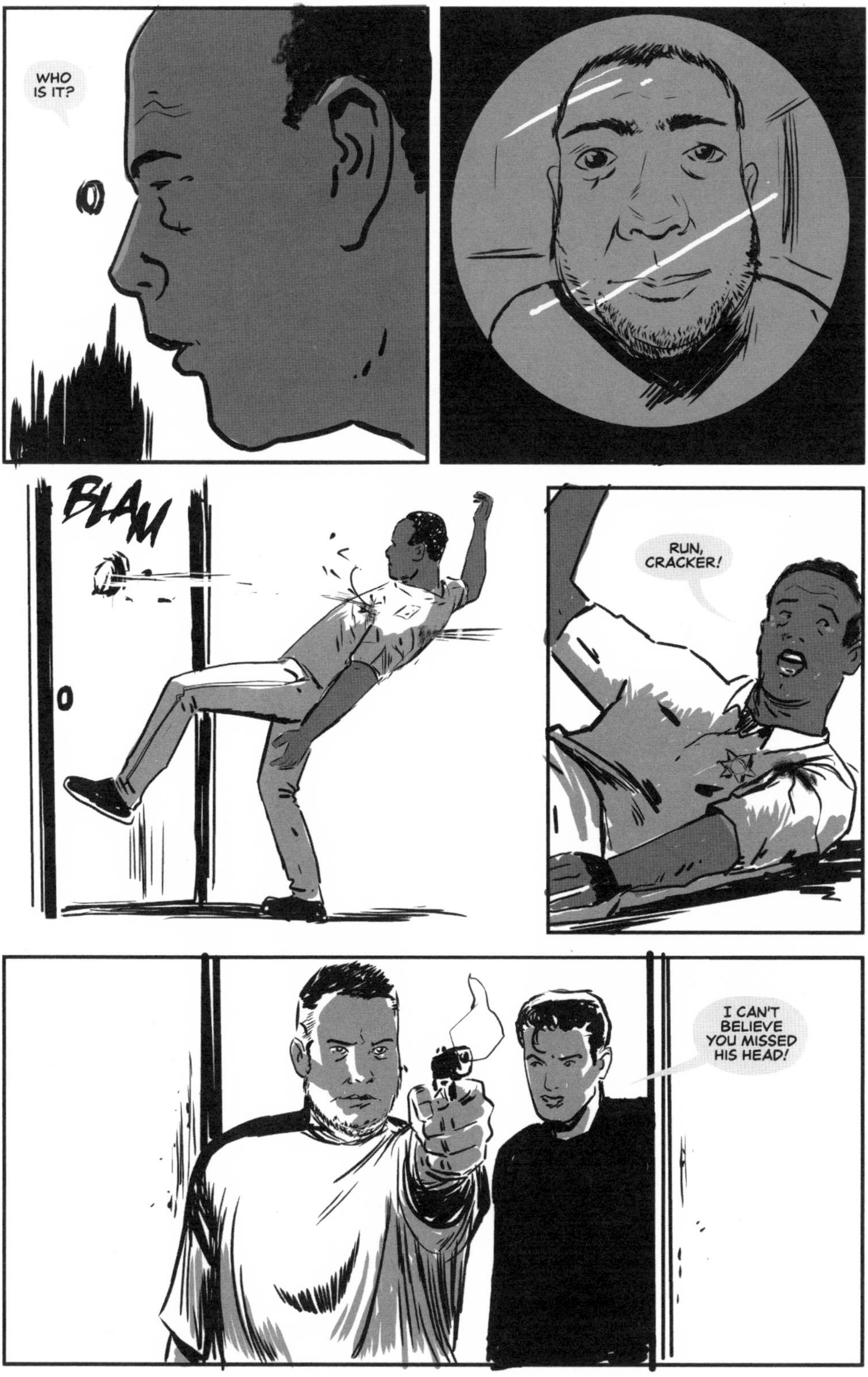
WHO IS IT?
BLAM
RUN, CRACKER!
I CAN'T BELIEVE YOU MISSED HIS HEAD!

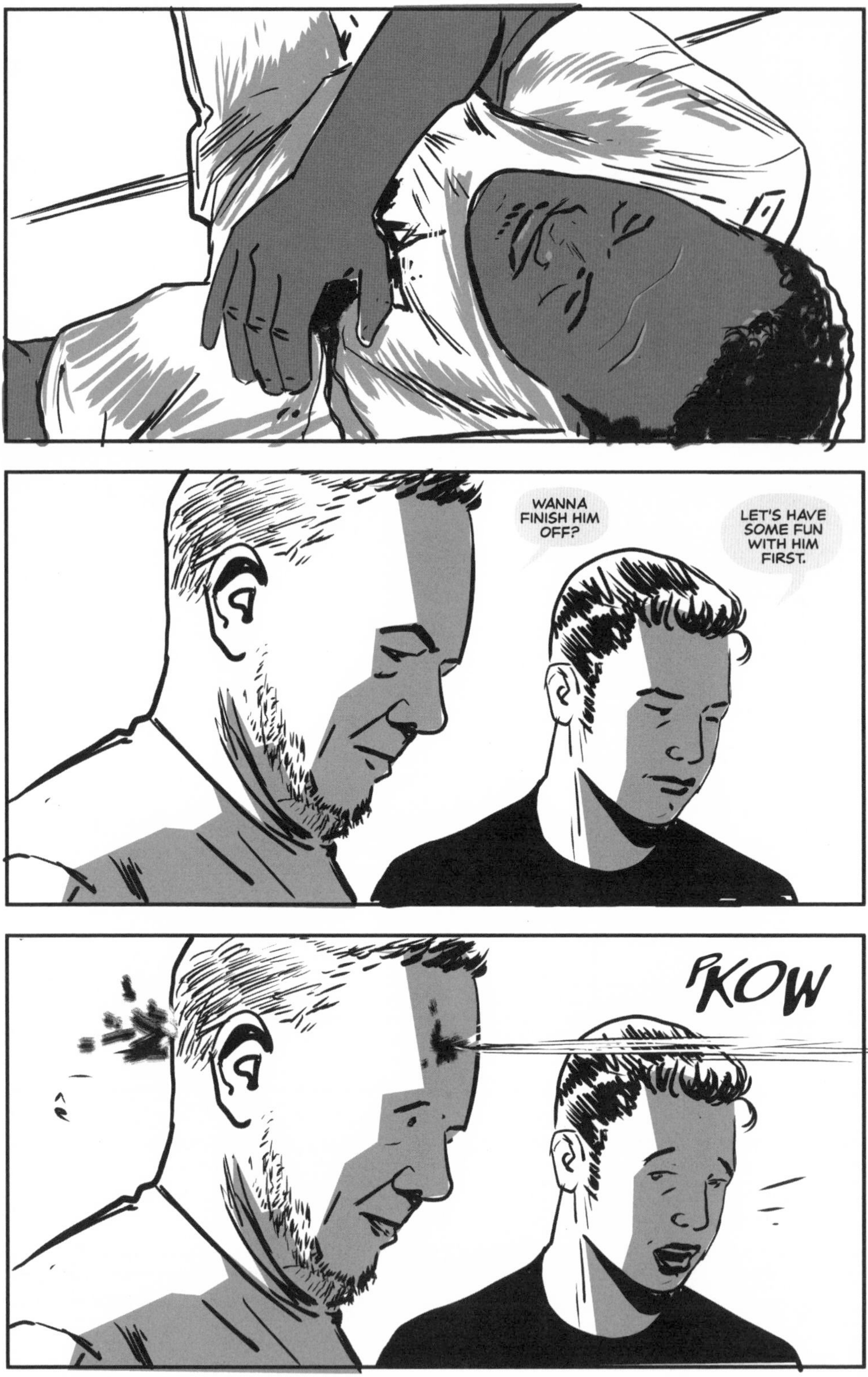
WANNA FINISH HIM OFF?
LET'S HAVE SOME FUN WITH HIM FIRST.
PKOW

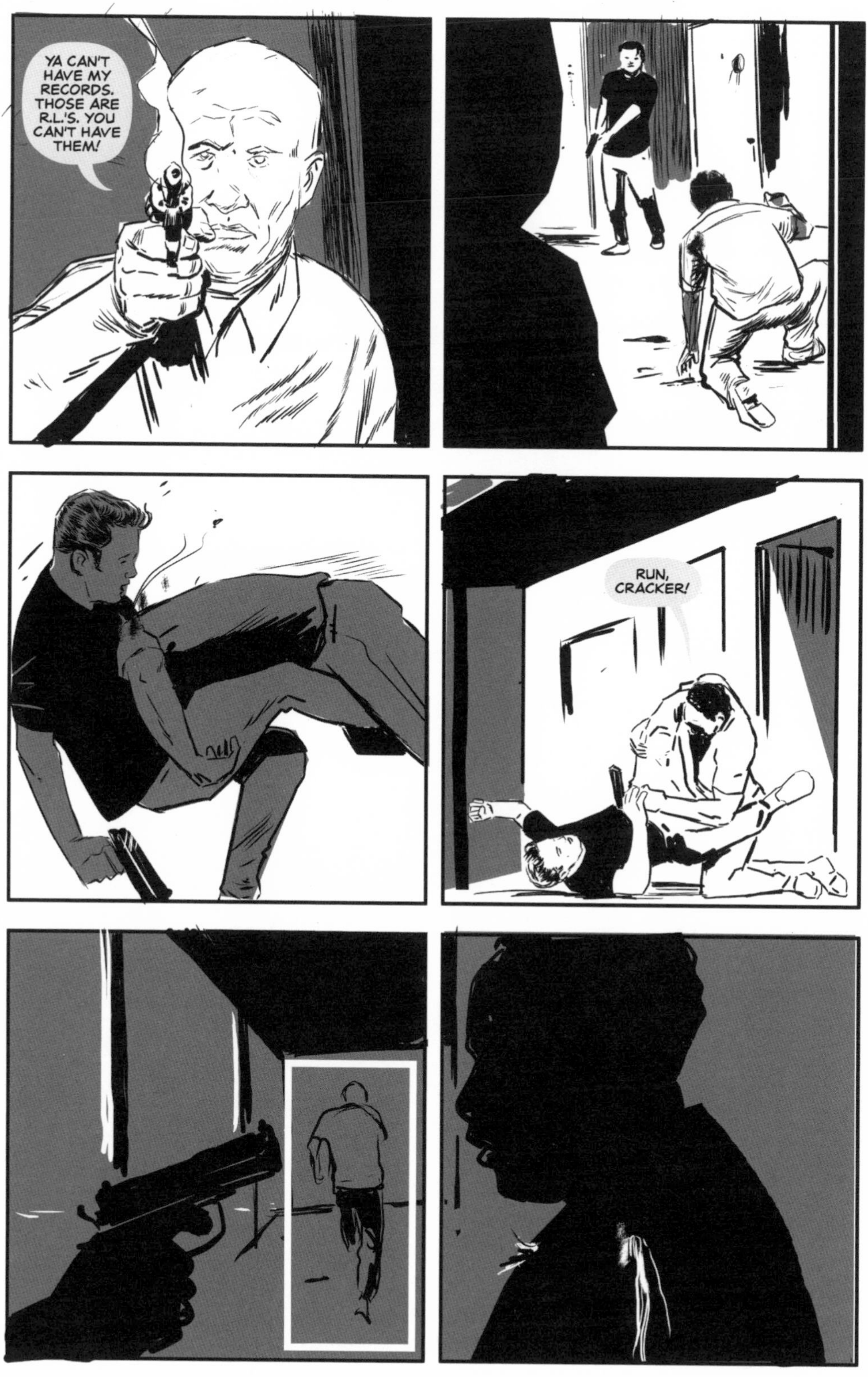
YA CAN'T HAVE MY RECORDS. THOSE ARE R.L.'S. YOU CAN'T HAVE THEM!
RUN, CRACKER!

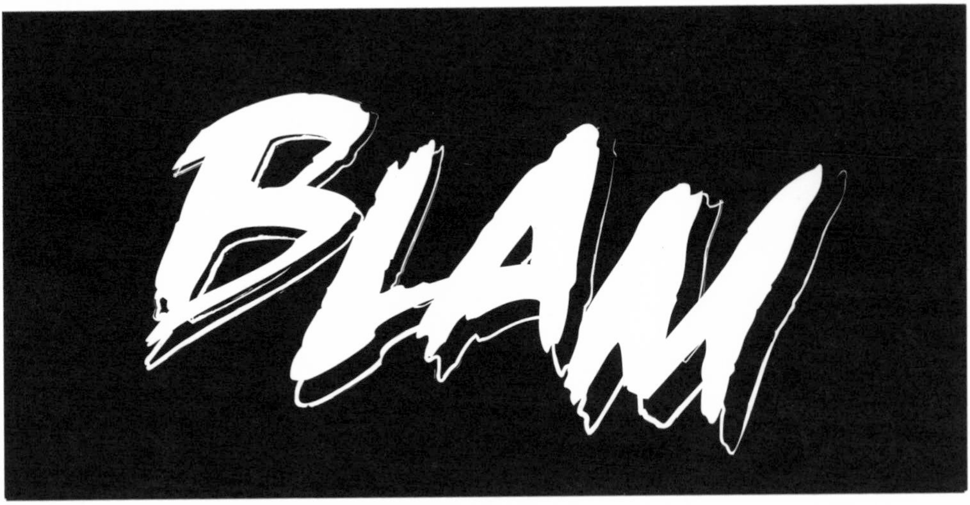
BLAM

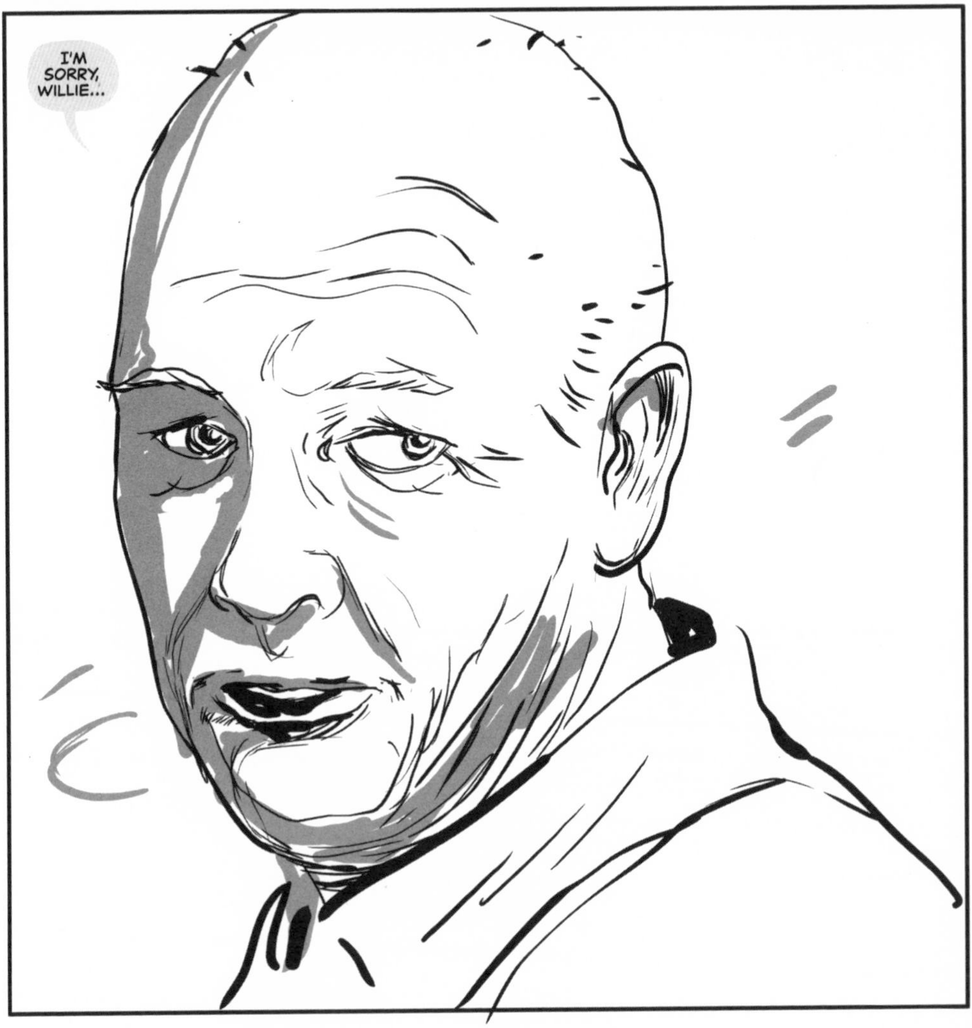
I'M SORRY, WILLIE...

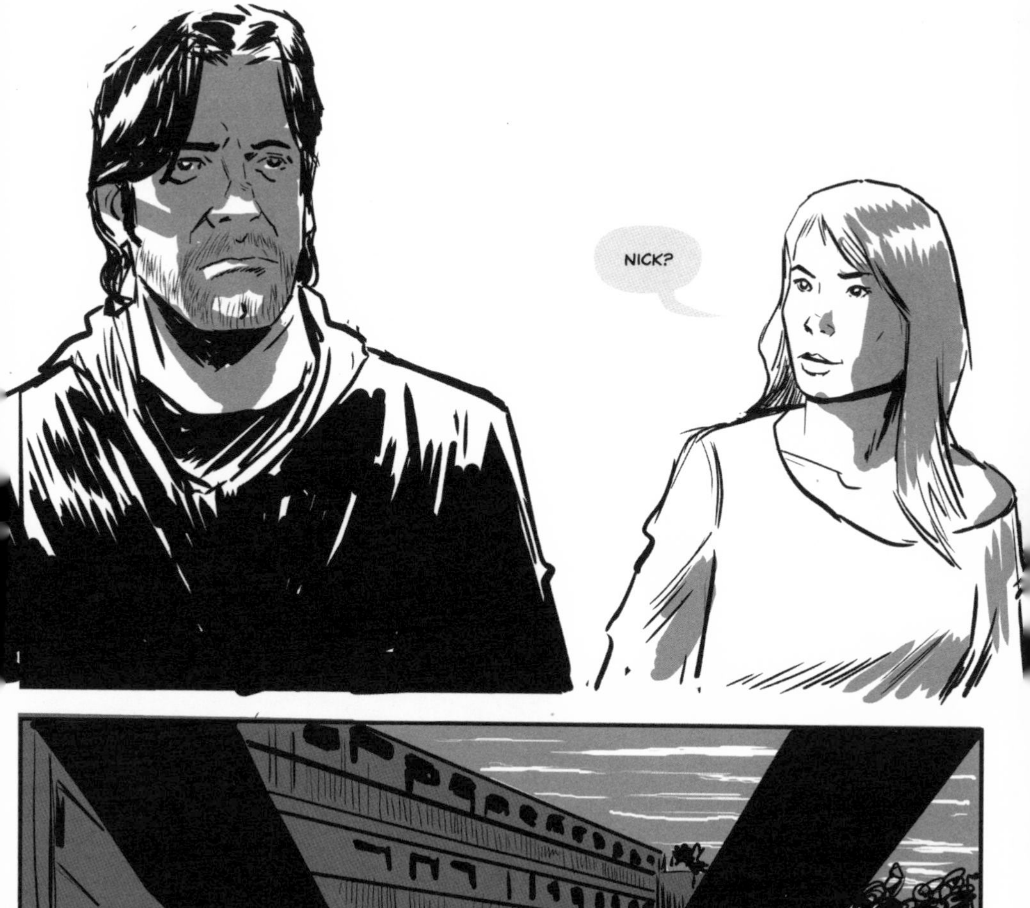
They were waiting for me at the motel the next morning.
NICK?

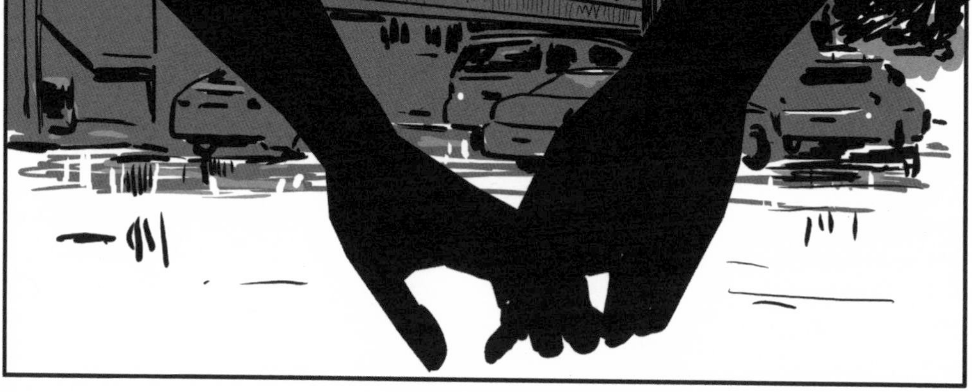

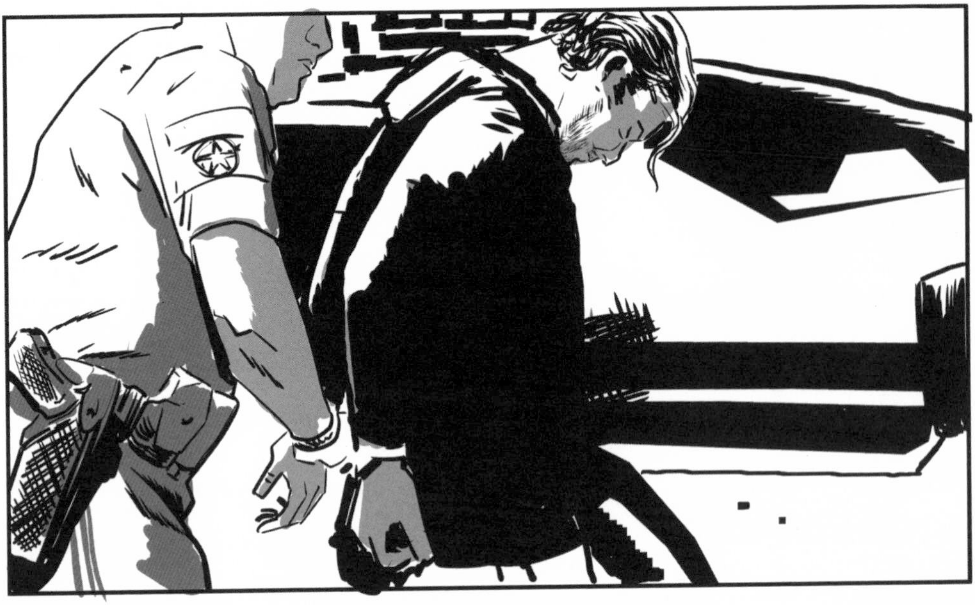

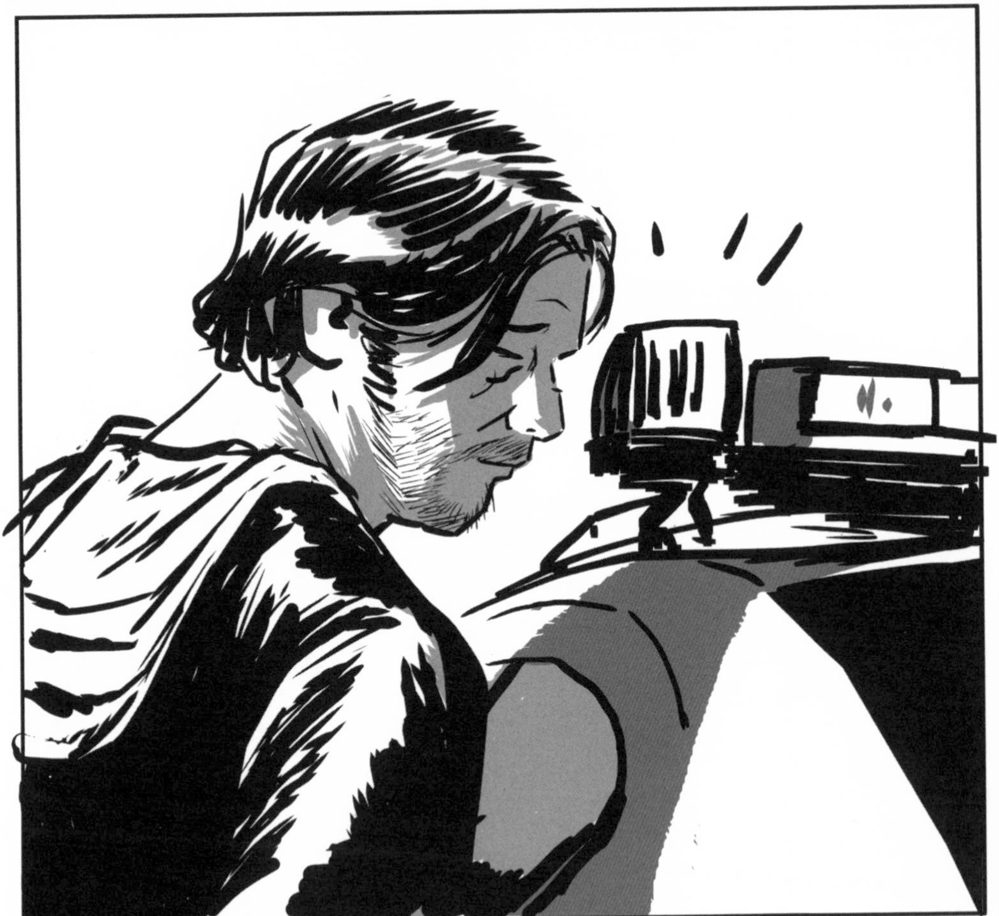

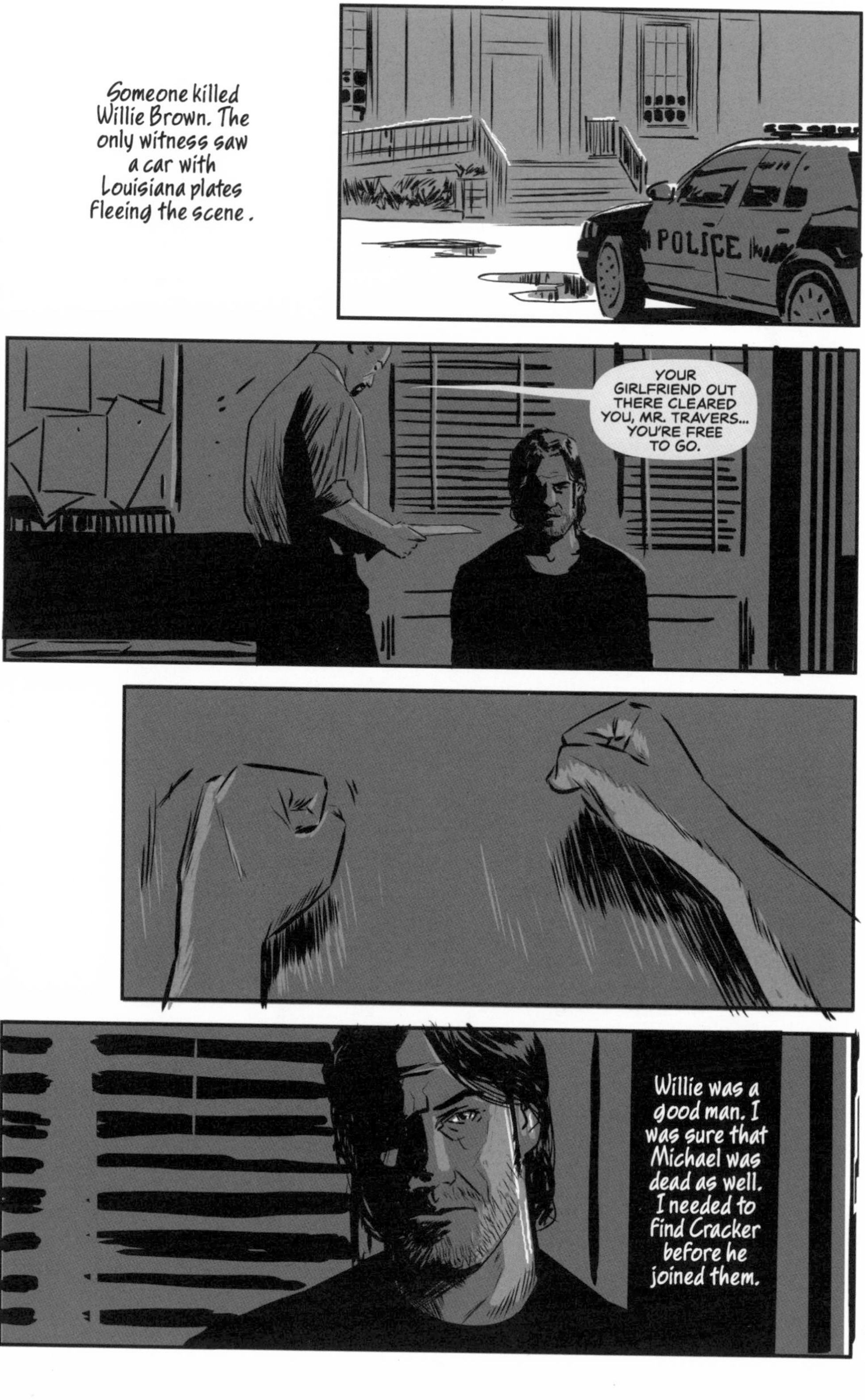
Someone killed Willie Brown. The only witness saw a car with Louisiana plates fleeing the scene .
POLICE
YOUR GIRLFRIEND OUT THERE CLEARED YOU, MR. TRAVERS... YOU'RE FREE TO GO.
Willie was a good man. I was sure that Michael was dead as well. I needed to find Cracker before he joined them.

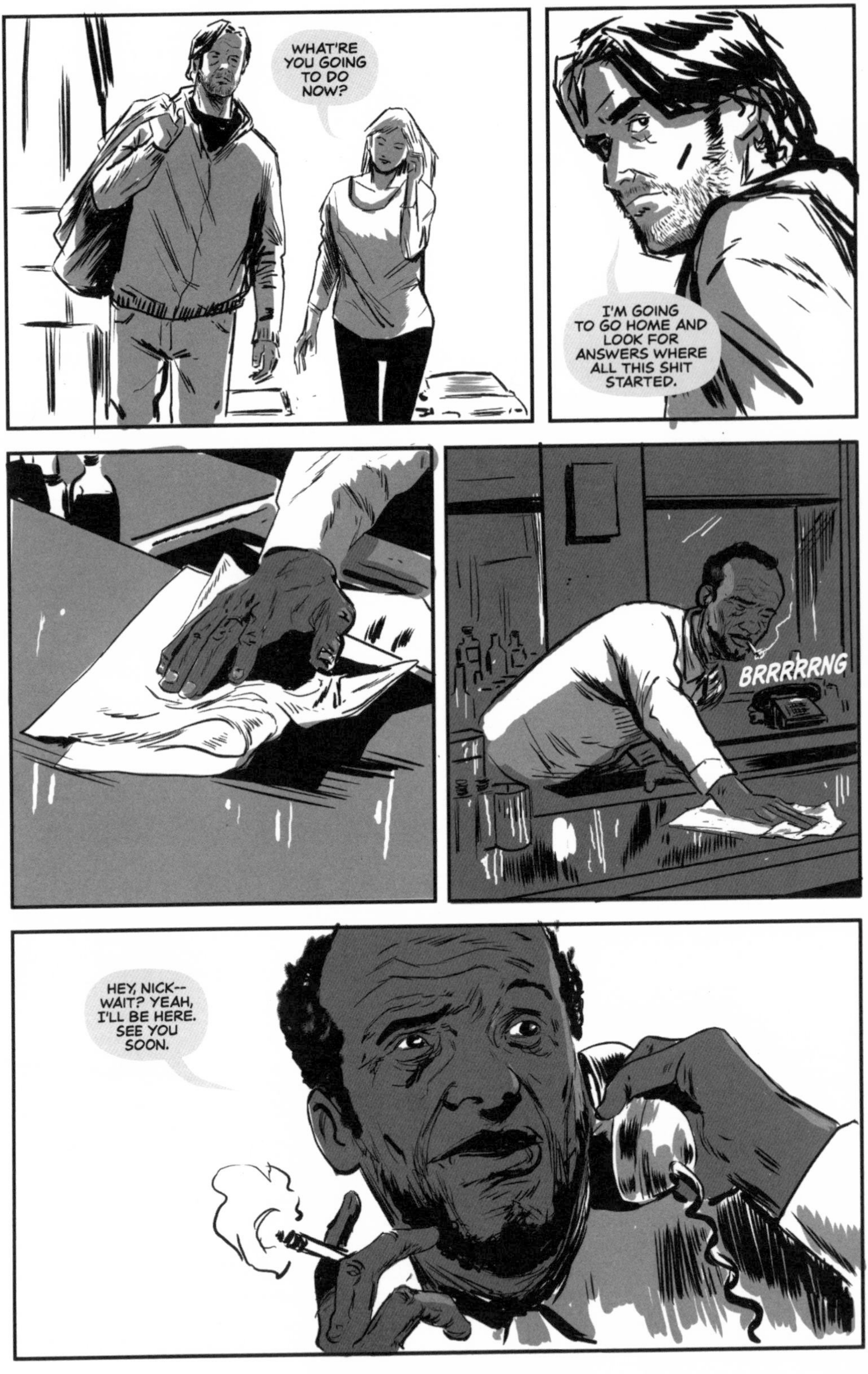
WHAT'RE YOU GOING TO DO NOW?
I'M GOING TO GO HOME AND LOOK FOR ANSWERS WHERE ALL THIS SHIT STARTED.
BRRRRRNG
HEY, NICK-- WAIT? YEAH, I'LL BE HERE. SEE YOU SOON.

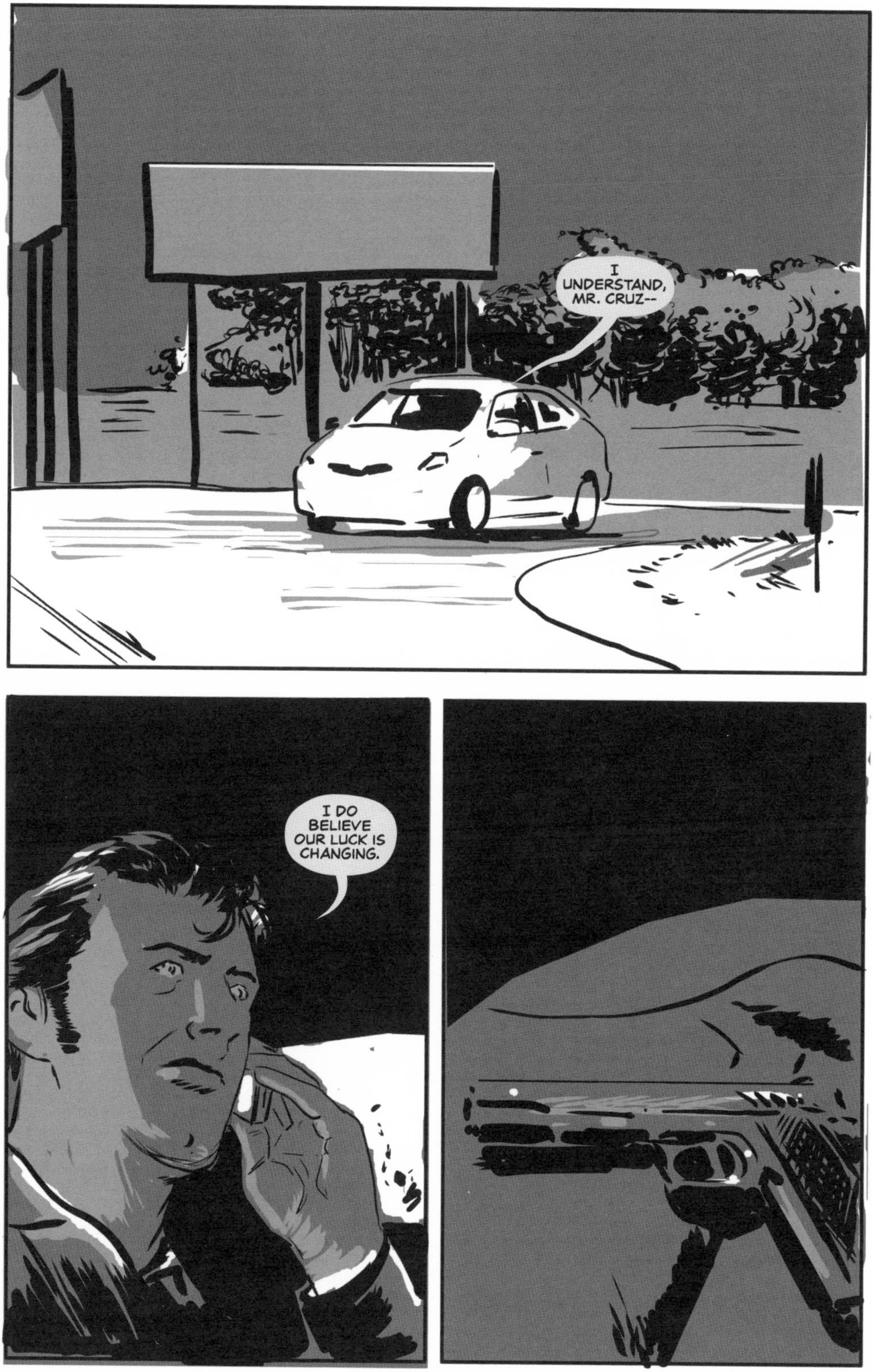
I UNDERSTAND, MR. CRUZ--
I DO BELIEVE OUR LUCK IS CHANGING.

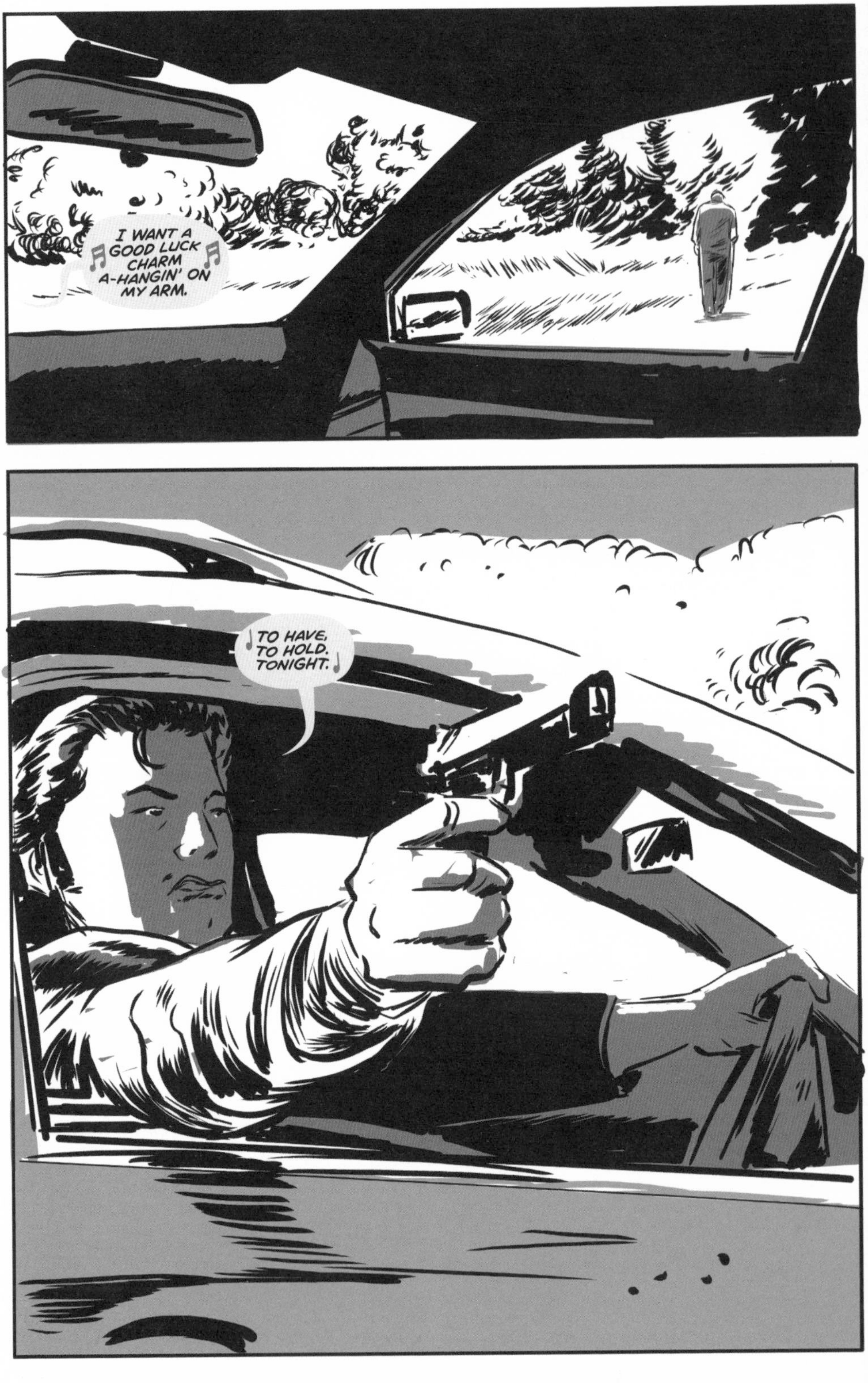
I WANT A GOOD LUCK CHARM A-HANGIN' ON MY ARM.
TO HAVE, TO HOLD. TONIGHT.

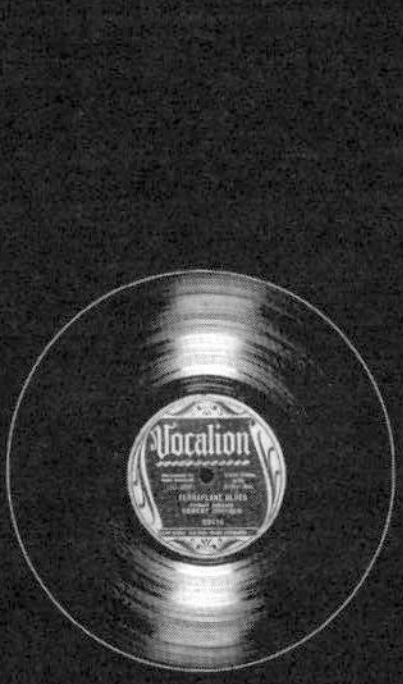
Vocalion

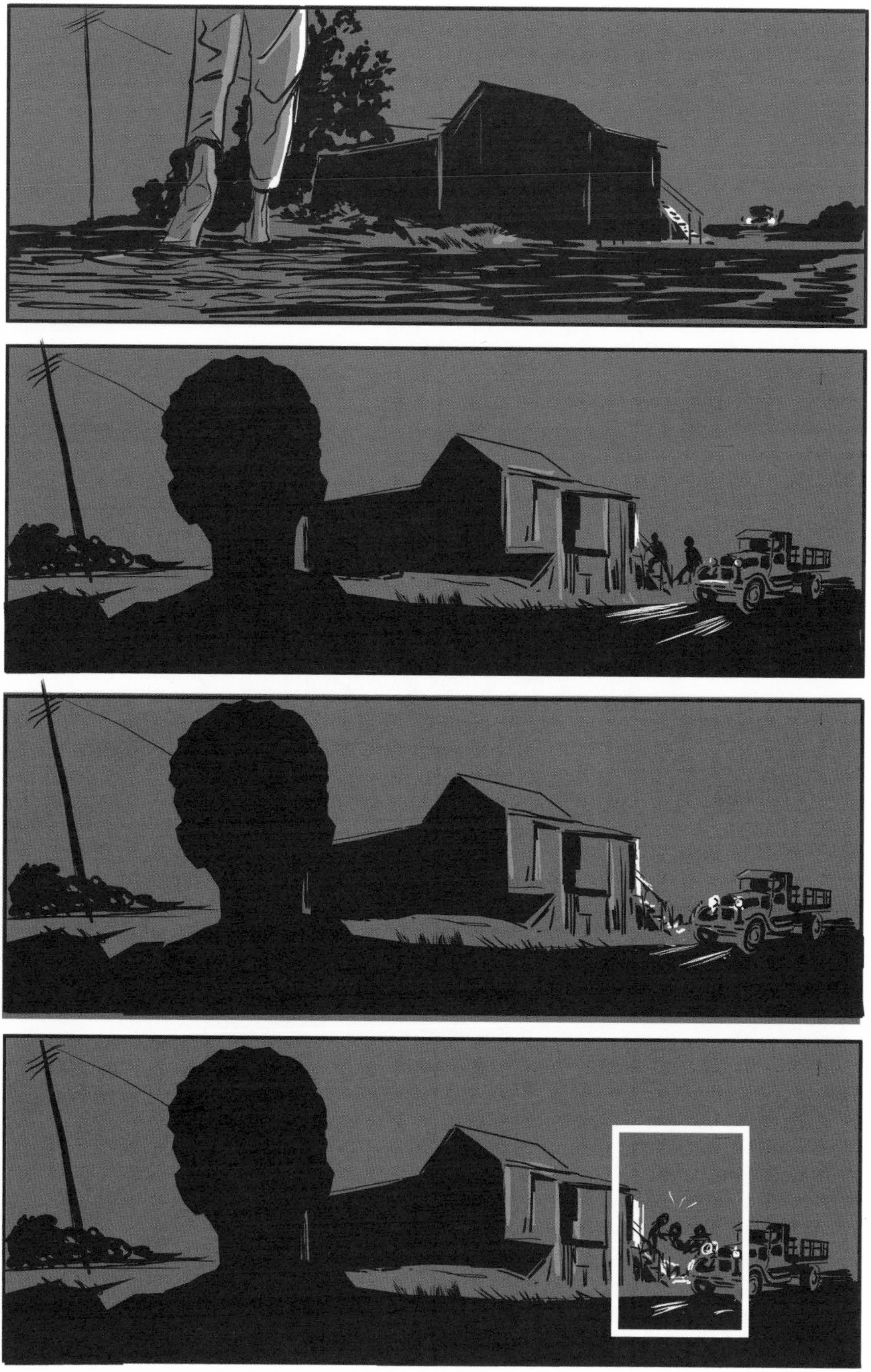

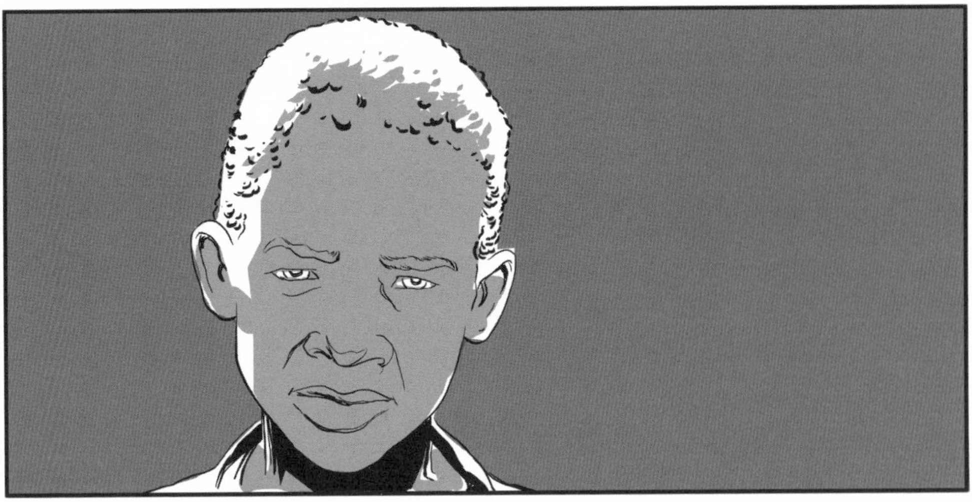

CHAPTER FOUR

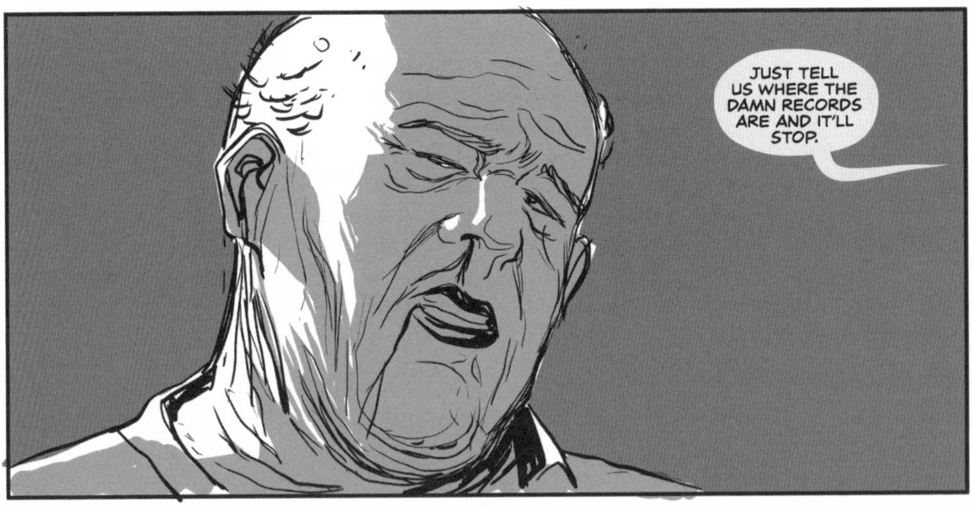
JUST TELL US WHERE THE DAMN RECORDS ARE AND IT'LL STOP.

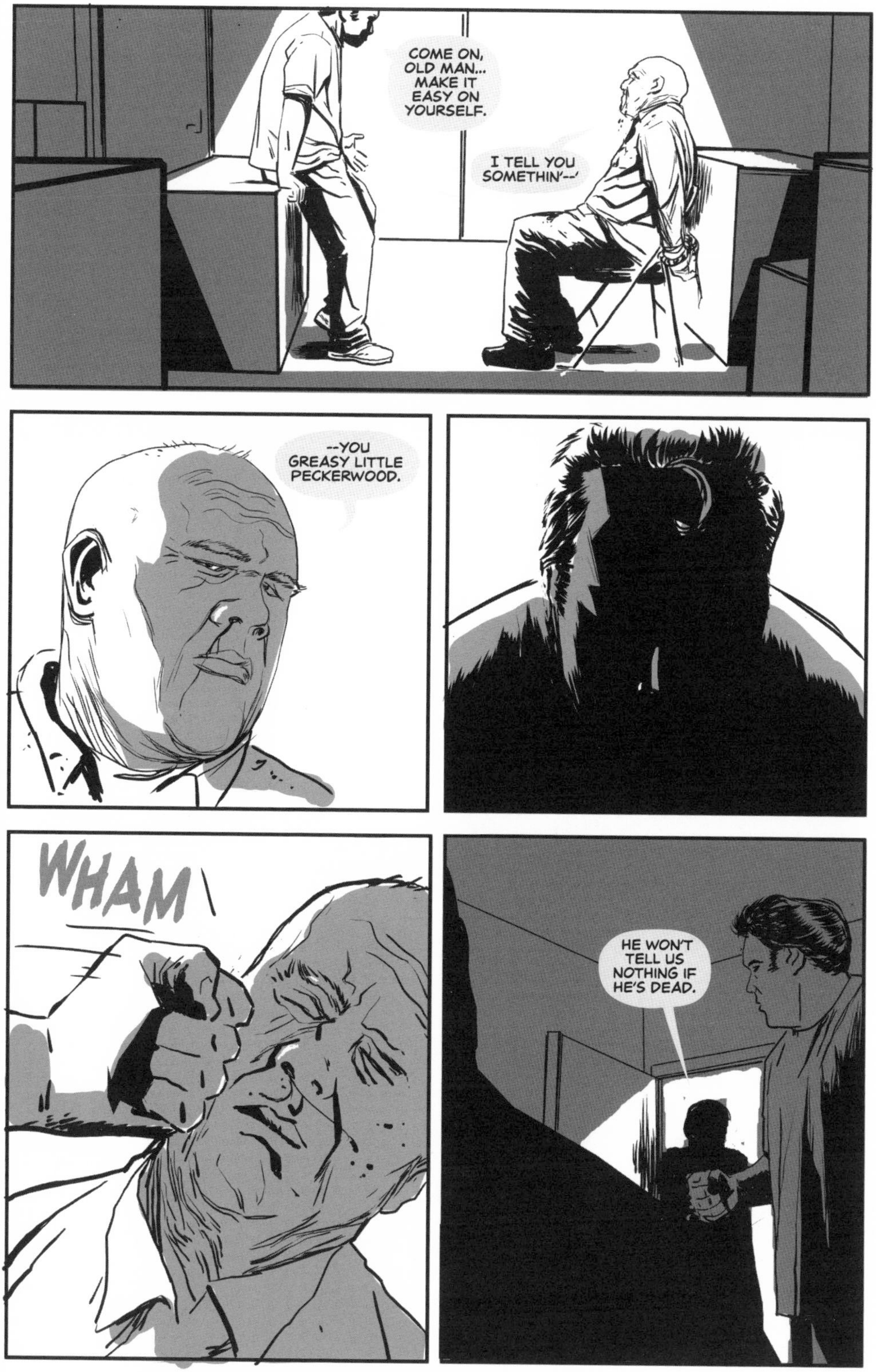
COME ON, OLD MAN... MAKE IT EASY ON YOURSELF.
I TELL YOU SOMETHIN'--'
--YOU GREASY LITTLE PECKERWOOD.
WHAM
HE WON'T TELL US NOTHING IF HE'S DEAD.

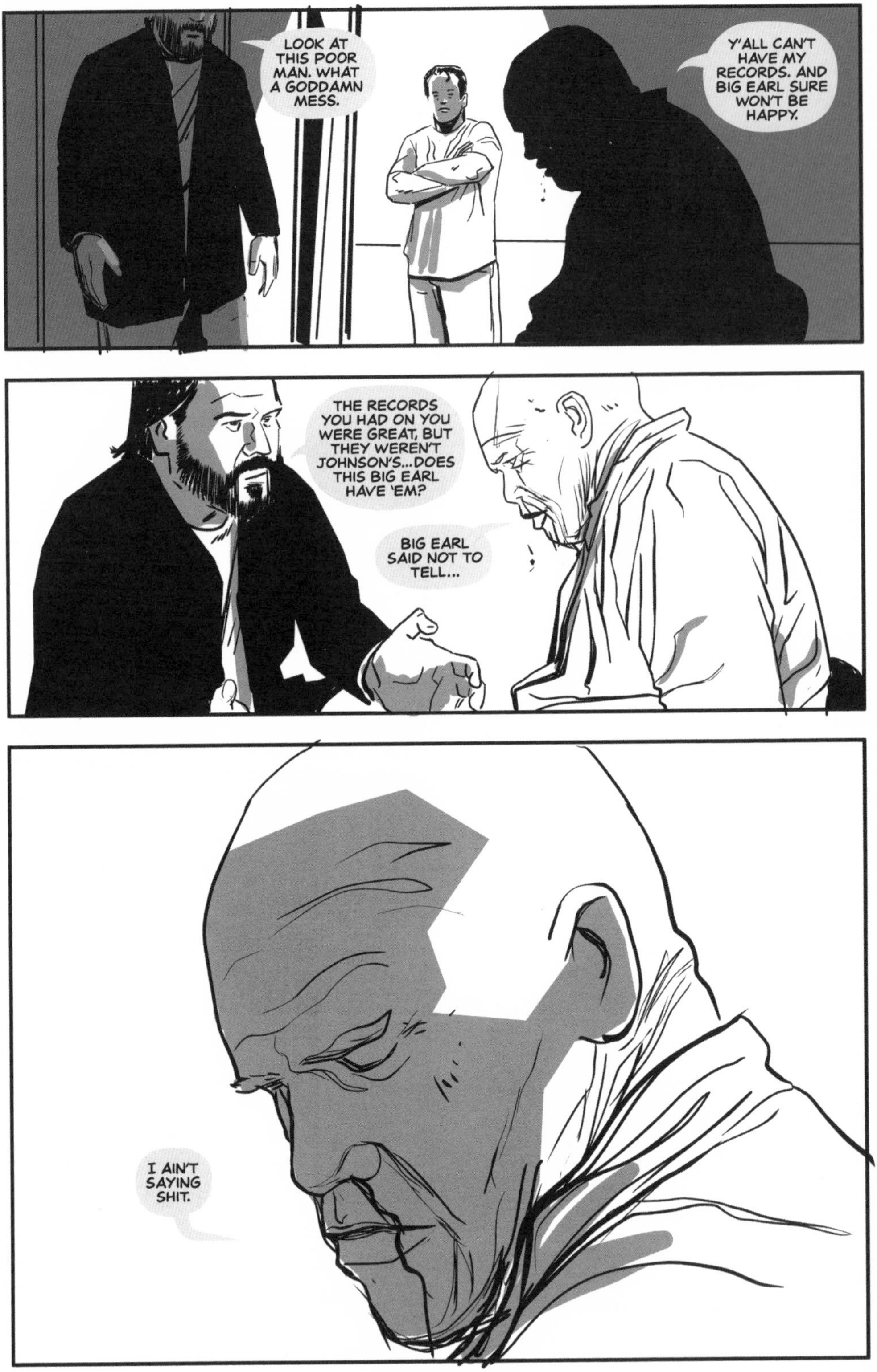
LOOK AT THIS POOR MAN. WHAT A GODDAMN MESS.
Y'ALL CAN'T HAVE MY RECORDS. AND BIG EARL SURE WON'T BE HAPPY.
THE RECORDS YOU HAD ON YOU WERE GREAT, BUT THEY WEREN'T JOHNSON'S...DOES THIS BIG EARL HAVE 'EM?
BIG EARL SAID NOT TO TELL...
I AIN'T SAYING SHIT.

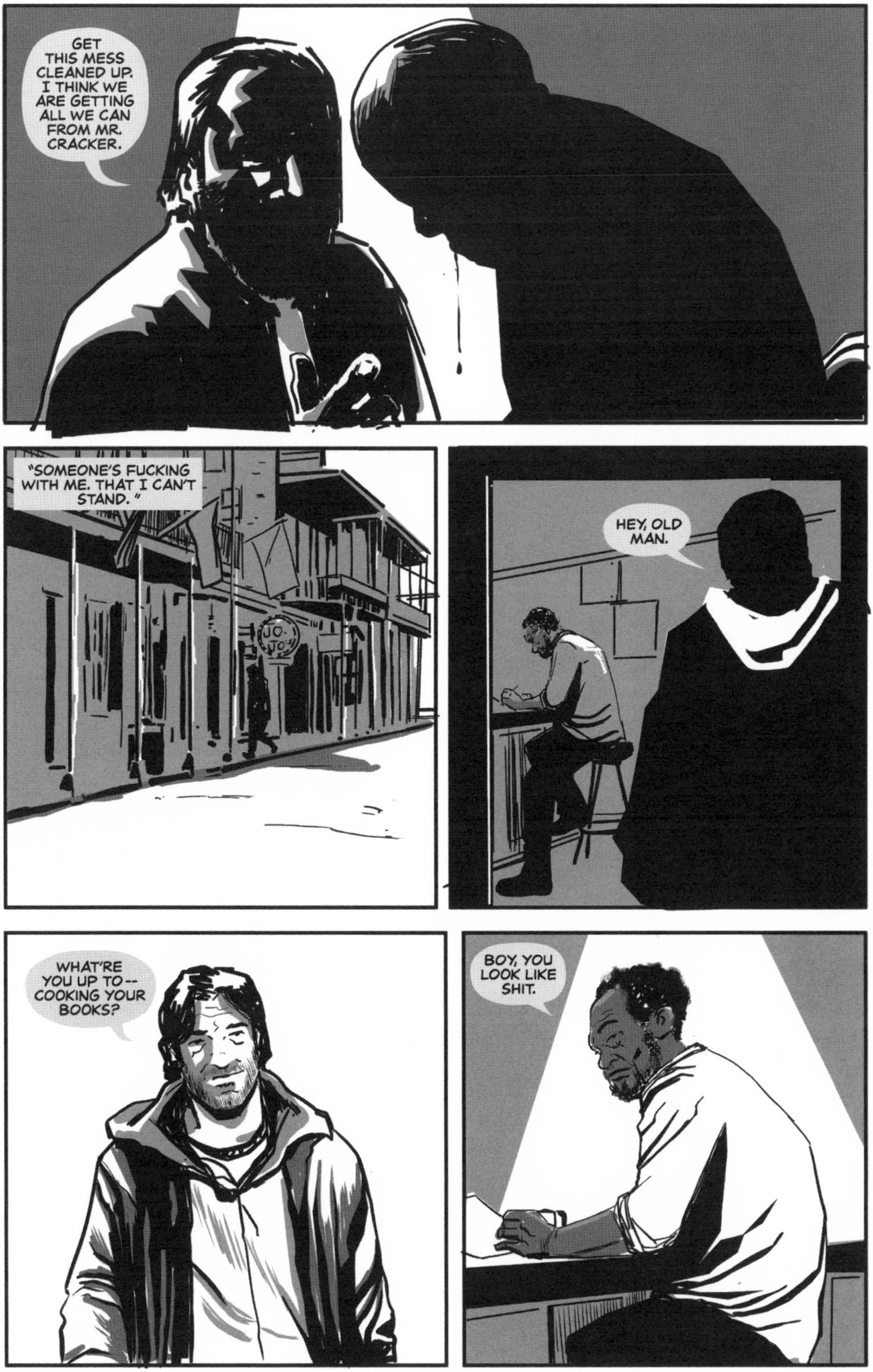
GET THIS MESS CLEANED UP. I THINK WE ARE GETTING ALL WE CAN FROM MR. CRACKER.
"SOMEONE'S FUCKING WITH ME. THAT I CAN'T STAND."
JO-JO'S
HEY, OLD MAN.
WHAT'RE YOU UP TO-- COOKING YOUR BOOKS?
BOY, YOU LOOK LIKE SHIT.

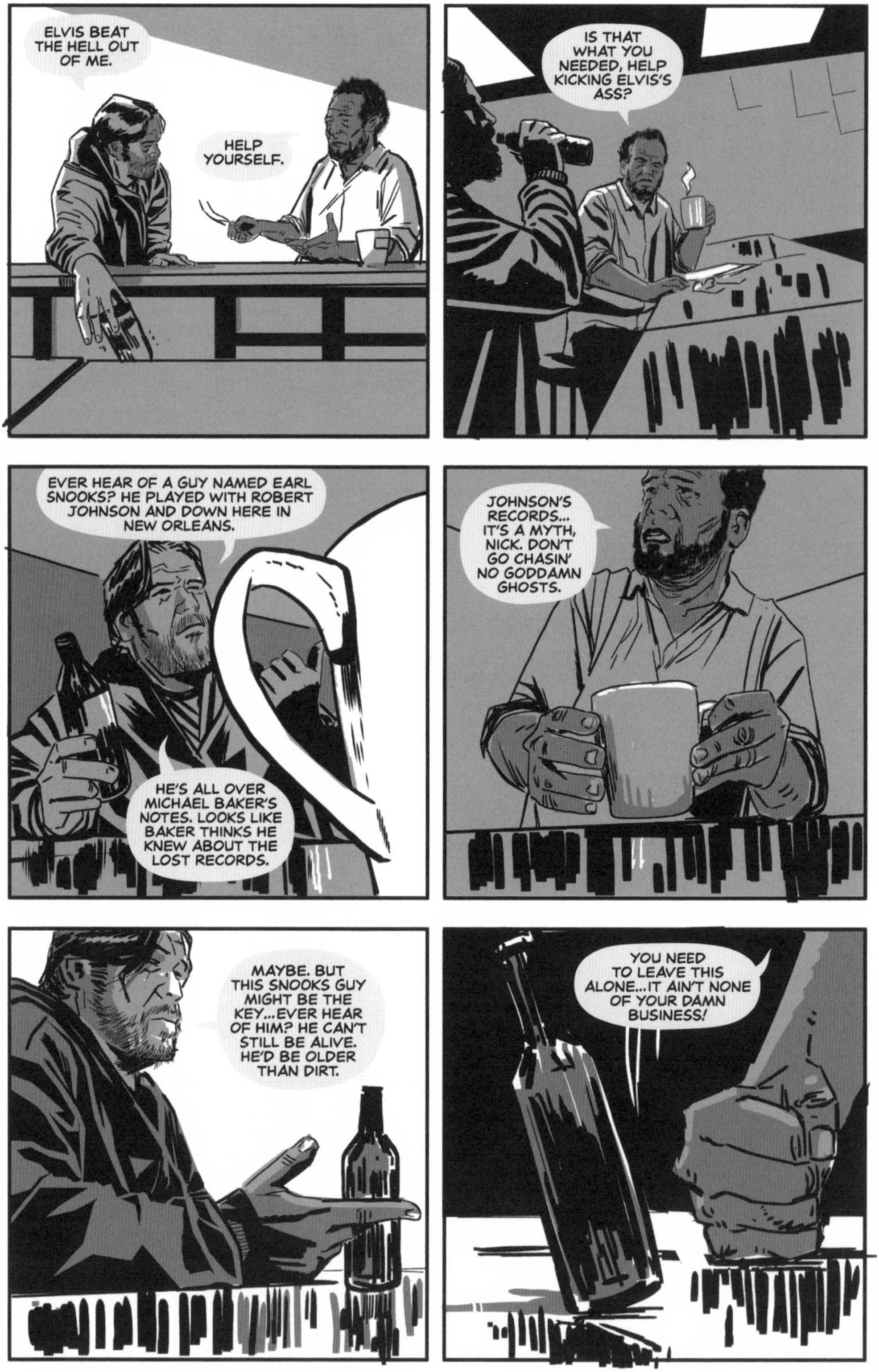
ELVIS BEAT THE HELL OUT OF ME.
HELP YOURSELF.
IS THAT WHAT YOU NEEDED, HELP KICKING ELVIS'S ASS?
EVER HEAR OF A GUY NAMED EARL SNOOKS? HE PLAYED WITH ROBERT JOHNSON AND DOWN HERE IN NEW ORLEANS.
HE'S ALL OVER MICHAEL BAKER'S NOTES. LOOKS LIKE BAKER THINKS HE KNEW ABOUT THE LOST RECORDS.
JOHNSON'S RECORDS... IT'S A MYTH, NICK. DON'T GO CHASIN' NO GODDAMN GHOSTS.
MAYBE. BUT THIS SNOOKS GUY MIGHT BE THE KEY...EVER HEAR OF HIM? HE CAN'T STILL BE ALIVE. HE'D BE OLDER THAN DIRT.
YOU NEED TO LEAVE THIS ALONE...IT AIN'T NONE OF YOUR DAMN BUSINESS!

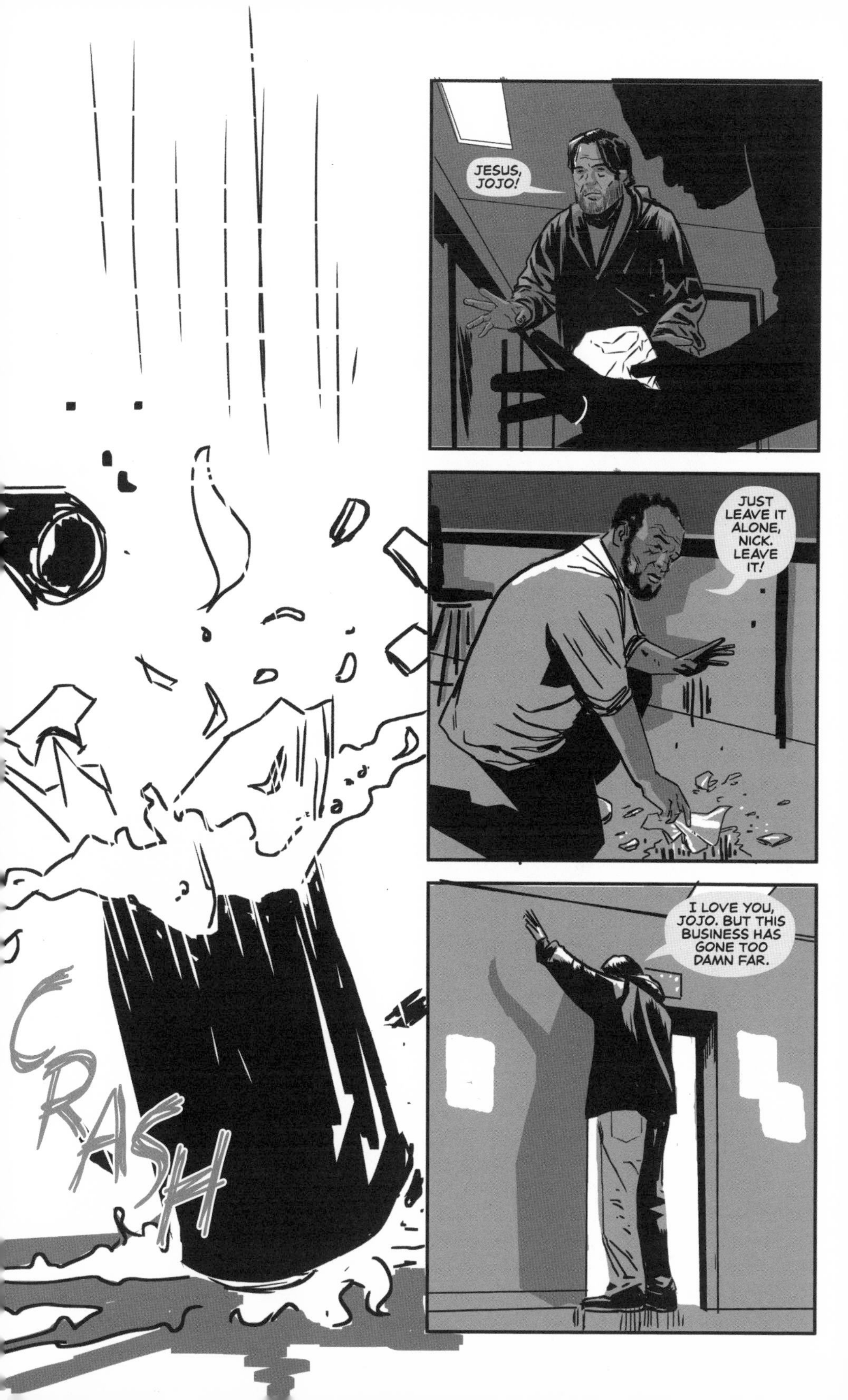
CRASH
JESUS, JOJO!
JUST LEAVE IT ALONE, NICK. LEAVE IT!
I LOVE YOU, JOJO. BUT THIS BUSINESS HAS GONE TOO DAMN FAR.

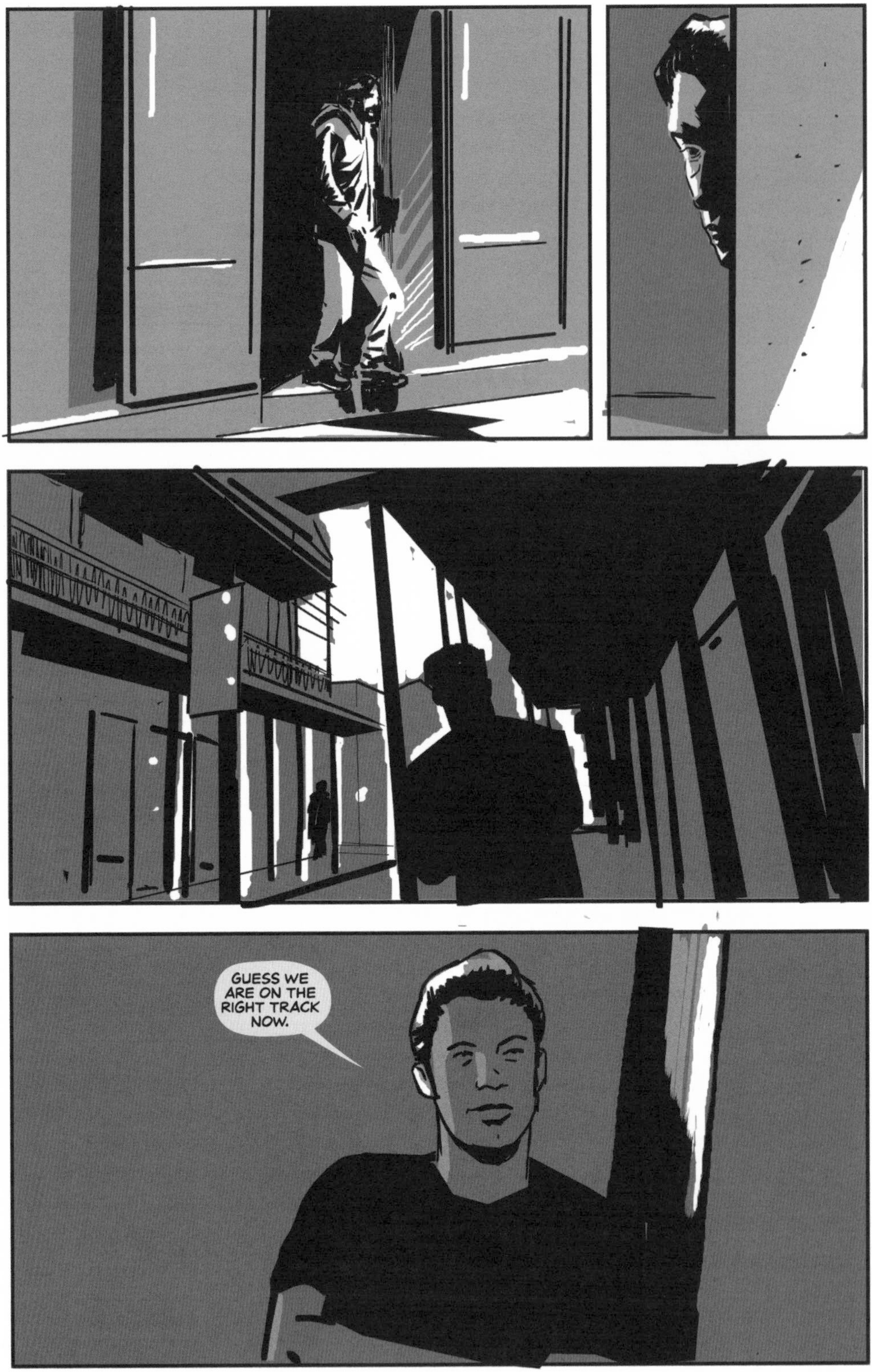
GUESS WE ARE ON THE RIGHT TRACK NOW.

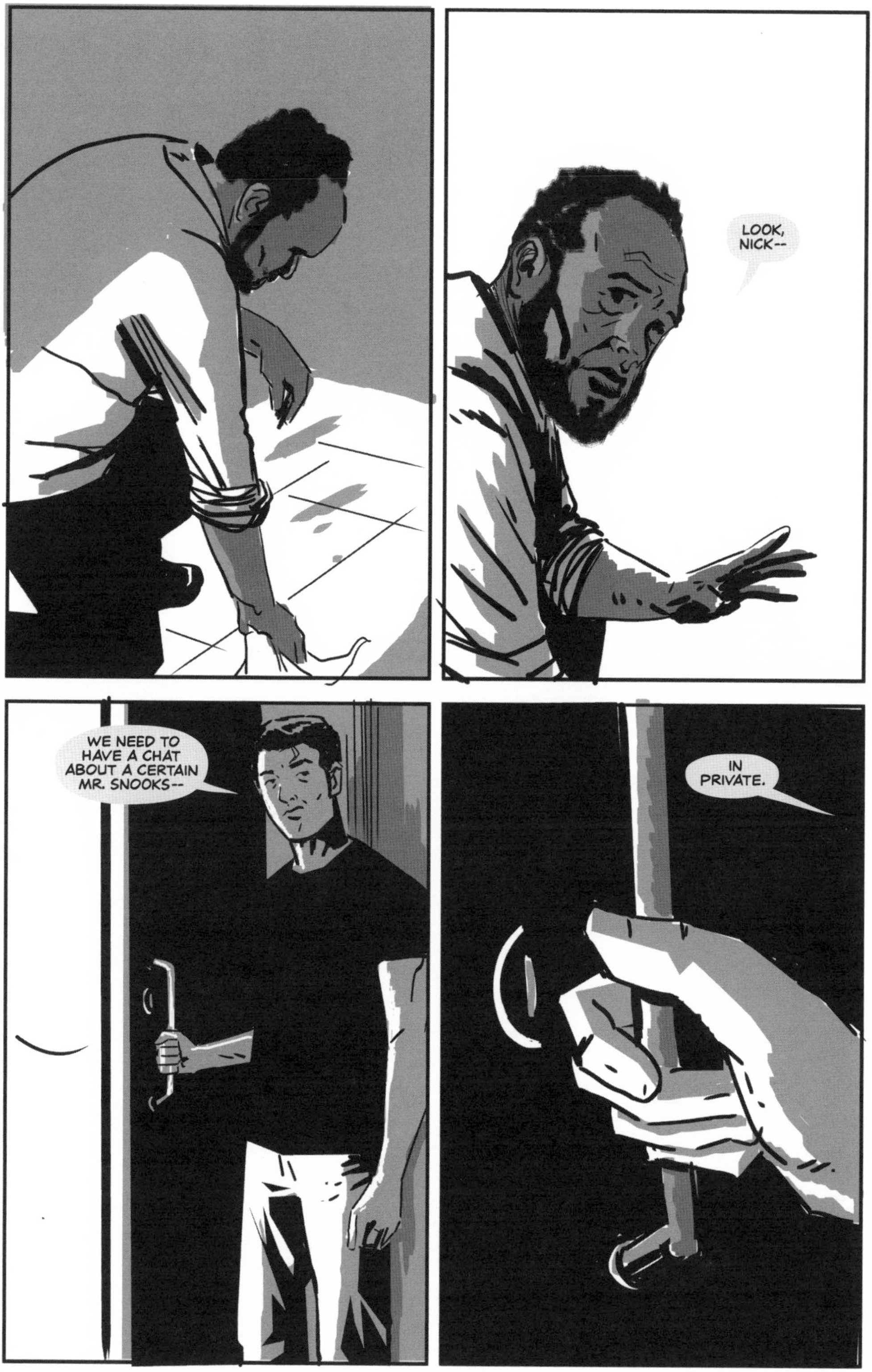
LOOK, NICK--
WE NEED TO HAVE A CHAT ABOUT A CERTAIN MR. SNOOKS--
IN PRIVATE.

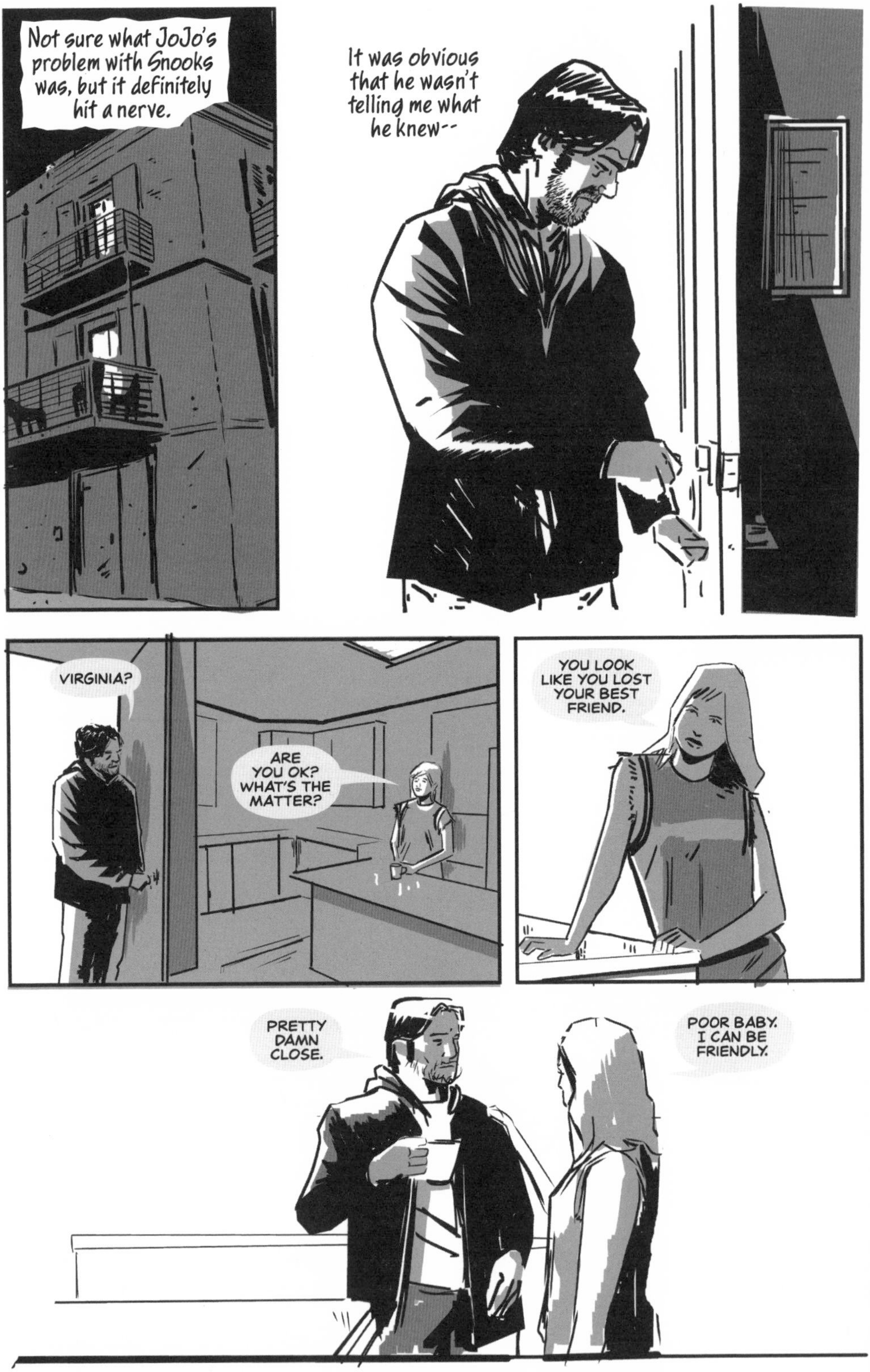
Not sure what JoJo's problem with Snooks was, but it definitely hit a nerve.
It was obvious that he wasn't telling me what he knew--
VIRGINIA?
ARE YOU OK? WHAT'S THE MATTER?
YOU LOOK LIKE YOU LOST YOUR BEST FRIEND.
PRETTY DAMN CLOSE.
POOR BABY. I CAN BE FRIENDLY.

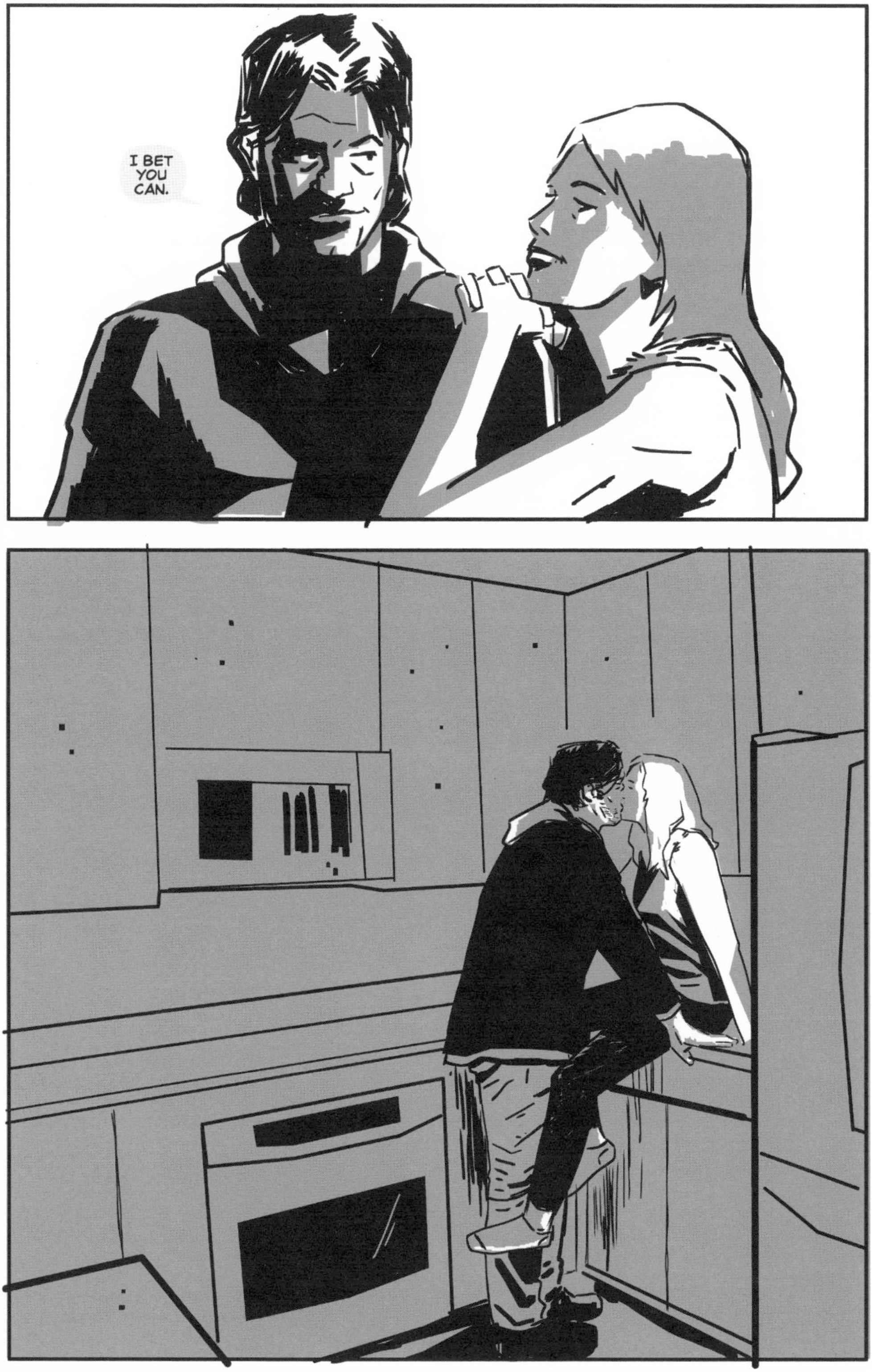
I BET YOU CAN.

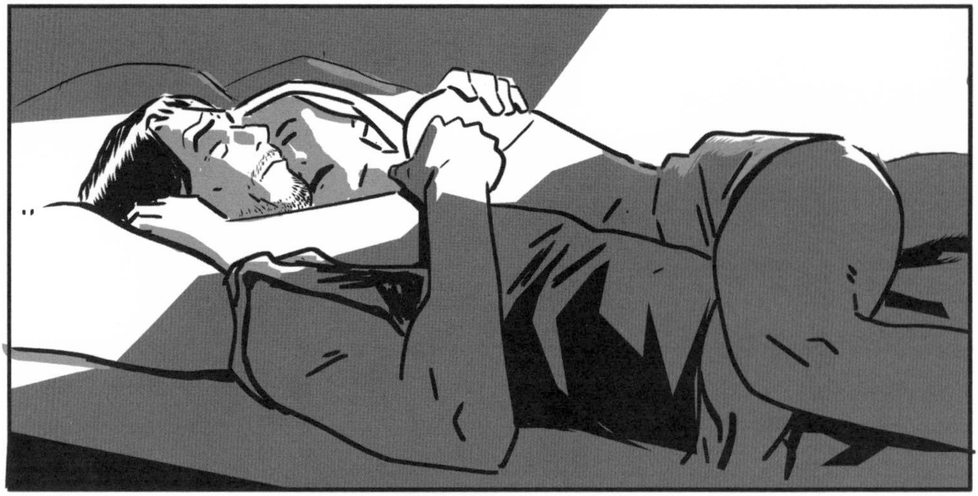

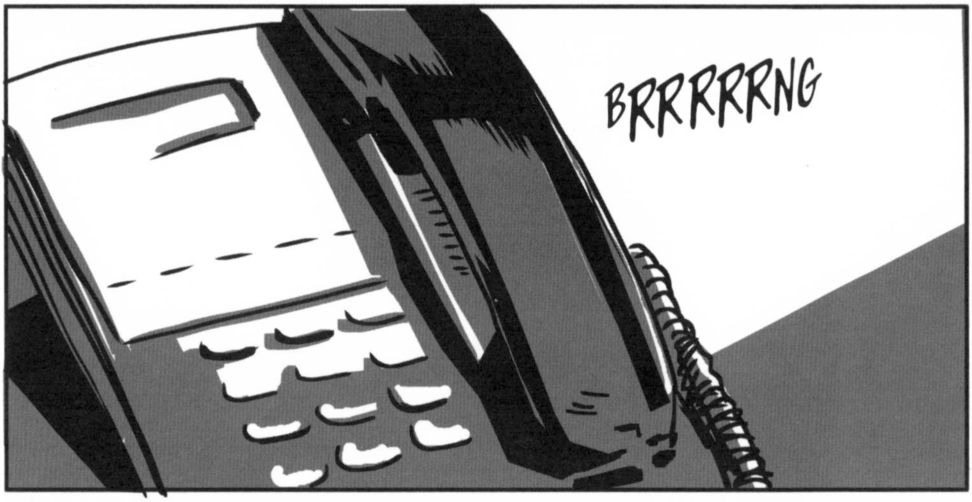
BRRRRRNG

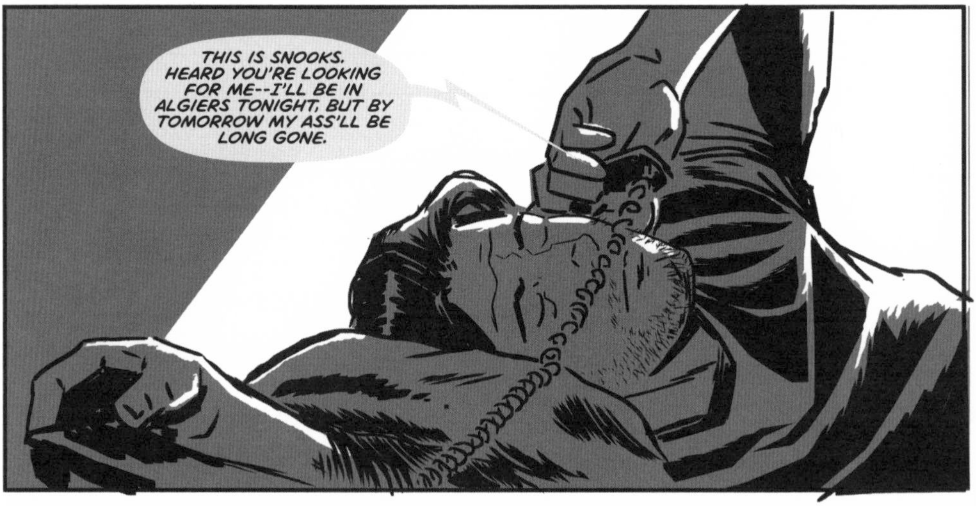
THIS IS SNOOKS. HEARD YOU'RE LOOKING FOR ME--I'LL BE IN ALGIERS TONIGHT, BUT BY TOMORROW MY ASS'LL BE LONG GONE.

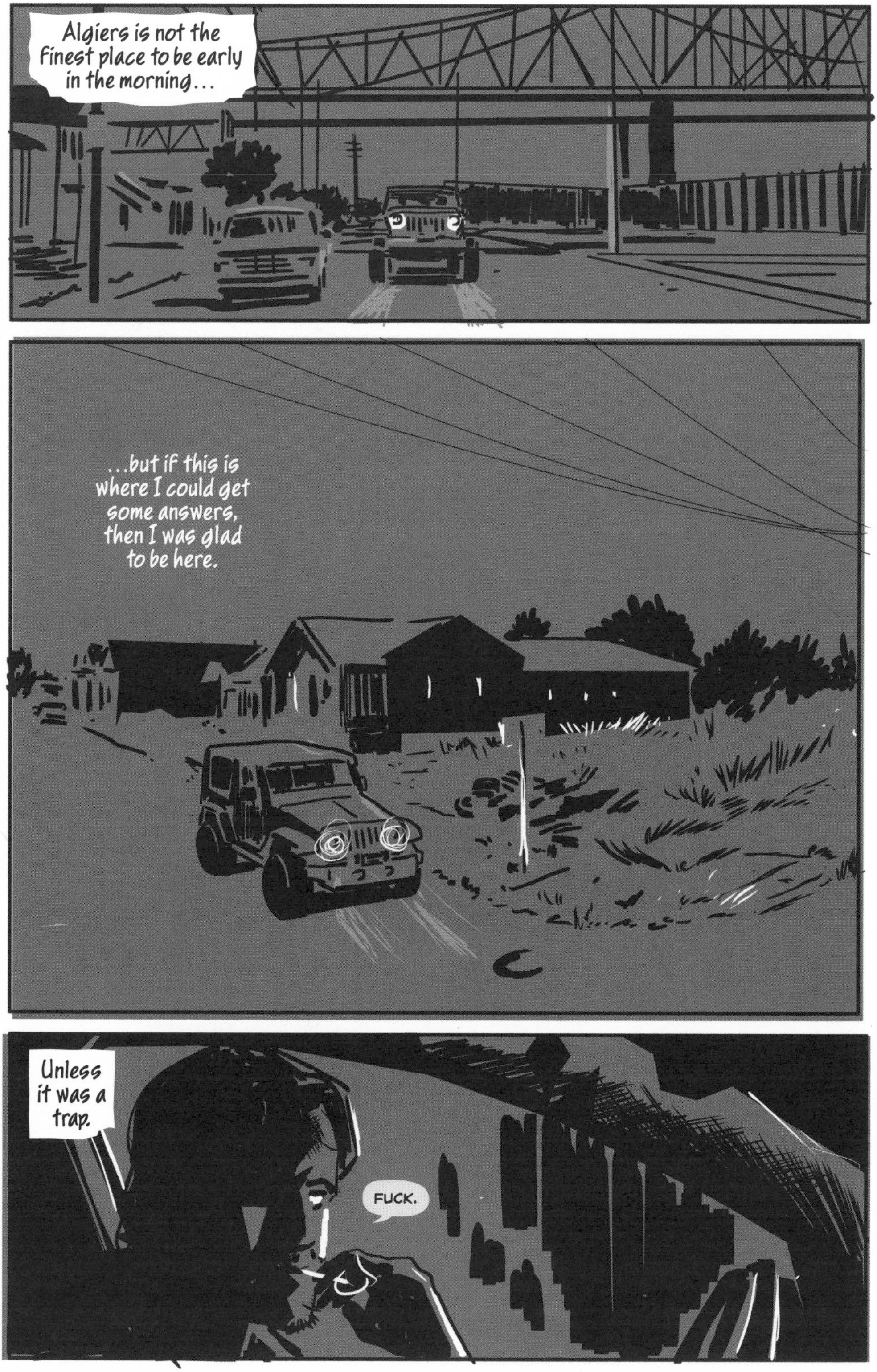
Algiers is not the finest place to be early in the morning...
...but if this is where I could get some answers, then I was glad to be here.
Unless it was a trap.
FUCK.

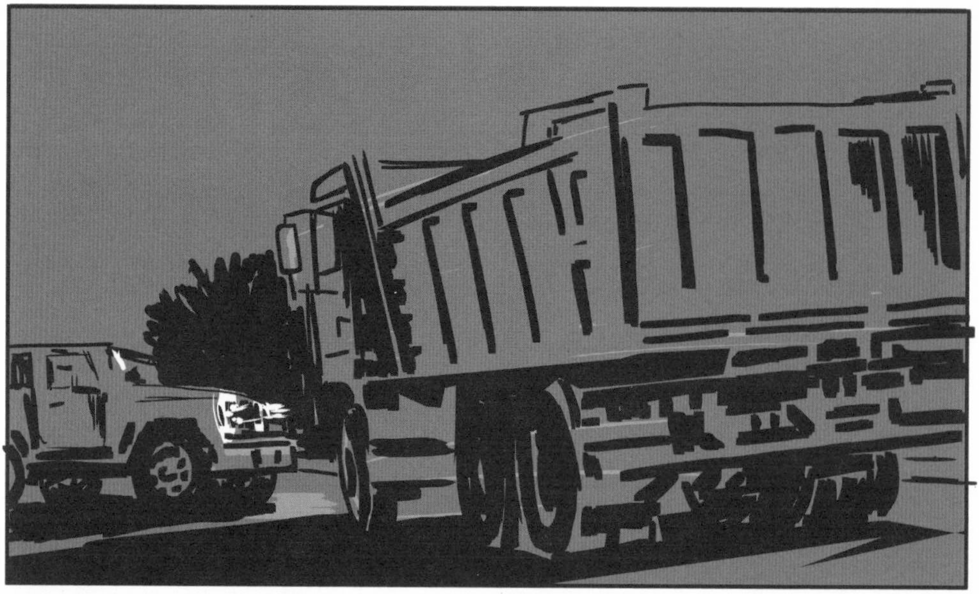

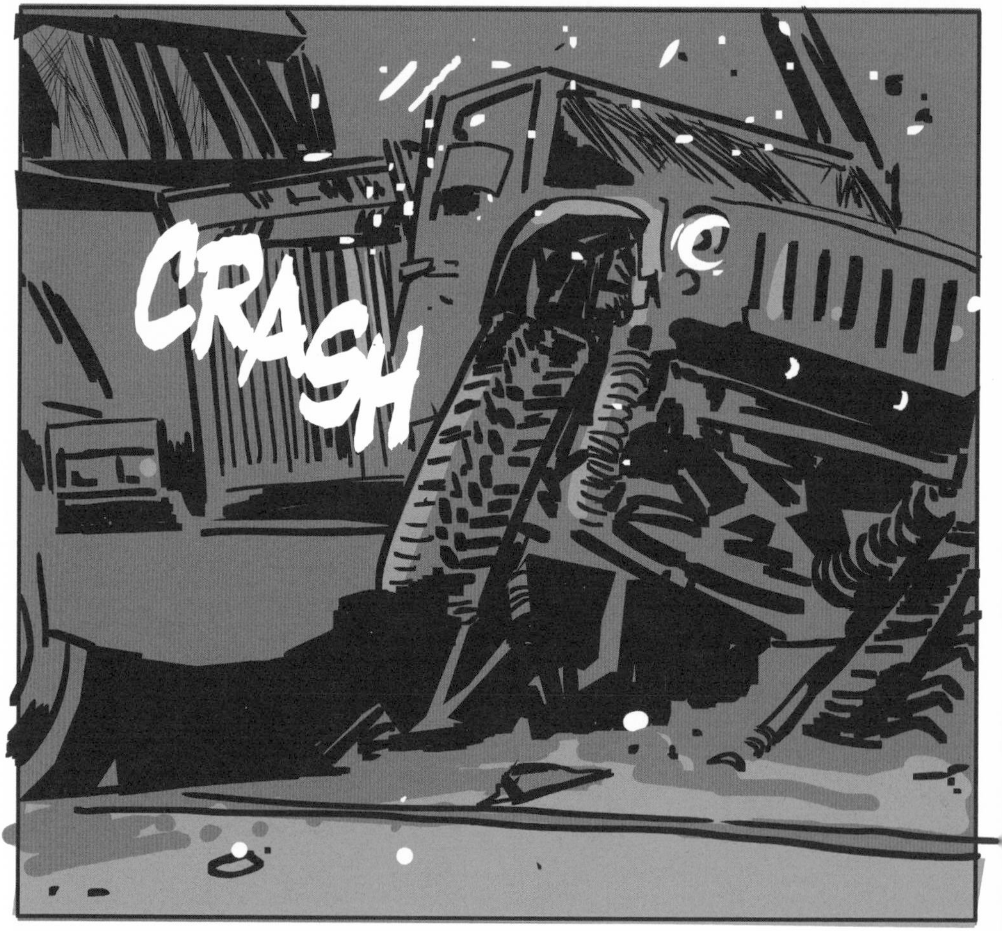
CRASH

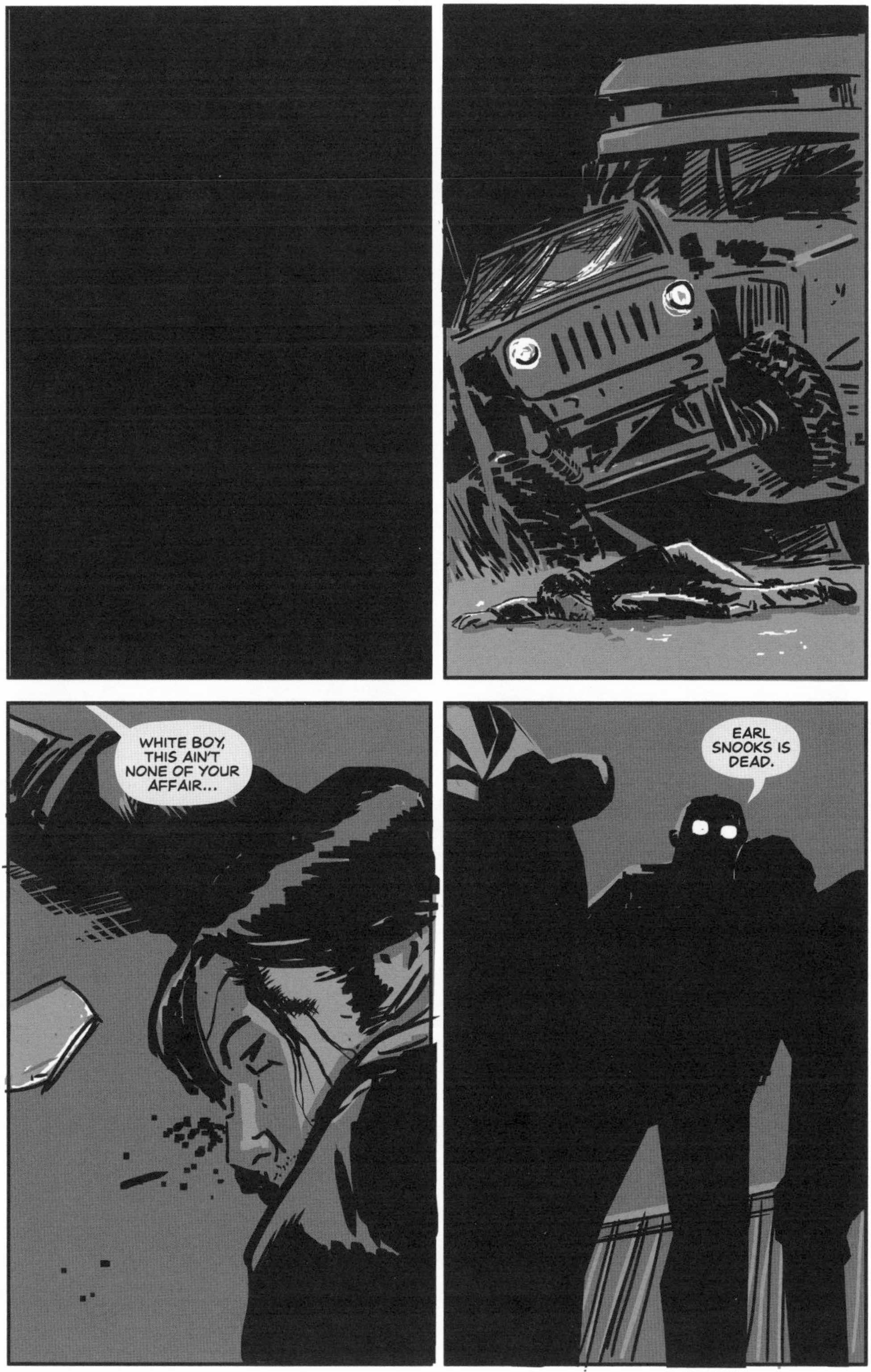
WHITE BOY, THIS AIN'T NONE OF YOUR AFFAIR...
EARL SNOOKS IS DEAD.

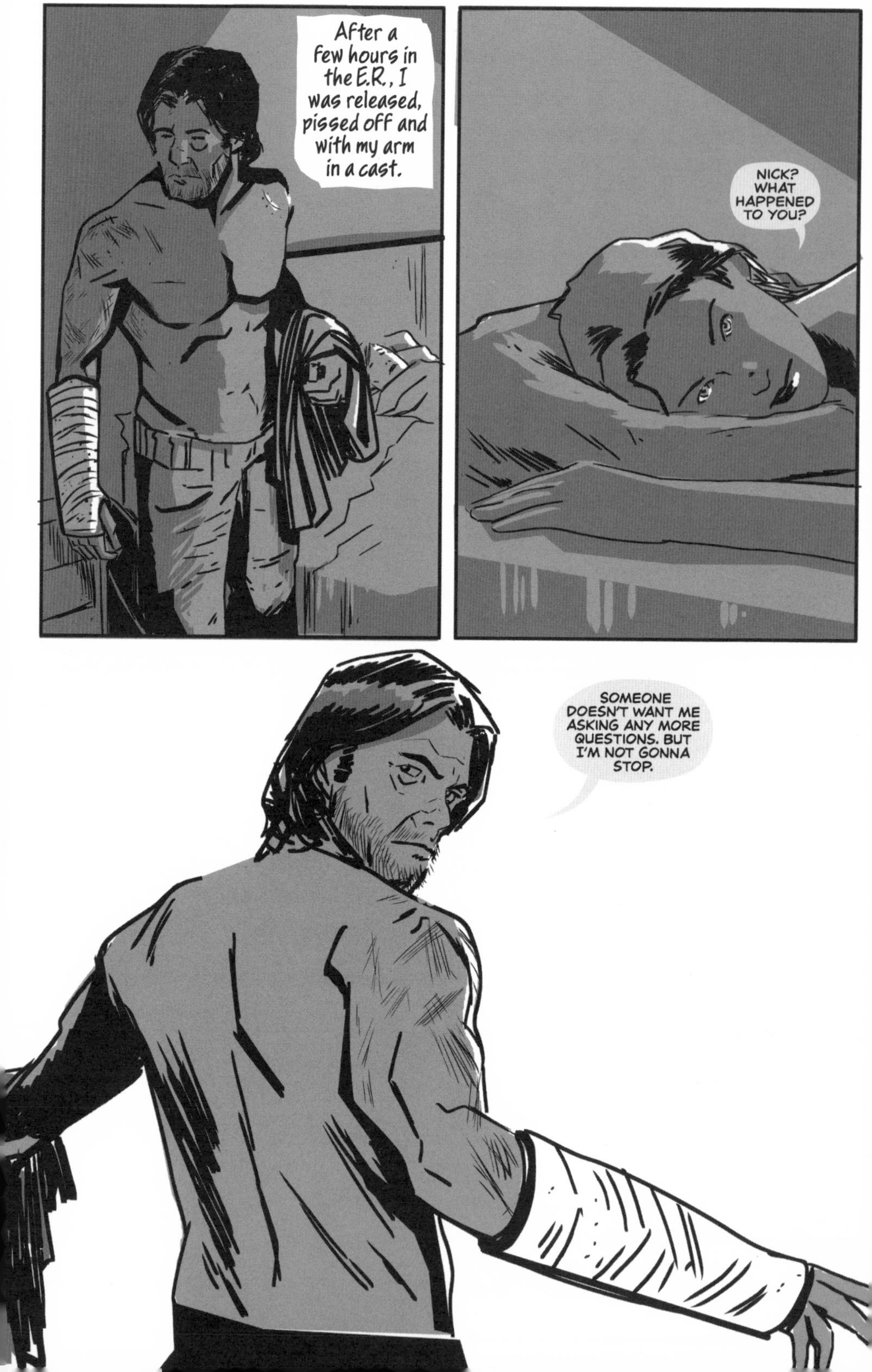
After a few hours in the E.R., I was released, pissed off and with my arm in a cast.
NICK? WHAT HAPPENED TO YOU?
SOMEONE DOESN'T WANT ME ASKING ANY MORE QUESTIONS. BUT I'M NOT GONNA STOP.

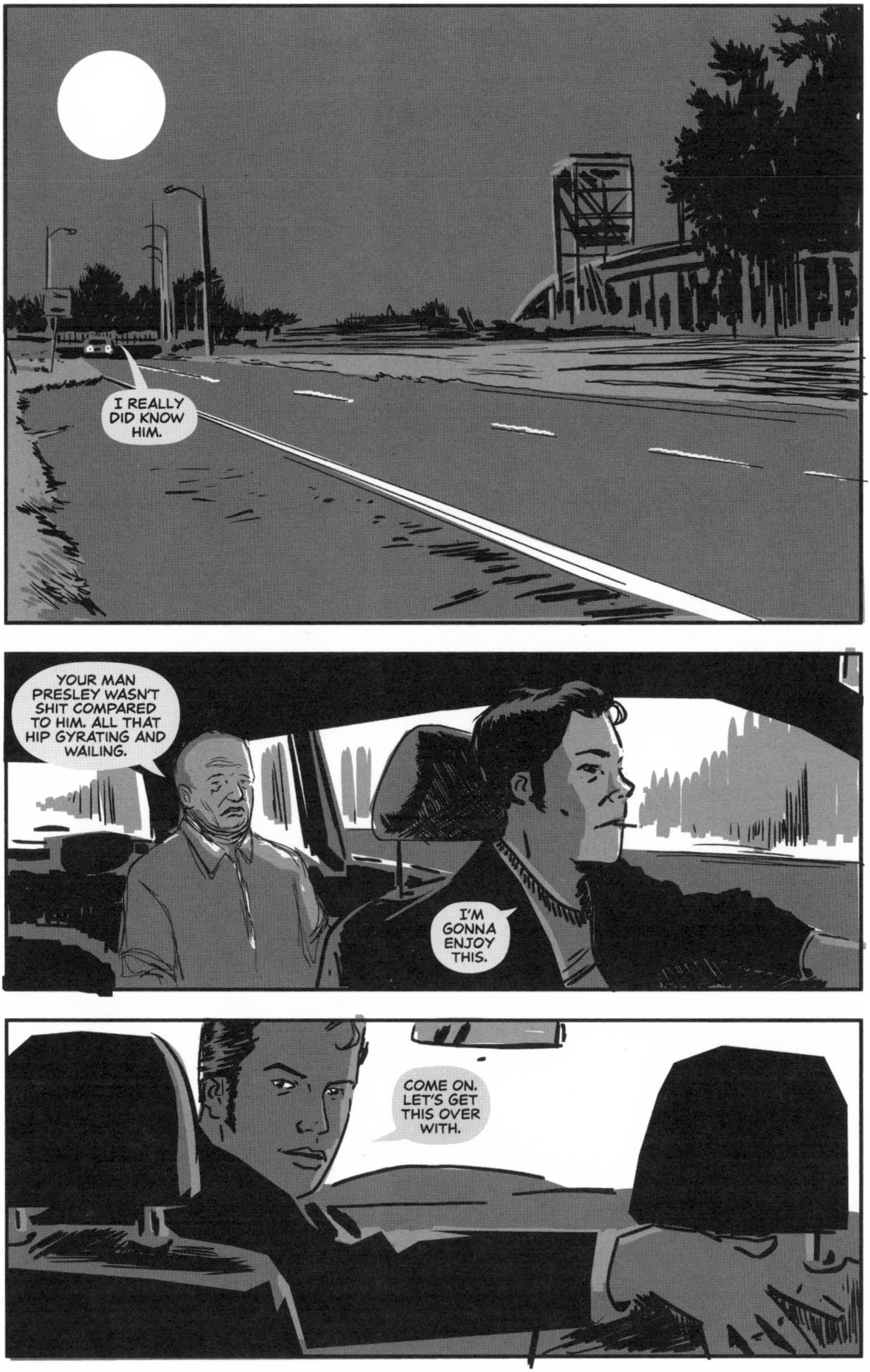
I REALLY DID KNOW HIM.
YOUR MAN PRESLEY WASN'T SHIT COMPARED TO HIM. ALL THAT HIP GYRATING AND WAILING.
I'M GONNA ENJOY THIS.
COME ON. LET'S GET THIS OVER WITH.

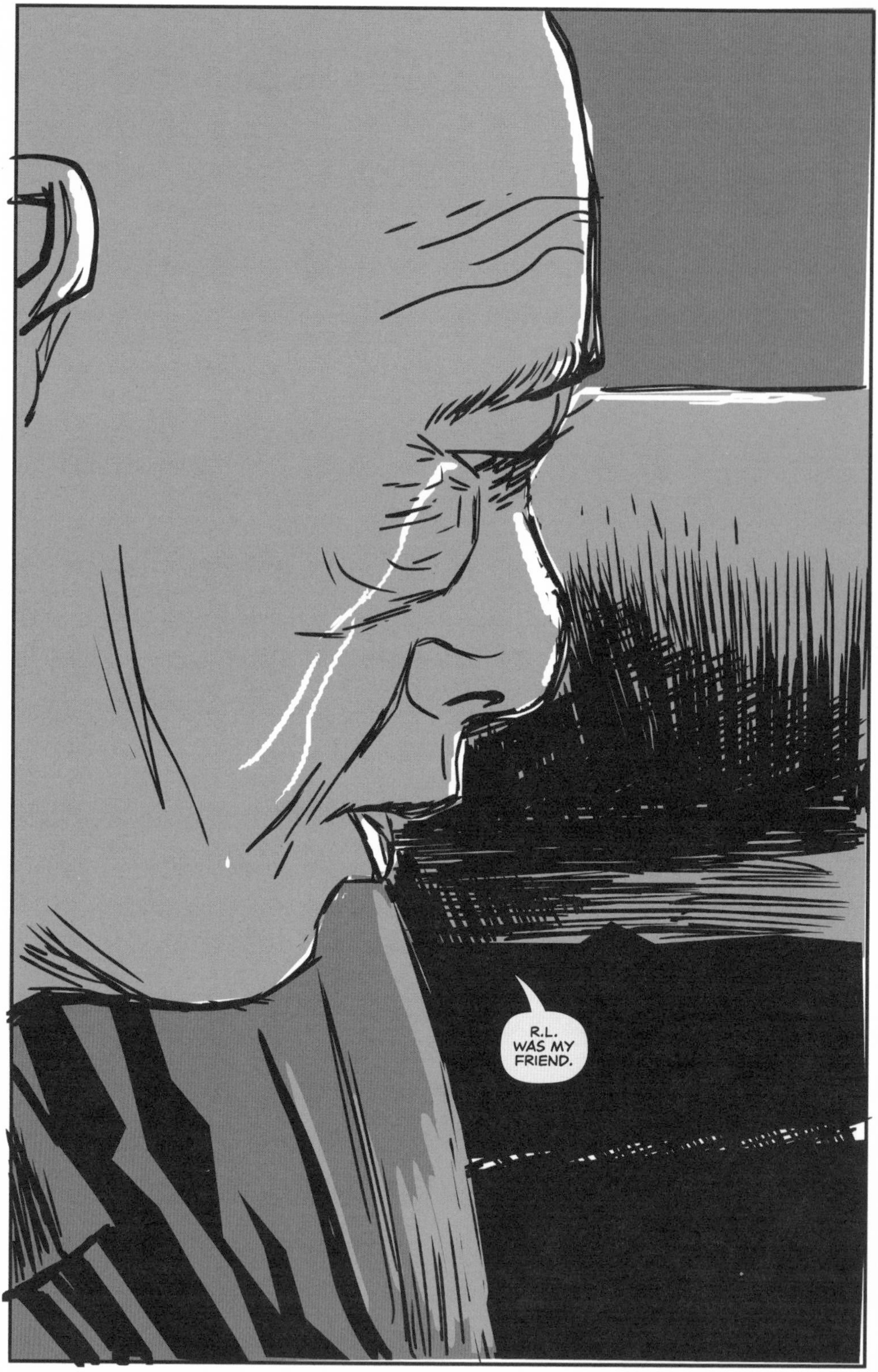
R.L. WAS MY FRIEND.

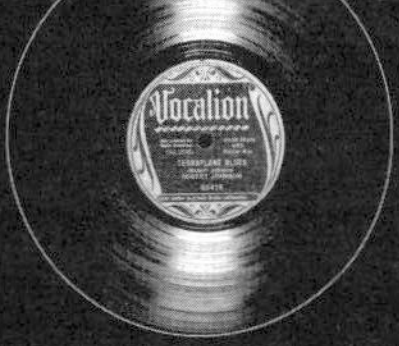
Vocalion

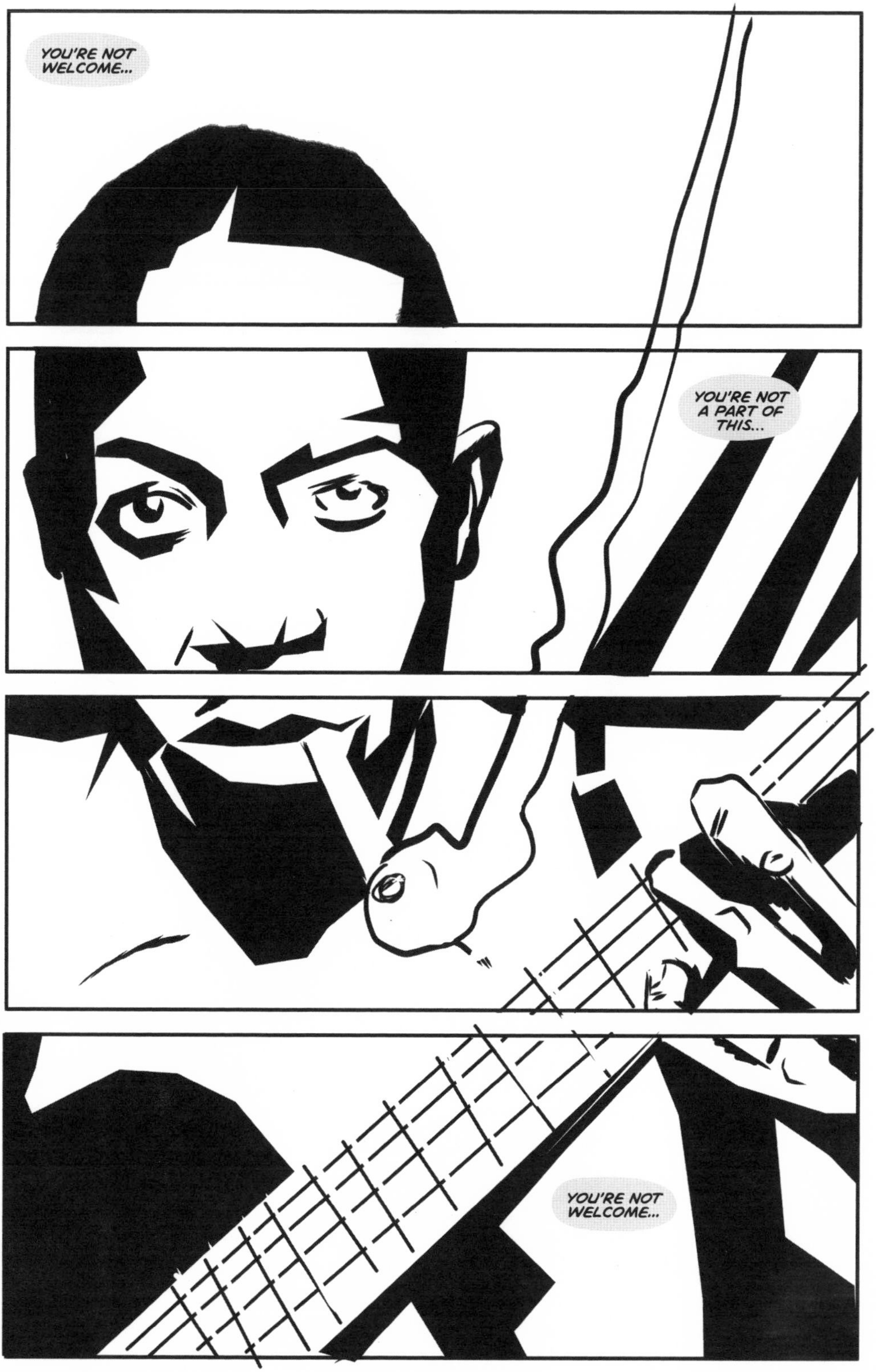
YOU'RE NOT WELCOME...
YOU'RE NOT A PART OF THIS...
YOU'RE NOT WELCOME...

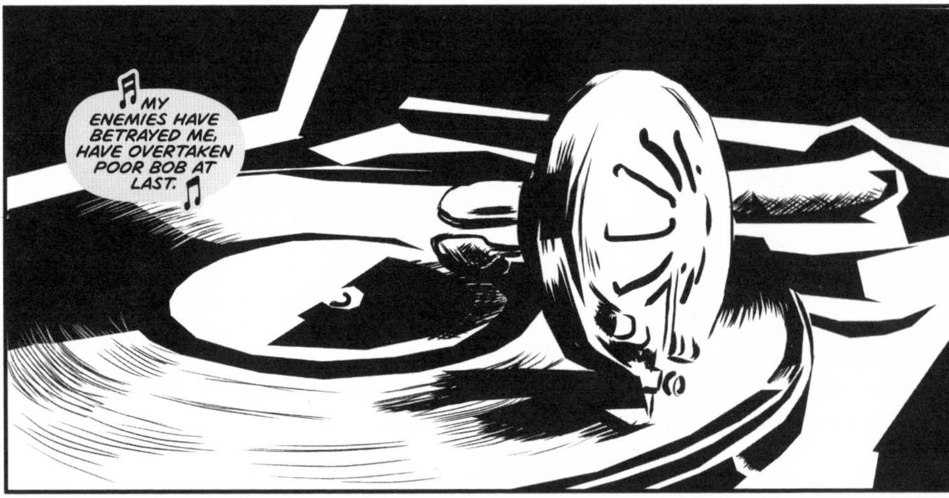
MY ENEMIES HAVE BETRAYED ME, HAVE OVERTAKEN POOR BOB AT LAST.

CHAPTER FIVE

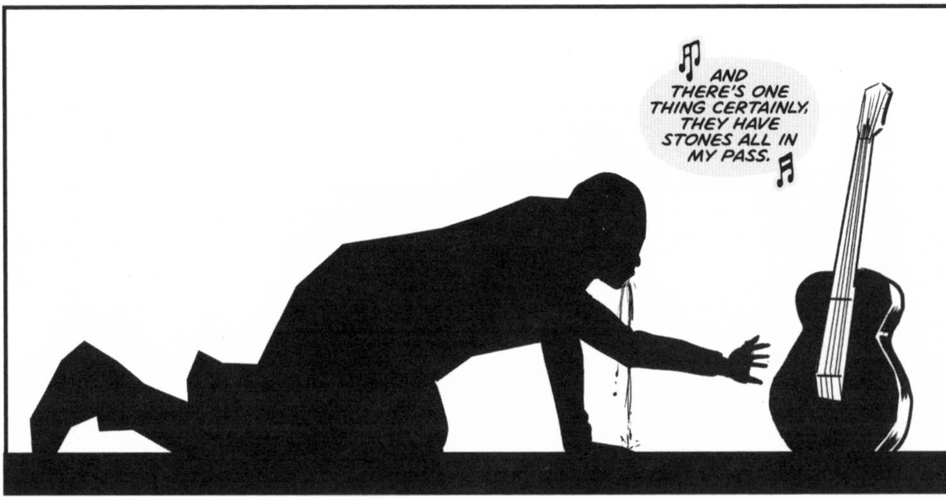
AND THERE'S ONE THING CERTAINLY, THEY HAVE STONES ALL IN MY PASS.

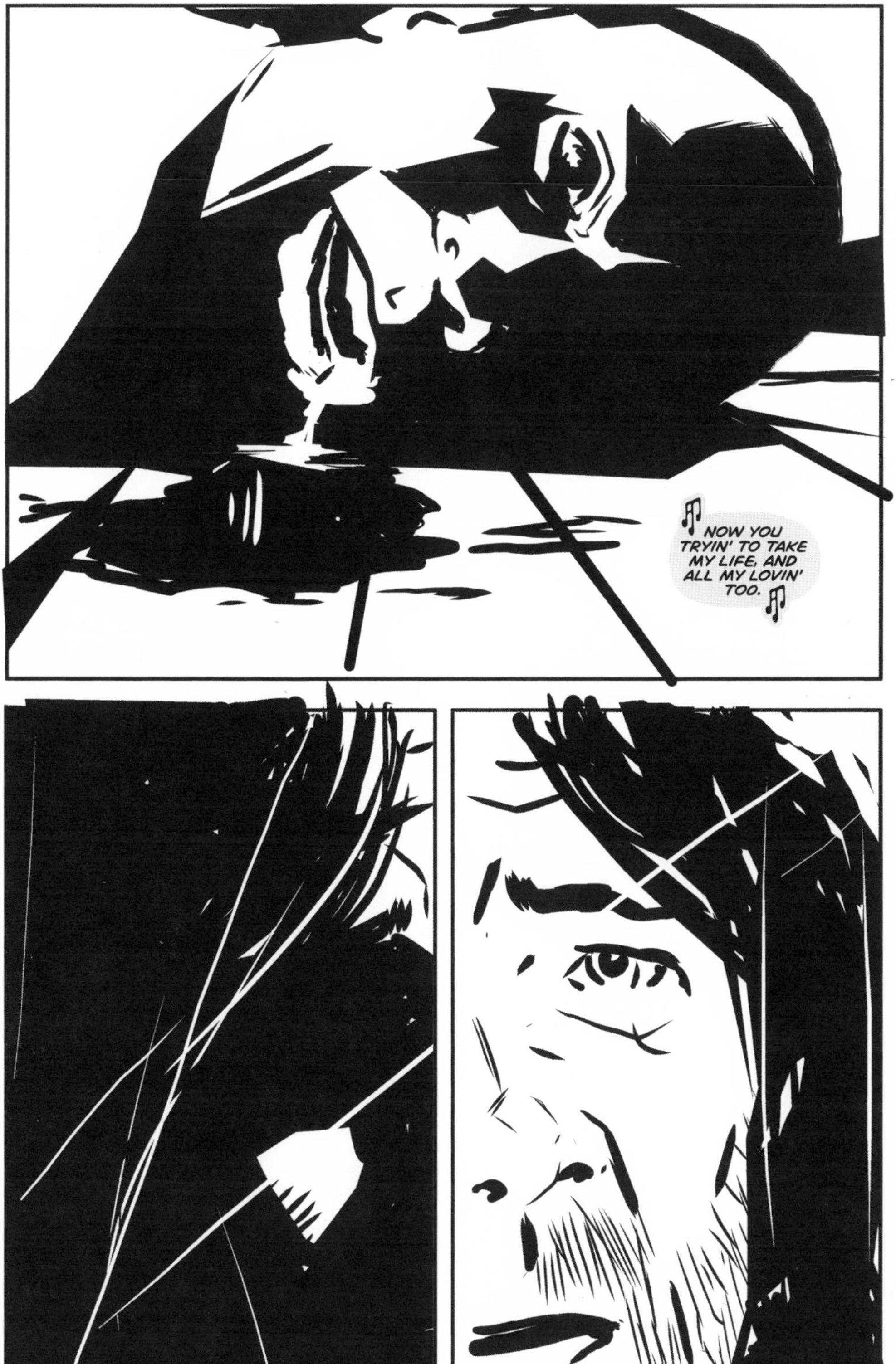
♫ NOW YOU TRYIN' TO TAKE MY LIFE, AND ALL MY LOVIN' TOO. ♫

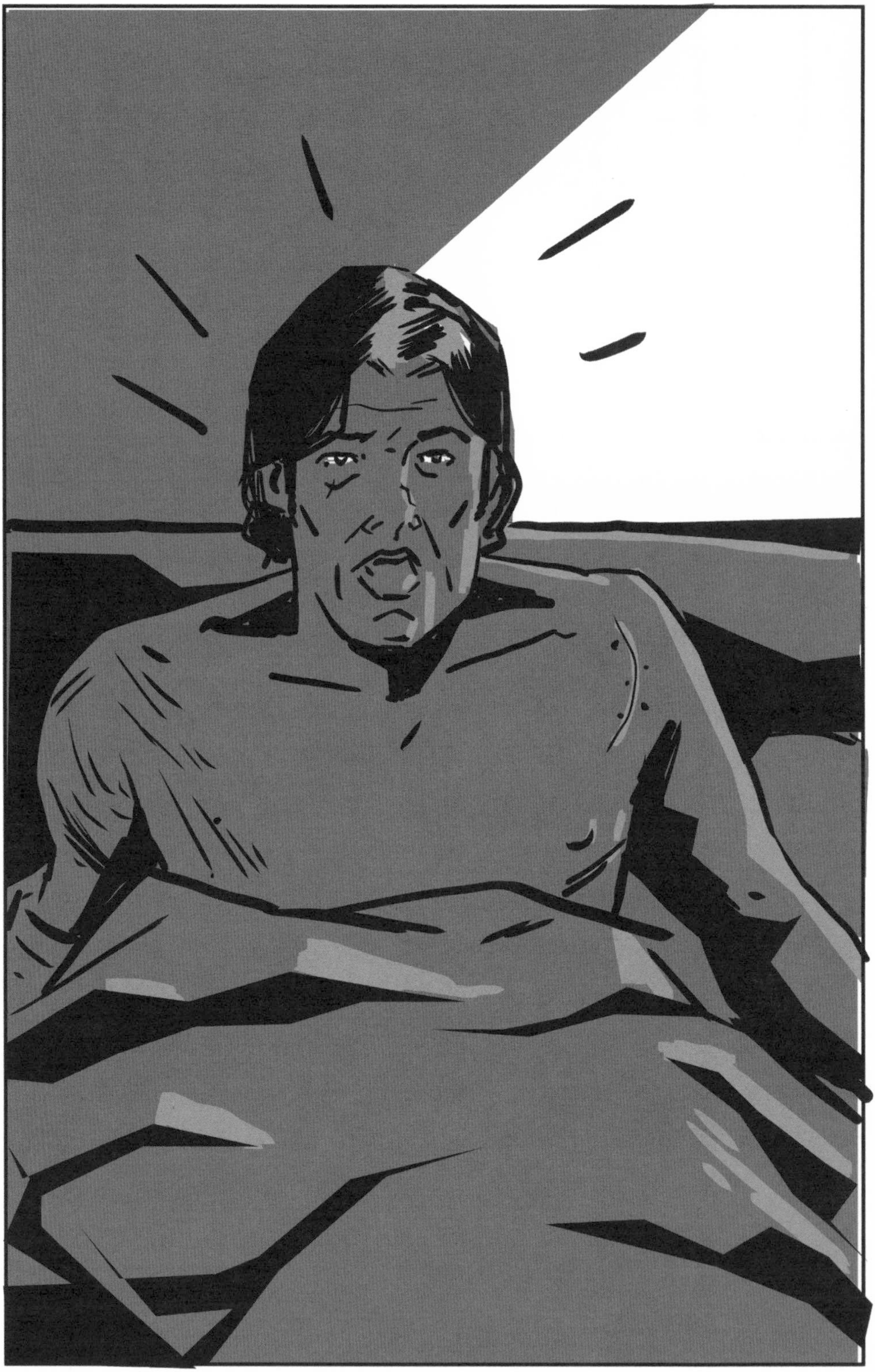

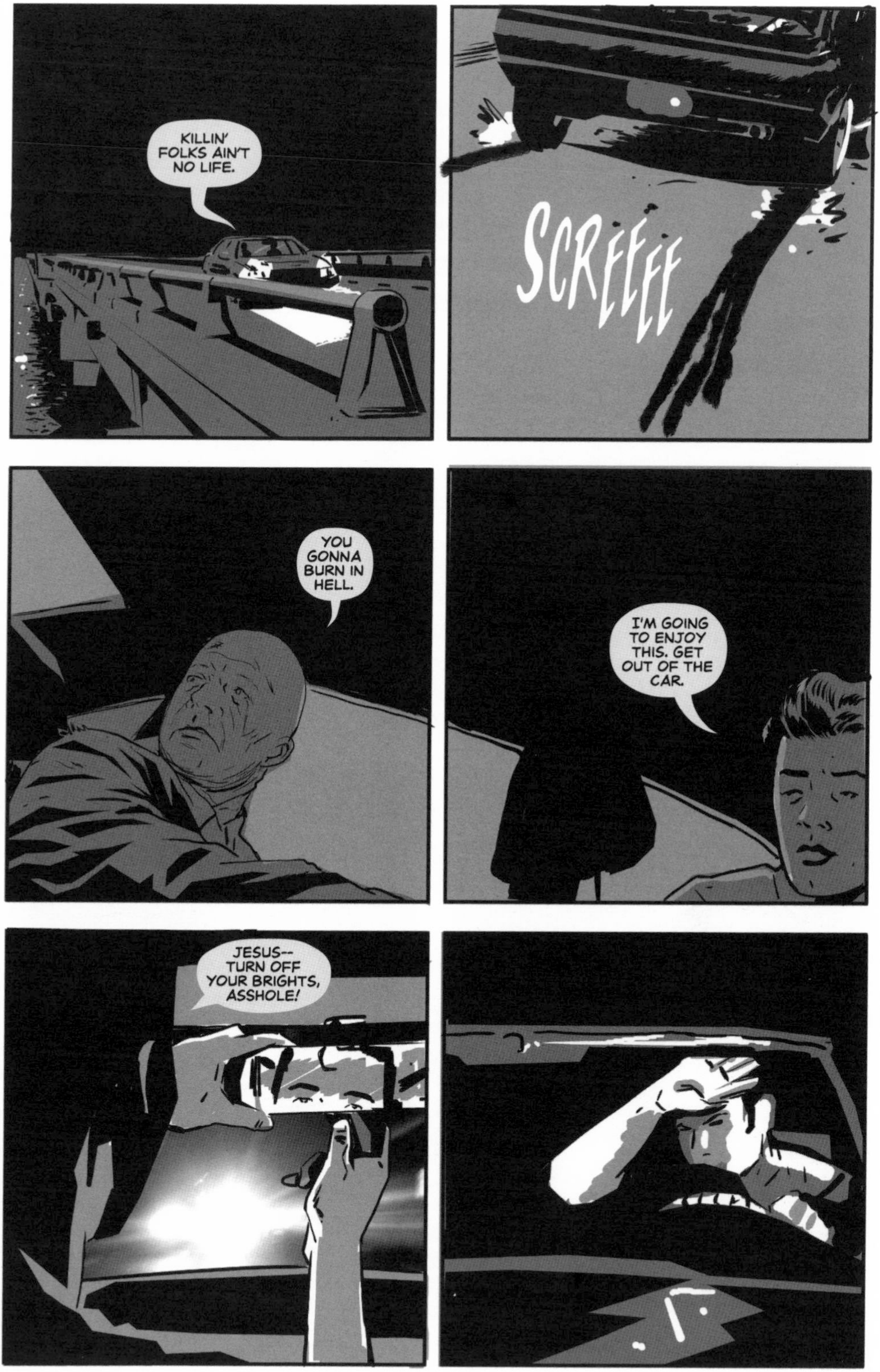
KILLIN' FOLKS AIN'T NO LIFE.
SCREEEEE
YOU GONNA BURN IN HELL.
I'M GOING TO ENJOY THIS. GET OUT OF THE CAR.
JESUS-- TURN OFF YOUR BRIGHTS, ASSHOLE!

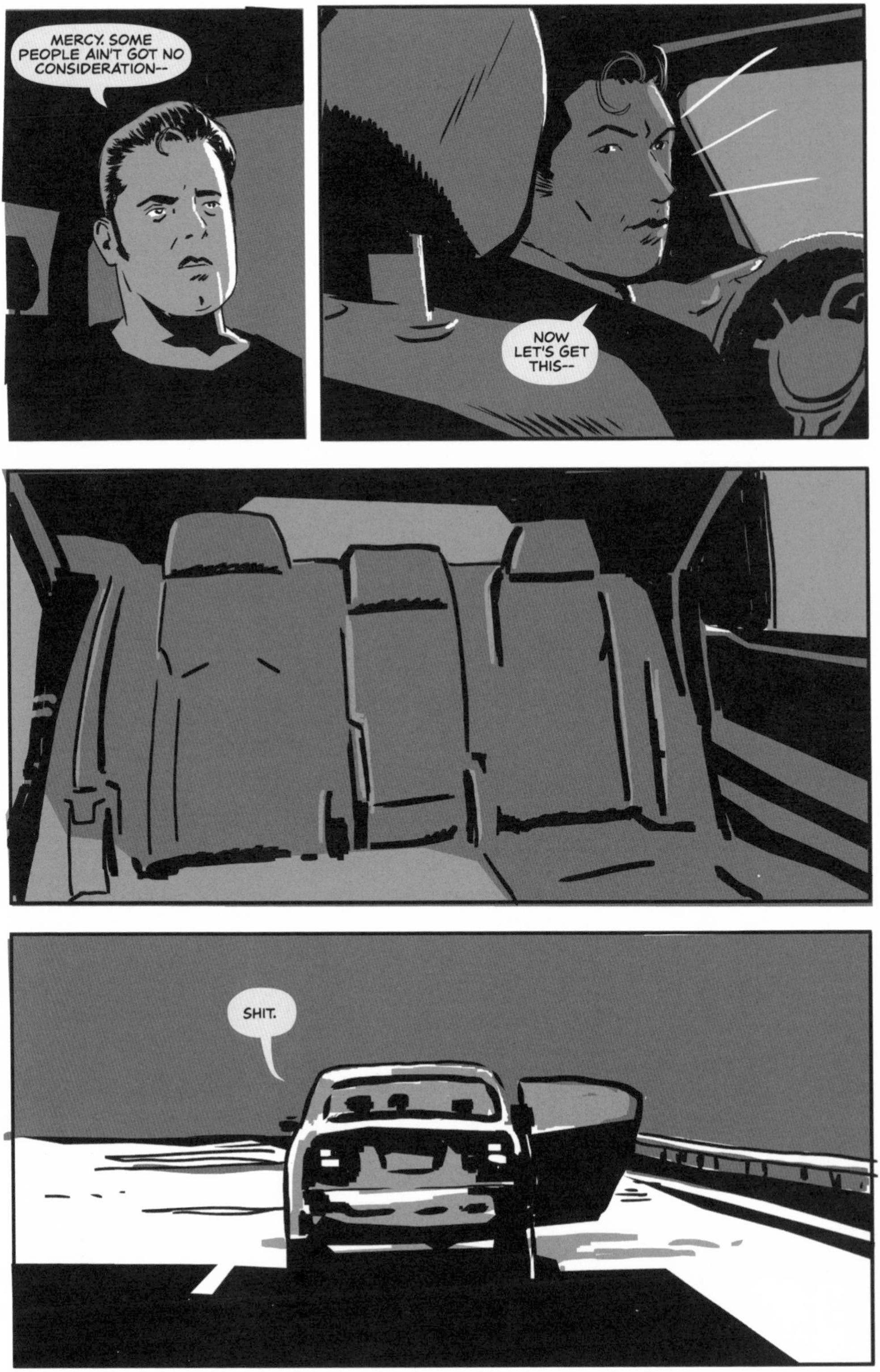
MERCY. SOME PEOPLE AIN'T GOT NO CONSIDERATION--
NOW LET'S GET THIS--
SHIT.

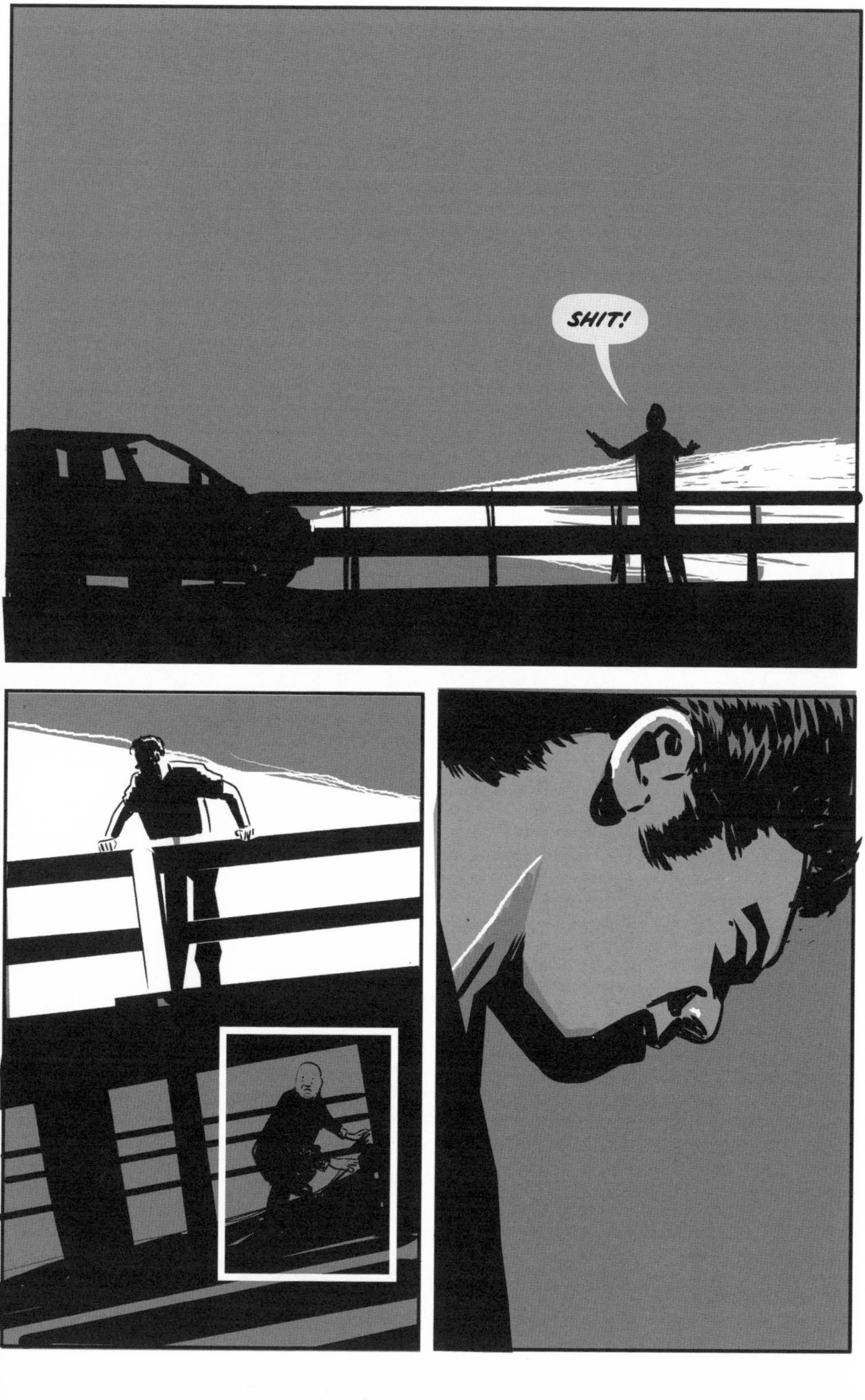
SHIT!

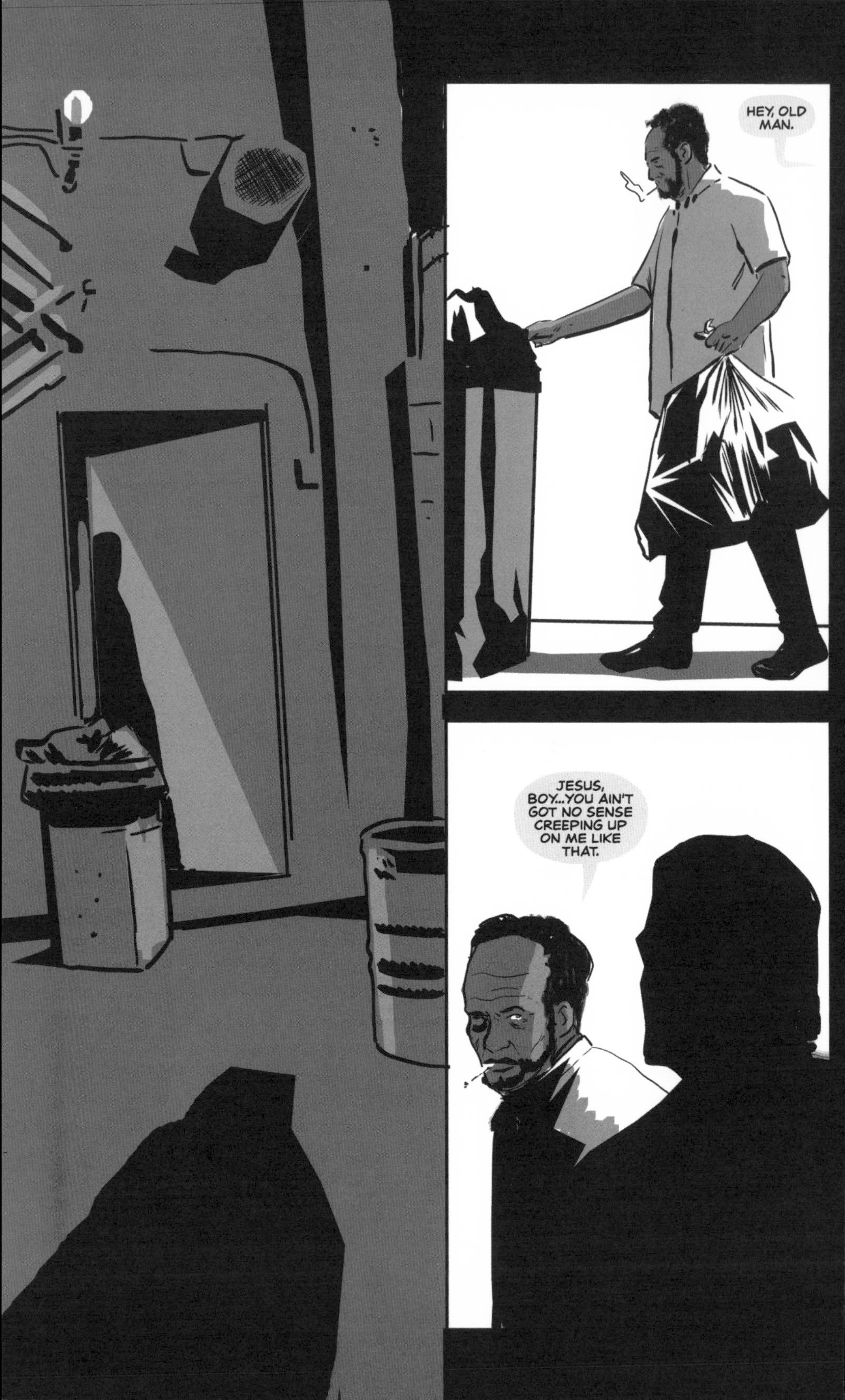
HEY, OLD MAN.
JESUS, BOY...YOU AIN'T GOT NO SENSE CREEPING UP ON ME LIKE THAT.

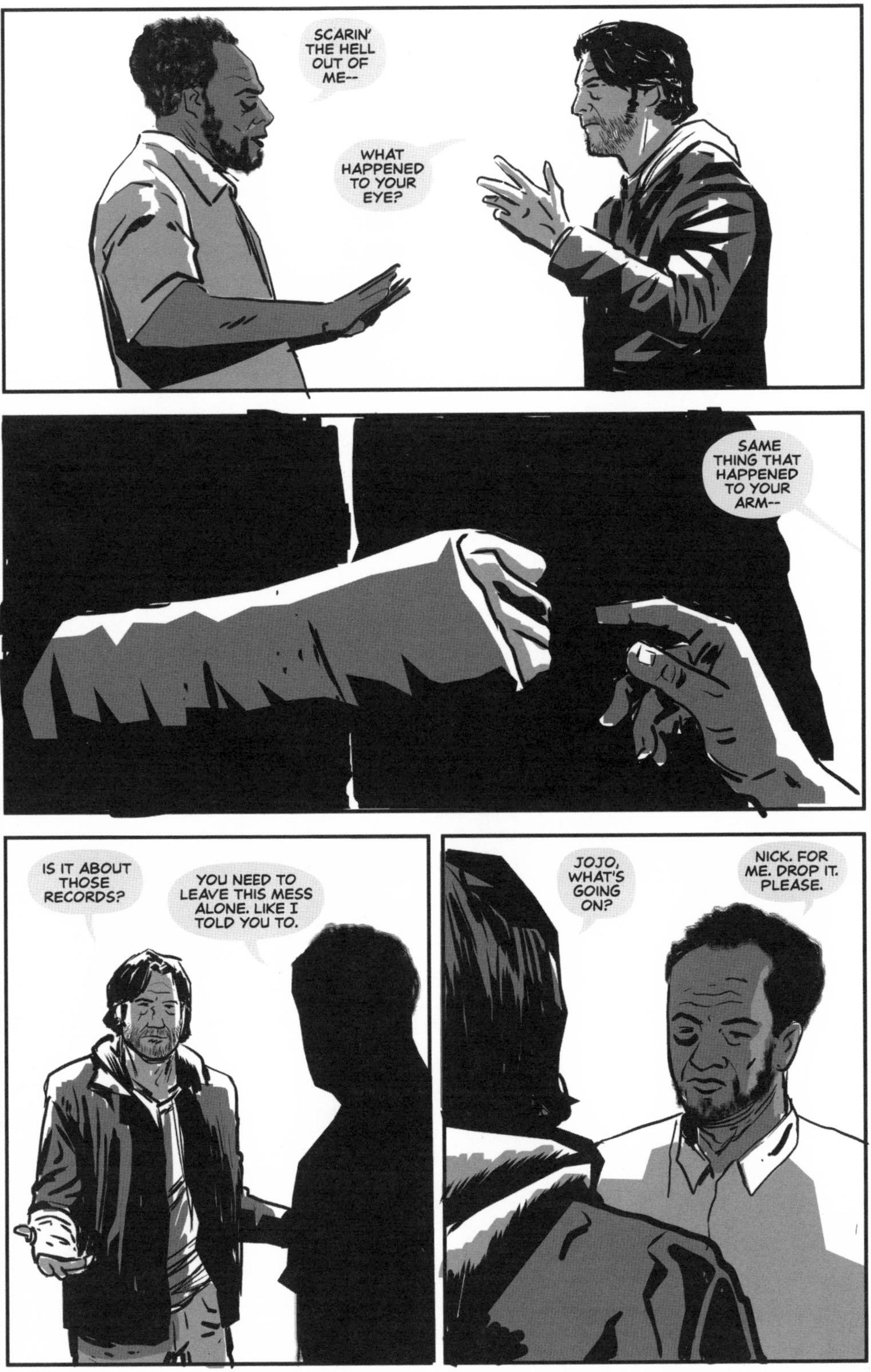
SCARIN' THE HELL OUT OF ME--
WHAT HAPPENED TO YOUR EYE?
SAME THING THAT HAPPENED TO YOUR ARM--
IS IT ABOUT THOSE RECORDS?
YOU NEED TO LEAVE THIS MESS ALONE. LIKE I TOLD YOU TO.
JOJO, WHAT'S GOING ON?
NICK. FOR ME. DROP IT. PLEASE.

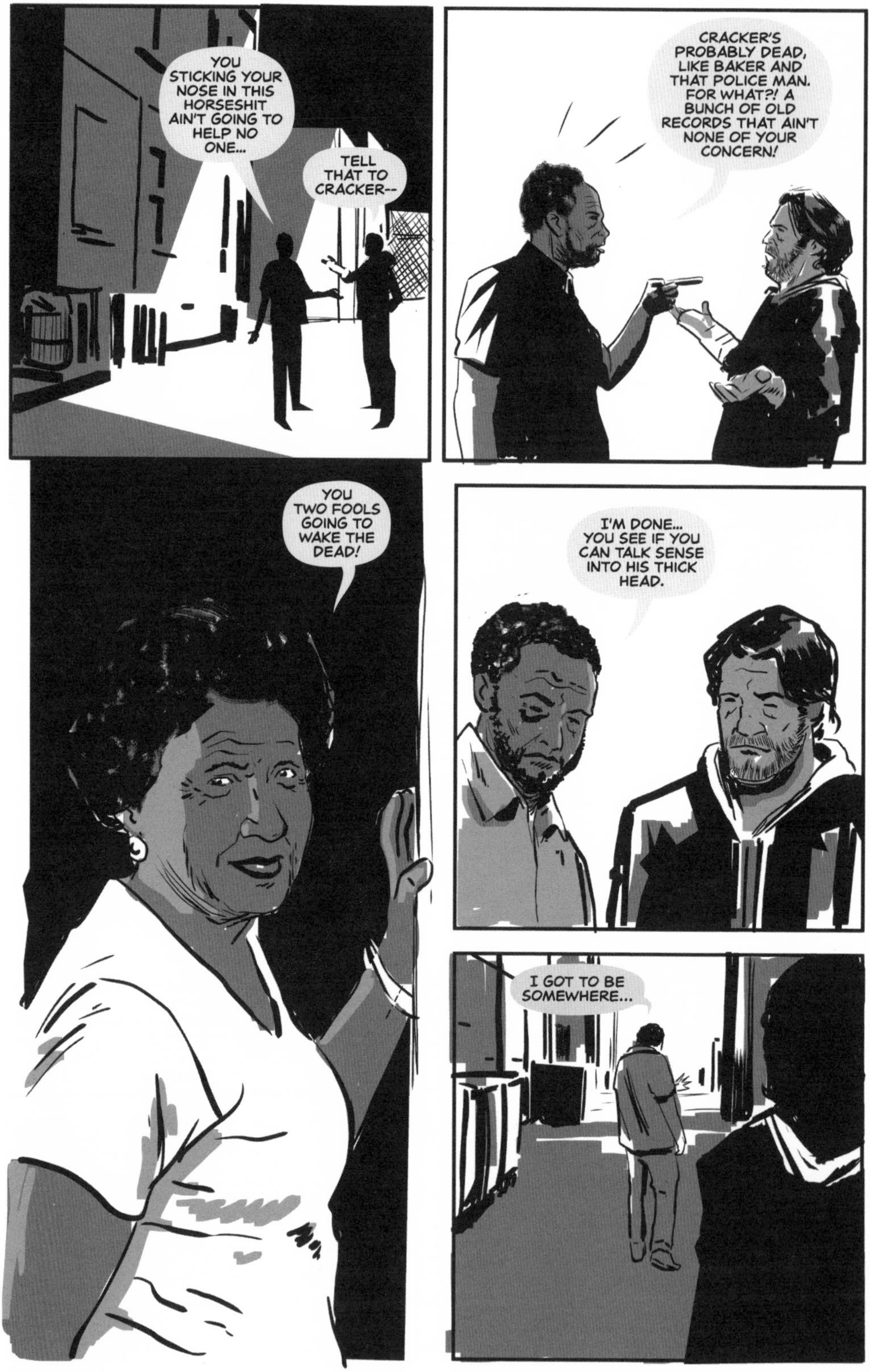
YOU STICKING YOUR NOSE IN THIS HORSESHIT AIN'T GOING TO HELP NO ONE...
TELL THAT TO CRACKER--
CRACKER'S PROBABLY DEAD, LIKE BAKER AND THAT POLICE MAN. FOR WHAT?! A BUNCH OF OLD RECORDS THAT AIN'T NONE OF YOUR CONCERN!
YOU TWO FOOLS GOING TO WAKE THE DEAD!
I'M DONE... YOU SEE IF YOU CAN TALK SENSE INTO HIS THICK HEAD.
I GOT TO BE SOMEWHERE...

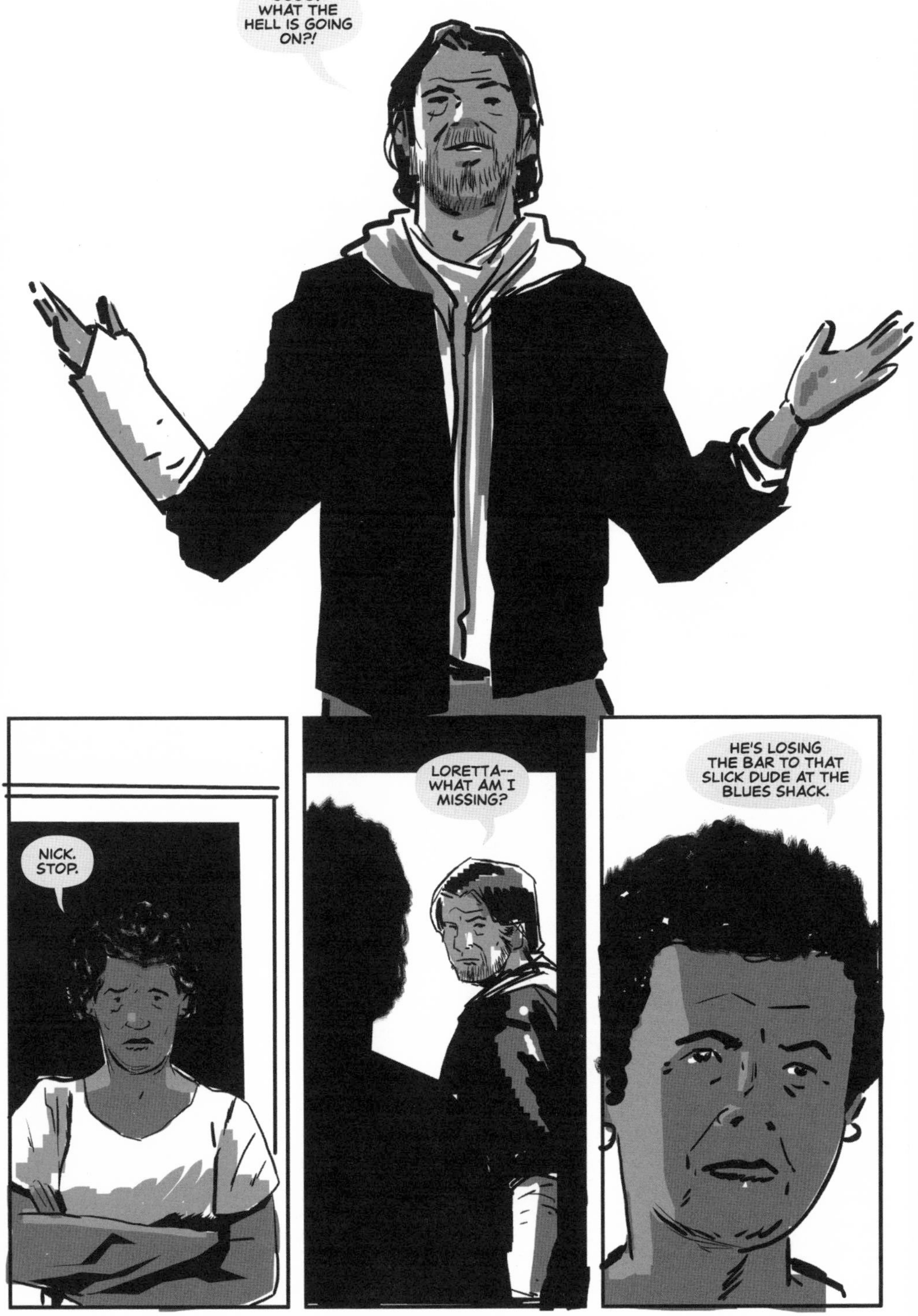
JOJO!
WHAT THE
HELL IS GOING
ON?!
NICK.
STOP.
LORETTA--
WHAT AM I
MISSING?
HE'S LOSING
THE BAR TO THAT
SLICK DUDE AT THE
BLUES SHACK.

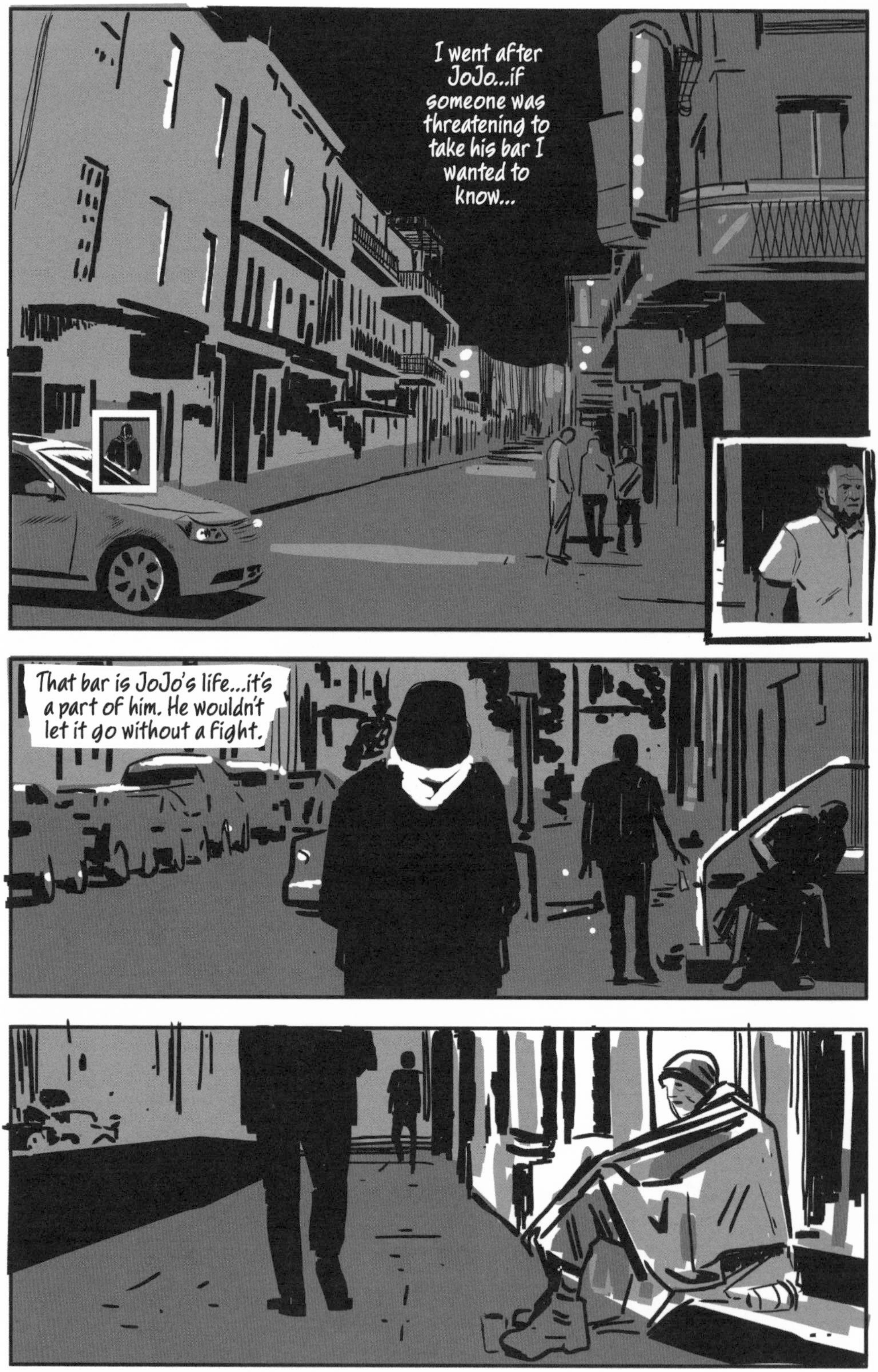
I went after JoJo...if someone was threatening to take his bar I wanted to know...
That bar is JoJo's life...it's a part of him. He wouldn't let it go without a fight.

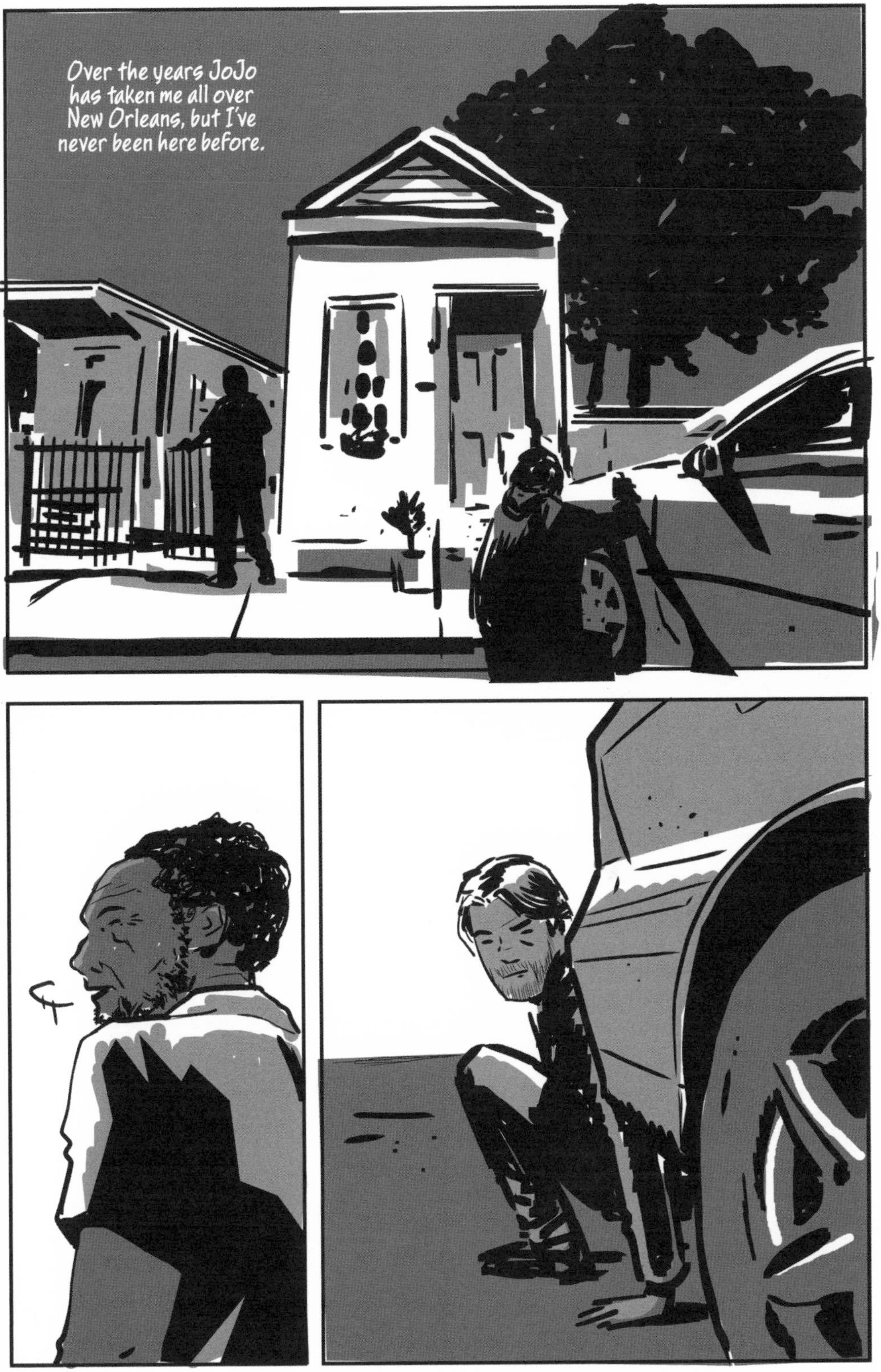
Over the years JoJo has taken me all over New Orleans, but I've never been here before.

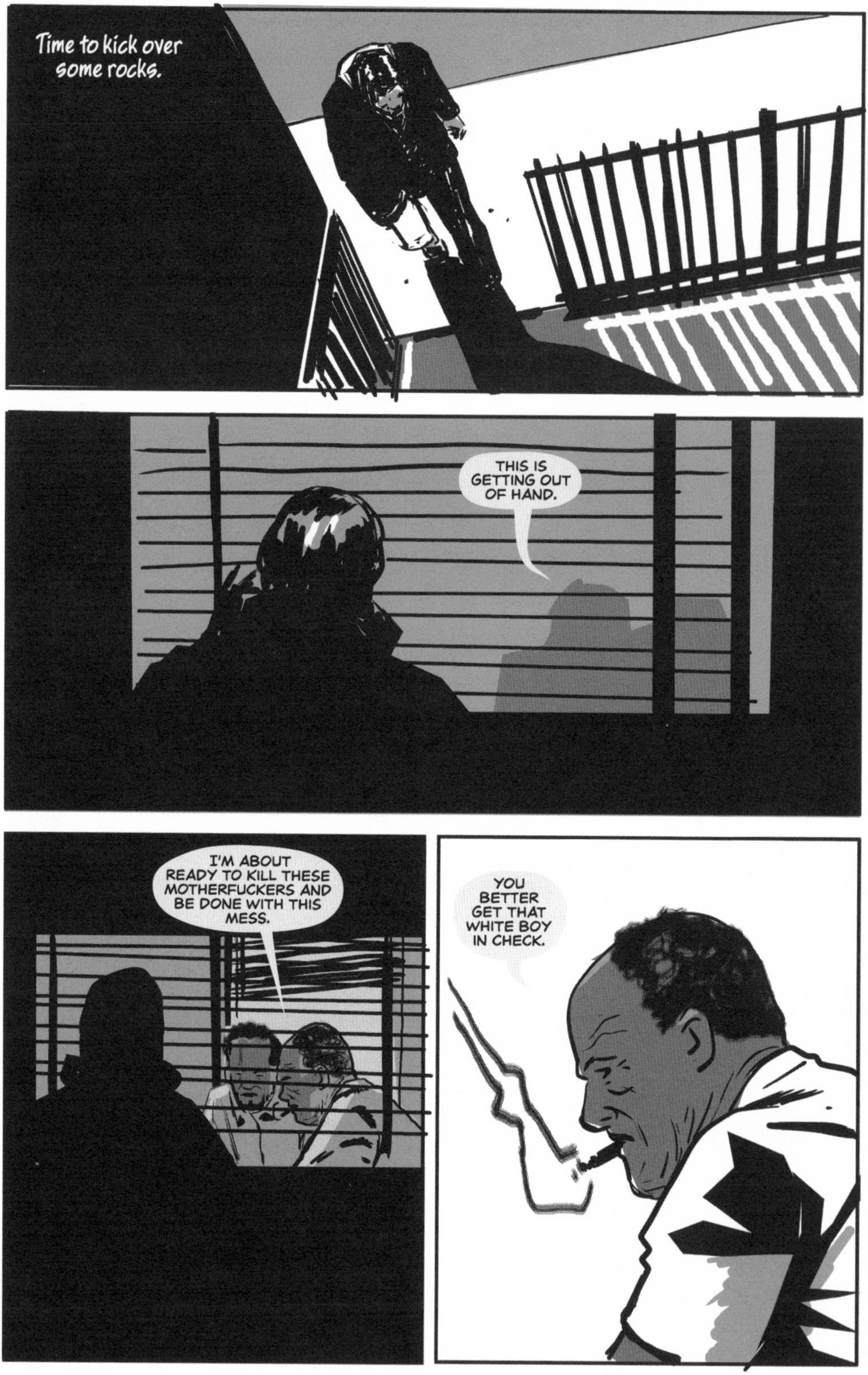
Time to kick over some rocks.
THIS IS GETTING OUT OF HAND.
I'M ABOUT READY TO KILL THESE MOTHERFUCKERS AND BE DONE WITH THIS MESS.
YOU BETTER GET THAT WHITE BOY IN CHECK.

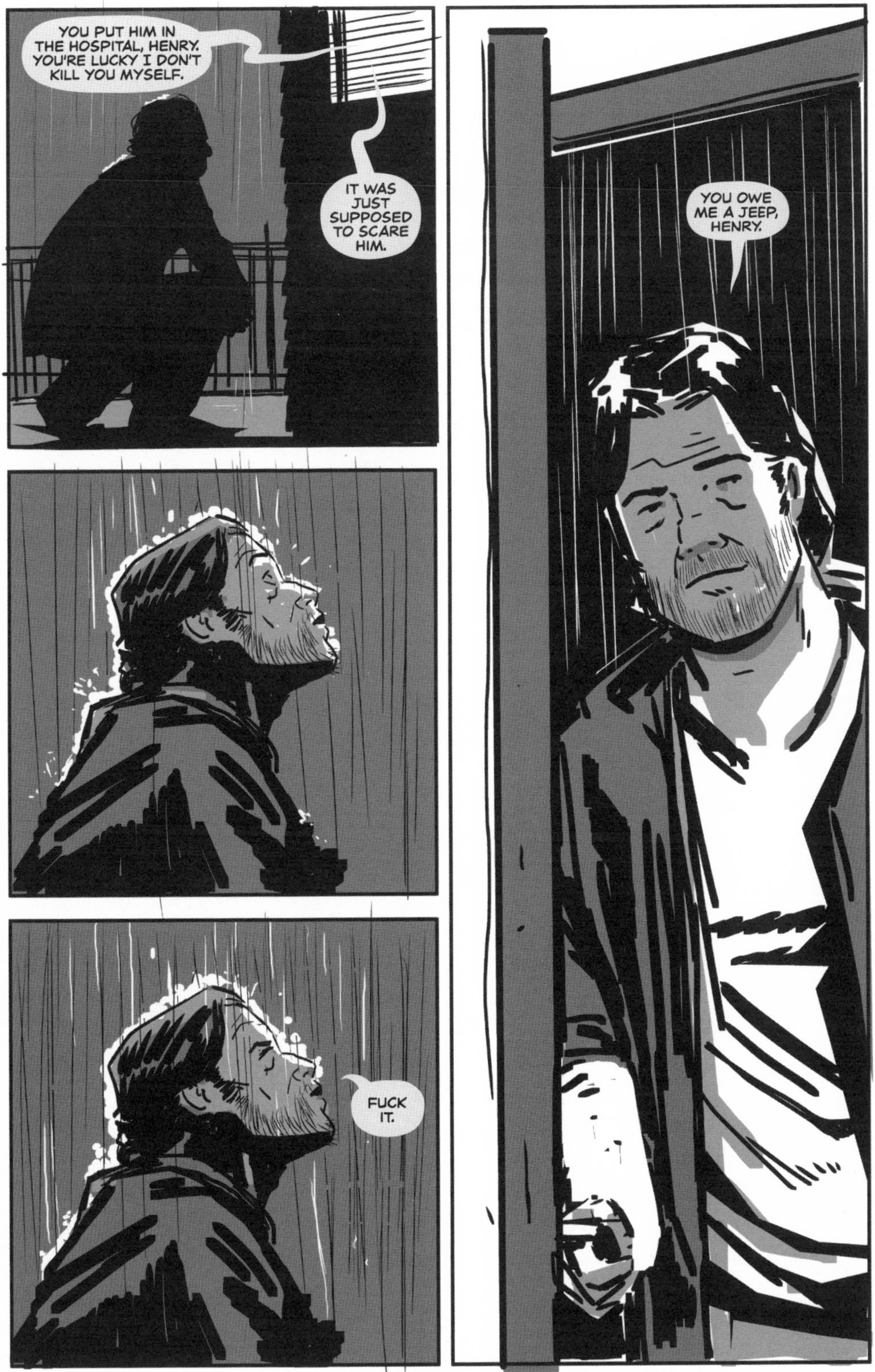
YOU PUT HIM IN THE HOSPITAL, HENRY. YOU'RE LUCKY I DON'T KILL YOU MYSELF.
IT WAS JUST SUPPOSED TO SCARE HIM.
FUCK IT.
YOU OWE ME A JEEP, HENRY.

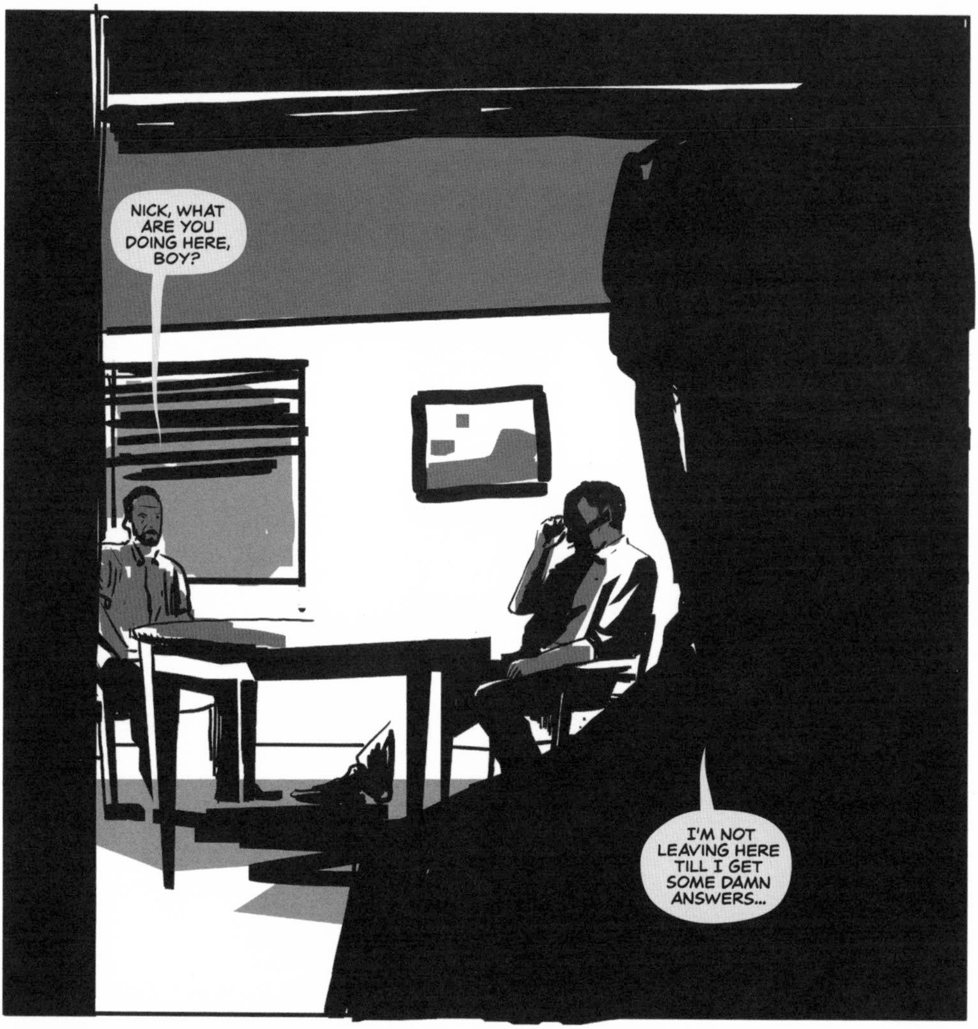
NICK, WHAT ARE YOU DOING HERE, BOY?
I'M NOT LEAVING HERE TILL I GET SOME DAMN ANSWERS...

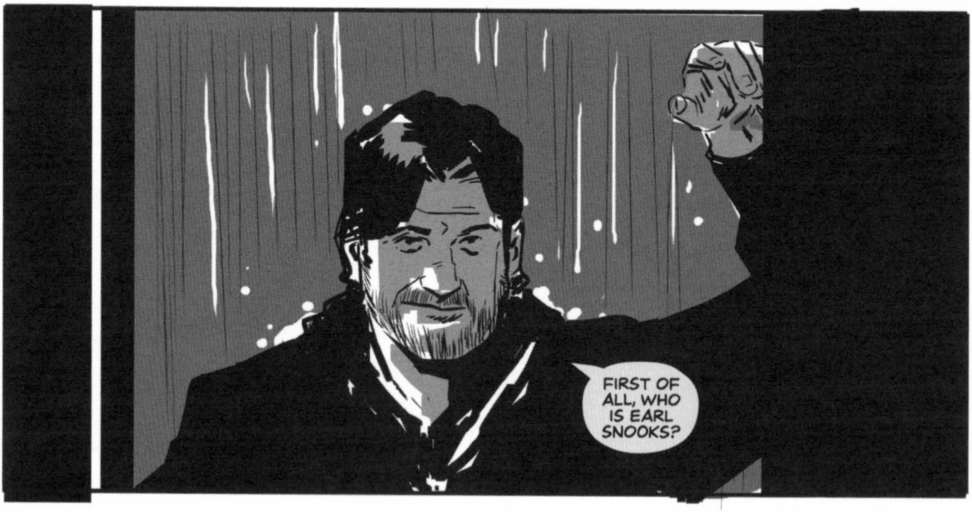
FIRST OF ALL, WHO IS EARL SNOOKS?

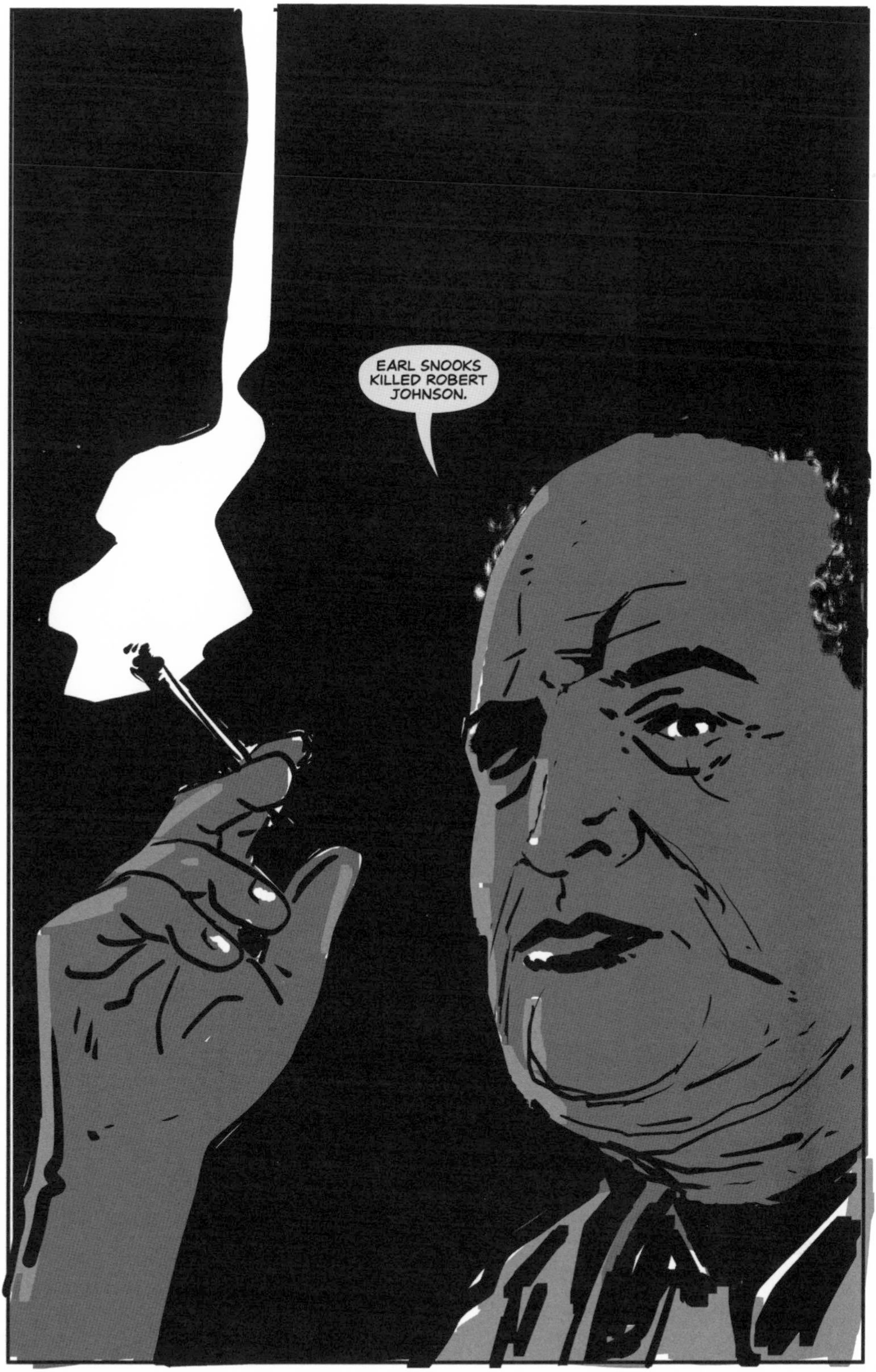
EARL SNOOKS KILLED ROBERT JOHNSON.

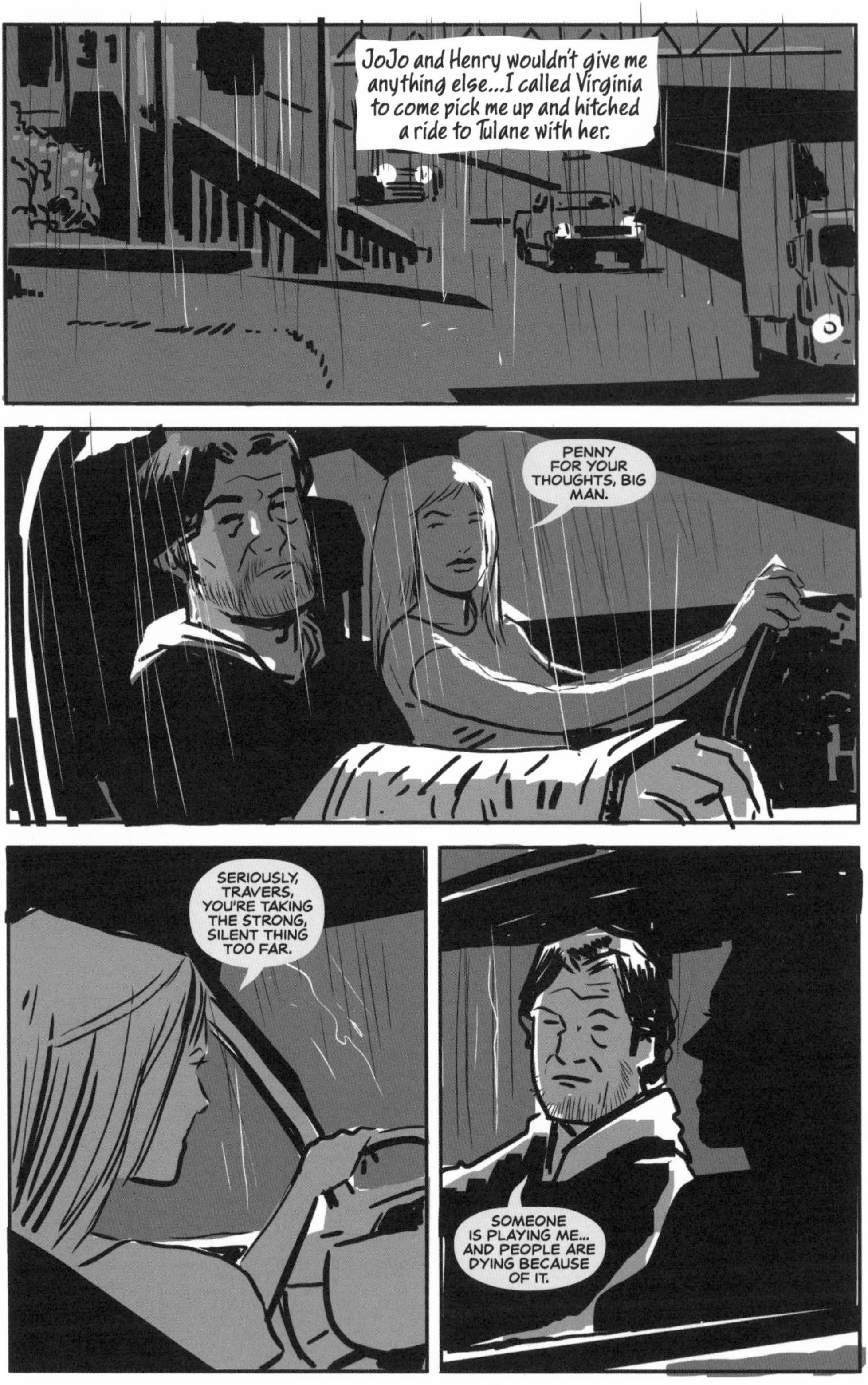
JoJo and Henry wouldn't give me anything else...I called Virginia to come pick me up and hitched a ride to Tulane with her.
PENNY FOR YOUR THOUGHTS, BIG MAN.
SERIOUSLY, TRAVERS, YOU'RE TAKING THE STRONG, SILENT THING TOO FAR.
SOMEONE IS PLAYING ME... AND PEOPLE ARE DYING BECAUSE OF IT.

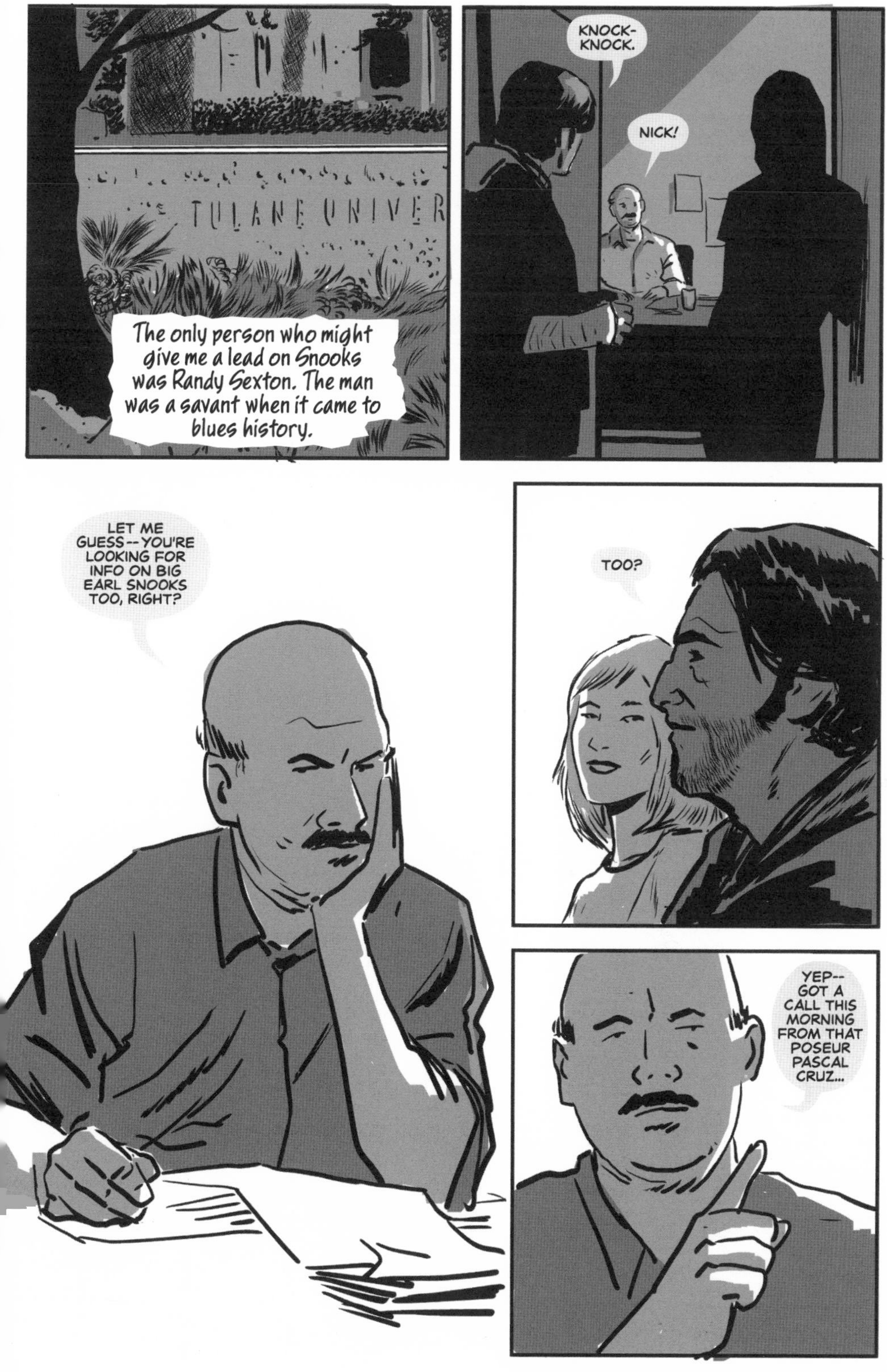
TULANE UNIVER
The only person who might give me a lead on Snooks was Randy Sexton. The man was a savant when it came to blues history.
KNOCK-KNOCK.
NICK!
LET ME GUESS--YOU'RE LOOKING FOR INFO ON BIG EARL SNOOKS TOO, RIGHT?
TOO?
YEP--GOT A CALL THIS MORNING FROM THAT POSEUR PASCAL CRUZ...

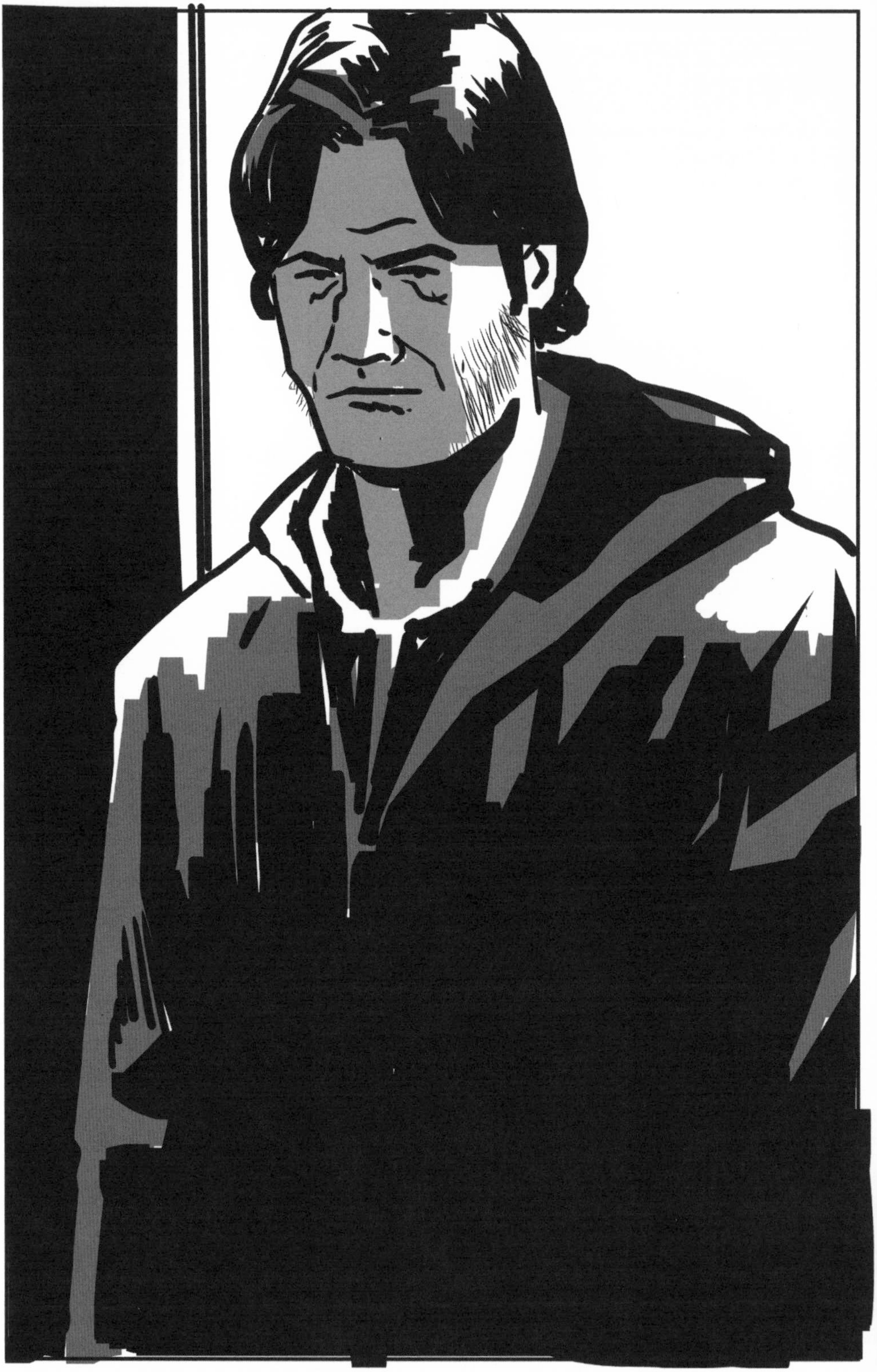

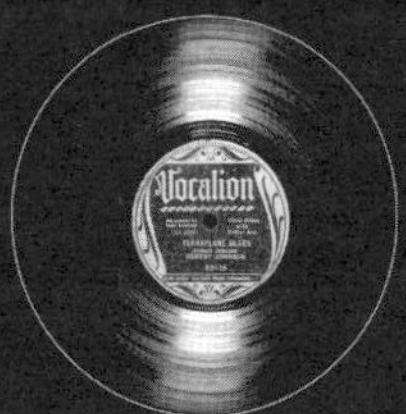
Vocalion

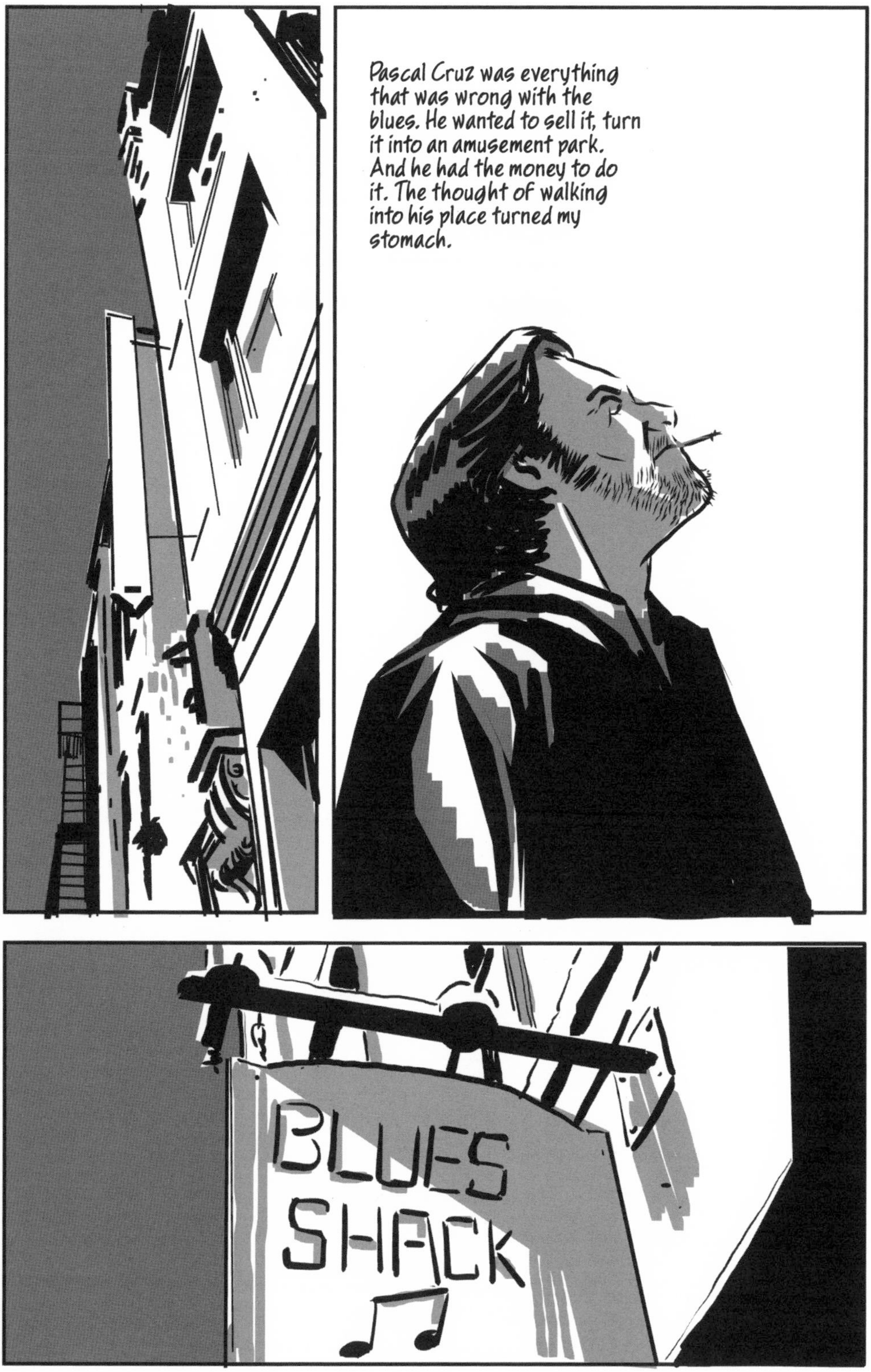
Pascal Cruz was everything that was wrong with the blues. He wanted to sell it, turn it into an amusement park. And he had the money to do it. The thought of walking into his place turned my stomach.
BLUES SHACK

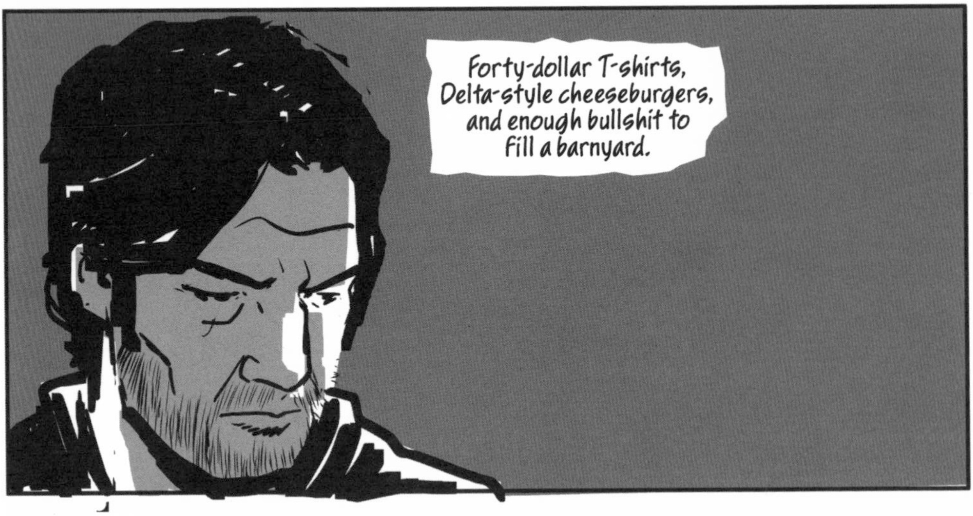
Forty-dollar T-shirts, Delta-style cheeseburgers, and enough bullshit to fill a barnyard.

CHAPTER SIX

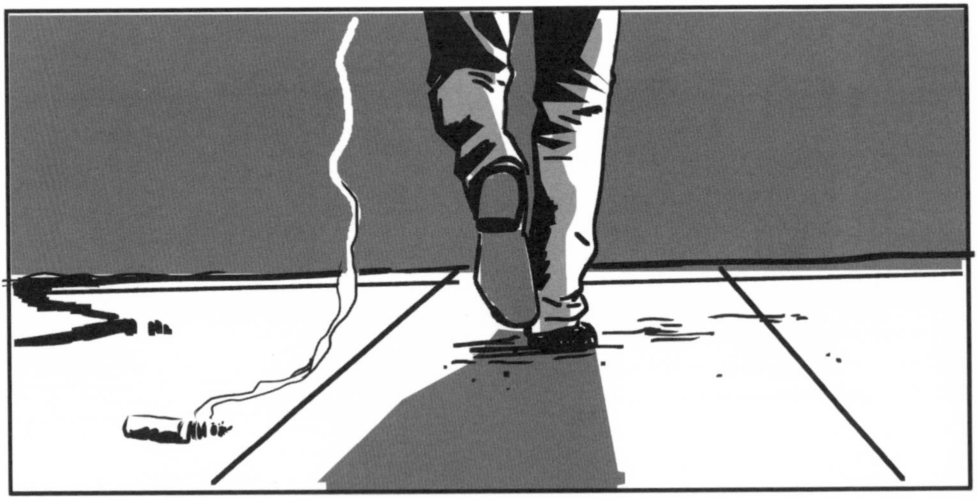

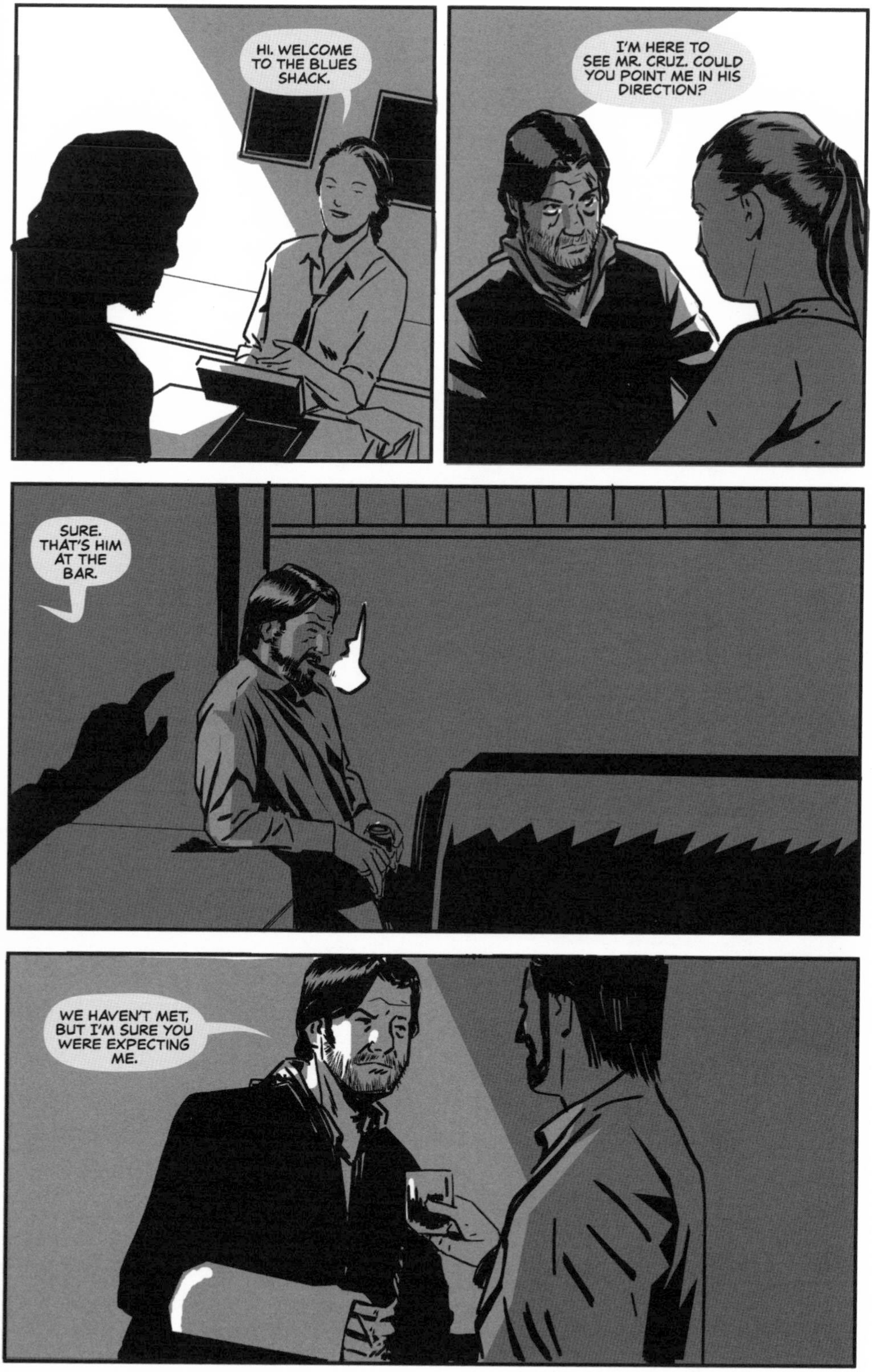
HI. WELCOME TO THE BLUES SHACK.
I'M HERE TO SEE MR. CRUZ. COULD YOU POINT ME IN HIS DIRECTION?
SURE. THAT'S HIM AT THE BAR.
WE HAVEN'T MET, BUT I'M SURE YOU WERE EXPECTING ME.

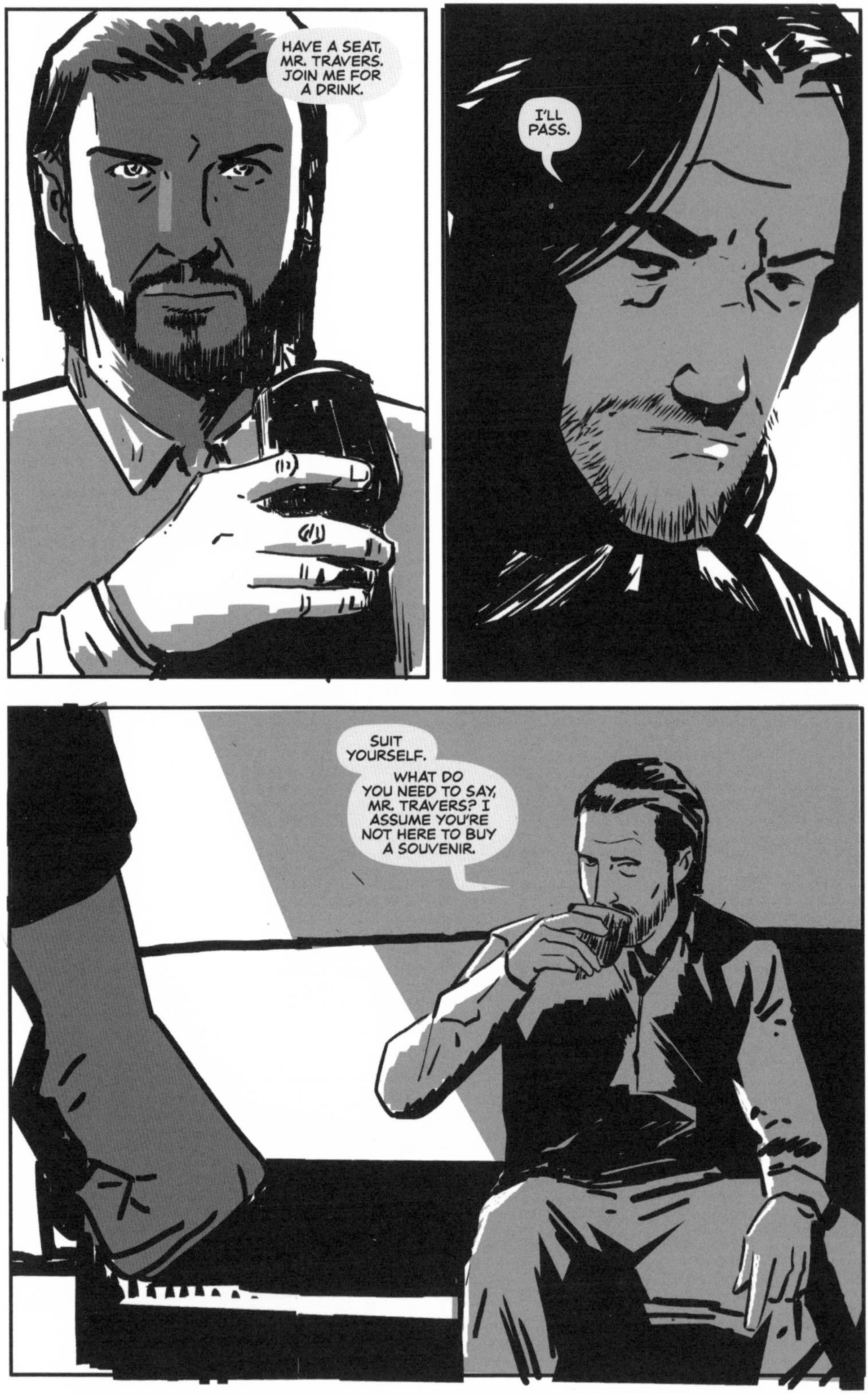
HAVE A SEAT, MR. TRAVERS. JOIN ME FOR A DRINK.
I'LL PASS.
SUIT YOURSELF.
WHAT DO YOU NEED TO SAY, MR. TRAVERS? I ASSUME YOU'RE NOT HERE TO BUY A SOUVENIR.

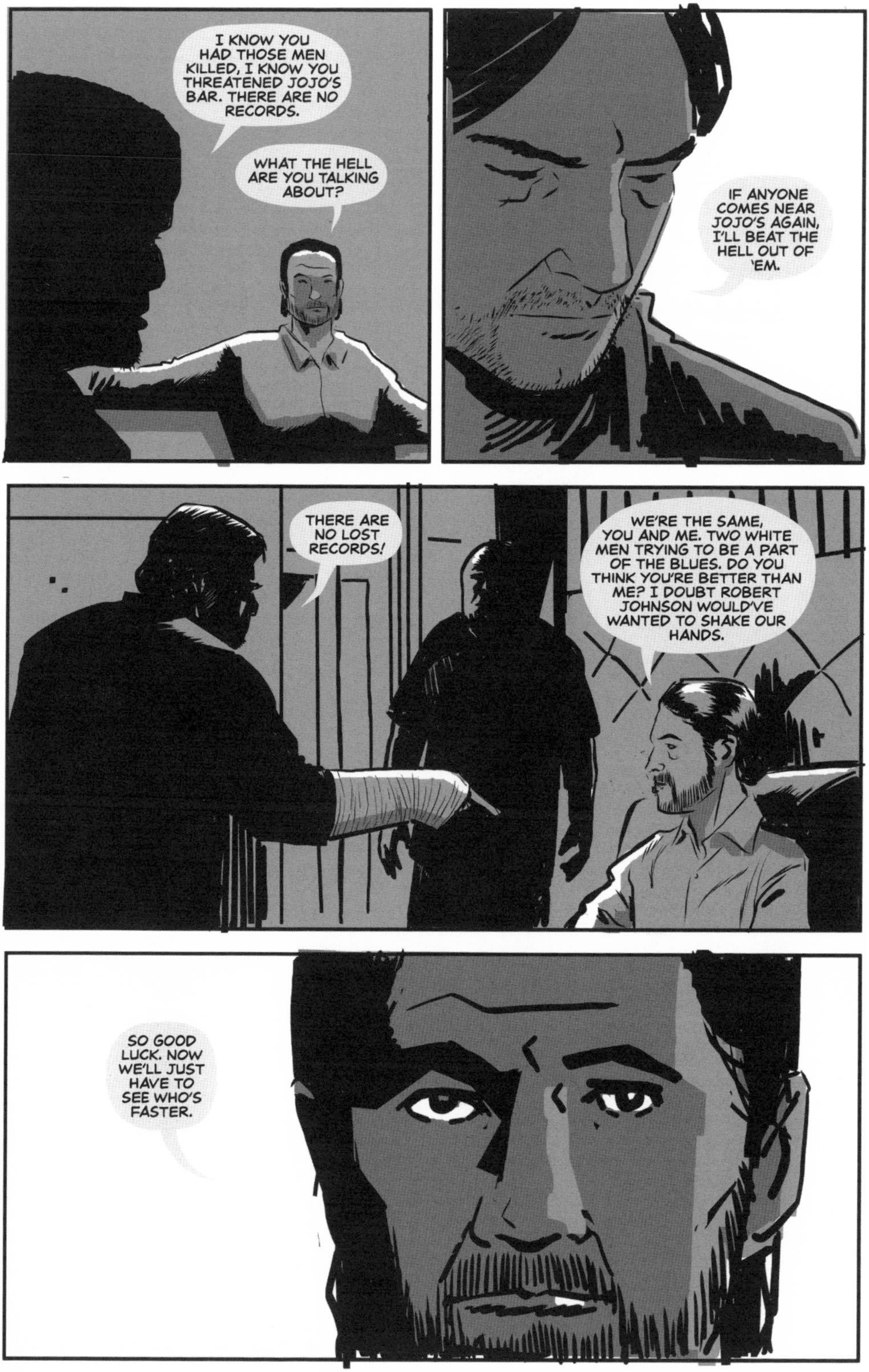
I KNOW YOU HAD THOSE MEN KILLED, I KNOW YOU THREATENED JOJO'S BAR. THERE ARE NO RECORDS.
WHAT THE HELL ARE YOU TALKING ABOUT?
IF ANYONE COMES NEAR JOJO'S AGAIN, I'LL BEAT THE HELL OUT OF 'EM.
THERE ARE NO LOST RECORDS!
WE'RE THE SAME, YOU AND ME. TWO WHITE MEN TRYING TO BE A PART OF THE BLUES. DO YOU THINK YOU'RE BETTER THAN ME? I DOUBT ROBERT JOHNSON WOULD'VE WANTED TO SHAKE OUR HANDS.
SO GOOD LUCK. NOW WE'LL JUST HAVE TO SEE WHO'S FASTER.

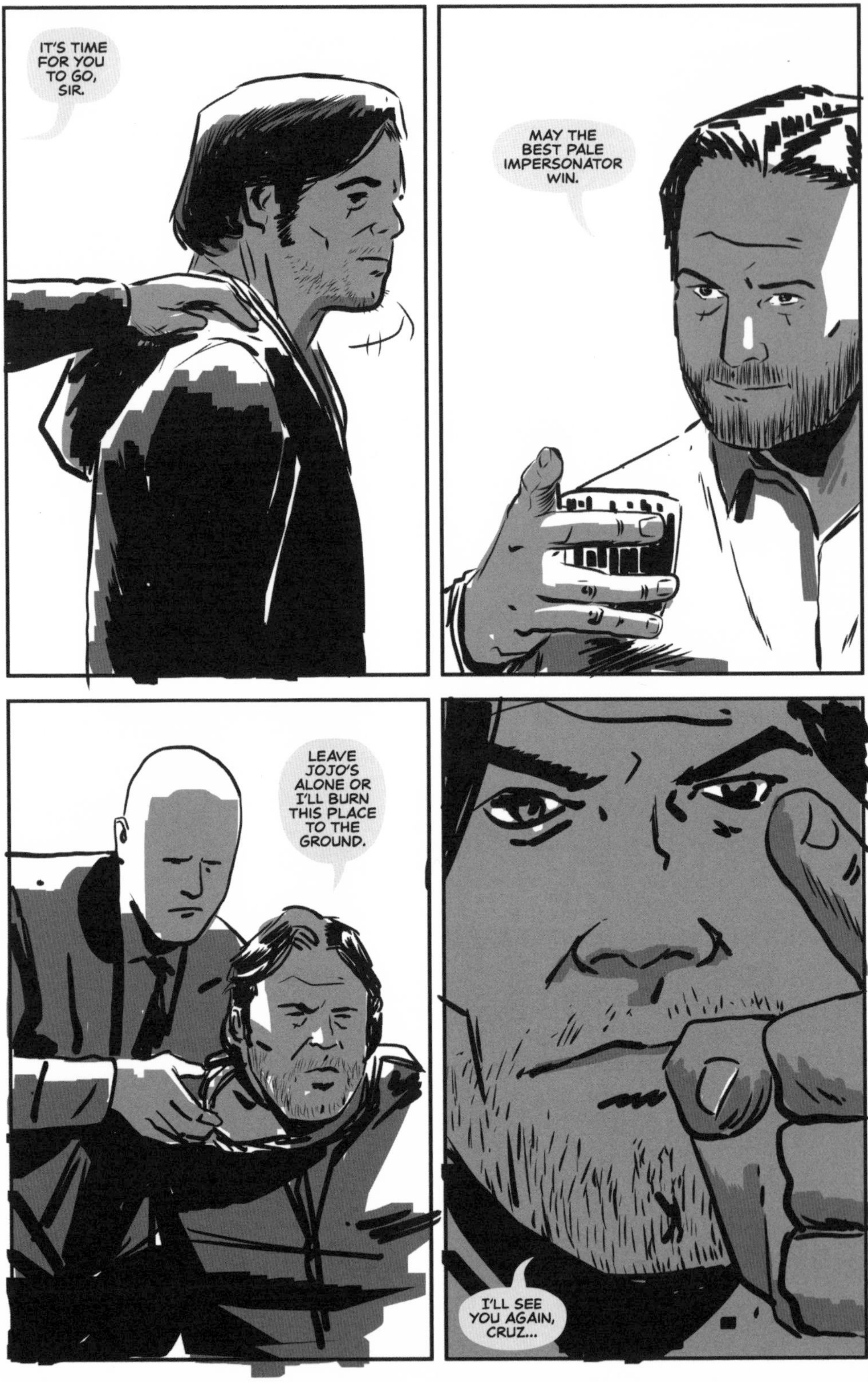
IT'S TIME FOR YOU TO GO, SIR.
MAY THE BEST PALE IMPERSONATOR WIN.
LEAVE JOJO'S ALONE OR I'LL BURN THIS PLACE TO THE GROUND.
I'LL SEE YOU AGAIN, CRUZ...

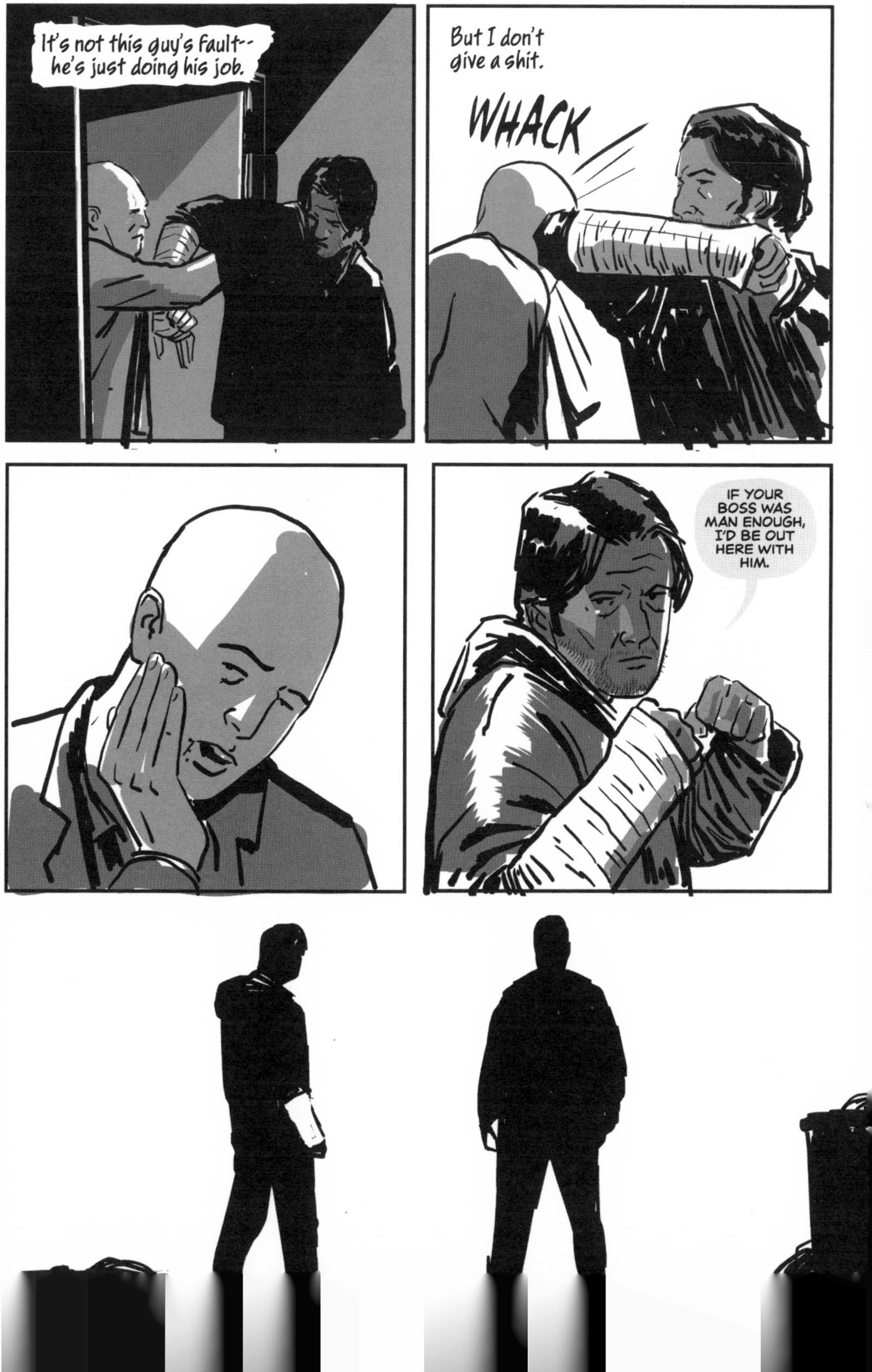
It's not this guy's fault--
he's just doing his job.
But I don't give a shit.
WHACK
IF YOUR BOSS WAS MAN ENOUGH, I'D BE OUT HERE WITH HIM.

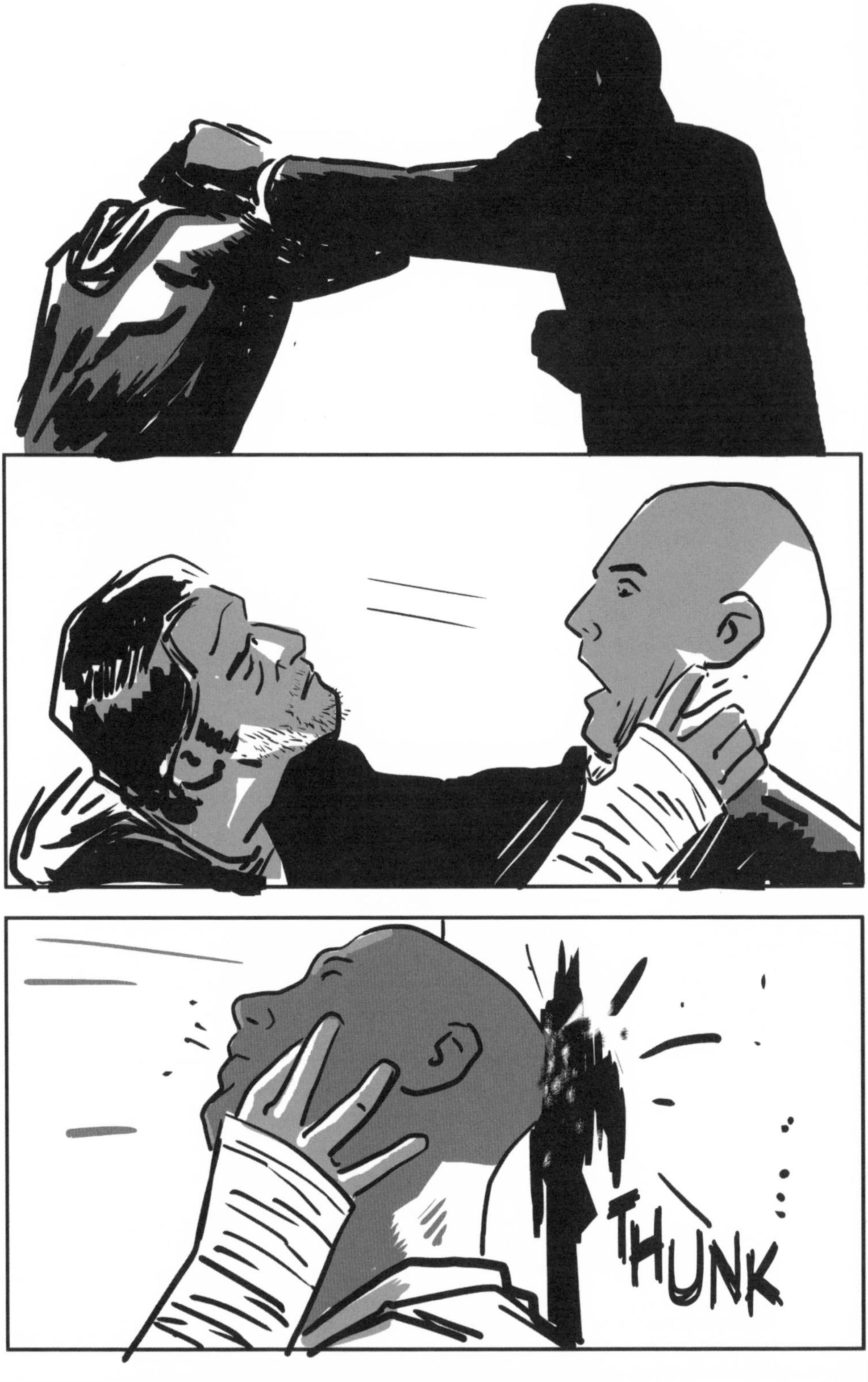
THUNK

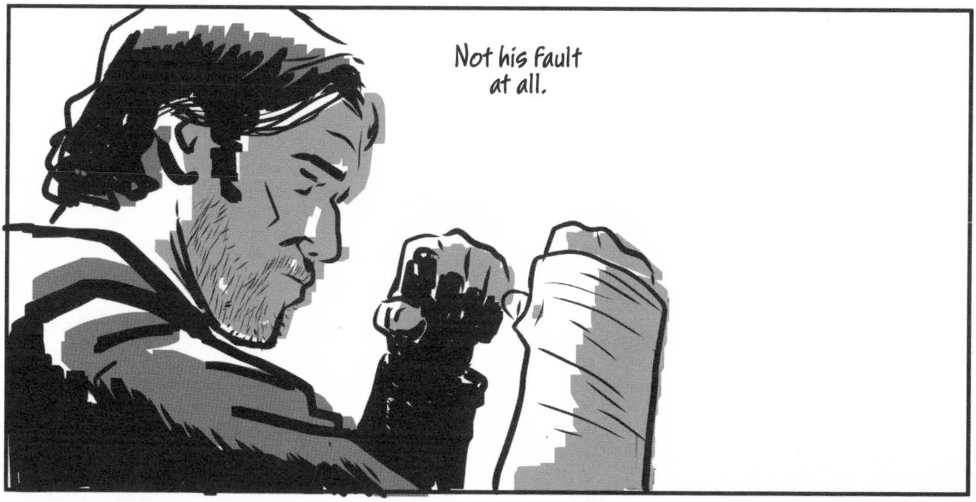
Not his fault
at all.

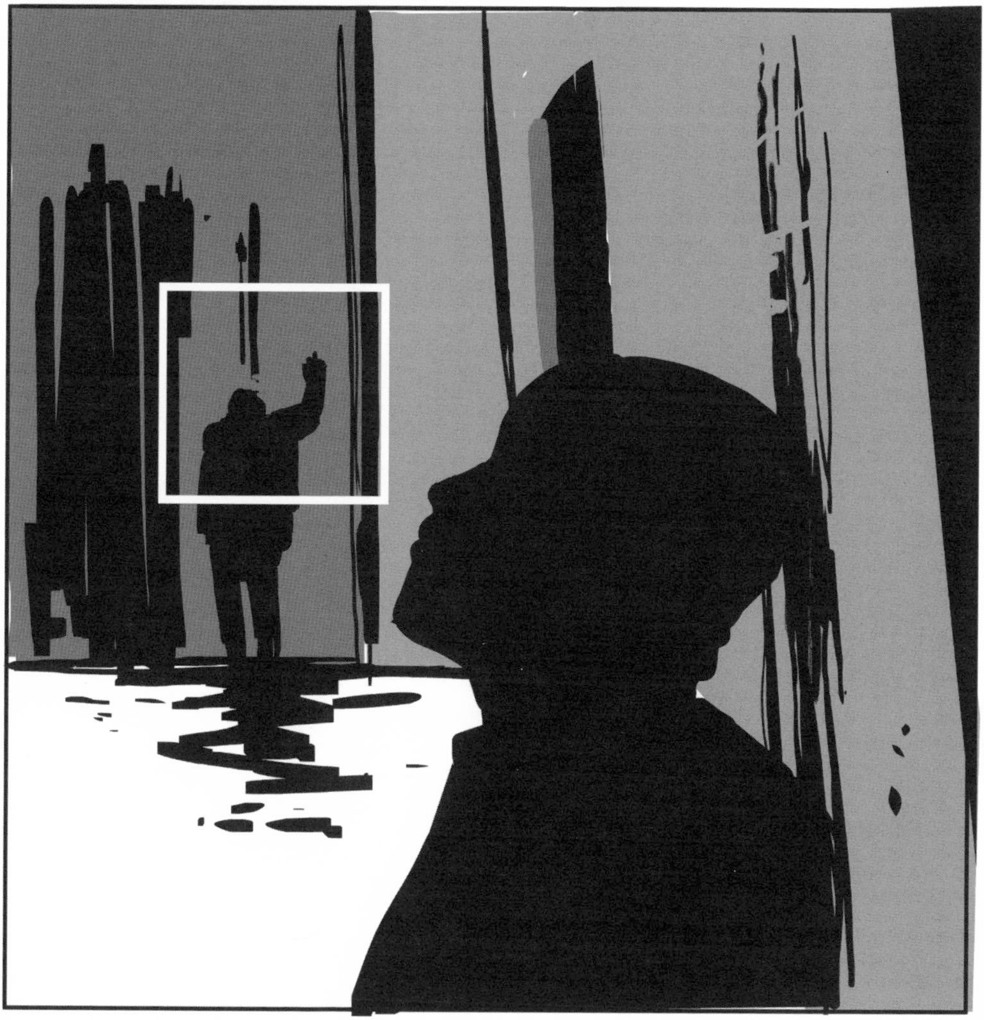

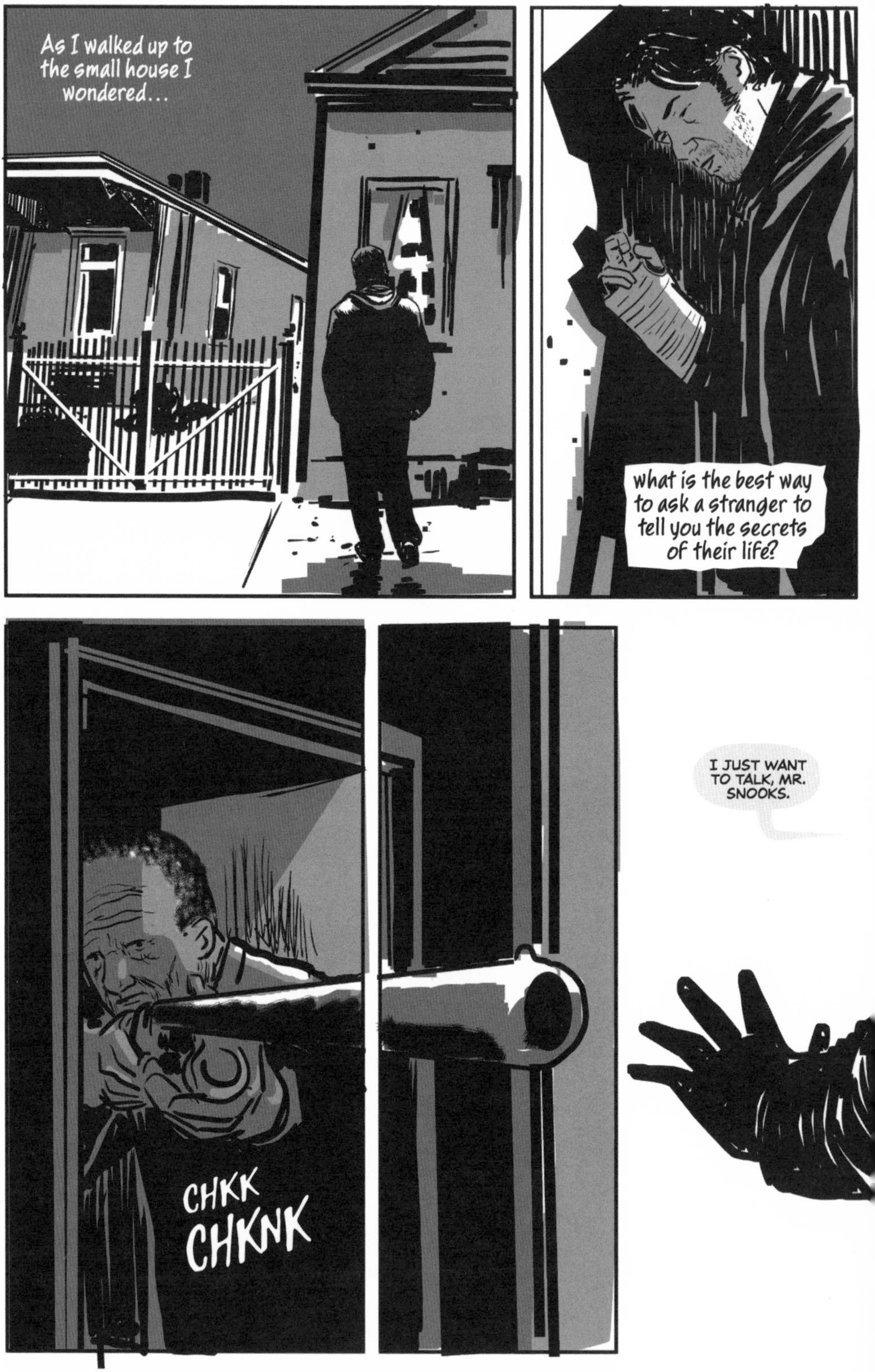
As I walked up to the small house I wondered...
what is the best way to ask a stranger to tell you the secrets of their life?
CHKK CHKNK
I JUST WANT TO TALK, MR. SNOOKS.

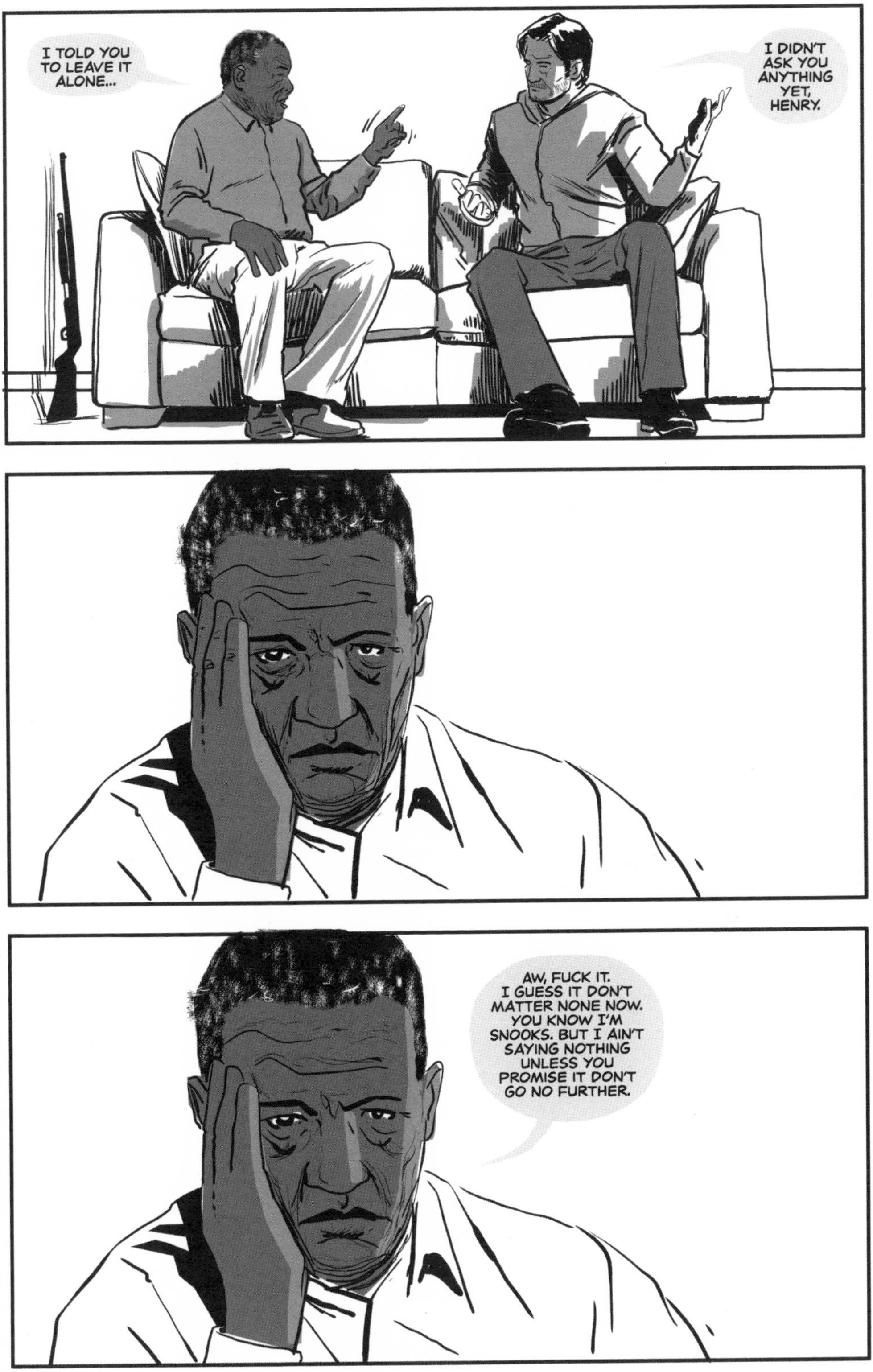
I TOLD YOU TO LEAVE IT ALONE...
I DIDN'T ASK YOU ANYTHING YET, HENRY.
AW, FUCK IT. I GUESS IT DON'T MATTER NONE NOW. YOU KNOW I'M SNOOKS. BUT I AIN'T SAYING NOTHING UNLESS YOU PROMISE IT DON'T GO NO FURTHER.

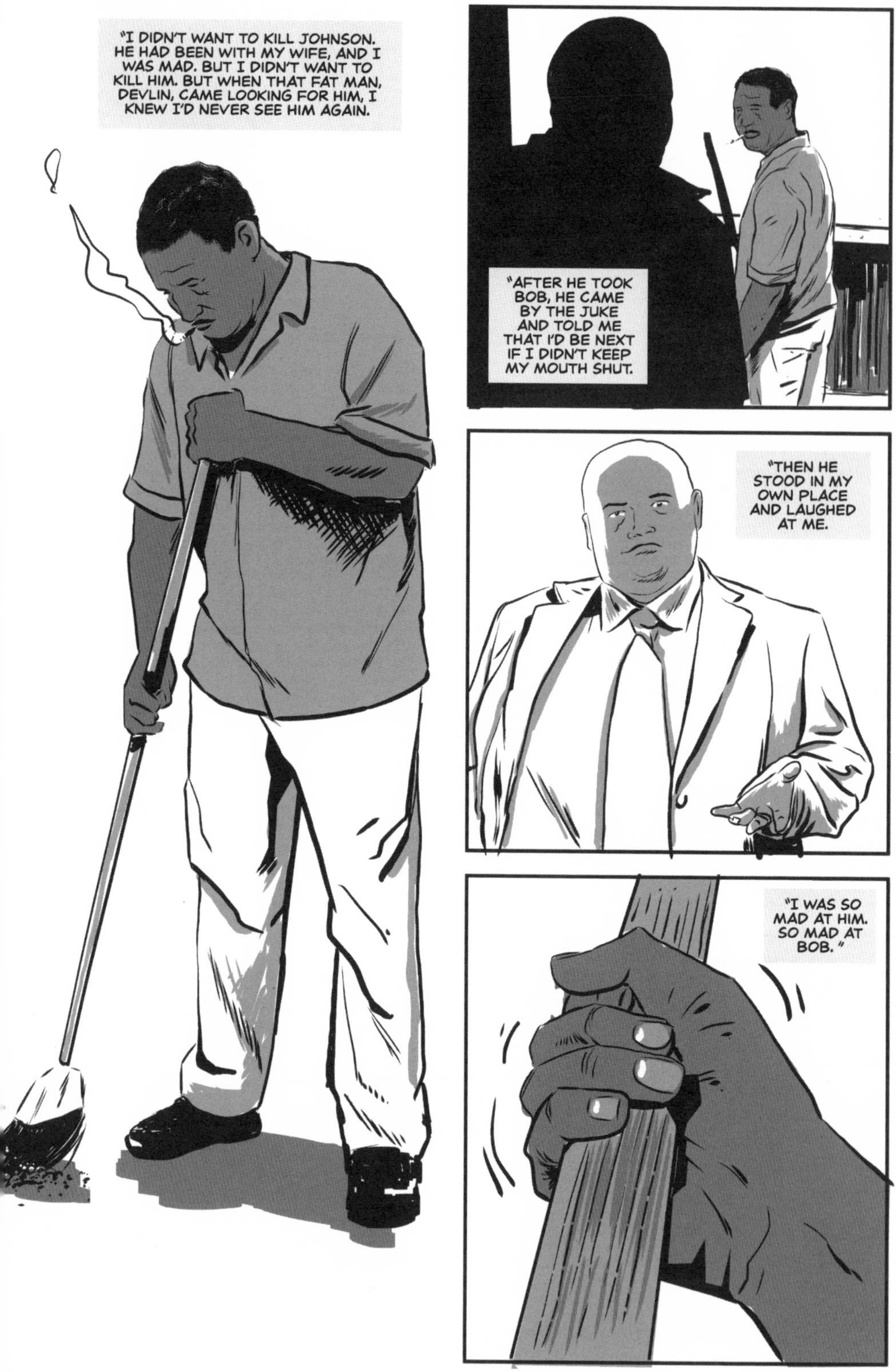
"I DIDN'T WANT TO KILL JOHNSON. HE HAD BEEN WITH MY WIFE, AND I WAS MAD. BUT I DIDN'T WANT TO KILL HIM. BUT WHEN THAT FAT MAN, DEVLIN, CAME LOOKING FOR HIM, I KNEW I'D NEVER SEE HIM AGAIN.
"AFTER HE TOOK BOB, HE CAME BY THE JUKE AND TOLD ME THAT I'D BE NEXT IF I DIDN'T KEEP MY MOUTH SHUT.
"THEN HE STOOD IN MY OWN PLACE AND LAUGHED AT ME.
"I WAS SO MAD AT HIM. SO MAD AT BOB."

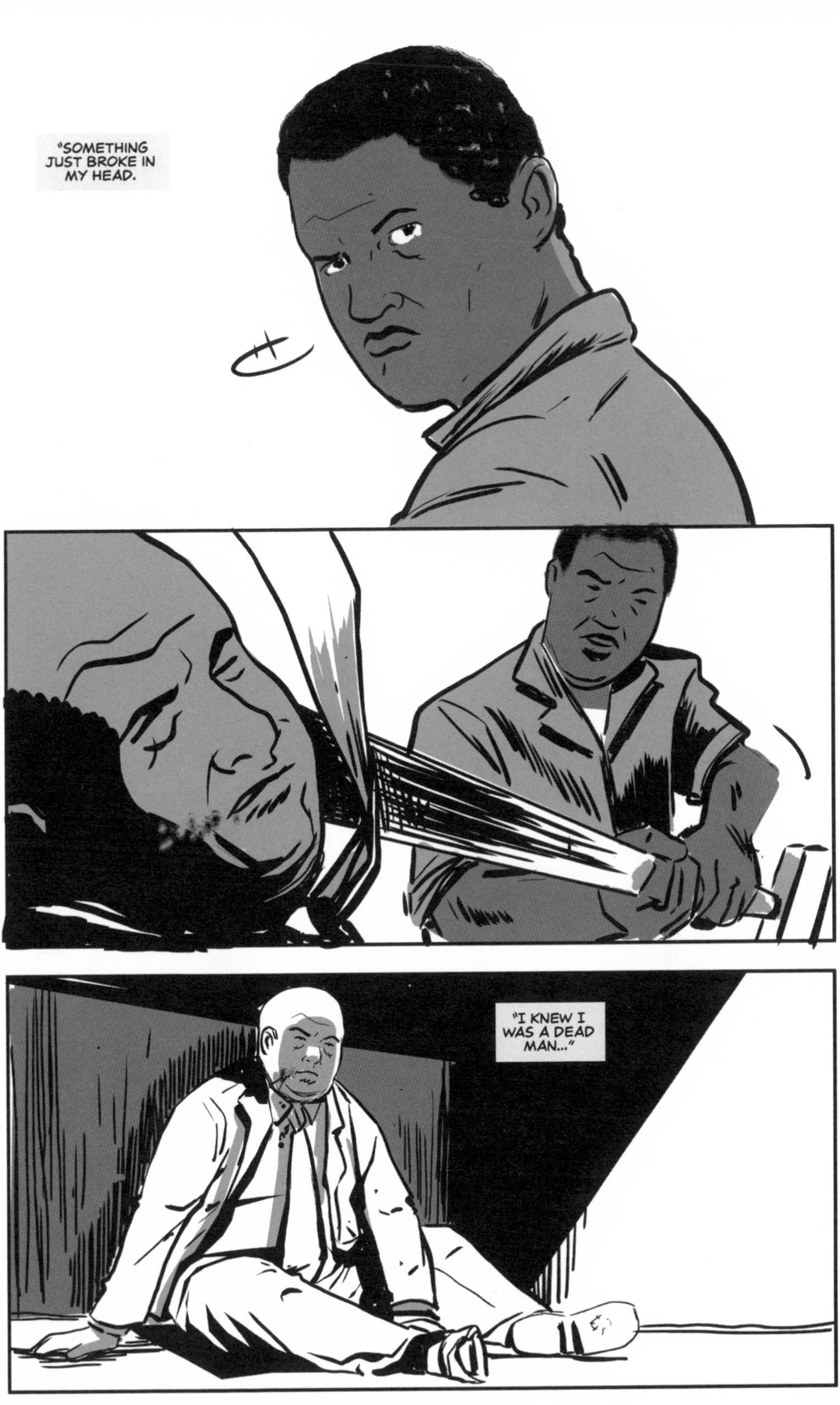
"SOMETHING JUST BROKE IN MY HEAD.
"I KNEW I WAS A DEAD MAN..."

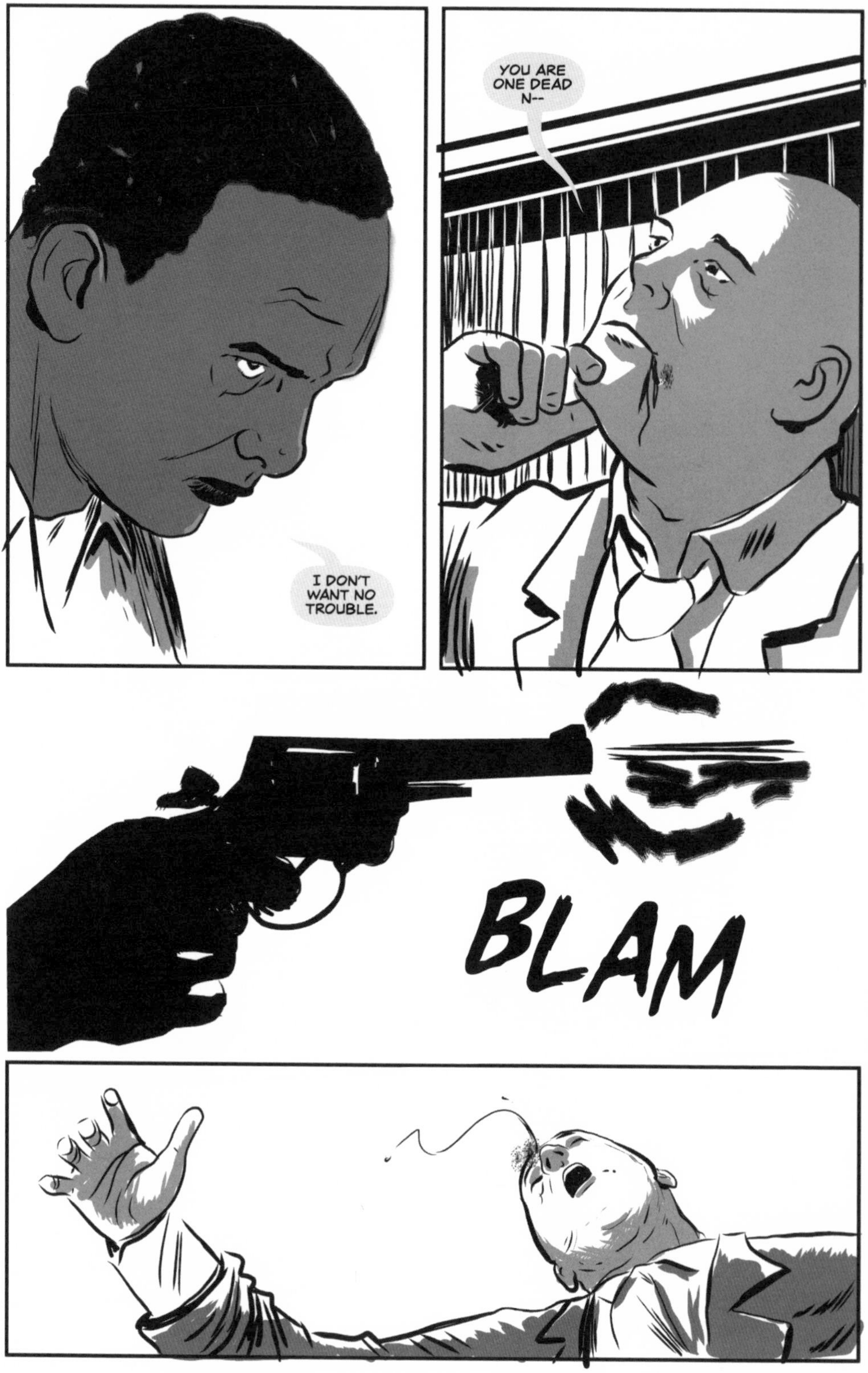
I DON'T WANT NO TROUBLE.
YOU ARE ONE DEAD N--
BLAM

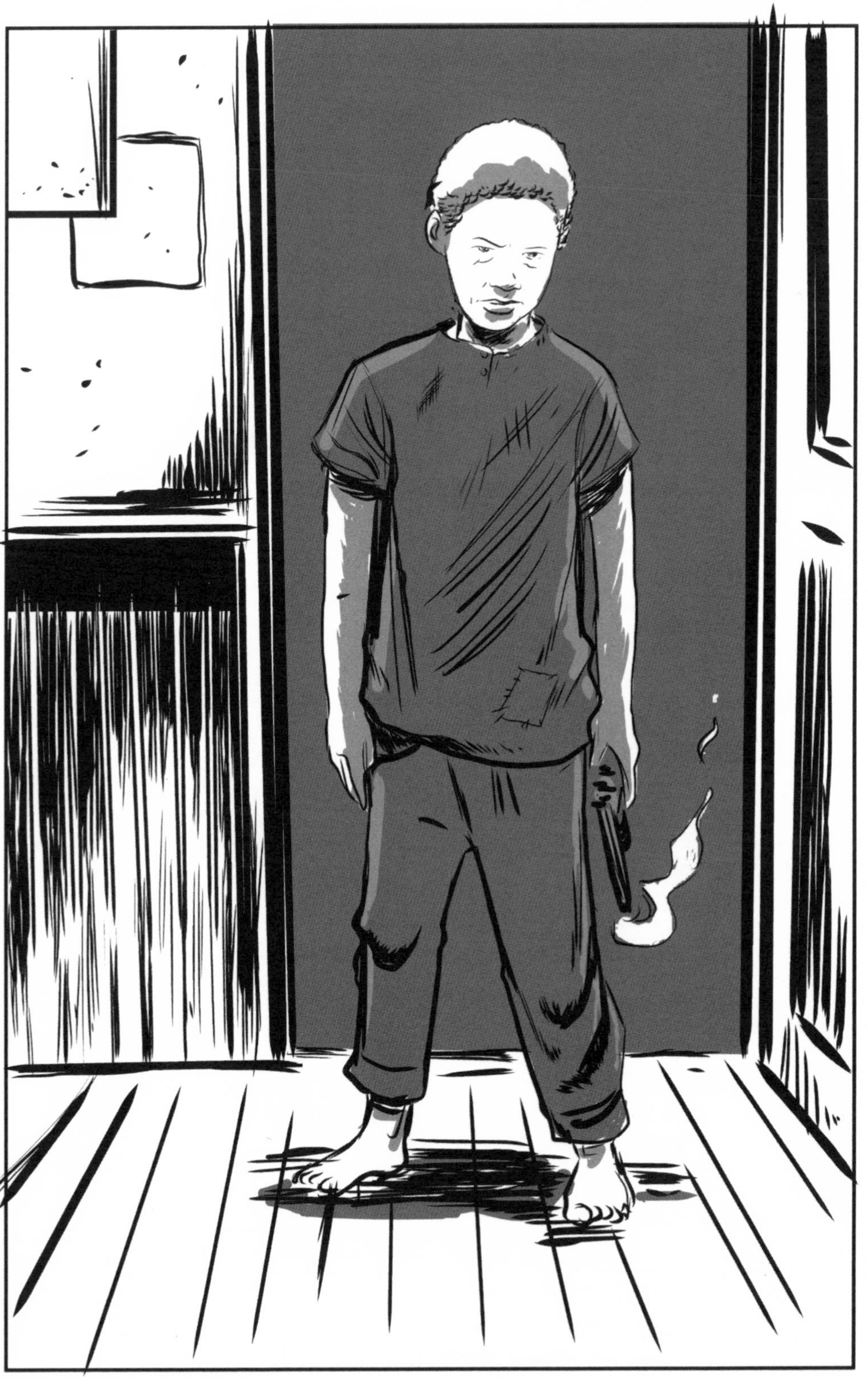

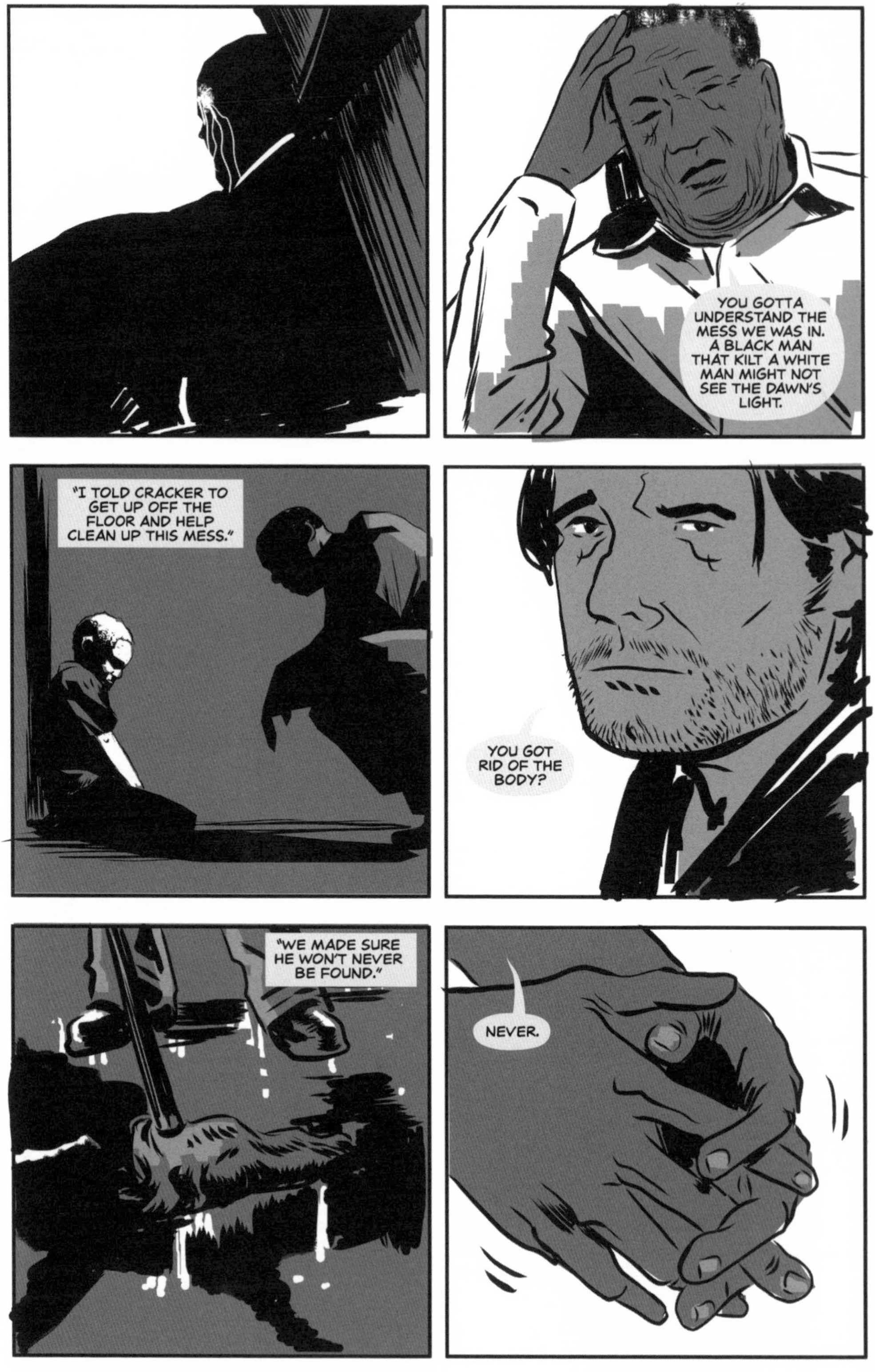
YOU GOTTA UNDERSTAND THE MESS WE WAS IN. A BLACK MAN THAT KILT A WHITE MAN MIGHT NOT SEE THE DAWN'S LIGHT.
"I TOLD CRACKER TO GET UP OFF THE FLOOR AND HELP CLEAN UP THIS MESS."
YOU GOT RID OF THE BODY?
"WE MADE SURE HE WON'T NEVER BE FOUND."
NEVER.

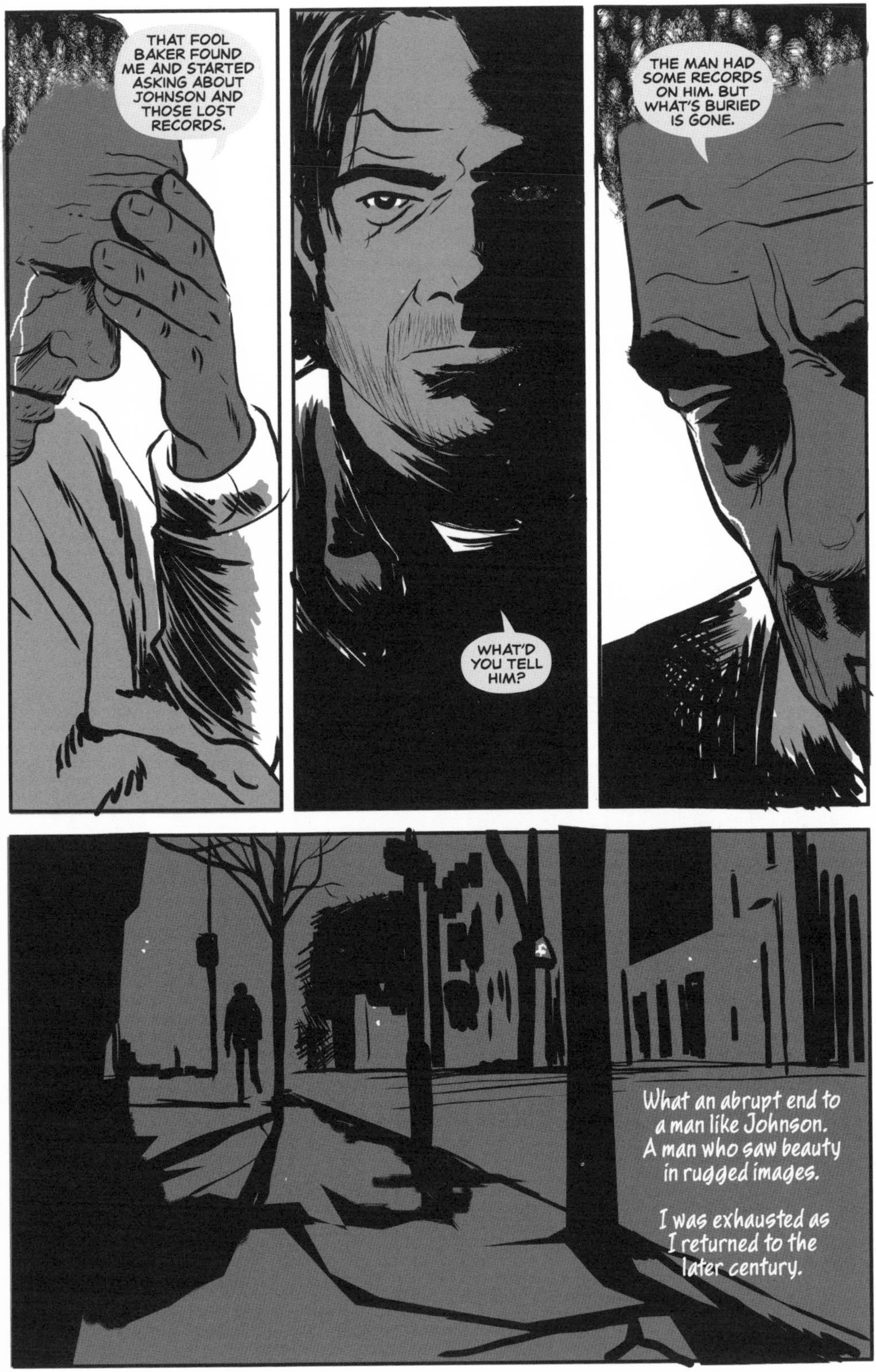
THAT FOOL BAKER FOUND ME AND STARTED ASKING ABOUT JOHNSON AND THOSE LOST RECORDS.
WHAT'D YOU TELL HIM?
THE MAN HAD SOME RECORDS ON HIM. BUT WHAT'S BURIED IS GONE.
What an abrupt end to a man like Johnson. A man who saw beauty in rugged images.
I was exhausted as I returned to the later century.

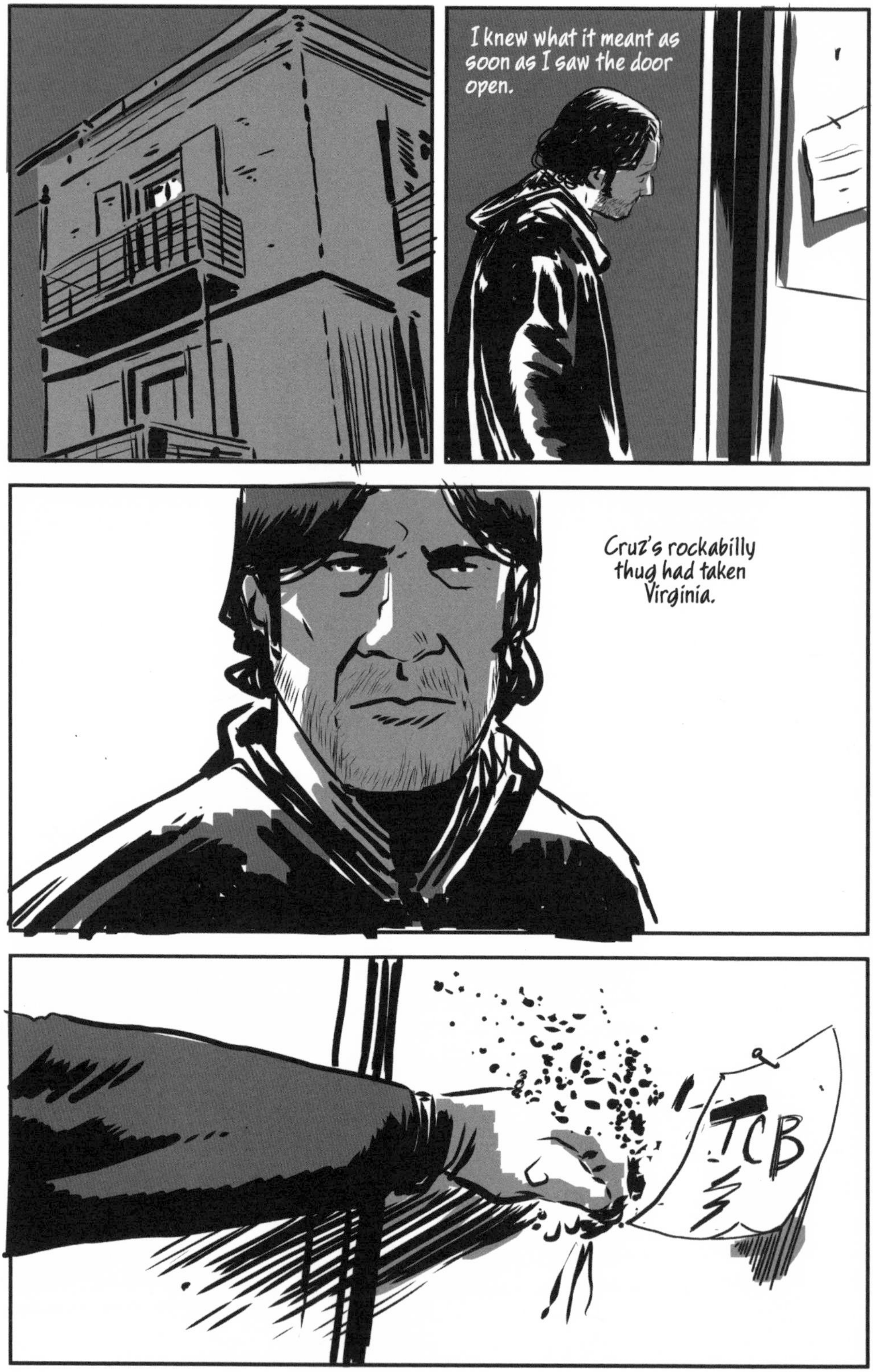
I knew what it meant as soon as I saw the door open.
Cruz's rockabilly thug had taken Virginia.
TCB

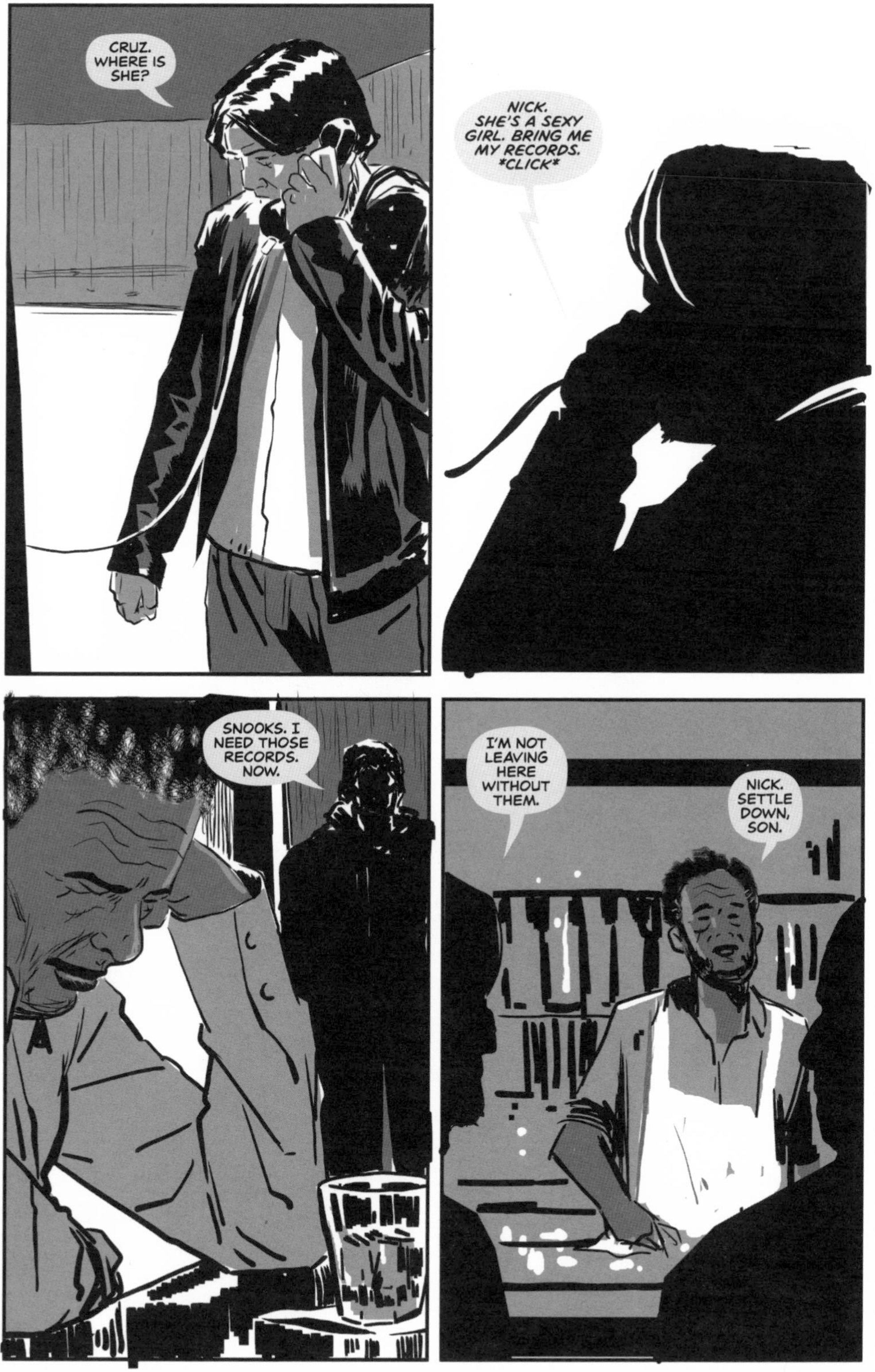

CRUZ. WHERE IS SHE?
NICK. SHE'S A SEXY GIRL. BRING ME MY RECORDS. *CLICK*
SNOOKS. I NEED THOSE RECORDS. NOW.
I'M NOT LEAVING HERE WITHOUT THEM.
NICK. SETTLE DOWN, SON.

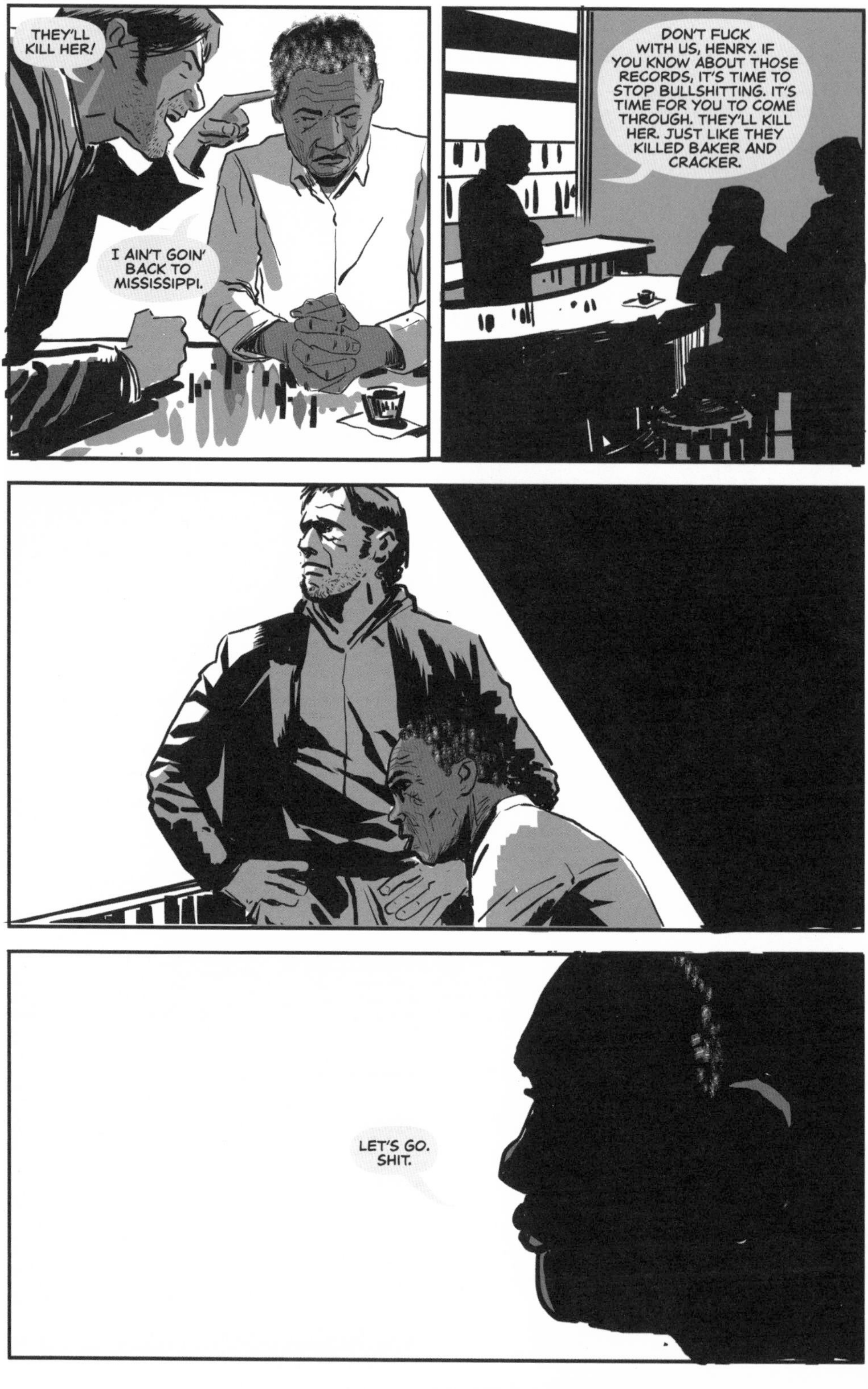
THEY'LL KILL HER!
I AIN'T GOIN' BACK TO MISSISSIPPI.
DON'T FUCK WITH US, HENRY. IF YOU KNOW ABOUT THOSE RECORDS, IT'S TIME TO STOP BULLSHITTING. IT'S TIME FOR YOU TO COME THROUGH. THEY'LL KILL HER. JUST LIKE THEY KILLED BAKER AND CRACKER.
LET'S GO. SHIT.

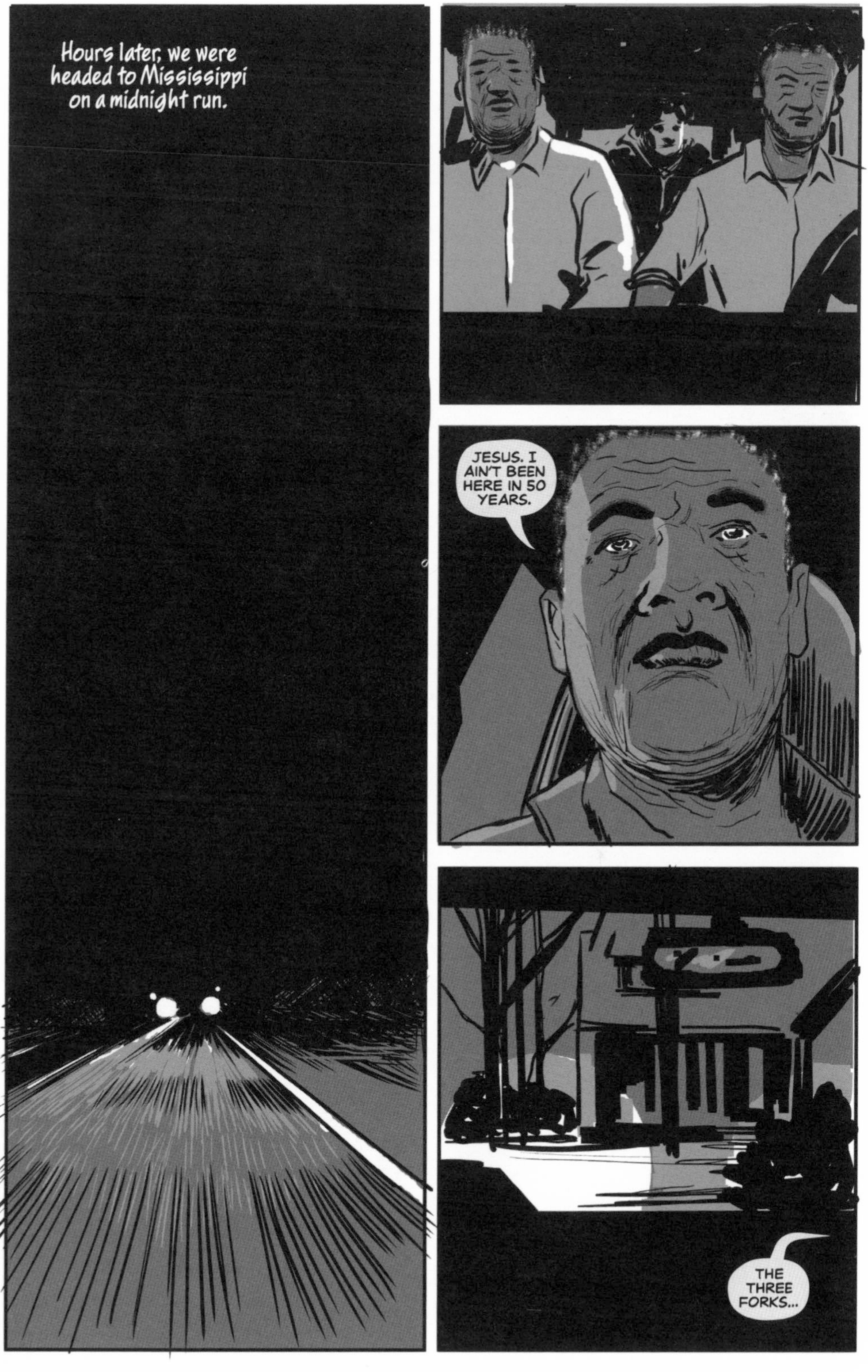
Hours later, we were headed to Mississippi on a midnight run.
JESUS. I AIN'T BEEN HERE IN 50 YEARS.
THE THREE FORKS...

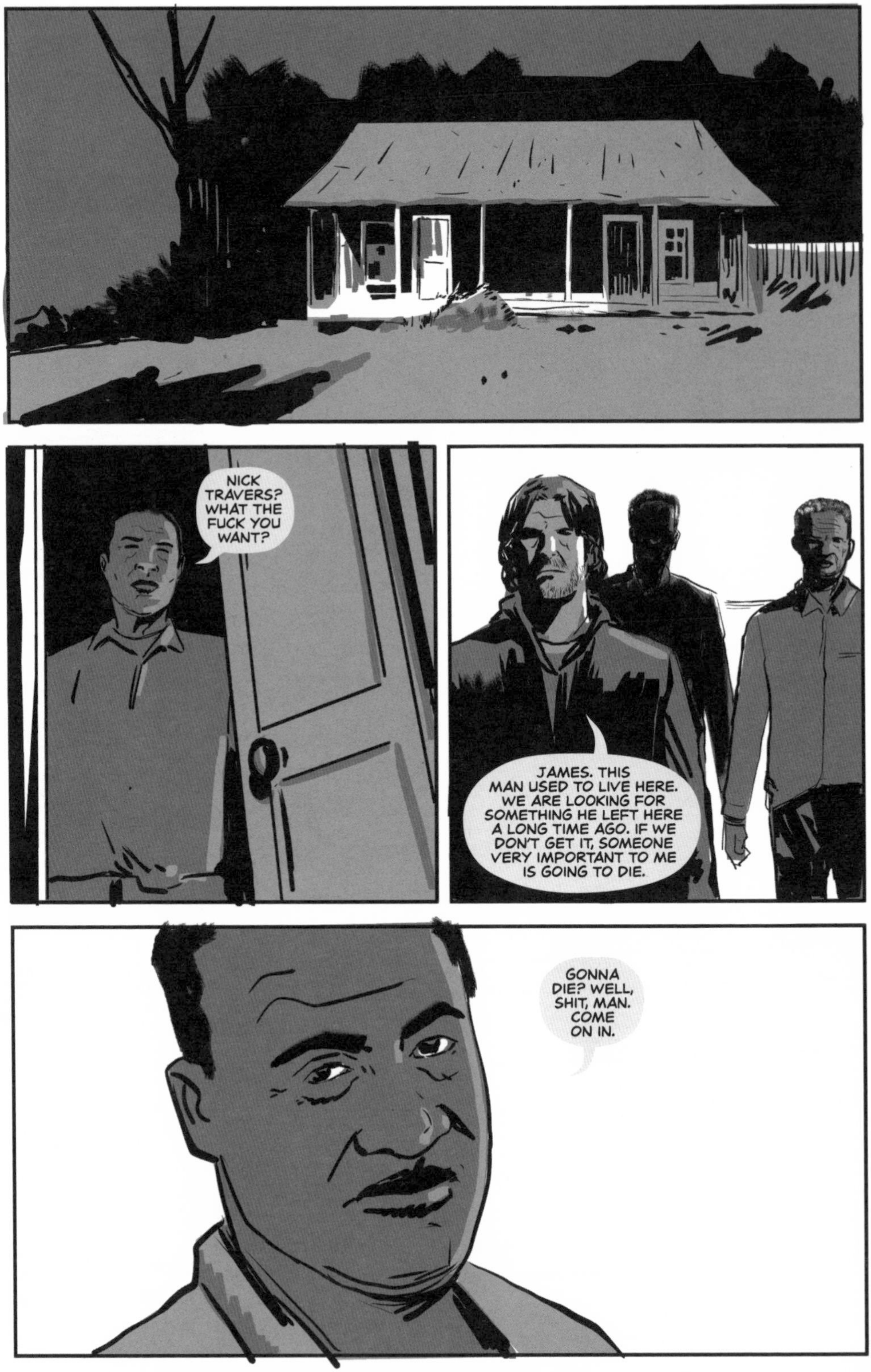
NICK TRAVERS? WHAT THE FUCK YOU WANT?
JAMES. THIS MAN USED TO LIVE HERE. WE ARE LOOKING FOR SOMETHING HE LEFT HERE A LONG TIME AGO. IF WE DON'T GET IT, SOMEONE VERY IMPORTANT TO ME IS GOING TO DIE.
GONNA DIE? WELL, SHIT, MAN. COME ON IN.

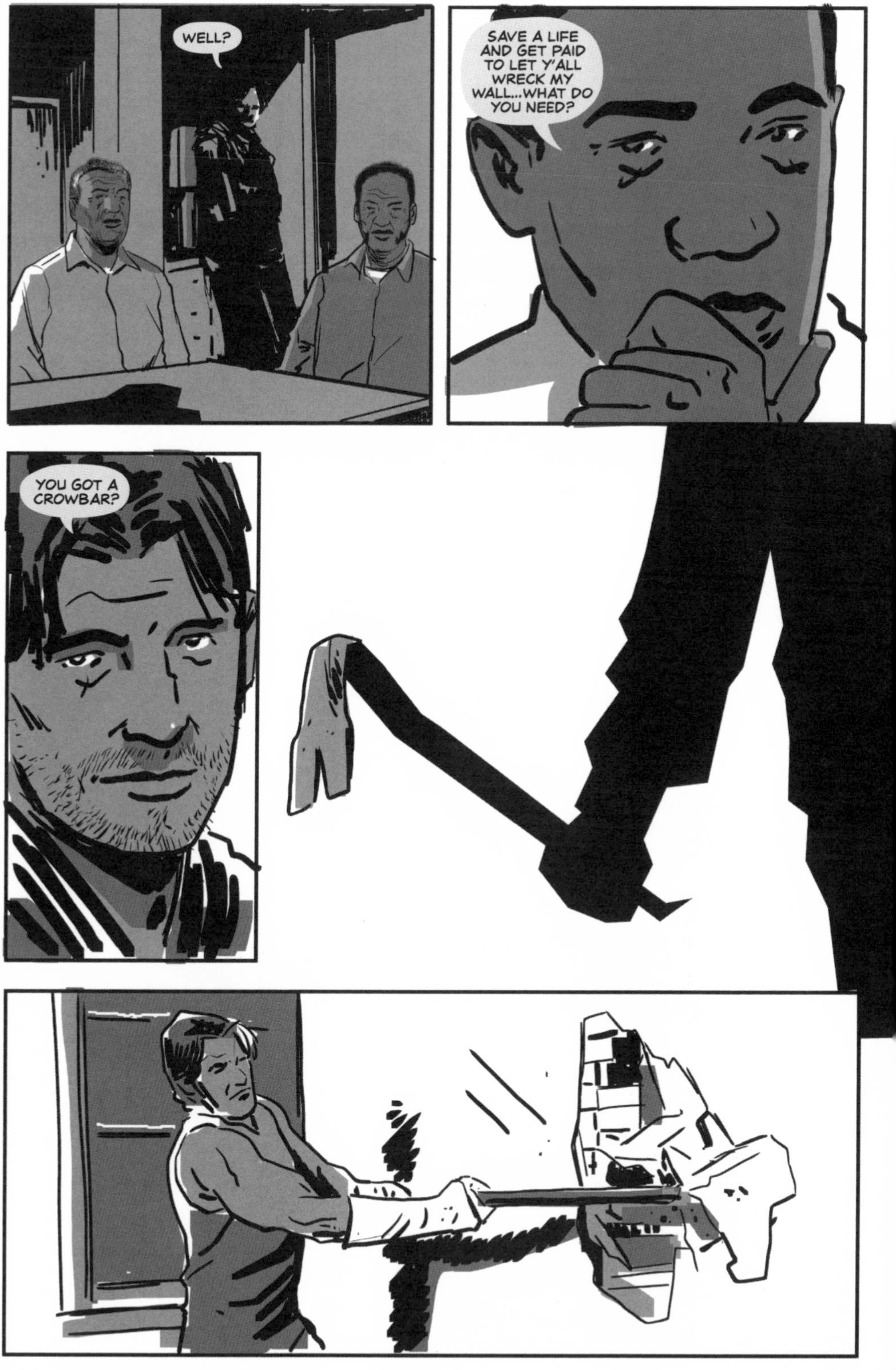
WELL?
SAVE A LIFE AND GET PAID TO LET Y'ALL WRECK MY WALL...WHAT DO YOU NEED?
YOU GOT A CROWBAR?

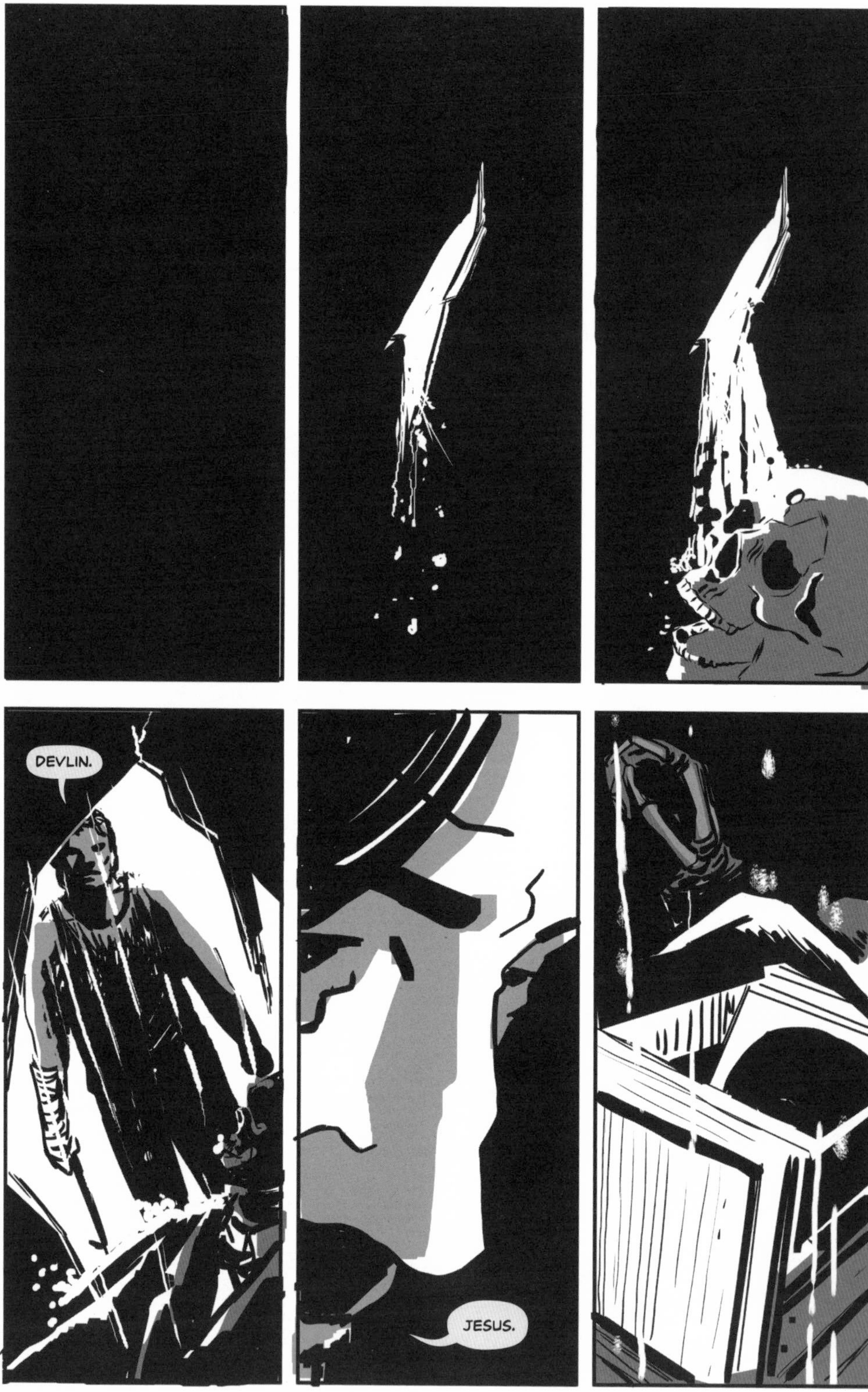
DEVLIN.
JESUS.

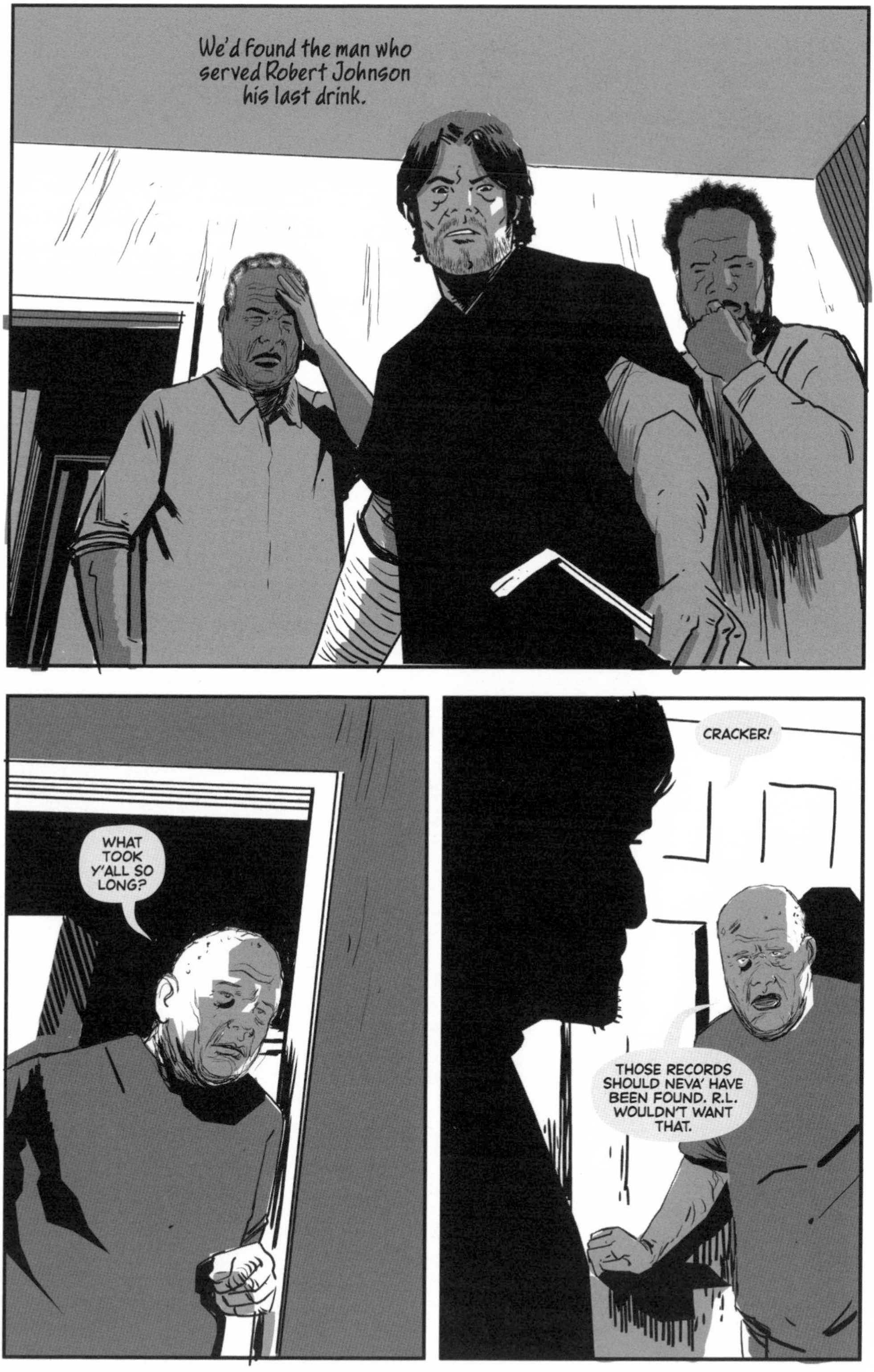
We'd found the man who served Robert Johnson his last drink.
WHAT TOOK Y'ALL SO LONG?
CRACKER!
THOSE RECORDS SHOULD NEVA' HAVE BEEN FOUND. R.L. WOULDN'T WANT THAT.

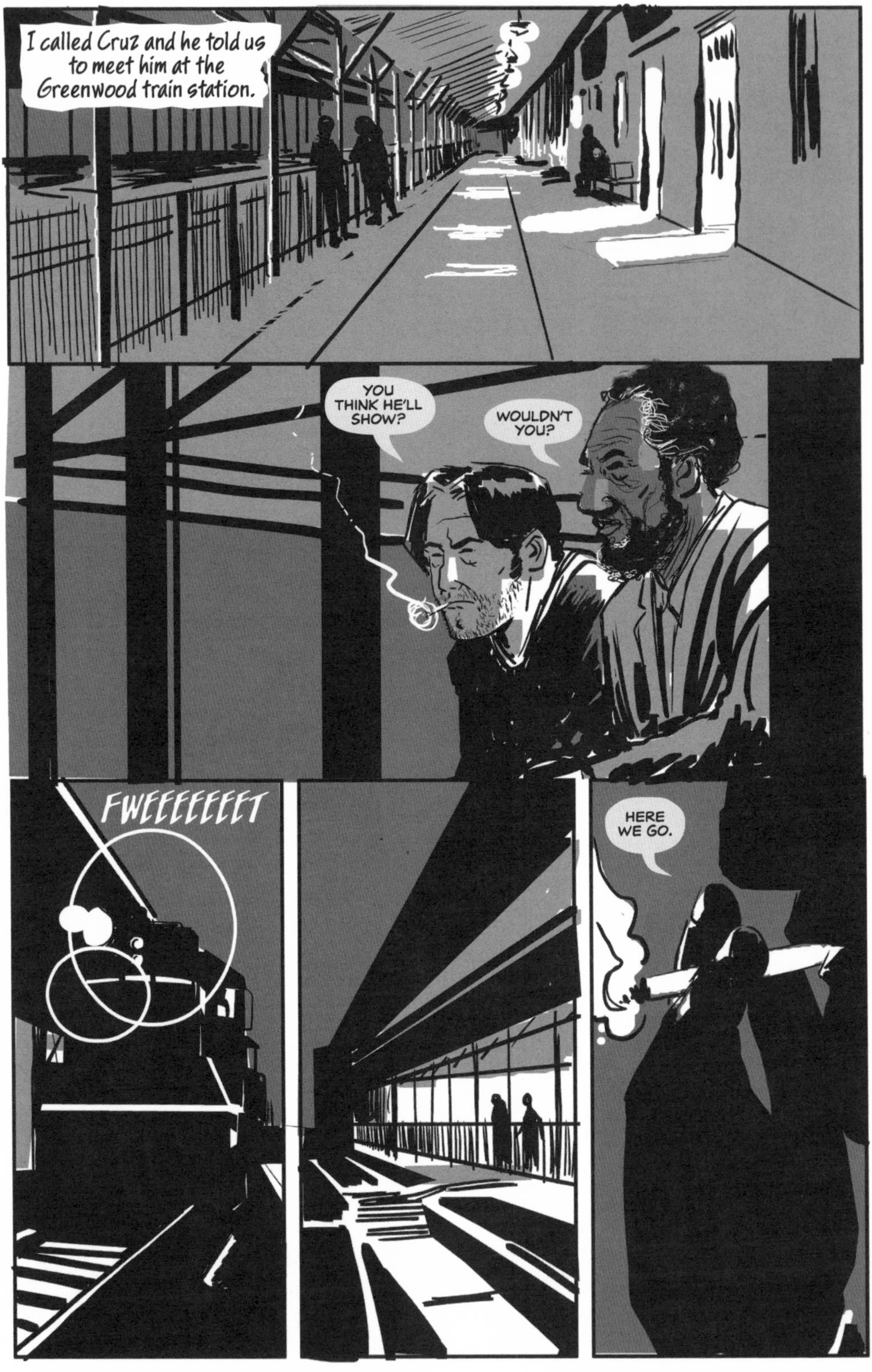
I called Cruz and he told us to meet him at the Greenwood train station.
YOU THINK HE'LL SHOW?
WOULDN'T YOU?
FWEEEEEEEET
HERE WE GO.

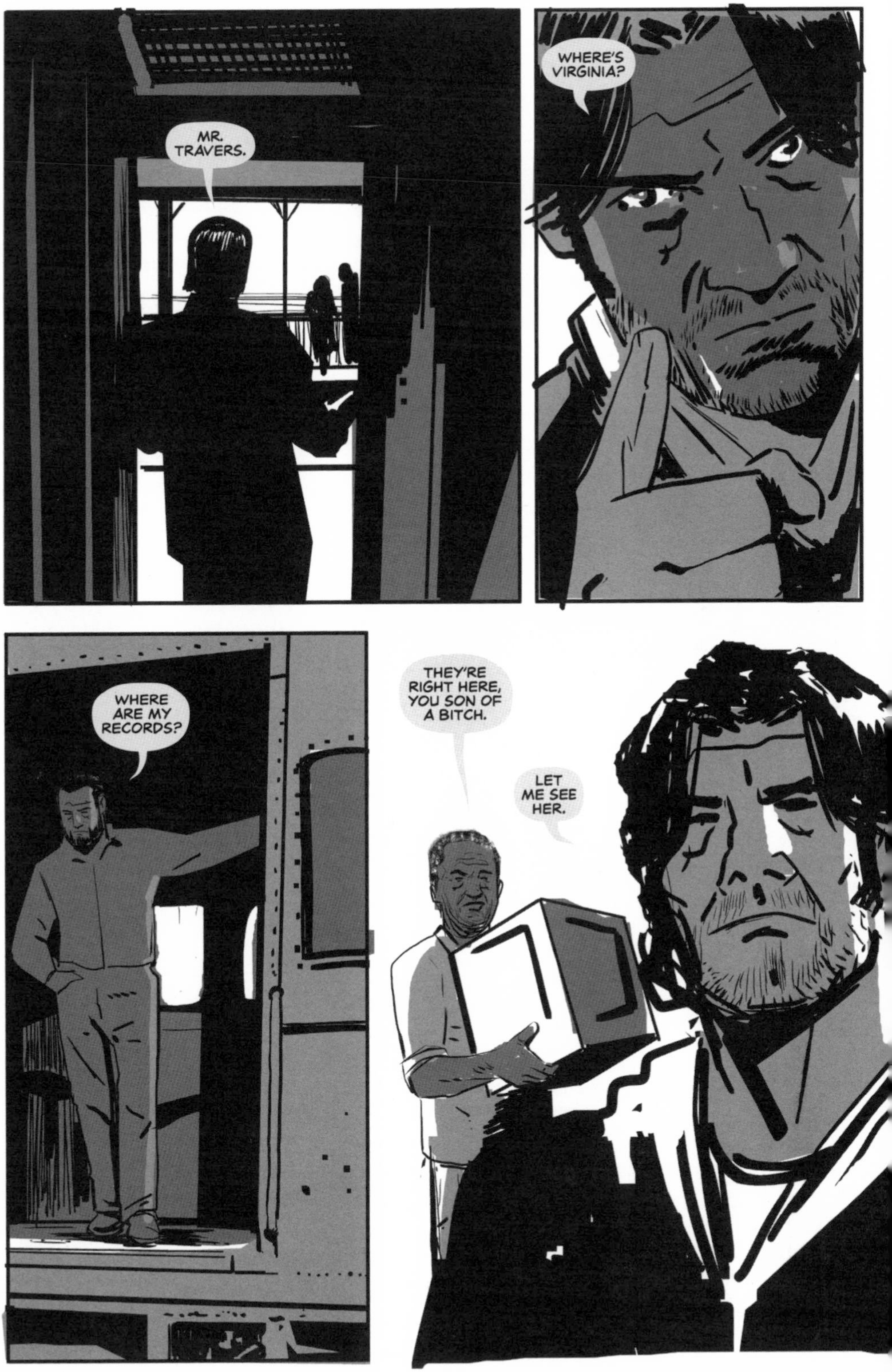
MR. TRAVERS.
WHERE'S VIRGINIA?
WHERE ARE MY RECORDS?
THEY'RE RIGHT HERE, YOU SON OF A BITCH.
LET ME SEE HER.

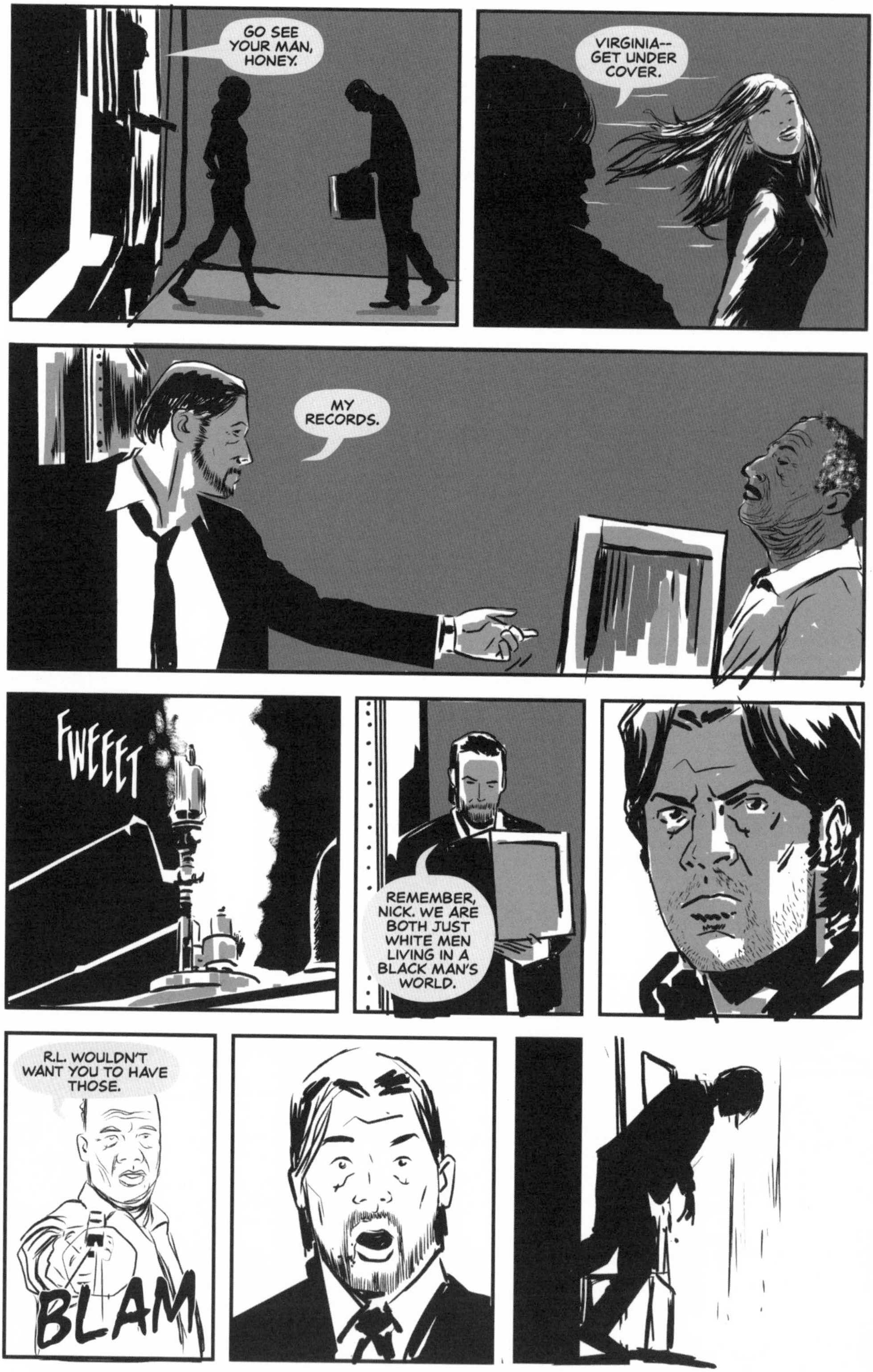
GO SEE YOUR MAN, HONEY.
VIRGINIA-- GET UNDER COVER.
MY RECORDS.
FWEEET
REMEMBER, NICK. WE ARE BOTH JUST WHITE MEN LIVING IN A BLACK MAN'S WORLD.
R.L. WOULDN'T WANT YOU TO HAVE THOSE.
BLAM

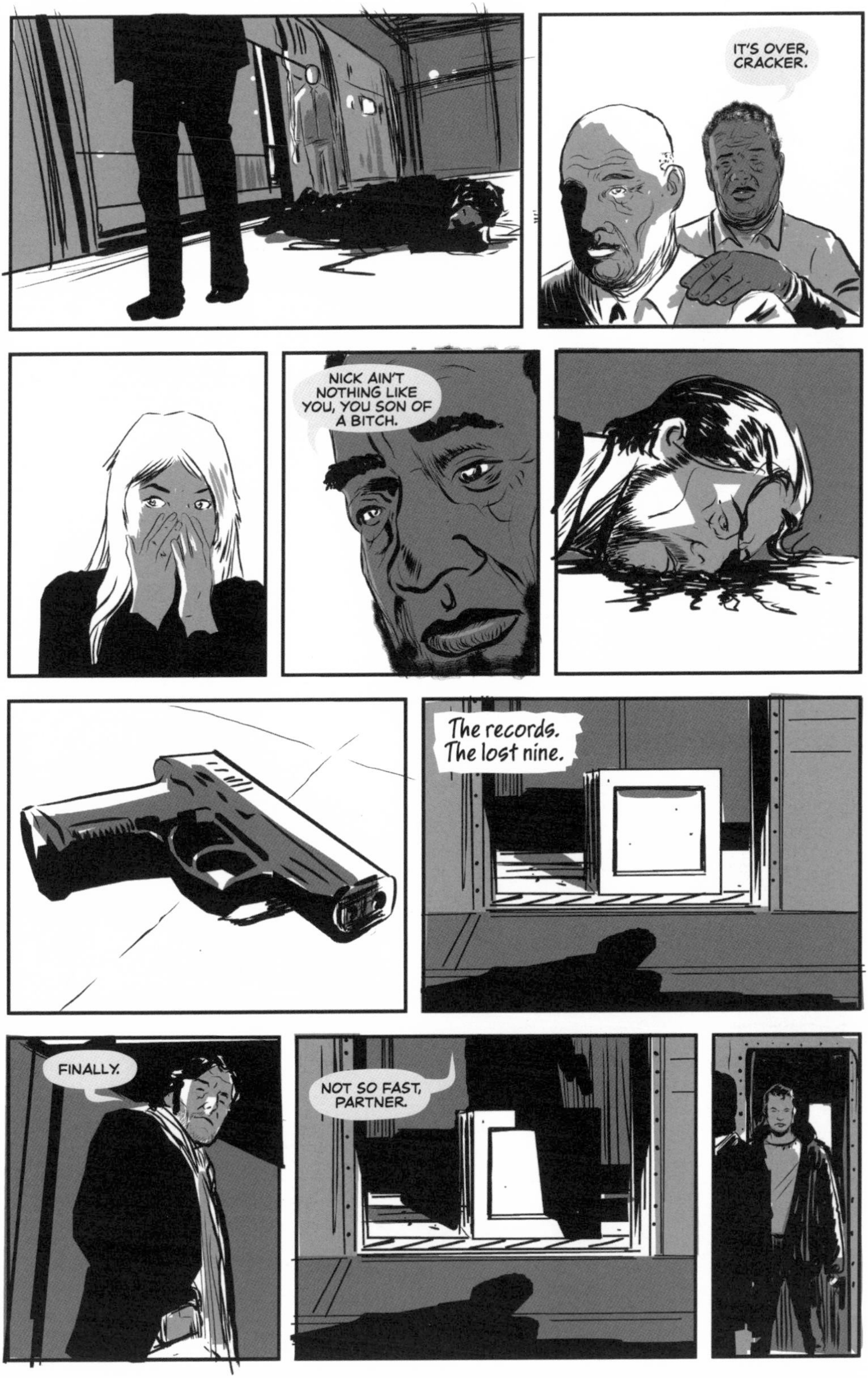
IT'S OVER, CRACKER.
NICK AIN'T NOTHING LIKE YOU, YOU SON OF A BITCH.
The records. The lost nine.
FINALLY.
NOT SO FAST, PARTNER.

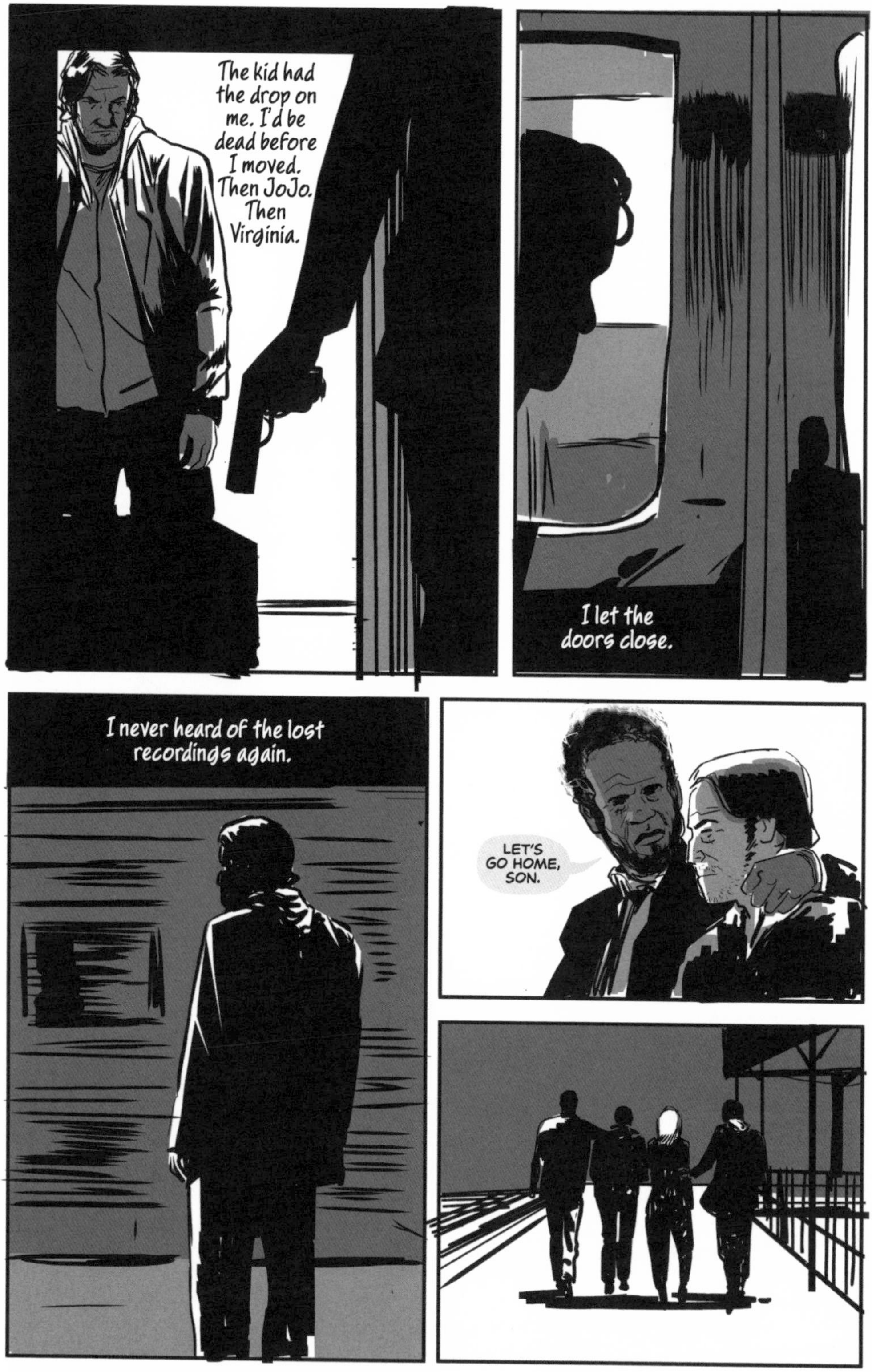
The kid had the drop on me. I'd be dead before I moved. Then JoJo. Then Virginia.
I let the doors close.
I never heard of the lost recordings again.
LET'S GO HOME, SON.

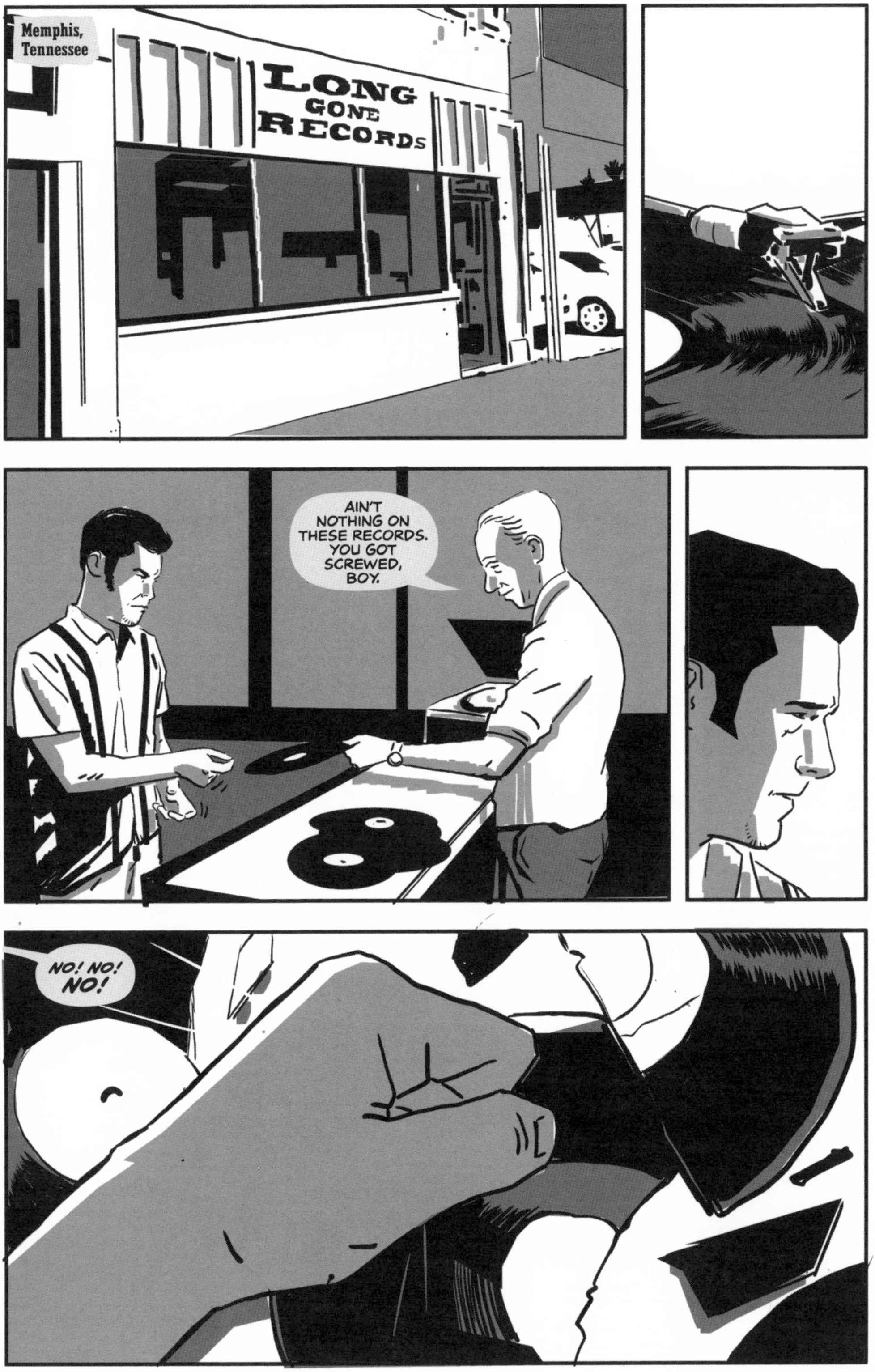
Memphis, Tennessee
LONG GONE RECORDS
AIN'T NOTHING ON THESE RECORDS. YOU GOT SCREWED, BOY.
NO! NO! NO!

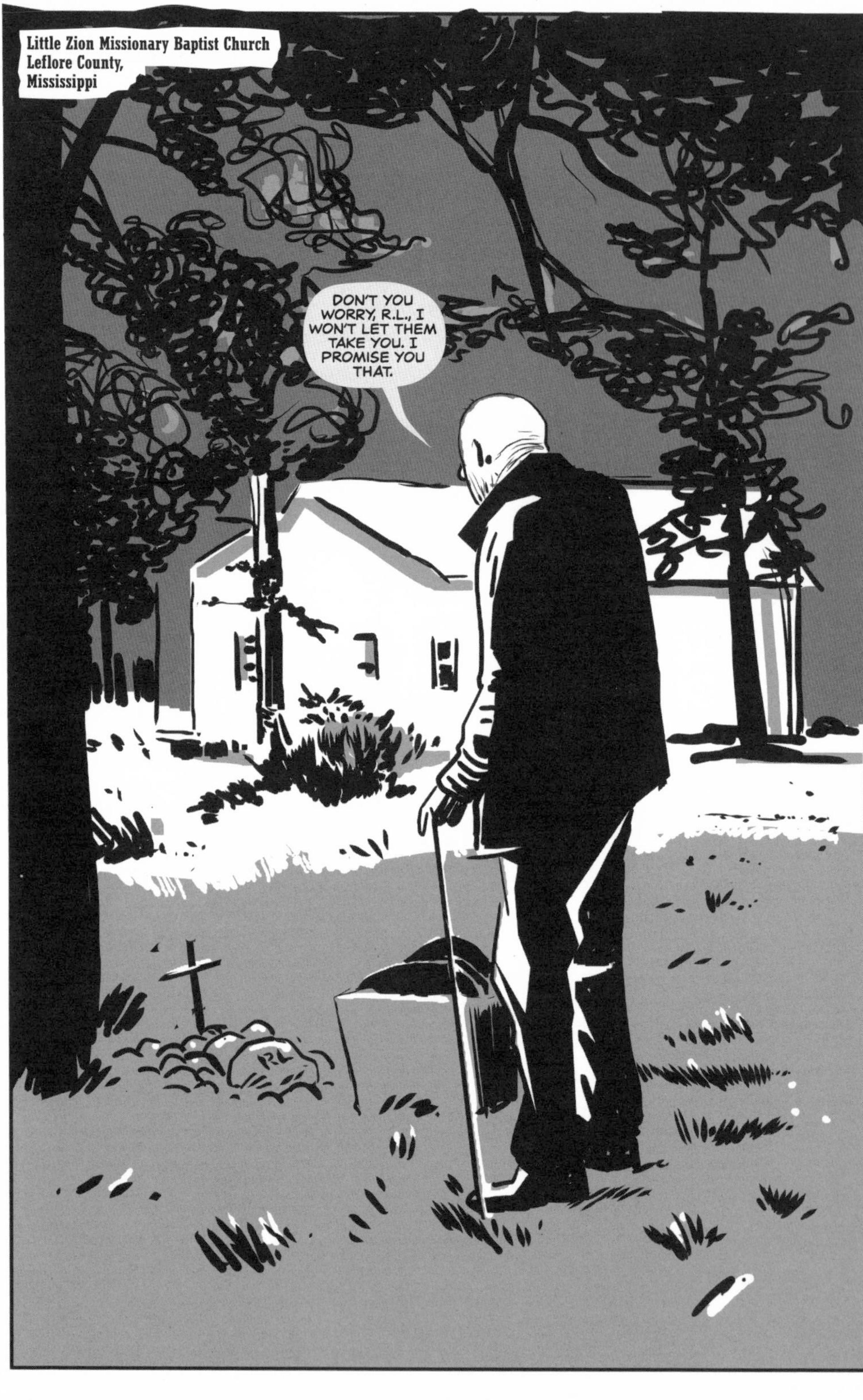

Little Zion Missionary Baptist Church
Leflore County,
Mississippi
DON'T YOU WORRY, R.L., I WON'T LET THEM TAKE YOU. I PROMISE YOU THAT.
R.L.

THE
END

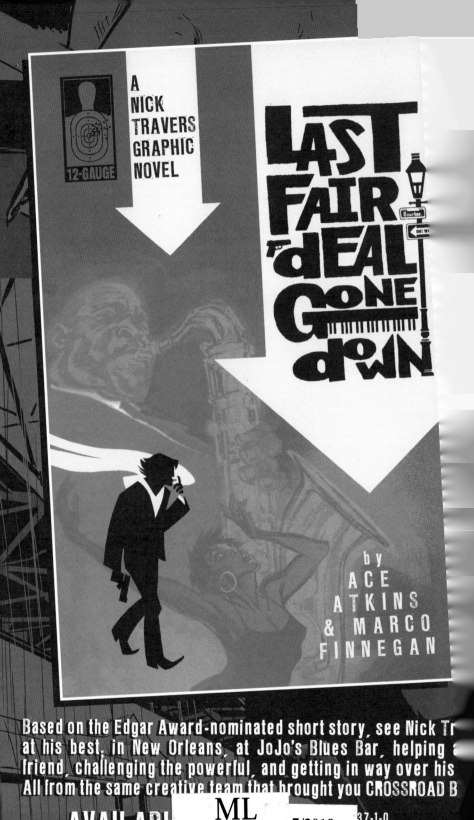

A NICK TRAVERS GRAPHIC NOVEL

12-GAUGE

LAST FAIR dEAL GONE doWN

by ACE ATKINS & MARCO FINNEGAN

Based on the Edgar Award-nominated short story, see Nick Tr
at his best, in New Orleans, at JoJo's Blues Bar, helping
friend, challenging the powerful, and getting in way over his
All from the same creative team that brought you CROSSROAD B

AVAILABL **ML** 7/2018 37-1-0
EB161858